A BANNER IS UNFURLED

ABIDE WITH ME

4

OTHER BOOKS AND AUDIO BOOKS
BY MARCIE GALLACHER AND
KERRI ROBINSON:

A Banner Is Unfurled (Volume 1)

Be Still My Soul (Volume 2)

Glory from on High (Volume 3)

ABIDE WITH ME

4

MARCIE GALLACHER
KERRI ROBINSON

Covenant Communications, Inc.

Cover: background painting *Spring Hill* © Al Rounds. For more information please visit www.alrounds.com; model reference photo by McKenzie Deakins. For photographer information please visit www.photographybymckenzie.com.

Cover design © 2010 by Covenant Communications, Inc.

Published by Covenant Communications, Inc.
American Fork, Utah

Printed in Canada
First Printing: February 2010

16 15 14 13 12 11 10 10 9 8 7 6 5 4 3 2 1

ISBN-13 978-1-59811-883-4

In memory of our great-great-grandfather Benjamin Franklin Johnson,
for his legacy of courage and faith.

And to our mother and father LaRae and Tal Huber,
with love and gratitude.

ACKNOWLEDGMENTS

Our hearts are filled with thanks for all those who have supported us through this journey, especially husbands, parents, and children. We would also like to acknowledge our editor, Kirk Shaw, and the entire Covenant Communications family, whose dedication and hard work made this possible. We are grateful to all of our readers whose kind words of enthusiasm and encouragement have often kept us going through busy days and sleepless nights.

We continue to be indebted to the journal keepers and letter writers of the past and to the professional and family historians of the present. We are especially grateful to the recently departed E. Dale LeBaron, historian and author of *Benjamin Franklin Johnson: Friend to the Prophets.*

EZEKIEL AND JULIA JOHNSON FAMILY

1838

Joel Hills [b. 1802] [m. Annie Pixley Johnson, 1826]
  Julianne [b. 1827–d. 1829]
  Sixtus [b. 1829]
  Sariah [b. 1832]
  Nephi [b. 1833]
  Susan Ellen [b. 1836]
Nancy Maria [b. 1803–d. 1836]
Seth Guernsey [b. 1805–d. 1835]
Delcena Diadamia [b.1806] [m. Lyman Sherman, 1829]
  Alvira [b.1830]
  Baby son [b. 1830–d. before 1831]
  Mary [b. 1831]
  Albey [b.1832]
  Seth [b. 1836]
  Daniel [b. 1837]
Julia Ann (Julianne) [b. 1808] [m. Almon Whiting Babbitt, 1834]
  David Homer [b.1835–d. 1836]
David [b. 1810–d. 1833]
Almera Woodward [b. 1812] [m. Samuel Prescott, 1836]
Susan Ellen [b. 1814–d. 1836]
Joseph Ellis [b. 1817]
Benjamin Franklin [b. 1818]
Mary Ellen [b. 1820]
Elmer Wood [b. 1822–d. 1823]
George Washington [b. 1823]
William Derby [b. 1824]
Ester Melita [b.1827]
Amos Partridge [b. 1829]

1

In all my trials, great and small
To God for help I fly,
He is the anchor of my soul
When foes are thick and nigh . . .

Oh, Father, in my grief and tears,
This joyful thought to me occurs,
No Good or evil visits me
But what is known or sent by Thee.

Joel Hills Johnson

Late January 1838

The morning sun shone deceivingly in the seamless blue sky. The air was dry and bitter cold. Delcena Sherman sat silently in the wagon with her younger brothers, nineteen-year-old Benjamin Johnson and fourteen-year-old George. They pulled up to the house in Kirtland that Delcena had vacated three weeks ago. The front door was broken and splintered, gaping like an open wound. Her brothers bolted from the wagon. Delcena climbed down and followed them, her heart pounding.

George let out a low whistle. "It's good you and the kids have been staying at our place. Whoever broke in wasn't fooling around."

A hard lump formed in Delcena's throat, and her hands shook. Her thoughts huddled around the circumstances that had brought her here. Shortly after the Prophet's departure a few weeks ago, their enemies had illegally gained ownership of the Church's printing press. Lyman had overheard a plot to use the press to publish lies that would destroy Joseph Smith. In a split-second decision and acting alone, he had started a fire that consumed the building. Lyman had gone on a mission the next day. She had moved in with her mother and watched in terrified silence as local authorities searched for the unknown arsonist, the different factions blaming each other. Only Delcena and her brother Benjamin knew the truth. They had told no one—not their parents, not their brothers and sisters. No one.

"Delcie, George and I will go in and get your furniture—if we can," Benjamin said in a low voice, his eyes focused on the broken door.

Delcena nodded and tried to stop shaking. A cold wind blew. She remembered Lyman holding her tightly before slipping away and promising to come back and take her to Missouri in early spring. Delcena bit her lip, clinging to brighter thoughts. *We'll settle in Far West. All this will be behind us. We'll have a home there, a safe, peaceful place for the children to grow. Zion.*

But the gaping door loomed in front of her. She thought of her furniture: the oak cupboard her father had built for her, the pine table and chairs, the feather bed with the children's trundle underneath, the rocking chair, and Lyman's walnut desk, left to him when his father died. Down the street a dog barked. Delcena pivoted toward the sound.

Two hundred yards away, two men strode briskly in her direction. Frightened, Delcena dared not stare at them long enough to determine who they were. After a momentary hesitation, she stepped quickly into the chilly house. Her kitchen cupboard was gone, dust blanketing the floor planks where it had stood.

Her brothers walked out of the bedroom. Benjamin spoke somberly. "The furniture's stolen."

Delcena's eyes stung. Benjamin put his arm around her shoulders. They stood without speaking, the only sound the rustling of George's feet.

George broke the silence. "Let's go report this to the constable."

Benjamin's eyes smoldered. "Luke Johnson won't help us."

"Help you with what?" a voice boomed. Two men stepped through the doorway and into the house.

"Speak of the devil," Benjamin muttered under his breath.

Delcena struggled to remain composed. Her jaw clenched. She turned to face the constable, a handsome man with blue eyes and wavy black hair. His last name was Johnson, her maiden name. But he was *not* a relative. Once an Apostle, now an apostate, a friend turned enemy.

"Mrs. Sherman." Luke nodded to her.

"Constable Johnson." Delcena's voice was strangely high as anger melded with fear. "Someone has broken into my house and stolen my furniture."

Luke studied her but did not answer immediately. His lips were tinted blue from the cold.

The second man, a stranger, said, "Ma'am, your property has been confiscated to help pay Joseph Smith's debts."

Delcena's jaw quivered. "How is this possible?"

"We have evidence that your husband was a business associate of Smith's."

"I'm sorry," Luke said.

Delcena's tear-filled eyes darted to his. "Are you?"

The stranger interrupted. "Where's your husband? Perhaps he could help straighten this out."

"My husband left town to preach."

Luke took a quick breath. "That's unfortunate. We have a warrant for his arrest."

The second man glanced sharply at Luke. "Are you a fool? If she's lying, Sherman will now abscond."

"I'm constable here," Luke snapped. He turned back to Delcena. "Get word to Lyman that he needs to answer these charges for his own good."

"I don't know where he is," Delcena said.

Luke looked closely at her. Delcena lowered her eyes. Luke said, "There are a number of people who're missing. Father Smith clean disappeared from his jail cell. We went to arrest Benjamin Wilbur, but he's gone. Now your husband. I've a hunch that these men are somewhere in Kirtland. Delcena, do you know where?"

She knew of the hidden cellar at the Huntington farm, the hiding place for the Mormon underground. She told a blatant lie, something she had not done since a young child. She looked back up into Luke's eyes. Her voice remained steady while her heart pounded. "No."

"You understand that if it turns out that you're lying, I could arrest you."

Delcena did not respond.

The other man took out a gun and pointed it toward Benjamin and George. "If the lady won't talk, take these boys in. There's ways to get information out of them."

Delcena's legs shook. Benjamin clenched his fists. George's brown eyes were wide and scared.

Luke turned briskly to his companion. "No. These are Zeke Johnson's boys. You know Zeke, our carpenter friend in Mentor. These boys are honest. They'd tell us if they knew anything. Let's go."

As the men left the house, Delcena heard Luke say loudly to his companion, "I'm going home to eat first. Then I'll write up a warrant for Don Carlos Smith, and we'll go get him."

* * *

Benjamin knew it was dangerous, making the horse trot with patches of ice on the road. The wagon lurched forward.

Delcena, who sat next to him, stared straight ahead, and her voice shook as she said, "Poor Agnes. It's nearly her time. Hurry, Ben."

"I'm hurryin'."

"They'll be on horseback." George's voice edged with panic. "They'll catch us."

Benjamin said, "Maybe not. Maybe Joe was right about Luke Johnson. Maybe he's not as bad as the rest. Maybe Luke was talking loud on purpose, giving us the chance to warn Carlos."

George shook his head. "Don't count on it."

Benjamin's mind spun backward in time. Years ago, Don Carlos had been his brother David's closest friend. They had both admired the lovely Agnes Coolbrith. David had died, leaving Don Carlos to marry her. Then Benjamin had lost Seth too—then Susan and Nancy. He could almost hear their voices now, speaking to him from a distant realm, telling him not to be afraid, to get to it. With a thudding heart, Benjamin put the whip to the horse's rump and prayed that the wagon wouldn't turn over.

* * *

Fifteen minutes later, Don Carlos welcomed Delcena and Benjamin into his home. Once inside, Delcena quickly closed and latched the door behind them. A fire blazed in the hearth. While Benjamin told Don Carlos the news, Agnes moved to the other side of the room and lowered herself into a rocker. Her shoulders sagged.

Leaving the men to speak alone, Delcena went to Agnes.

"I just have to sit for a moment," Agnes whispered apologetically. Her light brown hair fell slightly in her face, laying a shadow across her hazel eyes. Her piquant little girl climbed into her lap.

Agnes spoke again, stronger this time as her little girl wrapped her arms tightly around Agnes's neck. "I prayed that we would be able to stay here until the baby comes. But we knew this might happen. Our things are packed. We can leave within half an hour."

"The constable could be here in ten minutes," Delcena warned.

"We'll hurry. Luke meant to warn us." Agnes took a shaky breath as she stood up. Her frame looked too slender to carry her pregnancy, not to mention the little girl in her arms.

"I wouldn't count on Luke Johnson's goodwill," Delcena commented.

A barely perceptible smile softened the worry in Agnes's eyes. "Luke arrested Father Smith like he was a common criminal. Then he and John Boynton helped him escape."

Sudden tears stung Delcena's eyes. How strange that the apostates, Luke Johnson and John Boynton, had helped Father Smith! Had Luke spoken truthfully when he said he was sorry about her furniture? Sometimes it was impossible to know who your enemies were.

Benjamin and Don Carlos walked over. Don Carlos took his little girl from Agnes. His voice was gentle as he addressed his wife. "It's time to leave." Agnes nodded.

Delcena hugged Agnes tightly. Agnes swallowed and brushed a tear away.

"May God be with you on your journey," Delcena said.

"And you as well," Agnes responded bravely.

"Sister Sherman," Don Carlos said. Delcena's eyes met his. In the waning light, his features were chiseled and handsome. He stood straight, tall, and slender. So much like David. "I wish I'd been able to go preach with Lyman. When he returns, tell him that we'll meet in Missouri under fairer skies."

"I will," Delcena responded.

A moment later she walked with Benjamin out to the wagon. George, who had been lookout, glared at them as they approached. "What took you so long?"

"It must have felt like an eternity, but it was really only a few minutes," Delcena responded as Benjamin helped her into the seat and tucked a blanket around her. Then he climbed in next to George.

"It was a lot longer than a few minutes," George growled. "Let's get home. I'm frozen and starved."

"Count your blessings," Benjamin said. "Think of Carlos having to leave his home. And think of Lyman on a mission, freezing cold, never knowing where his next meal and bed are coming from."

Delcena did not find the thoughts comforting.

"You weren't out here waiting, wondering if Luke Johnson was going to ride up and shoot you," George quipped.

Delcena took a deep breath as the wagon jerked over the frozen ground. "Constable Johnson is not who he pretends to be," she stated. "He helped Father Smith escape."

* * *

Ontario, Canada—Late February 1838

It was nearly dark, and an icy rain fell when Almon Babbitt and John Snider knocked on the door of William Law's modest but well-built home in Churchville, Canada. Almon's wife, Julianne, had remained in Toronto with John's family. Tomorrow Almon would be leaving Canada to travel by water to Far West, Missouri, where he would meet up with his friend Anson Call to buy land for themselves and many of the Canadian Saints.

William answered the door, and within minutes the men were seated around a roaring fire. His wife, Jane, a petite, impeccably groomed woman in her mid-twenties, brought them steaming bowls of venison stew with thick slices of bread. A moment later, she excused herself in order to take care of the children.

William made himself comfortable in a cushioned chair. "What brings you here, lads?"

"A visit to you before I leave for Missouri," Almon answered, feeling warm and comfortable. William and John were his favorites among the Canadian converts. William, a twenty-nine-year-old, stocky, blue-eyed Irishman, was articulate, intelligent, passionate, and amiable. A born leader, William would be an asset to the Church.

"Are you leaving too, John?" William asked.

John shook his head. "No. Almon's buying land for a group of us then coming back to lead us to Zion. We plan to leave by the first of May. Invest and join us. That's why we came tonight."

William shook his head. "Not yet. I don't want to leave those in the Churchville Branch who are still without means. They are preparing and one day soon we will all join you."

"It's worse in Kirtland," Almon commented. "There are so many poor." He thought of Julianne's family.

John spoke. "Every day I pray that a way will open for those suffering."

William looked affectionately at John. "God hears the prayers of a man as faithful as you."

Almon nodded and voiced his agreement. He lived under John's roof and knew the quality of the man.

"How are things with your father?" John asked William, turning the conversation away from himself. The Laws and the Sniders had been friends for many years.

William tilted his head and shrugged slightly. "His health is fine, but he's no closer to forgiving me for becoming a Mormon." William's brow furrowed, and his eyes flashed. "But this doesn't discourage Jane and me.

We're determined to hold out to the end no matter what we suffer. And how fares Mary, and your lasses and laddies?"

The flames leaped and sputtered in the hearth. Almon sat slightly apart and watched his friends chat. He crossed his legs and thought of how he liked them equally. John, nearly a decade older than William, didn't have William's Irish flare, ambition, or suavity of manners, but he made up for it in kindheartedness.

"My property is sold," William suddenly commented.

Almon sat up straight, returning to the conversation. "That's wonderful news!"

William continued. "My fortune gets even better. Jane's father's estate in Pennsylvania is about to be divided. We'll travel there to obtain her share. Then we'll come back to Churchville and prepare to leave with all who are ready. When we arrive in Zion, we'll have capital to invest."

Almon grinned broadly. "The Church needs money nearly as much as it needs revelation."

William's eyes widened at Almon's comment, and he added, "My brother Wilson is coming too."

Almon raised his eyebrows. "Really?"

William scratched his well-trimmed beard. "Wilson wants an adventure, to go look after his younger brother's interests, even though he doesn't believe a whit of Mormonism."

"Doesn't he realize that you're the smarter brother?" Almon joked.

William smiled. "Wilson claims that he's too smart to listen to your silver-tongued preaching."

"Tell him I'm glad that he's coming to Missouri where I'll continue using my silver tongue in his behalf. And I'll be on the lookout for a pretty wife for him."

"And I wish you luck," William said, his blue eyes warm as he looked into Almon's.

* * *

March 1838—A steamboat along the Missouri River

Almon stretched out his legs as he sat in a steamboat cabin with his friend Anson Call. Accompanying them were Anson's father, Cyril; Anson's older brother Harvey; and Asael Smith, the Prophet's uncle.

While the other men rested, Almon and Anson sparred with their wits.

"I knew better than to marry for money," Almon joked. "After all, it didn't do you any good."

Anson guffawed. "I didn't mind being disinherited. Mary's worth her weight in gold. But if you'd been a better preacher and converted my father-in-law, I'd be sitting pretty right now!"

Almon raised his eyebrows. "I believe Mr. Flint used the Church as an excuse. You'd already laid hands on his daughter, and he didn't want your hands on his money as well."

Anson's father, Cyril, opened his eyes and chuckled.

Anson grinned at Almon. "Not so! He disinherited Hannah too. All blame falls on you! If you hadn't cuffed me around with your knowledge of the gospel, I wouldn't have read the Book of Mormon and would now be a very rich young man."

Asael Smith sat up and stretched. Harvey Call opened his eyes. Asael said, "Take the blame, Almon. But you must share it with the Lord. After all, He called a Latter-day Prophet and restored His ancient gospel."

Almon opened his hands wide and laughed. "Then I gladly accept it!"

Anson's blue eyes were merry as he continued to talk. "Remember how we taught the gospel to nearly the entire Methodist congregation? That was a time!"

Almon nodded, but a shadow passed over his heart. "Those were the days, my friend." *Before the apostasy. Before my little son's death. Before Julianne's grief.* Almon pushed the shadow away and grinned at Anson. "But cracking through your stubborn skull, that was my greatest triumph!"

The men's conversation abruptly halted at a knock on the door.

"Come in," Asael Smith called out.

A middle-aged gentleman of average height with slightly graying hair entered the room. He appeared distinguished in his white shirt, cravat, and well-cut broadcloth suit. "Gentlemen, I recently learned that there were Mormons on board this boat."

Asael Smith nodded. "Yes, we are Mormons: members of The Church of Jesus Christ of Latter-day Saints."

"Where are you going?"

"To Far West, sir," Almon replied as he stood and sized up the man. Was he a gentleman or a Missourian looking for a fight? Were there more waiting outside the door? Was he interested in the gospel?

The man's jaw tightened, and he shook his head as he looked from Almon to each of the other men. "I am sorry to see so respectable looking a company journeying to that place."

"Why so?" Anson asked.

"Because you will be driven from there before six months pass."

Almon stiffened. He would soon bring a group of more than one hundred Canadian Saints to Far West. He eyed the man and forced his voice to sound pleasant. "By whom?"

"By the Missourians, gentlemen."

Father Call said, "Are there not human beings in that country as well as others?"

The man straightened his shoulders. "Gentlemen, I presume you are not aware of to whom you are talking."

Anson snorted. "One of the Missourians, I presume." Almon frowned. Anson was too quick to speak his mind and make his opponent defensive.

The man eyed them sternly. "Yes. I am General Wilson. I expect that I will soon be engaged in driving your people from Caldwell County. I carry here a letter from Grandison Newell of Mentor, Ohio."

"I know Newell," Cyril Call growled. "You'd do well to keep other company."

"That is undoubtedly a matter of opinion. Perhaps some in *your* company need enlightening." General Wilson pulled the letter from his pocket and read aloud:

> Good Sir,
>
> I perceive that you need further information about the notorious Joe Smith. This will aid you as you pursue a course of action. Joe Smith's moral course is so serpentine that the devil himself might be puzzled to follow him, yet the fear of sheriffs and constables have been ghosts on his track. No wonder. He has committed such incredible wickedness in pretending to direct revelations from Heaven, in ruining so many deluded but innocent families. In Kirtland, he has been successful in collecting over four hundred honest but ignorant and credulous people. They are now on their way to their supposed Zion in Missouri which they claim is theirs alone. Joe Smith has basely perverted their religious sentiments; and by pretending to act by the authority of that great Being whom all the conscientious revere, he has subjected them to a system of tyranny and plunder as he swindled the community by means of rag money. Some are overwhelmed in ruin, some are in a state of starvation, some are mad, and all are in despair.

"Gentlemen, I implore you to leave the company of such a man before it is too late."

"These facts are twisted, General," Almon said evenly. "Propaganda. Grandison Newell plotted the economic downfall of the Mormon community. Sit down and we will enlighten you."

General Wilson eyed Almon with more pity than contempt. He continued as if Almon had not spoken. "Gentleman, I implore you to go to some other place. You appear to be worthwhile men. If you go to Far West, you will eventually be butchered. I find no joy in that thought."

"We are no better than our brethren," Harvey Call said, his deep-set eyes narrowing with ferocity. "If they die, we are willing to die with them."

Wilson exhaled sharply. "You appear to be very determined in your minds. Regardless, Mormonism must be put down. Thrice false, Joe Smith's career shall be stopped!"

The general turned and headed toward the door. Anson Call suddenly stood up and called out, "If you will stop for a moment or two, I will tell you the way it can be done, for there is but one way of accomplishing it."

Turning back around, Wilson focused on Anson, a questioning look in his eye. "What is that, sir?"

Anson stepped up and stood next to Almon. "Dethrone the Almighty and Joe's career is ended. But never until then."

Almon smiled slightly. Anson had scored a point. General Wilson turned on his heel and left abruptly, slamming the door behind him.

Hours later, during a delay at Jefferson City, Almon and Anson got off the boat to stretch their legs. A few minutes after they had disembarked they were surrounded by General Wilson and over a dozen men whom they hadn't seen before. Most were rough looking and uneducated. They leaned on their guns, chewing and spitting tobacco. One man, somewhat older than the others and more genteel, spoke quietly to General Wilson while eyeing Almon and Anson.

General Wilson cleared his throat and turned to the two Mormons. "Let me introduce you to some of the Jackson County Boys. And this gentleman beside me is Governor Boggs. Perhaps they can help you change your minds."

Almon swallowed, knowing that Boggs was not a friend to the Mormons. Would he and Anson be able to get back to the boat in one piece? The moment felt familiar. A memory flashed through his mind. He and David Johnson had been surrounded after cutting hay on a hot summer day, while thunderclouds mounted the sky. Almon had been a boy then, just seventeen years old and sick with fever and terror. But Samson-like, David had wielded his scythe and frightened off the attackers. David was gone now and Almon was not just a man but a leader of men. Almon squared his shoulders. If Anson kept his mouth shut, Almon would find a way to get them out of this.

Boggs said, "I hear that you boys are Mormons on your way to Caldwell County."

Almon tipped his hat. "That we are. And we are grateful, sir, to a Mr. Alexander Doniphan. We had heard that through his efforts, Caldwell County has been set aside for our people. Because of this, all good citizens of Missouri can now live in peace. Thank you, Governor Boggs. And, thank you, General Wilson, for the pleasure of this introduction. Our boat is nearly ready to leave. Farewell."

Some of the men began to laugh derisively. One said with a sneer, "If you fellows have any brains in your pretty heads, you'll clear out while you can."

Governor Boggs smiled, and there was more laughter.

Almon turned and began walking back the way they had come. Anson followed. The Missourians parted just enough to let them through.

* * *

The next morning, Almon arrived in Far West. The wind was chill and the sky fair. While the Calls went in search of large tracts of land, he purchased a farm on the outskirts of the city. He stood alone in the late afternoon, feeling the approach of evening as he looked out at the fields and trees. This was the western edge of the country, a slave state, with little refinement. It wasn't Kirtland, but it would do. It had to do. He would build a log house for Julianne and farm this land. He would preach on Sundays and study law at night. A time would come when he no longer labored with his hands. A time would come when he built his family a mansion. A time would come when he would have the power at his fingertips to protect his Prophet and his people from ruthless judges and politicians. If he had time . . . if the mobs didn't come first . . . he would make this Zion.

An hour later, Almon met Anson at the boardinghouse for supper. His friend's face was grim. "There's not nearly enough land left in Caldwell County for all of the people we represent."

Cyril, Anson's father, joined them. He sat down next to Almon, across from his son. "I found out about land north of here, at the three forks of the Grand River. It's outside Caldwell County, but the land's cheap. If we pool the rest of the money, we can buy a thousand acres."

"Will it be safe?" Anson asked.

"I don't see that we have a choice," Cyril responded.

"Should we ask Joseph?"

"Joseph has enough on his mind."

* * *

That night Almon slept soundly. The next morning he arose early and began his journey back to Canada. Anson stayed behind to purchase the thousand acres.

With yearning look upon each face
And heartfelt grief that none can tell
With hurried kiss and short embrace
That whispered to each one farewell.

Joel Hills Johnson

Kirtland, Ohio—April 1838

Fifty-eight-year-old Julia Johnson sat up in bed, wondering if she had heard a knock at the front door or if she were dreaming. Her dark hair streaked with gray fell down her back. Her shoulders were straight and regal. It was past ten and the house was quiet. She strained to listen but heard nothing unusual. Then the sound came again, perhaps a branch tapping in the wind.

Lying back down and tightening the covers around her, Julia shivered. Bitter men still threw torches into Mormon cellars. When would the hate cease? Would they ever have the teams and wagons they needed to move? Yesterday she had heard that the Quorum of the Seventies was holding meetings, trying to put together a plan to help the poor get to Missouri. But the task seemed insurmountable.

Yet they were trying so hard. Julia's twenty-year-old, Joe, was determined to move them. He and Benjamin hired themselves out each day. How strange that Joe, who had been a delicate child, was now her strength. It was Benjamin she worried about; Benjamin whose patriarchal blessing promised that he would live to fulfill Seth's mission. But Benjamin grew thinner and coughed as he labored. At night when darkness pressed in upon her, Julia's faith wavered. She swallowed hard. She had lost four children in Kirtland.

She heard the tapping again. Louder this time. It was clearly not the wind, but a knock. Julia stood and wrapped a cloak over her white nightdress. She walked from the room, following the sound down the hallway toward the front door. Stopping briefly in the kitchen, she lit a candle, placed it in a sconce, and gripped the dinner horn. She would blow it if she needed to.

Putting her hand to the latch, she called out, "Who is it?"

"Mother Johnson, it's me, Lyman," came the whisper.

She quickly opened the front door. Hatless and clean-shaven, her son-in-law stood before her in a threadbare coat. The reflection of candlelight glittered in the lenses of his glasses. Julia noticed an ugly scar above his right eye.

Lyman took a deep breath. "Some thugs in New Portage tried to stone me, but I ran fast."

Julia embraced him. "Oh, Lyman, thanks to God you're safe!"

"Yes, thanks to God. Is my family well? Are they here?"

"Yes, yes. Go upstairs. The bedroom to the left."

"Thank you." Lyman ascended the staircase.

An instant later, Julia heard Delcena's gasp of surprise. Then she heard her daughter weep tears of relief and joy. Julia blew out the candle and walked back to her room. Why was her heart heavy? It was a great blessing that Lyman was back safely. But now her daughter and grandchildren would be leaving. The constable came by every ten days or so, asking if Lyman had returned. They would be gone before his next visit. How would she ever get the means together to follow them?

* * *

Two days later it was a windy afternoon following a day of rain. Ezekiel Johnson rode to his wife's house with his married daughter Almera sitting behind him on the horse. They rode bareback, letting the horse pick his way through the mud. Almera's arms wrapped around Ezekiel's waist, and her head rested on his back as if she was still his little girl. Ezekiel had received word that his son-in-law, Lyman, was back. They were on their way to say farewell to Delcena before she left for Missouri.

When they arrived at the house, the first thing Ezekiel noticed was the wagon packed and ready. The wind kept his eyes dry as he waited for Almera to slide off the horse before he dismounted. He followed Almera to the front door, and Julia greeted them and invited them inside. She was hardly his wife anymore. They had been separated for three years now, ever since Seth's death, when the pain of their differences had become too much for both of them.

He watched as Julia embraced Almera warmly. Then, with her arm still around Almera's waist, Julia looked at him. "Hello, Zeke."

"Hello, Julia. How are the children?"

"Fine. Amos wants to go home with you tonight if that's all right."

"Of course. Amos and I will take turns walking beside old Leo so Almera can ride."

Julia looked at her daughter then back at Ezekiel. "I was hoping that Almera could stay the night and spend tomorrow with me."

Almera interrupted. "I can't, Mama. Sam wouldn't like it. I'll look after Amos while Papa's working."

Julia's eyes clouded with concern. Ezekiel changed the subject. "Have you heard when Julianne's coming back from Canada?"

Julia nodded. "She sent a letter. They hope to be here by May. Then Almon will take her on to Missouri."

Ezekiel cleared his throat. Delcena came down the stairs with her husband and children. Ezekiel hugged his grandchildren, teasing the three oldest, Alvira, Mary, and Albey, about how they had stretched up like bean-stalks since he had seen them last. Then he kissed Seth and Daniel, the dark-haired babies, inwardly trying to convince himself that this wasn't as bad as the loss of David, Seth, Susan, and Nancy. It was a cruel fate when parents buried their children. Today was a natural part of life. Grown children moving away. But when would the ache stop?

Lyman shook his hand. Ezekiel noticed the scar at his temple but didn't ask where it came from. If this son-in-law were not such a good man, Ezekiel would hate him for fanatically embracing Mormonism and for taking Delcena along with him.

"Father Johnson, thank you for everything."

"You're welcome. When are you leaving? It won't be long until your enemies get wind of your arrival here."

"We leave before dawn tomorrow."

Ezekiel nodded. Delcena handed baby Daniel to Lyman. There were tears in her eyes as she hugged her father. "I'll think of you every day."

"And I you, princess." He held her tightly for another moment. Would he see her again? She had five babies and a husband who traipsed all over the country preaching. She wouldn't be able to drop everything and travel a few hundred miles to Kirtland, the town that had cruelly turned against them. Ezekiel would only see her if he made the journey. And at the moment, he felt very old. It wouldn't be long until the rest left—Julianne and Almon, his eldest son Joel and his family, then his wife, Julia, and the younger children, all except for Almera.

Eleven-year-old Esther, with her long dark braid, skipped into the room. "Papa, see this apron? I sewed it myself."

"It sure is pretty, sweetheart."

"Hey, Pa!" His blond-haired, brown-eyed nine-year-old Amos ran down the stairs, grabbed him around the waist, and nearly knocked him over.

"I hear you're coming home with me."

"Yep!"

"Pa," Will, his fourteen-year-old, interrupted from the doorway. "This new mare is giving us trouble. George and Mary are waiting in the barn. Could you come look at her?"

"I'll come directly," he responded.

Then he turned back to Delcena. "Don't you run off before I get back."

She smiled at him with tears in her eyes. Those tears meant the world to him. "I won't, Papa."

As he followed Will out to the barn, he thought about how in a few hours, after the good-byes were over and he was home, he would tuck Amos into bed, go to the tavern, and drink brandy until the sadness subsided.

* * *

Later that evening when all was packed and ready, Lyman and Delcena took Baby Daniel with them to bid farewell to a few close friends. When they were at Oliver Granger's home, Brother Granger pulled out a letter that the Prophet had written to the Kirtland Saints containing the latest news from Missouri. As Lyman read, tension moved through his limbs and torso, culminating in a knot in the pit of his stomach. He forced himself to continue as if nothing was wrong.

"Is Brother Joseph all right?" Delcena asked. She sat opposite him in a rocking chair, holding Daniel. Lyman knew that she sensed his mood swing, the vulnerability that he tried to hide. He nodded his head but did not look up.

Oliver Granger said, "Joseph's right as rain, Sister Sherman. You're welcome to read his letter too. You're fortunate to be leaving tomorrow. If the Seventies can get the poor out, that will be the greatest undertaking since Moses led the children of Israel."

"Do you think it's possible?" Delcena asked. "My mother, brothers, and sisters are among them."

"One thing's certain. If it's the Lord's will, they won't be left behind. You're brother Joel made sure their names were at the top of our list."

Lyman did not hear the rest of the conversation. The Prophet's words stared at him like a snowstorm whiting out any other thought.

> We have heard of the destruction of the printing office, which we presume to believe must have been occasioned by the Parrish party, or more properly the aristocrats or anarchists.

Anarchist. Lyman knew the definition. A lawless man who uses terrorism to achieve his means. *The Prophet believed that the person who set that fire was an anarchist. How would Joseph feel when he found out who the anarchist was?*

Lyman forced himself to read the remainder of the letter. It was a cheerful, kindly letter meant to comfort the Saints. The Prophet included a note to Mother Beamon whose husband had died recently. It was like Joseph to remember a suffering widow. The Prophet spoke of Far West as a safe haven. He concluded the letter referring to himself as "their servant in Christ."

Lyman carefully folded up the paper. Forcing a smile, he stood, took the baby, and handed the letter to Delcena. Lyman sat back down, bouncing little Daniel on his knee while he and Brother Granger talked about Far West and Kirtland. In the back of his mind, he thought about how he used to be open and frank with all his friends. Since setting that fire, there was a hidden part of him, a disparity between how he acted and what he was thinking. This gnawed at his energy and peace of mind. He wondered at men who lived lives of falsehood. How could they keep it up?

When Delcena had finished reading the letter, she handed it back to Brother Granger. Lyman thanked him and stood up. It was time to go. Brother Granger stepped over to his desk and retrieved a handful of letters for Lyman to take to Far West. Then Brother Granger escorted them to the door, where he embraced Lyman and wished him Godspeed.

The night was cold, and a penetrating fog lanced through Lyman as he drove the wagon home. Delcena sat next to him wrapped in quilts with Daniel nursing at her breast. For the first five minutes they traveled in silence. Tomorrow they would be leaving Kirtland forever.

Delcena said, "Lyman, do you think the Seventies will be able to get the poor to Far West? That Mama will come?"

"God willing," Lyman replied. He realized that his wife was thinking about her mother, not his act of arson. How easily the word *anarchist* had slipped from her mind.

"But they're so poor," Delcena responded. "You're fortunate that Electa and her husband were able to take your mother with them. If only Mother and the children were coming with us tomorrow!"

"I can't help that," Lyman said, his voice uncharacteristically sharp.

Delcena stiffened. "I'm not criticizing you. I'm just thankful that we're together. Brigham had to leave without his wife."

"But Brigham didn't burn down a building! Didn't you read the letter? How can I face Brother Joseph, knowing what he thinks of the man who set that fire? How can I expect the Lord to guide me when I acted rashly and faithlessly; when I am an anarchist?"

Delcena breathed out. "I wish that you hadn't set that fire, but Joseph will understand. You did it out of love for him."

Lyman moaned. "I wish to God that I'd been wiser. If the apostates find out, they'll follow me to Missouri. This will never end."

"It has ended," Delcena said. "We're moving forward, not backward."

Lyman's grip on the reins loosened a bit, allowing the horses to step out more freely. The air felt cold against his sweaty palms.

* * *

Three weeks later—a mile west of the Wabash River

From the wagon seat, Delcena stared out at the low, soft prairie stretching before them as far as the eye could see. Much of it was covered with water. There wasn't a cloud in the sky above, but distant lightning flickered on the horizon. Lyman sat next to her holding the reins. Once again she held Baby Daniel close, protecting him from the wind. The journey had been slow going, the roads badly cut up from alternate freezing and thawing. Now there was no road, just endless prairie. They traveled with another family, the Shurtliffs, whose team and wagon trailed behind them.

The quiet expanse of country was broken by the sound of the little girls singing in the wagon. Delcena thought of how it had been a stroke of luck when they had run into the Shurtliffs in Indianapolis. They were Ohio converts who had joined the Church shortly before the bank failure. Although scarcely knowing each other, the families had decided to travel together.

From the start, Lyman had liked Luman Shurtliff, an intelligent, precise, and talkative man. But it was different for Delcena. Eunice was quiet and observant, but not a skilled conversationalist. The lapses of silence between them felt uncomfortable.

On the other hand, traveling with another family made all the difference for the children. The little Shurtliff girls, Elsa and Mary, were the same ages as Delcena's Alvira and Mary. Elsa and Alvira became fast friends, and the two little Marys behaved angelically when together and only cried if they were separated. Eunice often offered to have Delcena's two little boys ride in her wagon and play with her youngest, three-year-old Lewis. As they traversed the prairie, Delcena thought about how this act of kindness significantly eased the burden of traveling with five young children.

A zigzag of lightning riddled the sky. Suddenly, it felt as if the wagon was slipping downward. Delcena held the baby tightly. The horses struggled, their legs deep in mire as the wagon's wheels sank. Once the wagon settled, Lyman turned to her. "I'm climbing out to see how bad it is."

He swung down and was looking at the wheels when Brother Shurtliff walked toward him through the sludge. He was much shorter than Lyman, and his knees churned up and down like eggbeaters. "Any ideas?" he called out.

Lyman took a deep breath. "We're going to have to carry the women and children to where the land's higher then come back and get one wagon out at a time. Hitch a chain to the tongue. It'll probably take all three span of horses pulling together. We ran into a similar mess when I was with Zion's Camp."

Lyman turned to Delcena. "Hand me the baby. I'll give him to Alvira and get you out first."

After giving the baby to the girls, Lyman slopped back through the mud and instructed Delcena to climb on his back. She complied but felt terribly unladylike with her legs apart and her skirt flapping behind her in the wind. Brother Shurtliff followed with two of his children in his arms. They left Delcena and the little ones on a high, fire-blackened section of prairie. The men went back for the others. Eunice was the last to be carried over on her husband's back.

After putting Eunice down, Brother Shurtliff turned to his children. "Don't run off and play in the mud. You'll get wet, and it's going to be cold tonight."

Delcena and Lyman both eyed five-year-old Albey. Keeping him out of the mud was like telling a horse not to graze. "Same goes for you," Lyman said sternly.

"I won't 'less I have to get Seth and Lewis out," Albey piped. Lightning flashed.

"You won't at all," Lyman commanded. "If you get wet, you'll freeze."

"But you're wet, Papa. You gonna freeze?"

"I'm wet for one reason alone—so that the rest of you stay dry and warm. Obey Mama, or you'll hear from me. Understand?" Albey sighed and nodded in defeat.

The men trudged back down into the mire as the children began digging in the soot. Delcena spoke more to herself than to Eunice. "This part of the prairie must have been burned by a lightning fire." The thought made her uneasy. They were on high ground, and lightning flashed in the distance.

Eunice nodded. "Must have."

The afternoon stretched on. Occasionally Delcena tried to carry on a conversation, but Eunice's responses were short and sometimes awkward. Eventually the women fell into silence, watching their husbands, who looked like toys in the distance, struggling with the horses and wagons.

"Their shoulders will be sore," Eunice commented.

"Especially from carrying us," Delcena added with a small smile.

Eunice took a breath. "I was thinking about the horses' shoulders. But you're right. The men too."

"And wet and cold."

"And nothing to make a fire with." Eunice gazed out at the prairie.

The temperature dropped as evening approached. Still the men labored in the distance. Lightning illuminated the western sky. The tired, hungry children huddled around their mothers. Baby Daniel wailed. Delcena sat down in the soot, feeling dirty and miserable as she nursed the baby.

Ten minutes later, the baby messed his clothes. There were no rags or water to clean him with. The little girls kicked up the ashes and yelled at each other. Two-year-old Seth whined and tried to push Daniel away from Delcena.

"Alvira," Delcena called out to her oldest, "come hold Daniel while I nurse Seth."

Alvira walked over then plugged her nose. "I won't. Daniel stinks!"

Seth screamed and pushed harder.

"It can't be helped until Papa gets here with the wagon. Please take him now," Delcena insisted.

"No!" Alvira shouted. "I'll throw up!"

"Right now!" Delcena snapped. Alvira ran off sobbing. Seth hit Daniel, and both little boys shrieked in unison. Mary burst into tears. The wind picked up, and Delcena felt like she might cry as well.

The Shurtliff children, who had previously been fussing, were shocked into silence and stared wide-eyed. Eunice took the screaming baby from Delcena and walked around with him, bouncing him in her arms. With a deep breath, Delcena began nursing two-year-old Seth.

Alvira squatted on the ground, still sobbing, her face buried in her hands. Elsa Shurtliff, who was also seven, placed her hand on her friend's shoulder and said commandingly, "Bear up, Alvira."

Eunice choked and Delcena caught her eye. Eunice shook her head. "I say that to her every day. Oh the things children learn! Poor Alvira has such a bossy playmate, and poor Elsa with such a high and mighty mother!" And suddenly Eunice was laughing and crying at the same time. Delcena joined in, crying and laughing at the absurdity of it all while Seth nursed at her breast.

It was nearly dark when the men arrived with the teams and wagons. They were exhausted, soaking wet and shivering with cold. But there wasn't a piece of wood to make a fire with, and there were the children to feed and put to bed. Exhausted, Delcena went about her work, until at last, the children collapsed on their bedrolls and, limp with exhaustion, slept.

After tucking a blanket around Seth, Delcena saw the orange glow on the western prairie. She knew at once what it was. The wind rustled the grassland, and the fire, ignited by lightning, crawled onward. She hurried to join Lyman and the Shurtliffs who were tending to the horses.

"What are we to do?" Delcena asked.

"It won't harm us," Lyman assured. "There's no grass to burn where we are."

"It will help us instead," Brother Shurtliff suddenly exclaimed. His grin looked garish in the orange and black night. "Surely the Lord watches over us. Come, let us get warm and dry!" With that, he took his wife's hand, and the two ran toward the blaze.

Lyman reached for Delcena, and they ran alongside the Shurtliffs. She felt a strange energy infuse her. A moment later, the men left their wives and raced each other toward the fire. Delcena and Eunice held up their skirts, and it felt like they were dancing with the flames parallel to them, the dry grasses rustling at their feet. Delcena's heart filled with the night's dark brightness, the wind and smoke, the miles of emptiness full of fire and stars.

When the men were warmed and dried by the flames, and the fire had passed them by, extinguishing itself in the mire, the couples walked back, the men with their arms around their wives under a black sky full of stars. After the couples divided and headed toward their separate wagons, Lyman pulled Delcena to him and kissed her with a passion and warmth that matched the vast prairie and wild beauty of the night. She shivered, feeling the need for oneness, to fill the darkness and emptiness with intimacy and love. At that moment at least, she did not play second fiddle to God in her husband's heart.

They slept soundly that night and in the morning awoke to the cooing of prairie hens and the croaking of frogs. Lyman saw a speck in the distance, and the men went to investigate. They discovered a good log from which they made a roaring fire, and the women cooked a warm breakfast. But before eating, they kneeled down together and Brother Shurtliff said a prayer, thanking the Lord for their comfortable situation and imploring God to continue blessing them, their horses, their wagons, and all they undertook. Afterward, the families ate their breakfast, hitched up their teams, and traveled on.

3

Father, Oh, forget me not
In my grief and sorrow,
May this bondage be forgot
Through Thy grace tomorrow

Joel Hills Johnson

Kirtland, Ohio—May 1838

It was early morning when Almon and Julianne knocked at the home of Julianne's eldest brother, Joel Hills Johnson. They had camped the previous night with their company of Canadian Saints on Anson Call's land in Madison, Ohio, a town near Kirtland.

Joel's wife, Annie, answered the door with a squeal of surprise and delight. She warmly hugged Julianne, her best friend since childhood. Annie was the shorter and rounder of the two, her unruly auburn hair tamed under a white, knitted cap. "Oh, Juli, when did you get back?"

"Last night. We stopped here before going on to Mother's."

Annie's four children, Sixtus, Nephi, Sariah, and Susie, jumped up from the breakfast table and ran over, pushing each other out of the way while they shouted greetings.

"The only thing our offspring can agree on is that you two are their favorite uncle and aunt," Joel called out above the ruckus as he followed the children over. Julianne broke through the crowd and embraced her brother. Almon shook Joel's hand.

"Come in and have some breakfast," Joel invited.

When they were all seated, the conversation immediately turned to the Saints' removal to Missouri. Joel explained the situation, "With the Lord's help, the Seventies are organizing a camp to help the poor. Right now we're all working to obtain what means we can. When the time comes, we'll pool our money, get the necessary outfits, and travel together. Over five hundred have committed to go, including Annie and me, Mother, and the children."

"How's Papa taking it?" Julianne asked.

"He understands."

Almon glanced at his wife. There were tears in her eyes. Were they tears of happiness? Was she thinking that her mother would go to Missouri and be close to her? Or was she thinking that her father would stay here alone?

Almon turned to Joel. "But what if there isn't enough money to go around?"

"There will be. Some have seen visions, and we have all felt the Lord's hand in this undertaking. He will not leave us alone."

"Tell Uncle about the steamboat vision!" Sixtus, a gangly ten-year-old sitting next to Almon, exclaimed.

"What steamboat vision?" Almon asked.

Joel elaborated. "A few of the brethren were out working when they saw a steamboat in the air passing right over Kirtland and heading toward the west. It was a beautiful boat, painted in the finest style, with Old Father Beamon standing in the bow of the boat, swinging his hat and singing a hymn. The men heard the sound of wagons following the boat."

Almon laughed. "That vision beats all! What hymn was Old Beamon singing?"

Joel's brow furrowed. It was clear that he didn't appreciate Almon laughing about sacred things. "I don't know."

Sixtus interrupted. "Don't you believe in the steamboat vision, Uncle Almon?"

"It's not that I don't believe it." Almon grinned as he ruffled Sixtus's hair. He could feel the boy hanging on his every word. "But it sure does sound funny."

"Papa says the vision tells us that Heavenly Father hasn't left us all alone."

"Or that Father Beamon hasn't left us alone." Almon grinned as Julianne elbowed him in the ribs, but he did not stop talking. "I'll tell you what! If I died and came back in a vision, I wouldn't be driving a steamboat. I'd grab a pair of wings and be whistling and flying through the air, like Icarus himself. I'd fly right over your house shouting, 'Ho, Sixtus Johnson! Good luck to you, my boy!'"

"And your wings would melt, and down you'd go," Annie said with a smile. "There lies poor, dear Uncle Almon."

"You forget, Annie," Almon chuckled. "I'd already be dead."

"Your *tongue* will be the death of us all," Julianne commented and turned toward her brother. "Ignore my husband and tell us more."

Joel continued. "It's been a hard winter, but spring is here at last. The camp will succeed. Zerah Pulsipher had a marvelous vision. He was praying, and a messenger in white came to him and said, 'Be one and you shall have enough.'"

Almon did not speak. Joel had not marched with Zion's Camp as he had. They had promises hinging on their unity and obedience. But they had not had the strength to be one.

* * *

At noon Almera took a loaf of bread from the larder and sat it on the table in front of the two men.

"I stopped by your mother's," Ezekiel said while Almera's husband, Sam, tore off a piece of bread, dipped it into a bowl of milk, and began chewing.

"How is she?" Almera asked.

"She misses you," Ezekiel answered.

"And I her," Almera said as she eyed Sam, her stomach knotting. He allowed her only one visit a month with her family.

She turned, walked to the counter, and brought each of the men bowls of steaming pork stew. Her father thanked her, but Sam did not.

"Are my brothers and sisters well?" Almera asked.

"Esther and Ben had a fever last night but feel better today."

Almera watched her father's fingers drum the table. He did that when he was trying to make a decision. He had aged in the past five years. Only his hands looked the same. Wrinkled and callused, they were large for his average-sized frame. Ever since she was a little girl, she had loved and hated those hands: loved them for the way they built, planted, and sowed, for how they smelled of wood and earth, and for their gentleness; but she hated them when they lifted a bottle of brandy to his lips.

She turned her head and glanced at her husband. Sam bent over his bowl, spooning food into his mouth.

Ezekiel's fingers stilled. He cleared his throat. "Almon and Julianne just came from Canada."

Almera's heart jumped. "Where are they staying?"

"Julianne is at home tonight. Almon's in Madison helping Anson Call's wife and children get ready to go. A group from Canada came with them. They're leaving early tomorrow morning. I'll take you over tonight to say good-bye."

Sam stopped eating, his blond hair prominent in the shadowy kitchen. He spoke sharply to Almera. "You've had your visit this month. You're staying put and tending to things here."

"But they're leaving," Almera begged. "Please, Sam."

"I don't want you there at all, but I still give you a visit each month. I've kept my end of the bargain, and you will keep yours. They can come here if they want to see you."

"But there isn't time. They're leaving at dawn."

Sam spoke rigidly. "That's not my concern."

"I want to see my sister!" Almera cried out.

Her father interrupted her. There was a stern edge to his voice. "Almera, your husband has decided. I'll give Julianne your best."

Almera's face grew hot, and her hands shook. She got up from the table and ran from the room, tears stinging her eyes. She hated the fact that as a woman, she was bound to obey. How could her father support Sam in this? Susan and Nancy were dead. Delcena was gone. Julianne was leaving tomorrow. Soon her mother and siblings would all be in Missouri. Her heart was breaking! She wanted to scream at the men, to tell them that loneliness was eating her alive, that they were cruel and unfeeling, that she needed the women she loved close to her. Instead, she sat down on the edge of the bed, gasping for breath.

* * *

Monday afternoon in Kirtland

Julianne and her mother were mending shirts after an early supper, sitting in the small parlor—like they had all the time in the world . . . like Julianne wouldn't be leaving the next morning. Facing the window, Julianne saw her father approach on horseback, the sky surrounding him rosy from the setting sun. "Papa's here. I'll go outside to meet him."

"He'll like that," her mother commented as Julianne set her sewing down.

She stepped lightly toward the doorway. Nearly thirty, Julianne was slender, with an upturned nose. She had once looked much younger than her age, but pain had deepened her soul; and her eyes, which had formerly shone so brightly with girlish effervescence, now held a look of compassion and kindness, of suffering and faith.

She walked outside. Ezekiel dismounted and tied the horse. Without a word, he turned and hugged her tightly.

After the embrace, Julianne looked into his eyes. "Papa, where's Almera?"

Ezekiel shrugged. "Sam wouldn't allow her to come. It pained her. Can you visit her?"

"I promised the children that I'd play games with them tonight. But I'll stop by in the morning before we leave. How can Sam treat her this way?"

"Sam's her husband. He has his reasons."

Julianne swallowed. "They are cruel reasons."

"Sam is *not* cruel," Ezekiel said in a flash of anger. Julianne did not want to argue with her father. Not tonight. She tucked her hand in his elbow.

"Let's go for a walk, Papa."

Ezekiel took a deep breath as he moved in step with his daughter, the sun sinking in the sky.

* * *

At daybreak, Almera did not get out of bed and make Sam's breakfast. Instead, she closed her eyes tightly as she listened to him stomp around the kitchen.

He barged into the bedroom, gripping a cold biscuit. "When are you getting up? I can eat this garbage, but the cow needs milking, and I have to go to the shop!"

She turned the other way. He walked over and roughly turned her over.

"Don't ignore me," he hissed. "Do you want the cow to dry up?"

"Don't touch me. I'll milk the cow," she said, her eyes blazing and her voice shaking with rage.

Sam abruptly let go of her and stalked out of the room, cursing and slamming the door behind him. After he left, her body jerked, but she did not let out a sob. She would not give Sam the satisfaction of knowing how much he had hurt her.

Fifteen minutes later, full of anger and sorrow, Almera sat on the milking stool. The cow felt her tension, and the milk would not flow. Almera heard footsteps. Had Sam come back to tell her he was sorry? Looking up, she saw Julianne and Almon in the barn entrance. She began to cry uncontrollably.

Julianne ran to Almera and took her in her arms. "Mera, oh, Mera! Papa told us what happened."

"Sam wouldn't let me come." Almera wept, her words pouring forth. "He promised he would never separate me from my family or my religion! But he has! He doesn't care. I never wanted a marriage like Mama's. And mine is worse. You and Delcie were right when you warned me. I sinned when I married him."

"No," Julianne said, "we were just worried about you. Loving and marrying a man is not a sin."

"But I don't know if I love him anymore!" Almera clung to her sister. "Now I just want to run away."

Julianne held Almera while she wept. Almon stood at the door watching, his green eyes full of concern and determination. He spoke to Julianne. "I'm sorry, but we have to go now. A whole company is waiting for us."

Julianne hugged Almera and kissed her cheek. "How I wish you could come with us!"

"She can," Almon said suddenly. Almera stopped crying, and the women stared at him, shocked and silent. Almon repeated the offer, now addressing Almera. "If you want to leave Prescott, I'll take you with us."

A moment passed. Thoughts spun in Almera's mind. *Marriage is sacred. But Sam lied to me. I can go and be with my family and my people. But Sam loved me once. If I leave him, will a man ever love me again? And what of Papa? Marriage is sacred.* Almera wiped her eyes with her sleeve. "He's my husband. I-I can't leave. And Papa is here."

"But you can't live like this forever," Julianne whispered. "If things don't get better, we'll come back someday and take you away with us. And Papa too, if he wants."

Almera nodded. After they left, she took a shuddering breath. She turned back to her work. Tears continued to creep down her cheeks, but her fingers relaxed as she milked the cow. The warm, white fluid flowed freely.

* * *

A thin, predawn mist dampened Joe's sunburned cheeks as he and Benjamin rode the horses toward Madison, Ohio. They were on the way to see Almon, Julianne, and the Canadian Saints who would be leaving for Missouri that morning. Afterward, they planned to ride from farm to farm looking for work.

Joe glanced over at Benjamin. His brother looked all right this morning. But that did not mean that Benjamin's cough and fever wouldn't return by nightfall. Joe took a deep breath. The air was fresh and full of the smell of grass growing and trees budding. His thoughts lingered on Benjamin. Their differences as boys had followed them into manhood. It was strange how close they were, how well they got along despite these differences. Joe was naturally cheerful, intellectual, and witty, while Benjamin tended to be sensitive, intent, and sometimes moody. Joe believed in Christ and in Mormonism, but it wasn't a part of his very nature as it was Benjamin's.

Indeed the love between him and Benjamin was strong, stronger then jealousy and stronger than sorrow. But love alone wouldn't make Benjamin well or take their family to Missouri. They labored like slaves six days a week at whatever work they could find. Too often they were sent away or taken advantage of because of their religion. If only there was more kindness in the world. When Jesus came again, would it be kindness that conquered hate, love that defeated both sin and death? The trees were in bloom, and the sky turned rosy as the sun rose. Despite the hardships, Joe loved this exquisite and terrifying world.

"I don't need to meet another girl," Benjamin suddenly remarked, scattering Joe's thoughts. Joe knew exactly what Benjamin was talking about. Yesterday Almon had said that there were some pretty girls among the Canadian Saints. Part of the reason for their going this morning was to meet them. "I just want to get to know Zina better."

"Don't wrap your heart around one girl until you have more experience," Joe advised with a wise smile. "I made that mistake with Rachel Risley. Keep your eyes open, and remember that they all have faults."

"Not Zina."

Joe chuckled. "Miss Zina Huntington has faults like everyone else. Trust me on this."

Benjamin eyed Joe. "Her brother, William, never complained about her. That says something."

Joe raised his eyebrows. "It sure does. If a girl is really awful, her brother's bound to praise her to a man in order to marry her off."

Benjamin smiled but shook his head. "Not William. He's a true friend."

"Remember your namesake Old Ben Franklin's advice. 'To find out a girl's faults, praise her to her girlfriends.' When we get to Missouri, take some time to talk to Zina's friends. In the meantime, look around at other girls."

Benjamin was silent for a moment, perhaps chewing on Joe's advice. Then he changed the subject. "I don't know if I'll be going to Missouri with the rest of you. You know how it's been with me. One day I feel fine, and the next day I'm flat on my back. I won't be a burden to Mother and the camp. I could stay with Almera and Pa. Come later when I'm stronger."

"If anyone belongs with the Prophet and the Saints, it's you. It's at least another six weeks before the leaders will be ready to go. You should be well by then. And if you're not, I'm with you. I'll get you to Missouri."

"You have to get Mother and the children to Missouri," Benjamin countered. "That comes first, and we both know it."

Joe didn't respond, fully aware of the weight of truth in Benjamin's words. It was Joe's first responsibility as the oldest son living at home to make sure that his mother was safe and that there was food on the table.

They rode in silence for the next five minutes. When they approached Anson Call's farm, they saw about twenty wagons camped in a large field.

Families milled around, cooking, packing, and conversing in low voices. Horses and oxen grazed on the thick spring grass. A dog barked. Smoke rose from cook-fires and wound its way upward, smearing gray into a sky that grew bluer by the moment. Joe and Benjamin dismounted and led their horses into the camp.

"That's their campsite," Joe commented, pointing to Almon and Julianne's wagon, which was near the road. But there was no cook-fire or sign of life.

Benjamin's brow furrowed. "Where are they? Will brought Julianne out here last night so she'd be ready to go first thing this morning."

"Almon must be busy," Joe commented with a low whistle as he looked around. "It's hard to believe that he's the leader of all these people, our teasing, troublemaking Almon."

"It's not so surprising," Benjamin remarked. "I've been on a mission with him. Something about him draws people to him, and he's a great preacher. When Almon digs his heels into something, there's no stopping him."

A man strode up to them. He looked to be in his forties, clean-shaven with brown hair and blue eyes. "What brings you fellows here so early this morning?"

Joe sensed wariness behind the man's words and quickly reached out his hand. "I'm Joseph Johnson, and this is my brother Ben. Julianne Babbitt is our sister. We came to say farewell."

The man's weathered face thawed as he warmly shook Joe's hand. "I'm John Snider. I've heard good things about you boys."

Joe recognized the name. This was the man Julianne and Almon lived with in Canada. "It's a pleasure meeting you."

John turned and greeted Benjamin, who returned the handshake with a smile more forced than real. Joe sensed that his brother was either worried or not feeling well. Benjamin said, "Sir, do you know where we could find Almon and Julianne?"

"They went to Mentor before dawn on family business. We plan to roll out in an hour. They'll be back at any moment. Brother Almon's true to his word if any man is. Many of these people were baptized after hearing his testimony. Gentlemen, come and meet my wife and children. We'd consider it an honor."

Joe and Benjamin followed John to a neat campsite where a girl stirred mush in a kettle that hung over a small fire. She looked up. Hair the color of cherrywood curled around the edges of her bonnet, and her eyes were the exact blue of the morning sky. Joe smiled and nodded at her. Color rose in her cheeks, and her hand stilled on the spoon.

"My fourteen-year-old daughter, Harriet," John introduced. "Harriet, these are Sister Babbitt's brothers Joseph and Benjamin Johnson."

"It's nice to meet you," Joe said as he took off his hat. Benjamin nodded a greeting.

"The pleasure is mine," Harriet said quickly, her color rising as she went back to stirring. A woman carrying a little girl walked around from the far side of the wagon, followed by two boys who both looked to be around ten years old.

"My wife, Mary, and my sons, Ed and Johnny. And this little one is our baby, Julia." He turned to his wife. "These are Sister Julianne's brothers, Joseph and Benjamin Johnson." Sister Snider warmly shook Joe's and Benjamin's hands, then invited them to breakfast.

A few moments later, the group sat around the fire eating corn mush sweetened with maple sugar. At first the Sniders discussed the detailed plans for their journey. John mentioned that he had forwarded funds to Anson Call, who was in Missouri buying land and putting in crops for them.

"Joseph and Benjamin, when will your family move to Missouri?" Sister Snider asked.

Joe glanced at Benjamin, who stared at his bowl of mush. Joe cleared his throat and said, "The Seventies in Kirtland are organizing a camp to help the poor. We hope to travel with the camp and leave Kirtland sometime in midsummer and arrive in Far West by early fall." Unbidden, a numbing chill passed through Joe. They had been focusing so much on leaving that he had thought very little about their arrival. This late in the season, there would be no time to put in crops. How would he sustain his mother and family once they were there?

As if perceiving his worry, Sister Snider continued. "John and I want our children educated. Last winter, your sister tutored them. She often mentioned you as an example of a superb scholar. Perhaps next winter, when we are all together in the land of Zion, you would be schoolmaster for the children in our company? It would be a large school."

Joe smiled. "I'd be delighted."

Suddenly the boy Johnny interrupted. "Sister Julianne told us riddles at school. Do you know any?"

"Absolutely," Joe said. "Johnny, how is your nose like the V in *civility*?"

Johnny shrugged.

"It lies between two I's. Eddy, this one is for you. Why is a windy, stormy day like a child with a cold in its head?"

"'Cause the cold gives the boy a cold?"

"A good try. But here's the better answer. It blows, it snows. Now say it fast. It blows its nose!"

The boys laughed. Following their example, Baby Julia joined in, clapping her chubby hands. Joe listened for a giggle out of their older sister, Harriet, but did not hear one. Yet he felt those clear blue eyes watching him. He dared not turn and look, for he was sure she would turn away. He wondered if she was smiling.

The next moment, Harriet stood up and gathered the dishes. She looked down as Joe handed her his bowl. Her hand looked small and strong, with a blue vein branching near her wrist and delicately traveling to her index and ring finger. Then Benjamin called Joe's attention to Almon and Julianne, who had rounded the edge of the woods bordering the road and now walked toward the camp. The Johnson brothers took their leave, tipping their hats to the Sniders and wishing them a safe journey.

Joe and Benjamin met Almon and Julianne at their wagon. Julianne hugged each of them tightly. "I will miss you terribly," she said. Joe noticed that her eyes were red and that there was a catch in her voice. But she was smiling, not crying. He hoped that someday he could find a wife like his sister, someone sweet and happy who smiled even when things were hard.

Almon cheerfully shook their hands. "Did you come across any pretty girls while waiting for us?"

"We met the Sniders," Joe said. "Harriet Snider looks like a charmer."

Almon cocked an eyebrow at Joe. "That she is."

Benjamin cleared his throat. "But she has faults, remember? You better get a list of her girlfriends from Almon."

Almon chuckled. "Don't pull me into this. He'd be better off sticking his hand into a den of rattlers than courting a girl and her friends at the same time."

Joe shook his head good-naturedly. "You've the wrong idea. Ben's referring to a quote by Benjamin Franklin. 'If you want to know a girl's faults, praise her to her girlfriends.' But I already know Miss Snider's faults. She's shy as a mouse and a mere fourteen years old."

Julianne humphed. "You men talk about girls like you're sizing up a mare. Harriet's a darling. She's only shy until you know her. And she won't be fourteen forever."

Before Joe responded, Almon put his arm around Julianne's shoulders. "It's time for us to roll. Joe, could you help me hitch up the oxen? And Ben, load those crates into the wagon. We'll continue this conversation when we're all together again in Missouri. Until then, don't be discouraged, boys—I've already corralled the finest filly in the herd."

Julianne shook her head and rolled her eyes.

As if he didn't notice his wife's response, Almon stepped back and glanced around the camp. Joe noticed that Almon's stature changed as quickly as a gentleman might don a new hat. A look of leadership, competence, and purpose entered his eyes. When Almon strode off to find his team of oxen, other men began hitching up their animals. Joe followed.

* * *

It infuriated Benjamin the way he felt shaky and tired after lifting a couple of crates. How was he going to make it through the remainder of the day, much less to Missouri when they left this summer?

"Are you all right?" Julianne asked.

Benjamin coughed as he turned to her. His face was red from exertion. "I don't know," he muttered.

Julianne's voice was gentle. "Our prayers are with you. You'll get well. I feel it. It won't be long until we're all in Missouri together."

Benjamin nodded stoically. "But what if I'm not strong enough to travel when the poor camp leaves? I don't like the idea of staying here."

"The Lord will open a way for you. You're so faithful." Julianne was quiet for an instant, then she exclaimed, "Oh, Benja! I'm so worried about Almera."

"Why? Did you see her in Mentor this morning?"

Julianne nodded. "She wants to go to Missouri with all her heart. But she can't right now. As long as you're here, watch over her. I pray that a way will open for her to join us."

Benjamin shook his head. "Sam won't consider it."

Julianne took a deep breath. "He isn't kind to her."

"In what way?" Benjamin asked quickly.

Julianne swallowed. "Sam doesn't strike her. And he hasn't been unfaithful. But he is angry and won't let her spend time with her family or worship as she chooses. She's so unhappy."

Benjamin took a quick breath. He hated the thought of Almera's sorrow. Was it God's will that he remain in Kirtland for a time and help her? But how could he help Almera when she was a married woman? A husband was the head. But Benjamin's mother had always acted independently.

Benjamin's thoughts were interrupted by the sound of Almon blowing a bugle, calling the company together for a prayer before they set off. Joe, who had just hitched up Almon's team of oxen, walked over to them. Julianne stepped between her brothers, tucking her hand into each of their elbows.

The three siblings walked over to the circle of travelers and knelt down together.

Almon's voice rose, expressive and resonant. He thanked Heavenly Father for His mercy and kindness then beseeched Him for guidance and protection on their journey. His prayer continued. He asked for blessings upon the Saints who had not yet found a way to gather to the land of Zion and that the Lord of Heaven open a straight pathway for their deliverance.

4

Oh Zion how I love
Thy great and holy cause
Could I thy wicked foes remove
And safe enforce thy laws—

How would I leap for joy
And labor day and night
Their evil works all to destroy
And put their hosts to flight—

That Zion may arise
And cause her light to spread
Till every people in surprise
Shall find her at the head—

Joel Hills Johnson

Far West, Missouri—May 1838

Two weeks after arriving in Far West, Delcena stood in the doorway of her newly constructed cabin and watched Lyman walk down the wide avenue toward the Prophet's residence. She took a deep breath. It was a lovely, cool morning with a light breeze and birds singing. Lyman was on his way to find Joseph, determined to at last confess that he had started the fire at the printing office. Delcena knew that her husband was uneasy, but she also knew that the Prophet would set his mind to rest. Then he would feel as she felt this morning: peaceful and happy.

It didn't matter to her that the log cabin was small, with one room downstairs and a simple loft above where the children slept. It was tightly built to protect them from the blistering sun and bitter wind. Two windows faced each other on opposite walls. At breakfast time, the eastern window filled with rosy light. At dinnertime, she could watch the sunset in the west.

Gratitude filled Delcena as she closed the front door and turned around. She walked to the corner and touched the smooth steps leading up to the loft. She gazed at the hearth, the chimney, the rack where she kept her dishes, her new table and chairs, and she and Lyman's straw-tick mattress. Alvira, Mary, and Albey were off exploring their new surroundings. Seth and Daniel napped. She smelled the new wood and felt a familiar quickening deep within her abdomen, a life apart from her own. Just three months ago, she had been fearful of the unknown and terrified that she might not see her husband again. Now they were together in the land of Zion, in the city of Saints. Tonight she would tell Lyman that they would have another child in the fall.

* * *

Lyman took off his hat and held it between his hands as Emma Smith, eight months pregnant, invited him in. "Good morning, Brother Lyman. How is your family?"

"Very well."

Emma smiled. "Tell Delcena that I will come visit tomorrow. Little Joseph misses Albey." Then Emma directed Lyman to the Prophet's study.

How can I find the words to tell him? Lyman struggled as he stood at the door.

"Come in." Joseph's voice was welcoming.

As Lyman entered, the Prophet stood and reached across his desk to shake hands. "Lyman, my beloved brother, how good it is to see you again!"

"To find you safe and well is an answer to my prayers," Lyman said. "Do you have a few moments to spare?"

"Yes, yes." Joseph indicated a chair for Lyman to sit in. Sitting back down, Joseph's blue eyes twinkled as he said, "I'm penning answers to questions I've been asked a hundred, no, a thousand times. What do you think of my answer to number ten? 'Was Joseph Smith a money digger?' 'Yes, but it was never a very profitable job for him, as he only got fourteen dollars a month for it.' Here's number eleven: 'Did not Joseph Smith steal his wife?' And I say, 'Ask her, she was of age, she can answer for herself.'"

Lyman forced a chuckle, but the laughter died on his lips. There was a lead weight in the pit of his stomach.

Looking into Lyman's eyes, the Prophet's mood shifted. "Ah, my faithful friend, we are in a refiner's fire, are we not? And the fire is not yet put out. Leading men who have shared visions of heaven continue to fall away from the Church: Oliver and David, witnesses to the Book of Mormon, and William McClellin, one of the Twelve. It has to end. But when will it? Will you always stand beside me?"

Lyman swallowed. He had told the Prophet this answer many times, and yet Joseph still questioned him. Didn't Joseph know that he would die for him? Lyman heard a knock outside the room. Thoughts crowded in his mind. Emma must be greeting another visitor. He did not have much time. Lyman said, "I will always stand beside you, if you will have me." He cleared his throat. "Joseph, I have erred to the other extreme. I have been overzealous in my faithfulness."

"If you have erred in being too faithful, it is a blessing to me," Joseph said with sudden warmth.

"You might not think so when you know what I have done."

"Now, Lyman, I know you haven't killed anyone," Joseph said with a tease in his eyes. Lyman knew that the Prophet wasn't making fun of him but trying to calm and encourage him.

"No, I haven't killed anyone."

Before Lyman could continue, Emma entered the room with tears in her eyes and a piece of paper in her hands. She handed it to her husband. "Forgive me for interrupting. But it's from the Marshes." Her voice broke, and she was unable to go on.

Joseph took a deep breath and read the note aloud.

> Our son, James, died this morning. He was fourteen years, eleven months, and seven days old. Brother Joseph, would you be so kind as to speak at his funeral on Wednesday?
>
> Yours in the bonds of grief and brotherhood.
>
> Thomas

Joseph stood up and stepped away from the desk. He embraced Emma and spoke gently, "James was a good boy. He died in full triumph of the everlasting gospel."

With an arm still around his wife and his blond lashes moist with tears, Joseph turned to Lyman. "My friend, I have to go and comfort the Marshes.

As to our previous conversation—we will talk of it again if you want to. But in my heart, I do not believe that you need to confess to me. If you fear you were in error, go to our Heavenly Father. I already know your faithful heart."

* * *

Far West, Missouri—July 4, 1838

Lyman's kiss on Delcena's forehead awakened her from a deep sleep. His lips were dry and warm like the brush of a late summer leaf just before it turns from green to scarlet. Baby Daniel snored softly in the crook of Delcena's arm. Groggy from tending to the baby much of the night, Delcena's vision slowly came into focus. Shaved, combed, and dressed, Lyman smiled down at her, his dark expressive eyes magnified by his glasses. "I'm off to hang the stars and stripes."

Delcena's memory jogged as her mind cleared. It was the Fourth of July. Yesterday Lyman, Brother Shurtliff, and several other men had felled a large white oak near Goose Creek. They had spent a good part of the day fashioning the trunk into a liberty pole for the Independence Day ceremony in which the temple's cornerstones would be laid. Lyman was going now to set up the liberty pole and hang the flag.

"Did you find the hominy and wild plums I left out for breakfast?" Delcena asked.

"Yes. The procession starts at ten. Is Daniel well enough for you to leave the children?"

Delcena nodded. "He isn't sick. His teeth are coming in. I'll send for the Shepherds' girl."

Two hours later as Delcena left the cabin, words of the Prophet's revelation echoed in her mind. *Let the city, Far West, be a holy and consecrated land unto me . . . The ground upon which thou standest is holy. Therefore, I command you to build a house unto me . . . And let the beginning be made on the fourth day of July . . .*

The sun shone brilliantly in the cloudless sky, and Far West teemed with activity. Delcena joined the crowd of Saints moving toward the public square. The procession was led by the militia, followed by the Prophet, his brother Hyrum, Sidney Rigdon, the Twelve, other priesthood leaders, and finally the congregation of ladies and gentlemen. The cavalry and band brought up the rear. When they reached the square, they began forming a large circle around the site excavated for the temple.

The site was more than a hundred feet long and eighty feet wide. Someday the temple would have three floors, the first for worship and the other two for educational purposes. Delcena imagined the blossoming of the city, the wide avenues, the beautiful buildings, the exquisite temple, a gem gleaming in the sunlight.

"Ladies in front and gentlemen behind," a voice boomed out.

A thrill coursed through Delcena as she moved with the throng of women, feeling the strength of their sisterhood. There were many that she loved: Emma Smith, Mary Feilding who had recently married Hyrum Smith, Clarissa Hancock, Nancy Tracy, and Eunice Shurtliff. The ceremony began. She was so close that she could nearly reach out and touch the cornerstones as the men carried them. Each cornerstone was laid by officers in the priesthood assisted by twelve other men. The band played a tune as each stone was set into place. Tears gathered in Delcena's eyes as she watched Lyman help lay the southwest corner. Years ago, he and Seth had helped lay the cornerstones of the Kirtland Temple. David, Nancy, and Susan had been with her that day.

Heavenly Father, her heart cried out, *bless my family. Help us to be able to stay in this land and raise our children in freedom and peace.*

The final stone was laid. The band quieted. Sidney Rigdon moved to the center of the temple site, the flag of the United States buckling and flapping in the breeze. Sidney stood straight and dignified, with his dark, arching eyebrows, his straight nose, his thin lips. His distinctive voice rose above the wind, resonating through the square.

The first part of the speech was patriotic. Sidney expressed his admiration for the free institutions of the United States government. He spoke of freedom and declared "all attempts, on the part of religious aspirants, to unite church and state, ought to be repelled with indignation." He reviewed the establishment of the Church of Christ in this new dispensation and spoke of the suffering the Saints had endured; how they had been smitten and had turned their cheek again and again, only to suffer more abuse from both within and without.

It grew warm. Delcena took a handkerchief out of her pocket, dabbing the perspiration forming on her forehead and temples.

The tone of President Rigdon's speech changed. "Better, far better to sleep with the dead than be oppressed among the living. But from this day and hour we will suffer it no more. Our rights shall no more be trampled on with impunity; the man, or the set of men who attempt it, do it at the expense of their lives. And the mob that comes on us to disturb us, it shall be between us and them a war of extermination; for we will follow them until the last drop of their blood is spilled.

"Remember it then, all men. We will never be the aggressors, we will infringe on the rights of no people, but shall stand for our own until death.

We claim our own right and are willing that all others shall enjoy theirs. No man shall be at liberty to come into our streets, to threaten us with mobs, for if he does he shall atone for it before he leaves the place; neither shall he be at liberty to vilify and slander any of us, for suffer it we will not, in this place. We therefore take all men to record this day, that we proclaim our liberty this day, as did our fathers, and we pledge this day to one another our fortunes, our lives and our sacred honors, to be delivered from the persecutions which we have had to endure for the last nine years or nearly that time. We this day, then, proclaim ourselves free with a purpose and determination that never can be broken. No, never! No, never! No, never!"

A cheer broke out after Sidney finished speaking, yet Delcena's heart pounded in her chest. Weren't threats more likely to beget violence rather than peace? Was the safety and peace she felt a sham? Were they on the precipice of war? Glancing over at Eunice, she saw fear in her quiet friend's eyes.

The leading Brethren stood and announced the Hosanna Shout. Delcena joined in, waving her white handkerchief, with tears running down her cheeks as her soul begged God for peace.

Levi Hancock stood up on the southeast cornerstone. "The Prophet Joseph asked me to write a song for this occasion. I was up most of the night doing it. It's called "A Song of Freedom," and my Uncle Solomon will help me sing it to you folks."

Solomon Hancock joined Levi on the stone, and their voices rang out free and strong.

To Celebrate this day of freedom, Don't let it ever be lost.
Remember the wars of our Fathers. And also the blood they have cost.
Go children, and tell the same story to your children's children unborn.
How English lords, tyrants and Tories, have once caused your fathers to mourn.
'Twas honor that nerved up your Fathers and caused them to go forth and fight
To gain us this great day of freedom, In which we can now take delight.
Yes, daughters, you too have your freedom, You too have your country most dear,
You love well your own Independence, Your Forefathers gained for you here.

Exalt then the standard of Freedom, and don't leave upon it a stain.
Be firm and determined forever, Your freedom and rights to maintain.
Remember the God of your Fathers. Ye Sons and ye Daughters give ear;
Then with you 'twill be well hereafter, And nothing you'll then have to fear.

* * *

The next day, Lyman and Delcena ate supper with their children when thunder clapped, then a flash of light followed by a crashing, tearing sound so loud that it sounded as if the earth split open. Alvira's eyes widened. Little Mary began crying. Albey climbed out of his chair. "Papa, let's go see what happened!"

Lyman quickly shook his head as he stood up. "All of you stay with Mama. I'll be back soon. Don't worry."

A moment later, Lyman joined the other men, women, and barefoot youth running toward the temple site. When there, Lyman stopped short. The white oak liberty pole had been struck by lightning and lay in splinters on the ground. Lyman bent down and picked up a piece of wood. A moment later Luman Shurtliff was next to him.

Brother Shurtliff took a deep breath. "Is this a sign from God? A farewell to our liberty in Missouri?"

Lyman stared at the splinter of wood in his hand. "I hope not. Not when we have finally come to Zion."

"You heard Elder Rigdon's speech," Brother Shurtliff said. "If the Missourians try to drive us out, there will be war."

"I marched with Zion's Camp," Lyman countered. "The Prophet hates war."

Brother Shurtliff continued. "I was called to a meeting last week—under the direction of Sampson Avard. The brethren are organizing into groups—calling themselves Danites. They've already driven out the dissenters and are ready to do whatever it takes to keep us safe and free. Some talk of fighting and of lynching those who break their oaths."

Lyman felt a sudden coldness. He thought of the dissenters whom he had testified against, of Luke Johnson, who had helped Father Smith escape. "Does the Prophet sanction this organization?"

Brother Shurtliff went on. "I think so. Brother Avard says he speaks for the Presidency. Remember President Rigdon's sermon two weeks ago, where he talked about salt losing its savor, and asked us to rise up and rid ourselves of those who would destroy the Church? The Danite preaching is in line with that and with what President Rigdon said yesterday."

Lyman nodded, not taking his eyes off Brother Shurtliff. "Yes, but the Prophet stood up after President Rigdon and said that he didn't want the brethren to do anything unlawfully."

"But what is unlawful in a lawless state, where the governor states that the voice of the people is the voice of God? Where a Mormon, an Indian, or a free Negro can be lynched without cause?" Brother Shurtliff asked.

A thought ran through Lyman's mind—a quote by Benjamin Franklin—one of Seth's favorites. Lyman couldn't remember it word for word, but it was something about how a democracy should not allow wolves to vote to eat the lamb; rather it should arm the lamb.

Lyman shrugged. "I don't know. But I will follow the Prophet Joseph, not Sampson Avard."

Brother Shurtliff nodded. "And I. There's Joseph now." The men did not speak further but watched as Joseph walked through the crowd and stood where the liberty pole had been. His shoulders were straight, his voice clear when he said, "A time will come when the Saints will triumph over every foe just as I now walk over these splinters."

* * *

Kirtland, Ohio—July 5, 1838

The morning of Julia's last full day in Kirtland was beautiful, with a thin layer of clouds and a soft breeze breaking through the summer heat. She supervised as her family hung the chicken cage, the butter churn, and barrels of cornmeal and flour to the outside of the wagon. Soon the house was virtually empty. Most of Julia's furniture and goods had already been shipped by water, first to St. Louis, then up the Missouri River, and on to Richmond, Clay County, Missouri.

Later that afternoon, they would leave the house and gather with the Kirtland camp to a large field about one hundred rods south of the temple where they would spend the night in order to begin the trek the following day. Julia swept the plank floor for the last time as morning stretched into midday and the clouds lingered, still insulating them from the sun.

"Good news, Mother," Joe said as he strode into the house. His face was red from activity and there was dark stubble on his narrow chin. He smiled. "Everything's coming together. Ben stayed to help Joel finish packing. There's some refractory stock that needs driving. Ben's agreed to start with us and do the job. If he can't bear up, he'll head back to Pa's in a day or two. But for now, Ben's coming with us!"

Tears sprang into Julia's eyes like rain out of a clear blue sky. She had been strong for months, working tremendously hard and moving forward, tucking away any grief about leaving Benjamin, Almera, and Ezekiel. But now the fact that Benjamin was coming dissolved her defenses. His health had improved somewhat, and she had prayed that he would have the faith to come with them. Yet he had continued to refuse, fearing that he would be a burden to the camp. The Lord had answered her prayers by providing unmanageable oxen.

Joe wrapped his arms around her. They were wiry and tan from work. "Don't cry, Mother. It's Zion Ho! And Ben will be with us."

Julia dried her eyes and smiled. "Yes, son. And the Lord is with us as well."

* * *

The cloud cover dispersed at evening. Over four hundred people had set up camp in the field, with the temple to the north of them, a majestic structure cut out of the darkening sky. The temperature remained pleasant, and the sky shone clear from horizon to horizon. The moon rose, and the first star appeared.

Standing near his eldest son, Ezekiel looked forward, the lines of his face resembling carved stone in the waning light. He and Almera had come to the camp to spend a final evening with their family. Almera had saved her monthly visit for this night.

"How many are in the entire camp?" Ezekiel asked.

"Over five hundred," Joel answered. "But some won't be here until tomorrow morning."

"As conspicuous as an earthquake," Ezekiel stated. "If Mormon haters decide to attack you, they sure won't have trouble finding you."

"There's safety in numbers," Joel returned.

"Maybe. Are you divided into companies?"

"Yes. About thirty to each. We share a tent and provisions."

"Who's in your company?"

"Annie and me. Mother and the children. Samuel Hale and his family and a woman named Susan Bryant."

Ezekiel glanced over at the two oxen that were now placidly grazing. He had seen Benjamin working with them earlier. "Those oxen are going to give you trouble."

"Probably. That's why I need Ben."

Ezekiel took a deep breath. "Let's hope he's strong enough. Write when you can. Almera won't hold up without letters. I'm going go say good-bye to the others now. You have a heavy load, son."

"Pa, if you ever decide to come to Missouri, you're welcome in my home. Send me word, and I'll come back and help you make the trip."

"That's not likely," he returned rather gruffly. "I've a business here and Almera and Sam to keep me company." He shook his son's hand, feeling his own shame and helplessness. He was a man who could not protect nor direct his own family. This day had been a long time in coming. He had grieved before and would grieve later, but tonight he would not shed a tear. His next statement came through clenched teeth. "Take care of my wife and children."

"Of course, Pa."

Ezekiel walked over to his silver-trimmed shotgun that leaned against Joel's wagon. He turned and saw Julia, about a hundred yards away with Mary. They were hooking the kettle to the wagon. Benjamin and Joseph were talking with Almera, their heads inclined toward her. George and Will sat around a campfire with a group of youth roasting apples. His younger children were not in sight but somewhere with the hordes running and playing in the moonlight as if they were on a holiday with friends and without a care in the world. They had no idea what they were in for—the starving and sickness they were bound to encounter before their journey's end. He walked stiffly toward Julia, his arthritis bothering him more than usual.

"Pa!" Ezekiel turned toward the voice. Benjamin had left his brother and sister and was walking quickly toward him. He looked handsome and manly, more slender than David, but not as thin as Seth had been. His square jaw was sensitive, yet his features could harden in an instant if he became angry or afraid. Ezekiel swallowed the lump forming in his throat. What would Benjamin suffer as a Mormon? As he proved his new manhood?

"I was feeding the stock. And worried that you'd already be gone," Benjamin said with emotion. "I'll miss you, Pa."

"Take Betsy," Ezekiel said as he handed Benjamin his silver-trimmed gun.

"Are you sure, Pa? I have a gun."

"Not as good as this one. Give yours to George or Will. Those oxen will give you trouble. You'll trail behind the rest of the company. And who knows what you'll encounter when you get to Far West. Mormon haters are thick as flies. Seth took this gun with him to Missouri. Each time you raise it to your shoulder, remember me and Seth and the things we taught you. Be true and honest. Upright. Keep your word."

Benjamin blinked back tears and hugged his father. "I will. When things settle down, Pa, I'll visit and bring you back your gun."

Ezekiel nodded briskly. "I'll be going now."

He felt a hand on his shoulder and turned to see seventeen-year-old Mary. She was crying too hard to speak. She threw herself into his arms, and he held her as she wept.

Almera came and touched Mary's shoulder. Mary turned and clung to her sister. Almera's brown hair looked even darker in the night, while Mary's blond reflected the moonlight.

George and Will walked over. George flipped his bangs out of his eyes and shook Ezekiel's hand. He glanced over at Benjamin holding the gun, then he grinned at his father. "I wish you'd given me that gun, Pa. I'd take better care of it than Ben. And he already has one."

"Ben's older, son."

"But not smarter."

Ezekiel managed a crooked smile. "I've no opinion on that account. Do your best each day like David and Seth. See that you help your mother." He hugged George and turned to Will, who was just a year younger. Both these boys were shorter than their brothers, built more like Ezekiel. "You too, son. Keep in line and look out for your brothers and sisters. If either of you decide to leave Missouri, come back here and I'll help you get a start."

Will did not answer but briefly embraced his father. Ezekiel continued to look at his sons. Would he be able to remember their features? Will and George were almost grown now, but Ezekiel could hardly remember their boyhood. It had been lost somewhere in the tumult of the past six years.

Ezekiel looked up and saw Julia walking over with a lantern. For an instant he remembered when he first met her. She was fifteen then. When he had told her that he had no family, she had exclaimed, "If by wishing or praying I could bring back your family, I would." He had loved her from that moment on. But now, through cruel twists of fate or God, she was taking his family away. Yet she had the right to them. He had never been good enough. On the very day he had met Julia, he had learned the truth: his inheritance was one of illegitimacy and shame.

Julia was near him now. She said, "Joe went to find Esther and Amos. They'll be along in a moment."

Ezekiel looked down. How was he to say good-bye to this woman who had brought him so much joy and so much pain?

"I wish you a safe journey," he muttered.

"You will always be in my prayers," Julia said so softly that he could barely hear. Or perhaps it was his hearing that was going. He was an old man now.

He took a deep and painful breath. This might be the last time he ever saw her. He placed his hands gently on her shoulders and kissed her forehead. "And you are in my heart."

Then Julia was weeping, and Esther and Amos were in his arms. He hugged them tight then quickly separated.

Joe shook his hand. "I'll take care of them, Pa. We'll be together again someday."

Ezekiel nodded then called Almera over. She clutched her mother, weeping uncontrollably. Without a word, he untied Leo and climbed on. With tears falling unchecked, Joe helped Almera up behind Ezekiel. She buried her head between her father's shoulder blades and continued to weep. Together, through the dark streets of Kirtland, they began the lonely ride back to Mentor.

* * *

The same day, twenty-five miles west of the Mississippi River

Julianne's hands, dirty and callused from the two-month-long journey, trembled with exhaustion as she pulled the oxen to a halt. She was in the lead wagon.

"What is it?" Sister Call, who sat beside her, asked quickly. Sister Call's five-month-old baby, Moroni, continued to nurse.

"There are three riders in the distance. Coming toward us. I can't tell who they are." There was an edge in Julianne's voice. Almon and Brother Lathrop had ridden ahead hours ago to scout out a place to camp. Were they two of the three riders? Had a friend from Far West ridden out with news? Or were they Missourians who had intercepted Almon and now approached to terrorize the rest of the company?

John Snider and the Jackson brothers rode their horses up to Julianne's wagon. "In a few minutes we'll know if they're friends or foe," John said matter-of-factly. "Don't worry, Sister Julianne. The Lord has been with us." The three men stationed themselves in front of Julianne's wagon, their guns ready.

Julianne took a deep breath. With escalating tensions between the Mormons and the old settlers, they were pushing hard and were now twenty-five miles west of the Mississippi River. At the rate they were going, they would arrive in Far West in about twelve days.

Thus far all had gone well. They had been able to purchase adequate food and had not suffered an outbreak of disease. But relentless fatigue pressed upon them. Cold stares and jeers from Missourians drained their energy. But Almon could make friends with anyone. Surely he was one of the riders and had convinced some unsuspecting Missourian that the Mormons were the best people on earth.

Julianne jolted at the sound of Sister Call's voice. "It's Anson!"

"Are you certain?" Julianne asked, shading her eyes and straining to see more clearly. The wind caused her eyes to water, the tears making streaks through the dust on her cheeks.

"Yes. See how straight he sits in the saddle. And that's Brother Babbitt and Brother Lathrop with him. Would you hold the baby for me?"

Julianne nodded and took the child in her arms. Sister Call jumped nimbly down from the wagon seat, calling out to her two children riding in the wagon. "It's your papa coming!"

Sister Call and her children ran across the prairie. Now the riders were close enough for Julianne to recognize Almon among them. Then the horse bearing Anson Call sprang ahead of the other two and galloped toward them.

Anson and his family reunited while Almon and Brother Lathrop loped toward them. Julianne looked down at the baby in her arms. They would soon be in Far West. It would be wonderful to be with Delcena again. But how long would it be until she had a baby of her own? Since Little David's death, she and Almon had been busy, so busy—living through the terrible apostasy in Kirtland, then going on missions together when Almon was not traveling back and forth from Canada to Kirtland to Missouri. They had rarely been alone. She had been afraid, terrified of becoming pregnant, of opening herself again to such love and potential loss. But now her need and hope swelled greater than her fear. Perhaps if she and Almon could love each other in a house of their own in Zion.

"So, Anson," Sister Call's voice broke into Julianne's thoughts as the group approached, "come see the boy you left when he was scarcely a month old."

Anson Call walked over to the wagon and reached up. Julianne handed him the baby.

With a quick wink at Julianne, Almon put a hand on Anson's shoulder. "This child's a sight handsomer than you, my friend. A passerby wouldn't know he's yours."

Sister Call smiled and hooked her arm into her husband's. Then she leaned against him. Her excitement gave way to weariness. She sighed and looked at Julianne. "Just two more weeks of this." Then she said to her husband, "Have you built me a house in Far West?"

Anson smiled. "Not there, Mary. But we have land as far as your eye can see, and I'm building you a fine place at the Three Forks of the Grand River. But it's not ready yet. We need to cut hay and buy stock. "

"Where will we stay until it is ready?" Sister Call asked.

The baby began to fuss, and Sister Call took him from her husband. Julianne's thoughts echoed her question. When would she have a house of her own?

"There's a boardinghouse in Far West," Anson said. "But if it's full, we'll stay in the wagon. Those going to Three Forks with me will have to head out as soon as we're rested."

John Snider smiled, though his eyes were bloodshot from the rigors of the journey. "The sooner, the better. Brother Almon's told us that the soil's fertile."

"It's beautiful country," Anson said. Then he glanced at Almon. "Brigham Young's brother, Phineas, plans to settle at Three Forks with us. Almon, sell your land in Far West and come. It's getting mighty crowded in Caldwell County."

Julianne shivered. Three Forks was too far away from the bulk of the Saints. Almon had told her what General Wilson had said. *They would be driven away within six months. Joseph Smith must and would be stopped.*

Her eyes briefly met Almon's. He raised his eyebrows good-naturedly as he answered Anson. "I'll stay in Far West and be your eyes and ears. If I get wind of any trouble brewing, I'll be in Three Forks before the wind changes directions."

5

Feeling, too, within determined,
All my burden to leave there
When my heart I have examined
Humbly bow myself in prayer.

From the presence of my Father
Light and glory fills my soul;
Mercy, love and peace together
With his Spirit, make me whole.

Joel Hills Johnson

Near Hudson, Ohio—Monday, July 9, 1838

Annie lifted her feverish, screaming two-year-old out of the wagon. It was an hour past noon. The sun blazed overhead, and the air was thick with humidity. The Hales' wagon tongue had broken, and their entire division would not move on until it was repaired. Annie's auburn hair lay matted and damp beneath her bonnet. Emotionally and physically exhausted from being up all night, she could scarcely contain her tears as she waved flies away from her baby. *When would Susie's fever break? Where had her other children run off to?*

Susan Bryant, a twenty-six-year-old convert, walked over to Annie. She was alone in the company, not only because she was unmarried, but also because she was the sole member of her family who had accepted the gospel. Tall, extremely thin, and capable, Sister Bryant's shoulders were slightly stooped, and her eyes blue. She had made herself useful from the moment the camp set out, cooking and helping wherever needed.

"Is Susie any better?" Sister Bryant asked.

Annie swallowed and shrugged as she continued to soothe the baby whose wails slowly decreased. "She's still feverish, but she nursed this morning. How are the others?"

"The Gribbles' daughter is nearly well. But the Wilburs' baby boy worsens. He no longer will nurse."

Annie did not respond. At least Susie was a sturdy toddler. When a baby's body raged with fever, and he could not nurse . . .

Sister Bryant continued. "It looks like we'll be here awhile. I'll set up the crick bedstead so you can lay her down."

"Thank you," Annie whispered as she blinked back more stubborn tears. Sister Bryant saw what needed doing without being asked. In a few moments the bed was set up in the wagon's shade. Annie's sweat mingled with her baby's as Susie relaxed in her arms. When the child was asleep, Annie gently laid her down.

Sister Bryant's blue eyes fastened on Susie: the flushed cheeks, the bow mouth, the wet curls against the fair, smooth skin, the whisper of breath going in and out. "She's beautiful."

"If only the fever would break," Annie responded. "When I think of the Wilburs . . ."

Sister Bryant took a quick breath. "I know. Yet I would rather have a child to love for a little while than never have one at all."

Annie turned to Sister Bryant, who continued looking at Susie. Who would have known that such churning need lay hidden beneath the calm, settled exterior? But losing a child. Could anything be worse that that? The death of Annie's first, her little Julianne, gathered in Annie's mind along with the fear of losing another.

Then Annie trembled and saw clearly. Sister Bryant had a mother's heart, willing to risk everything to love, to hold a child in her arms, to give an infant her heart and living breath, even if God took that child away in a day, a month, or a year.

Tenderness filled Annie. She touched Sister Bryant's hand. "Thank you for your kindness to me. The man who finds you will be a lucky one."

Sister Bryant blinked in the sunlight. But when she spoke, her voice was matter-of-fact. "I'll go now and see if the other sisters want help. Sister Johnson, if you need anything, send someone for me. I'll come quickly."

Annie wiped away a tear. "Thank you. And call me Annie."

"Yes, Annie."

As Sister Bryant turned to go, Annie said, "Susan, I am here to help you as well."

Sister Bryant nodded. As she walked away through the dust, she stepped in one of Annie's footprints. Annie noticed that Sister Bryant's print was two inches longer than her own.

Susie whined and coughed. Annie turned and stepped over to the water bucket. She reached for the rag at the bottom and wrung it out. She squatted down, placing the damp cloth on Susie's forehead. Her legs felt lead heavy. The heat and humidity drained her. Annie crawled into the bed next to the baby.

Annie did not know how much time had passed when she opened her eyes to Joel beside her, bending down, putting his hands on Susie's forehead and blessing her with a return of health. When the blessing was over, Annie inched away from Susie, placed her feet on the ground, and sat up. She had to check on her other children. She reached for Joel's hands, and he helped her stand. Her head did not even reach his shoulder.

"When will we start moving again?" Annie asked.

"In an hour." Sweat dripped from Joel's brow.

"Have you seen the other children?"

"Sixtus is with Amos—watching the men work on the wagon. Esther and Mary Ann Hale took Nephi and Sariah to the creek to play and fetch water."

"Sister Bryant helped me with the bedstead," Annie commented.

"It's good that she makes herself useful," Joel remarked.

"I like her very much," Annie returned. "I hope she finds a husband someday."

Joel nodded and kissed Annie's forehead. "As I blessed Susie, I felt she would recover."

Before Annie responded, the couple's attention was diverted as Benjamin ran up, his linen shirt drenched with perspiration. He had been traveling with the herdsmen, far behind the rest of the camp, driving the stock.

"I heard about the Hales' wagon," Benjamin said, catching his breath. "But there's worse news. The animals are fatigued, and your cows have failed. I can't get them up."

Joel's brow furrowed. "Stay with them today. If they don't recover by tomorrow morning, sell them in Hudson for slaughter. Try to get ten dollars a head."

Benjamin nodded, taking the water pouch that hung from his shoulder and drinking deeply. Then he dipped it into the bucket of water and held it there as it filled up again. When finished, he turned and jogged back down the road.

"We're only four days out," Annie said as worry welled up inside her. "Susie's sick, and now there won't be milk for the children."

"The children will bear up if we have faith," Joel countered. "Like the Nephite women and children on their way to the sea."

"I'm trying," Annie said as she took a handkerchief from her skirt pocket. Swallowing, she wiped her eyes and blew her nose. She was hopeful one moment, fearful and crying the next. What was wrong with her?

Joel looked down at her, his features softening. "I'll talk to the council tomorrow morning about the milk."

Annie drew a deep breath. Her jaw quivered as she forced a small smile. "Just promise not to ask me to eat raw meat like the Nephite women."

Joel returned a crooked smile. But Annie saw the worry in his eyes. Though he chose faith, he too was fearful of losing the cows. Then Annie noticed that Benjamin was not coughing as he ran toward the herd, past fields of whitening wheat, under scorching sunlight, and through thick humidity.

* * *

That night, the moon was full overhead, and the ground damp beneath his feet as Benjamin laid out his bedroll. Hours ago, Thomas Butterfield, the camp herdsman, had gone ahead with the fourth division and the rest of the stock, leaving Benjamin behind to tend to Joel's cows. But Benjamin did not mind being alone tonight. His father's gun lay next to him, and the air was cool and comfortable. One of the cows had revived and grazed near him. He had sold the other to a butcher in Hudson and had ten silver dollars in his knapsack. During the past four days, his cough had ceased, and he could not remember ever feeling as strong and hearty as he did today.

Benjamin knelt by his bedroll and thanked his Heavenly Father for blessing and healing him. Faith and hope filled him. He would not die from consumption as he had feared. He would live to fulfill the mission God had in store for him, the work Seth had left for him to do. Lightning bugs flickered around him, the sound of crickets and frogs filled the night. After his prayer, Benjamin stretched out on the bedroll and pulled the quilt over him. He closed his eyes, and as he drifted to sleep, Benjamin thought about Seth, David, Susan, and Nancy. He thought about Joseph Smith, God's Prophet and his friend.

* * *

The next morning, Joe sat in the council meeting with the other men in the camp. He was exhausted. It had been midnight when their division had rolled into camp. Then the horn was blown at four that morning. He listened as his brother Joel spoke to the council, explaining his concern for his children because of the loss of his cows.

Another man raised his hand. "We traveled twenty miles yesterday rather than the usual fifteen. If we aren't careful, we'll all be in the same boat as Brother Joel. Our cows won't hold up, and it's a strain on our wives and children."

Other men voiced their agreement as Joe dozed. He jerked awake when Brother Allen spoke out. "When the horn blows at four each morning, some people worship and others don't. Shouldn't the entire camp worship at the same time so that no one's prayers are disturbed?"

The leaders of the camp said that they had the same feelings. Then they asked the overseers of each tent to report on the welfare of their companies. Joe's eyes grew heavy once more. He shook his head to stay awake. He was the eldest unmarried male in his household and needed to know what was going on. He listened to the reports. All of the sick children had recovered except the Wilburs' baby, who was still grievously ill.

After the reports, Brother Harriman put forward several resolutions:

"First, that the horn should be blown first at four each morning, then again at twenty minutes past four, at which time worship would commence throughout the entire camp at the same time, immediately following the blowing of the horn.

"Second, that every company in the camp is entitled to an equal proportion of milk whether the cows are owned by the individuals of the several tents or not.

"And third, that in no case shall the camp move more than fifteen miles in one day, unless circumstances shall absolutely require it.

"All in favor show by the raised hand."

Joe lifted his arm as the resolutions were unanimously adopted.

Following the council meeting, Joe left immediately, even though Joel stayed to talk with the leaders about the distribution of milk. As Joe walked past the first division, he thought about how Benjamin had been alone last night with the cows. Had he sold them for slaughter? When would he rejoin the camp?

Clouds darkened in the sky. It would rain today. Joe looked down the lane at the members of camp eating breakfast and taking down their tents. Then he saw his sister, Mary, sitting on a rock near a grove of trees, her long, blond braid snaking down her back and her face buried in her hands.

Joe quickly walked over to her and put his hand on her shoulder. "What is it?"

Mary looked up at him. There were tears on her cheeks. "The Wilburs' baby died half an hour ago. Sister Bryant told us. Our Susie is fine this morning, and we thank Heavenly Father for it, but Sister Wilbur's baby boy is dead. Why, Joe? Why couldn't he live too?"

Joe sat down next to his sister and put his arm around her. "I don't know. Maybe their baby was younger and not as strong."

"Doesn't God love the weak as well as the strong?"

Joe nodded, and his own jaw quivered. "Yes. And the dead as well as the living."

"You sound like Seth," Mary said, and she began to cry harder.

Joe bit down on his lip. Was it God, science, or luck that ruled the world? Did God direct things or clean up afterward, sweeping away sorrow with hope? Would they all live through the journey? Only one thing was certain. The camp would be rolling out soon. Everyone except those who would stay to bury the child. Joe's family was not in that division.

"Mary," Joe said gently, "it's time to go."

Mary wiped her eyes and stood up. They walked silently toward their tent. When they neared, Benjamin approached from the east. One of Joel's cows was with him.

Mary broke into a run. "I thought the cows had failed," she cried as she joined Benjamin. "And you sold them for slaughter."

Benjamin grinned. He patted the cow. "I couldn't save the other one, but this old girl didn't give up."

Mary swallowed and stretched her arms around the cow's neck. It blinked its large, dark eyes as she hugged it. Mary began to cry once more.

George and Will walked over. George tilted his head. "It's just a cow, Mare. Not your long, lost sister. Though I do see a resemblance."

"Shut up, George," Mary said as she let go of the cow and wiped her eyes.

"'Then shall two be in the field,'" Will quoted from the Bible. "'One shall be taken and the other left.' Who would have guessed this verse was about cows?"

Mary's eyes flashed at her younger brothers. It began to sprinkle.

"Let's go," Joe commanded. "It's time to roll out."

* * *

That afternoon a drenching rain fell. Susan Bryant drove one team while Annie and her three youngest children huddled in the wagon. Joel and Sixtus walked on either side of the team. Julia's wagon trailed behind. Will sat next to her and handled the team. George walked. Esther and Amos squeezed in the wagon bed, their feet bare, and their bodies sandwiched between bedrolls and barrels. They tried to make up riddles to pass the time, but the rain drummed loudly on the canvas, interrupting their conversation and filling their ears.

Joe, Mary, and Benjamin walked behind the wagons, through mud holes, and up and down inclines. Water and mud seeped between Benjamin's toes. His well-worn boots were stored in the wagon. He couldn't afford to wear them again until the weather turned cold—except on Sundays.

Mary's skirts were soaked as she followed her brothers with a stick in her hand, driving the cow through the downpour. Thunder clapped. Lightning riddled the sky.

Joe turned around and called out to Mary, "Get in the wagon before you get chilled."

Benjamin walked up and took the stick from Mary. "I'll drive her." The cow stopped and bawled, its feet sinking into the mud.

Mary shook her head and took the stick back from her brother. "She goes better for me." She waved the stick, and the cow moved forward willingly, despite the sludge sucking at its feet.

Her brothers watched. Joe shook his head. "Is it possible that this is the same sister who was crying this morning?"

Benjamin grinned. "That's Mary for you."

Mary turned around and called to her brothers. "We'll make it to Zion." Her head was high in the storm as water streamed down her face. "I don't care if it's eight hundred miles away."

Heavenly Father, fill thy Servant
With the gift of Inspiration
To advance the cause of Zion
In the work of her Salvation.

Lo! her foes are strong and many
Who have long her cause mistreated
Help me wage eternal warfare
Till they all shall be defeated.

Joel Hills Johnson

Far West, Missouri—July 1838

Baby Daniel whined and pulled on Delcena's skirt. Six months pregnant, Delcena reached down and lifted him up. In the kitchen, Alvira and Mary were at the table twisting bread dough. Seth sat in the corner building a tower of sticks. Albey was somewhere outside.

Daniel drooled and cried out. With a free hand, Delcena picked up a bag of caraway seeds and dipped it in honey. Recognizing the sweet toy to chew on, Daniel reached a chubby hand out and put the bag in his mouth. His hands were sticky, but the crying had stopped. Delcena sat Daniel down next to Seth. She picked up a towel and wiped the sweat off her forehead. It was nearly candlelight. The rosy glow in the western window would soon dim into darkness. She needed to find Albey and call him in for supper.

Opening the front door, Delcena had no further to look. The Prophet approached with Albey on his shoulders. His son, Little Joseph, skipped along beside them.

"Hello, Sister Sherman." Joseph smiled warmly as he deposited Albey on the narrow plank porch and lifted his boy to his shoulders.

"Thank you for bringing Albey home. I was just going out to look for him."

Albey wrapped Delcena's legs in a hug. She ran her fingers through his brown curls. Albey exclaimed, "I was chopping wood to surprise Papa, but Brother Joseph came and did it for me."

Delcena's color heightened, and her heart beat faster. She knew of children who had died from gangrene after cutting themselves with axes. She put her hands on each of Albey's rosy cheeks. "Thank goodness for Brother Joseph! Son, never touch the ax without Papa. It's dangerous. Promise me you won't again."

"I already promised Brother Joseph."

The Prophet grinned. "And don't forget your promise, Albey. Fortunately God judges the intent of the heart. All's well that ends well. Sister Sherman, I came by to speak to your husband. Will he be home soon?"

"Not soon. He went to a meeting hosted by Brother Avard."

The Prophet's eyes widened slightly. "I didn't know that Lyman was attending Brother Avard's meetings."

"This is the first he's been invited to."

The Prophet continued. "Sampson Avard is zealous in his defense of me and the Saints. Perhaps that's needed. But on the other hand, he tends to do as he pleases regardless of my counsel. I don't want any of the brethren to act unlawfully. Tell Lyman so."

Delcena nodded. "I will."

The Prophet went on cheerfully. "I've word that Brother Babbitt will arrive soon with a large group of Canadian Saints. I'm sure that you'll be pleased to see your sister."

Delcena smiled. "Very pleased."

"Tell Lyman that I'm riding to Di-Ahman tomorrow. In a revelation, the Lord said that there is room enough in the land where Adam dwelt for the gathering of His Saints. I'm going to see for myself."

Little Joseph interrupted. "Can Albey play tomorrow? My mama said he could."

"Of course," Delcena responded.

"As long as the two of you stay away from woodpiles," the Prophet added.

"We will!" Albey and Joseph cheered.

The Prophet tousled Albey's hair. "And now Joseph and I must get back for supper. Good-bye, Albey. Good-bye, Sister Sherman. May God bless your family."

* * *

Lyman sat silently on a bench in the shadowy barn. It was growing dark and lanterns hung from the ceiling, casting long shadows. Around seventy-five brethren were in attendance. Lyman knew many of them to be good, faithful men. Earlier in the day, someone had left a note on his doorstep with the time and location scrawled on the paper. The note had also contained a warning to tell no one else. It was signed by *S. Avard.*

Lyman knew that the Danite group had been in existence for over a month. Yet this was the first meeting he had been informed of. Why? He had been one of the foremost witnesses against the dissenters in Kirtland. He had been a President of the Seventy and a member of the Kirtland high council. If this group was sanctioned by Joseph, then why did they meet secretly? The Book of Mormon warned of secret combinations. The first thing Lyman had done was to tell his wife about the meeting he was attending. As Avard spoke, Lyman's jaw became tense and his mouth a hard line.

"If any man comes to disturb the Saints of God, it will be a war of extermination between us and them. We will no longer turn the other cheek. Vengeance will be ours. If there is blood and burning, so be it. We will stand by each other until death.

"Whatever the Presidency of the Church requires, we shall be ready to give up life and property for them. Here tonight, all shall enter into a covenant that the word of the Presidency shall be obeyed, and none shall be suffered to raise his hand or voice against it."

Was it conceivable that Sampson Avard spoke for Joseph, or did he speak for Sidney Rigdon, whose rhetoric had been more militant? Lyman had chosen burning in Kirtland. He prayed that the Lord had forgiven his rashness. Would he be forgiven if he chose burning or blood now?

Avard continued. "Whatever we are asked to do, no member of this group shall judge whether it be right or wrong but shall accomplish it. Know that I speak for the Presidency of the Church, who speak for God Himself."

Lyman did not join in as other men entered into oaths to stand by these principles until death. Sampson Avard walked over to Lyman, "Brother Sherman, come with me."

All eyes were on Lyman as he followed Avard out of the barn. A thin line of light balanced on the horizon as the moon rose in the sky. Avard's words were quick and pointed. "Why are you hesitant to raise your hand and promise allegiance to God's Prophet? Has the faithful Lyman Sherman joined the dissenters?"

Lyman looked Avard in the eye. "Don't ever accuse me of being a traitor to Joseph Smith! But I don't see him here. I make my oaths to God, not man."

"I speak for the Presidency of the Church!"

"Then let me hear those words from Joseph himself."

"Believe me, you shall. But for now, leave if you haven't the courage to join us."

Lyman turned and walked away, his heart troubled. Would the brethren now distrust him? Could he blame them? They had seen the strongest fall. Was Avard right? Had Sidney Rigdon spoken for Joseph in the Salt Sermon? In the Fourth of July address? Were such measures necessary in a time of war?

When Lyman arrived home, Delcena met him at the door. She hugged him tightly. While he ate a late supper, she nursed Daniel and told Lyman all that Joseph had said concerning Brother Avard. Regardless of her words, the weight in Lyman's heart did not diminish as he tucked his children in bed and kissed them good night.

* * *

Three days later

On the morning following their arrival in Far West, Julianne spun the peg dolly in the oak washtub. The load of soaked linen strained heavily against the dolly, and the pungent smell of lye filled her nostrils. Shoulders and arms aching, she continued to agitate the fabric, her hands raw from spinning the dolly in both directions, over and over again.

She looked at Delcena, who was hanging a sheet on a nearby line. Her sister was only two years older and was pregnant with her sixth child. Julianne wished she could scrub away the emptiness inside her, the ache to hold her own child.

Delcena stepped over and peered into the tub. "They're done," she commented with a quick smile. "Soaking them in lye helped."

Julianne sighed and let go of the dolly. "I doubted they would ever be clean again. Almon will be glad that his shirts are white."

"After our journey, I thought that my *children* would never be clean again," Delcena commented. "You could have heard Albey scream a mile away when I scrubbed him."

Julianne forced a smile. What she wouldn't give to have her own little boy to scrub clean. Together the sisters lifted the soaking clothing from the soapy water and submersed it in the copper tub filled with rinse water.

Julianne brought the dolly over and gently agitated the clothing. She watched as the fabric freed itself of the soap, the suds rising to the surface.

As they wrung out the clothes, Delcena chatted. "I remember wash day when we were little. It seemed like the piles of clothing were endless. Do you miss those days?"

Julianne nodded. "You and Nancy at the washboards, me and Almera rinsing and wringing, and Sue and Mother hanging them on the lines. How we used to complain!"

Delcena grinned. "Almera was the worst."

"And I used to sing just to rile her," Julianne added. "Once it made her so mad that she doused me with rinse water. I splashed her back. Mother wasn't happy. She made us go fetch more water. We continued our water fight at the well. When we came back sopping wet, Mother told us that we would do the entire wash alone next week. It took us three full days. It would only have taken a day and a half if we hadn't cried and moaned."

Delcena chuckled. "I remember. I was glad to get a break, but Nancy begged Mother to let her help! I think Susan cried even harder for you than you cried for yourselves."

Julianne swallowed. Her voice cracked as she said, "And now Nancy and Sue are gone. And Almera is so far away and so lonely. What I wouldn't give for one more washday with all of us together."

"But it wouldn't be enough," Delcena said, her eyes moist as she put her hand on Julianne's shoulder. "It would never be enough. I'm so glad you're here."

Julianne squeezed her sister's hand. "And Mother's coming. If only Almera was coming as well."

* * *

The sun grew hot as Almon and Lyman walked through the cornfields. The stalks stood shoulder high, straight and green, tipped with feathery ears. Two hundred yards away, cows, black and white under a blue sky, stood belly-high in deep mud holes, having found a cool reprieve from the summer heat.

"The soil is fertile here," Lyman commented.

Almon gazed at the sun. "But things are raw, and there are so many poor. We lost a great deal in Kirtland. And there was potential for real progress. It's a shame that the bank failed."

Lyman glanced at Almon. "On July eighth, the Prophet received a revelation. 'Let the properties of Kirtland be turned out for debts, saith the Lord. Let them go, saith the Lord. Is there not room enough on the land where Adam dwelt? Therefore come up hither unto the land of my people, even Zion.'"

Zion? Almon took a deep breath. He despised the old, slaveholding settlers. He had passed enough of them on the way, staring at him in doorways and fields, cold-eyed and threatening. He had doffed his hat to them and watched them spit on the ground after he passed. Too many of them were stupid and mean to the core. He shrugged. "Joseph also received a revelation that Kirtland would be rebuilt. I'd like to help with that. At least our enemies there are Yankee men and women."

"In God's own due time," Lyman said. "Right now Far West and Adam-ondi-Ahman are the sanctioned gathering places. I'm concerned about the Canadians going to Three Forks."

"Why? There's not enough land in Caldwell County to support the immigrants. Three Forks is a goodly land and the price is right. Crops are already planted. My people don't have a better place to settle. They'll go there as soon as they're rested. All except for me."

"Why did you decide to stay here?"

"Because I want to be in Far West. To keep a pulse on what's happening. I want to be close to the First Presidency."

"Did you or Anson ever ask the Prophet about the Canadians settling in Three Forks?"

Almon shook his head. "No. But we don't have to be commanded in all things. What's the difference between settling in Adam-ondi-Ahman in Daviess County versus Three Forks in Clinton County? Only Caldwell County was set aside by the legislature for Mormon settlement."

"The difference is that Three Forks isn't mentioned in the revelations. I think Joseph went to Di-Ahman to find a place for the Canadians to settle. It isn't wise to plunge ahead against his counsel."

"But we aren't going *against* his counsel, are we? We bought land. The hay is ready to be cut. Joseph should have said something long before Anson broke his back preparing for these people."

"The Prophet can't know what every single man is doing all of the time. There are nearly five thousand Saints here. He teaches correct principles and expects us to govern ourselves."

"That's exactly what we're doing."

"But you're about to move nearly two hundred people to a settlement not mentioned in the revelations."

Almon didn't respond. Lyman continued walking. Almon followed, his brow creased. The last thing he wanted to do was to put his friends in danger. "I wish Joseph was here. When will he be back?"

Lyman shrugged. "I don't know. A week, maybe two."

"If my people wait that long, they'll risk their crops. The hay could be lost. I can't tell them to wait, Lyman. They have to feed their families."

Lyman did not speak. After a moment, Almon broke the silence. "These are faithful Saints. *I* am a faithful man. We tried to buy land near Far West, but there wasn't enough of it, and the price was too high. We prayed about this. The tract at Three Forks fell into our hands like manna from heaven."

"I understand. Proceed if you feels it's right." Then the tone of Lyman's voice changed, becoming inward. "It's just that I, personally, fear God's judgment, the withholding of His blessings, if I don't act in accordance with His will."

"It's not God's judgment I fear, but the Missourians'," Almon said. "But I don't see a better option. If the Prophet doesn't get back in the next couple of days, I'll send my people on to Three Forks."

Lyman tilted his head and looked at Almon somewhat quizzically. "You call them *my people.* Whose are they? *Yours* or *Joseph's* or *God's*?"

Almon suddenly grinned. "God's people, of course. Don't worry, my friend. I am not that vain. And I know I don't speak for the Prophet."

Lyman sucked in a deep breath. "Not everyone in Far West feels that way. Sampson Avard has formed a secret militant group called the Danites. Many good men follow him. They make oaths among themselves and prepare to fight the Missourians. Joseph allows them to be, but he does not lead them. Yet Avard tells others that he speaks for Joseph and that Joseph speaks for God."

Almon whistled lowly. "Thus Avard speaks for God."

Lyman let out a breath. "I don't know Avard that well."

Almon looked carefully at Lyman. It seemed that he had changed, that some of his energy and passion had slipped away. "I know Sampson Avard. He is and has always been an opportunist. In Canada he tried to take the leadership of the Church out of John Taylor's hands. For a time, he lost his license as a high priest. Have you been to any of their meetings?"

Lyman nodded. "One. I refused to take an oath unless Joseph himself commands. I'm sick to death of all the pride and conflict. I want to preach the gospel of peace. I came to Zion to find safety, not to fight a war."

Almon had another question. "When you refused, did Avard threaten you?"

Lyman shook his head and smiled ironically. "No. He questioned my loyalty to the Prophet."

Almon choked in disbelief. "Any man who questions your loyalty is a fool and had better steer clear of me. That's a fight I'm ready for."

Lyman smiled, and Almon saw the life return to his friend's eyes. The man of action, who was ready to pick up a hoe or a sword, to do whatever needed doing, was still there inside.

Almon spoke once more. "Since old Avard encourages oaths, I'll promise you two things. First, I'll never follow Sampson Avard. And second, I'll never let my pride jeopardize the safety of those I love. Not for all the world. If the Prophet tells them to leave Three Forks, I will ride there as fast as I can and advise them to follow his counsel."

Lyman spoke with warmth. "In one way you remind me very much of Joseph. People are naturally drawn to you. Not because of oaths, but because of love."

Almon grinned. "The scriptures say that he who loves much is forgiven much. Lyman, my friend, I'm banking on that."

7

I may teach thy holy word
Through nations far and wide;
Directed by thy Spirit, Lord,
A sure, unerring guide.

Joel Hills Johnson

Clark County, Ohio—Saturday, July 28, 1838

It was midafternoon as Benjamin walked alone through a village in western Ohio. The blazing sun baked the earth beneath his bare feet. A dry wind blew, and layers of dust stuck to the sweat on his neck and forearms. It was his twentieth birthday. As he neared a busy tavern, Benjamin felt self-conscious. He appeared to be a filthy, overgrown, barefoot boy when he ought to look like a man.

He lagged behind the camp because he had spent the morning chopping wood for an elderly farmer in return for eggs and fruit. Ever since Mary had taken over driving the stock, he had made the sick and feeble his special responsibility. It was his way of thanking the Lord for renewed health. He tried to think about how the fresh food would strengthen Sister Willey, instead of how the townspeople stared at him curiously.

"Young man." A voice rose above the buzz outside the tavern. Benjamin glanced over at the group of people. Perhaps the call wasn't for him. Feeling vulnerable, he looked down and kept walking. There was a great deal of local prejudice against the Mormons because of runners who had come through Clark County with Kirtland money, swindling other people.

"Young man," the voice said again. Benjamin saw a middle-aged man with a neatly trimmed mustache take a step toward him. Behind him, on the tavern porch, men, women, and children fanned themselves in the sweltering heat, some sitting on benches, others with legs stretched out on the wooden planks, their backs resting against the brick front of the building. Only the boys playing marbles had something better to do than stare at Benjamin.

"Yes, sir," Benjamin answered.

"Are you part of the company of Mormons who passed through here this morning?"

Benjamin swallowed. "Yes, sir."

"I heard you Mormons worship Joe Smith instead of the Lord Jesus Christ. Is that so?"

Those on the porch were silent now, gawking. Benjamin's mind spun. If the crowd turned to a mob, he wouldn't have a chance. He would feel the heat of tar and feathers. There was nothing he could do. Nothing but answer the question. "No, sir. We worship our Heavenly Father and His Son, Jesus Christ, just as the Bible teaches."

"If you believe in the Bible, then why do you follow Joe?"

"Because he is the Prophet of God."

"God doesn't raise up prophets in these days."

Benjamin's racing heart slowed as he took a deep breath. Was this how Stephen felt before he was stoned? If he was going to go down, he would go down testifying of the truth. "With all due respect, sir, God is the same yesterday, today, and forever. Christ has restored His ancient church in these latter days through Joseph Smith."

More passersby stopped along the road. Women peered out the windows of the tavern. Benjamin's cheeks burned. Near a hundred people stared at him.

A grizzled old man lifted himself off a bench and stood next to the first gentleman. The old man leaned on his cane. "Joe's a swindler, boy. He deals in rag money."

There were nods from the crowd. Benjamin took a deep breath. There was something about the old man that reminded him of his father. Benjamin said, "When the Kirtland bank failed, Joseph Smith lost all he had. You see, he believed in that bank. He didn't try to swindle anyone."

"Then he sure can't foresee the future," the old man continued. "You call that a prophet?"

"Moses was one of the greatest prophets, but he made mistakes."

The first man cleared his throat. "I hear that Joe pretends to walk on water. You witnessed that?"

Benjamin shook his head. "No, sir. He was my neighbor in Kirtland. I never heard or saw him do anything like that. He's a plain-talking man, the best sort, who is only trying to accomplish the mission God has given him."

The old man said, "Boy, a plain-talking man don't claim to speak with angels. That's the talk of a liar or a loon."

Benjamin remembered the day Joseph had called him out of a crowd, had given him a blessing, and had comforted him after Seth's death. Benjamin's voice rose, firm and sure. "Unless angels do, in open vision, converse with that man. I testify of that reality."

For an instant there was no sound. A child coughed. Then the old man shook his head. "Foolishness."

A dog barked. The boys resumed their game of marbles. Benjamin looked down at his feet. He had failed. Who in their right mind would listen to a dirty, barefoot boy?

"Son, don't pay no mind to my husband."

Benjamin lifted his head and looked into the watery blue eyes of an elderly woman. Her white hair hung thin and lank. "Tell us folks about them angels."

Benjamin nodded and cleared his throat. He began by saying, "When Joseph was a boy of fourteen, he prayed to find out which church was true."

The sun moved through the sky, and hours passed as Benjamin told the people of the Restoration of the gospel, of the visitations of angels, of the Book of Mormon and the teachings, blessings, and visions which the Prophet had received. He bore his testimony. The sun set behind his back, crimson in the western sky. Benjamin closed his discourse in the name of Jesus Christ.

Tears were on the old woman's cheeks. Without looking at Benjamin, the old man took her arm. "Mother, it's time to go." The gentleman with the mustache stared quizzically at Benjamin but said nothing. He, too, turned to leave.

The rest of the crowd slowly dispersed, some going back into the tavern, others heading toward home and supper. Some said good-bye. Most did not.

Benjamin stood alone once more. With a pounding heart, he continued down the road. *So this was what it felt like to preach the gospel, like the Lord stood next to you.* No wonder Lyman yearned for it. No wonder Almon went on one mission after another.

Darkness fell, and the quarter-moon rose. The temperature dropped, and the wind stilled. As he walked the eleven miles to camp, Benjamin marveled at the preacher inside him, at the shy, barefoot boy whose tongue had been loosed.

* * *

The next morning after a breakfast of corn mush and honey, Benjamin made a poultice for Sister Willey. As he walked to the Willeys' wagon to deliver the poultice and food, he thought about Nancy. He and Joe had spent a great deal of time nursing her. The poultices, the medicines, the blessings, and prayers had not saved her life nor Susan's nor Seth's nor David's. Yet he and Joe had been spared. Was it so he could preach the gospel like he had yesterday? So that Joe could comfort their mother and get the family to Missouri? But Seth and David could have done that. How did God decide who would live and who would die?

After delivering the poultice and food, Benjamin went down to the Mad River to wash. Naked to the waist, he squatted on the rocky bank and scrubbed his tan face and arms, his pale stomach and chest. He shivered as the dust and dirt dripped from his body into the chilly water. Afterward, he trimmed and combed his hair then shaved. He covered his dirty shirt with a coat and pulled on his worn boots. It was the Sabbath, and at eleven o'clock the Saints had permission from a nearby farmer to worship in a large grove that was used for camp meetings.

Twenty minutes later, Benjamin and his family sat among more than four hundred Saints on logs that served as benches forming a semicircle around a makeshift pulpit. The Seventies sat in the front. After a hymn and prayer, Zera Pulsipher stood up to preach. Before he began, Brother Harriman pointed to a half dozen carriages driving up. With a booming voice, Brother Pulsipher called out and welcomed the strangers. After they settled their teams, the Seventies stood and offered the visitors their front-row seats. A shudder ran through Benjamin. These were people who had listened to him preach yesterday. Brother Pulsipher gave a rousing sermon on the first principles of the gospel. Following the sermon, he asked the guests if they had any questions.

A man raised his hand. "Yesterday a young man preached to us in town. Do you know him?"

Benjamin's face flushed deeply, and his long fingers nervously tapped his knee. Should he speak out? Brother Pulsipher turned to the other leading brethren who stood on his left. He asked if they knew of any elder who had preached the previous day. The brethren shook their heads. Elder Pulsipher apologized to the guests.

A little girl chimed out. "Maybe the young man wasn't real, Grandpa. Maybe he was one of the angels he told us about."

"Oh, he was real all right," the man answered shrewdly.

Amos, who was leaning on Benjamin, whispered. "Maybe he was one of the Three Nephites or John the Apostle."

Benjamin shook his head. "He was a man."

On the way home, Benjamin walked apart from his family. What was wrong with him? Why hadn't he claimed to be who he was?

Amos sidled up to him. "I've been reasoning, Ben. Was it you that preached to those people yesterday? Is that why you know it wasn't an angel?"

Benjamin nodded slightly.

"Why didn't you say so? Mama says not speaking up is the same as lying."

Benjamin eyed his little brother. His voice was low. "Not in this case. It didn't seem like *me* preaching. It seemed like someone else, like Seth."

"Like Seth's spirit was telling you what to say?"

"I guess."

"Then it wouldn't be completely honest to say it was you."

Benjamin grimaced. "I guess not."

Without another thought, Amos ran back to his mother. As Benjamin continued walking, he stared at the boots he wore, Seth's boots. Yesterday, dressed like a barefoot and filthy boy, he had stood before a crowd and boldly testified like a man. But this morning, dressed in boots and looking like he was twenty, he had behaved like a bashful child.

* * *

With bent shoulders, Almera gathered overripe peaches that had fallen to the ground. It was early afternoon, and a cloud shaded the sun. As she worked, Almera thought dismally about the rest of her day. She would make jam before cooking supper. Then after the meal was over and the dishes scoured, she would mend. She swallowed. Every day she cooked, cleaned, and sewed. Alone. Always alone. With an ache inside that never went away.

Did her mother or siblings yearn for her like she did for them? Tears stung her eyes, because she knew that they did not. Though they loved her, their hearts weren't broken. They were on their way to Missouri, to Zion. They had everything to look forward to.

Almera remembered before they left how her mother had tried to comfort her by telling her of a spiritual experience where she had felt the Savior's love, where her mother had seen her progeny and known without doubt that Heavenly Father was with them all. But right now the memory stung Almera. Her mother's life was full. She had children and grandchildren surrounding her. She had everything to look forward to.

Almera's lower lip quivered. She was nearly twenty-six. When her mother was twenty-six, she already had five children. Her mother could not understand what it was like to have nothing. And Sam had hurt her so deeply that Almera did not love him. Pausing, she stared at the sky, at the dark clouds billowing in the northwest. It would rain soon. She had chosen to marry Sam. Was she choosing this suffering? Could she do anything to combat the loneliness that pressed upon her, that darkened the brightest day?

These questions haunted her. Neighborhood women had tried to befriend her. Nearly every week someone stopped by with fruit or preserves to share. Why were they trying so hard? Did they feel guilty for their husbands' roles in driving the Mormons away? Yet a part of her wanted to be grateful, to be a part of the community. Last week she had gone to a quilting bee. The ladies had been careful and attentive, avoiding any mention of Joseph Smith or the Mormons. They had talked of the Bible and of their families, but Almera had dared not speak of her Prophet or her people, knowing that these Christian women had rejoiced when the Mormons left Geauga County, at the very events that had broken her heart. To enjoy their company would require cutting a part of her soul away. And she couldn't do that. Familiar tears slid down Almera's cheeks. Sam had been kind the night following the quilting bee. But even as she had tried to respond to him as a caring and affectionate wife, her heart had shuddered at the falsity of his kindness—acutely aware of his betrayal, of the way he had callously separated her from those things closest to her heart.

A black-and-white cat sidled up and rubbed against Almera's leg. Almera set the basket down, picked up the cat, and cradled him in her arms. The vibration of his purr felt warm and alive against her chest. He had come to her when he could be napping in the shade. Almera stroked him tenderly, cat hairs sticking to the peach juice on her fingers. The cat raised his head, his yellow eyes unblinking, unfaltering. A grim determination hardened inside Almera. She had to find a way to make her world bearable. *Heavenly Father, I can no longer be alone. Help me. Please, help me.*

"Sister Almera?"

At the sound of the voice, Almera started, and the cat leaped from her arms. She turned to see Rebecca Winters walking up to her. Almera's heart pounded. *Had Heavenly Father known the prayer that would be on her lips at that moment? Had he prepared the answer to her prayer even before it was uttered?* Rebecca and her husband, Hiram, along with their extended family, the Burdicks, were among the few faithful Saints who had remained in Kirtland. Almera had longed to visit them, but Sam had forbidden her from associating with any remaining Mormons.

Rebecca's blue bonnet shaded her eyes. Her fair cheeks were rosy from the warmth. Her jaw was square and her eyes very kind. Rebecca smiled at Almera and embraced her warmly. "I've been thinking of you. Praying for you."

Deeply touched, Almera spoke through tears. "I've longed to visit you. But my husband won't allow it."

"I'm so sorry," Rebecca said. "Can I help?"

Almera brushed away her tears. "You already have. Did you walk the whole way? Are you thirsty?"

Rebecca shook her head. "I'm fine. Hiram and Father Burdick are doing business at your father's shop. I only walked from there. I suggested to your father that you come tomorrow and sew with Mother Burdick, Jerusha, Anna, and me. He said it was a fine idea and that he would bring you to Kirtland."

Almera's eyes clouded with confusion. "Papa knows that Sam won't allow it. Was Sam in the shop?"

Rebecca shook her head. "No."

It began to sprinkle. Rebecca hooked her arm through Almera's. "Will Sam be angry if I help gather the peaches before they're ruined? Hiram plans to pick me up here."

Almera swallowed and answered quickly. "I . . . I don't know, but I want you to stay as long as you can. After we gather the peaches, maybe we can sit on the porch and visit. I hope Brother Hiram takes his time."

* * *

By dinnertime the sky had cleared. Cool, fresh air breezed through the open windows. Ezekiel watched Almera walk to the table, her hands gripping the chicken pie, her knuckles white. Ezekiel's brow furrowed. Since Julia had left, Almera had lost weight, and there were dark circles under her eyes. He had lived long enough to know what grief looked like, hope wilting like a dying flower. But tonight there was a hint of color in his daughter's cheeks. He could thank the Winters woman for that.

Almera cut her husband a large piece of pie and set it before him. Sam began eating without thanking Almera or blessing the food. Her long-lashed eyes glanced away from him, like he was a stranger to her, something foreign and cold.

Sam chewed quickly. Ezekiel sensed the anger in him. He saw it every day in Sam's eyes or heard it in his voice. How long before Sam struck, no longer able to cope with Almera's distance and melancholy? A part of Ezekiel identified with Sam. He knew what it was like to be furious with his wife. But Ezekiel was her father. He knew that Almera was doing her best. He knew that she was so lonely and discouraged that it took her whole strength just to get up each morning.

And there were the words that Ezekiel couldn't get out of his mind—the words Almera had spoken to him over three years ago when he had insisted that she accept Sam's advances. His daughter's eyes had been fiery that day, not defeated.

I'll obey you, Papa, and Sam will court me. But what if we marry and my faith comes between us? If my heart is broken, it will be your fault, Papa, not mine.

That day, his answer had come confidently. *I look to Sam to protect you, not break your heart.*

But he had been wrong. Her heart was broken. He had failed her, like he had failed Julia when Seth had died. But Almera was still here. If he could, he would bring her some shreds of happiness. She was his beautiful, spirited little girl, broken down but not alone—not as long as her father breathed.

Almera cut another piece of pie and handed it to Ezekiel. He briefly touched her hand. "Thank you, darlin'."

"You're welcome, Papa." She cut herself a small piece and set down with them. While Sam continued to eat, she said grace over the meal.

After the prayer, Ezekiel cleared his throat and said, "Almera, this morning I did some business with Gideon Burdick and Hirum Winters. Mrs. Winters came to the shop too. Said that she needs help with her sewing. I told her I'd take you into town tomorrow to help. Hope that's all right with you and Sam."

Ezekiel saw the hope in her eyes when she glanced at him. She dared not speak. Ezekiel's mind flew back to his boyhood, to the day he had wanted so desperately to go to the circus.

Sam looked up at Ezekiel. "You know that I don't allow my wife to go gallivanting off with Mormon women."

Ezekiel did not back down. "This has nothin' to do with religion. I've been doing work for the Burdicks for the past twelve years in New York as well as here. A man needs his family's support in his business associations. There's little enough work around here for you and me with the Mormons gone."

"Sounds like you wish they were still here." Sam's voice tightened. "But your wife didn't blink when she left."

Ezekiel's voice was low. "Boy, you've been hit harder than me. We both know that you won't have enough business to stay afloat if I leave the shop."

Sam leaped to his feet, his fists hard and his eyes smoldering. "Don't threaten me."

Almera paled and put her hand on her father's arm. "I'll stay, Papa," she said. "It's not worth it."

Ezekiel did not stand up to fight. Nor did he take his eyes off of Sam. "Is it worth it to you, Sam? You let Almera help these women sew, and I'll give you half of the profits I make from the work I do for Winters and Burdick."

Ezekiel watched Sam push his anger below the surface. Sam had decided to control his rage, to let it flame when he chose. Sam turned, strode to the door, and put his hat on. Before leaving the house, he looked back at Almera, his eyes cold. "Go sew for your father's friends. But make sure my supper is ready on time."

After Sam was gone, Almera stood up and put her hands on his shoulders. "Thank you, Papa."

Ezekiel reached up and took her hands in his. Though they were young and feminine, they too were callused from hard work. "Sometimes a man makes a mistake that can't ever be righted."

"What mistake?"

It was difficult to get the words out, but Ezekiel said them anyway. "Your marrying Sam."

"You've made your own mistakes, Papa. You don't need to take on mine. Do you really think that I would have married Sam because you told me to?" Almera smiled sadly, ironically. "After all these years, you ought to know me better than that."

"I do know you, darlin'," Ezekiel said, his hands vibrating from age. "I've known you all your life."

Then Almera's smile dimmed, and her body shook with sobs. Ezekiel gathered her onto his lap and held her close, rocking her back and forth like he had rocked her as a little girl when she had sobbed for hours because her mama was busy nursing the new baby.

* * *

Dayton, Ohio—Tuesday, July 31, 1838

The sun dipped behind the line of wagons as Susan Bryant, Julia, and Annie dried the supper dishes. A stone's throw away, the Johnson men pitched their tent. Two hours earlier the camp had moved to a lovely grove sandwiched between the dusky prairie and the thick foliage of the Mad River.

Julia slapped away a fly. The day had been tiring. The women had washed while the men had attended a council meeting. The camp no longer had the funds to continue to Missouri. After hours of talk, the brethren had unanimously agreed to hire themselves out as a group to build a section of the Dayton–Springfield turnpike. It would delay them for about four weeks, but there was no better option. During this time, they would live in tents, battling dust, heat, and insects while the men worked and the women taught the children in a summer school.

Following the decision, many in the camp struggled with discouragement. Families longed to be in Zion and to have the long, tedious journey behind them. But Julia's mind centered on a different thought. Cincinnati was only fifty miles away. Her brother, Joel, and her sister, Nancy, lived there. She had not seen them for nearly twenty years.

As Julia dried the forks, her mind fluttered around past memories. As children, Julia, Joel, and Nancy had clung to each other through their father's death and their mother's remarriage. Joel had been a tease like her David and an intellectual like Seth and Joe; Rhoda, his wife, had become her sweetest, dearest friend. Nancy, her sister, with snappy dark eyes and a forthright personality, had married the dashing George Taft. Julia loved Joel and Nancy so dearly that she had named her two eldest children after them.

"Where's Esther and Mary?" Susan Bryant said. "When I was a girl, I recall behaving like them, disappearing when there was work to be done."

"Mary is feeding the stock since the men are busy," Julia answered, a defensive edge in her voice. She bristled when others criticized her children. "And Esther is with Mary Ann Hale tending Annie's children."

Sister Bryant nodded satisfactorily as she slid her hands down the stack of trenchers, making a perfect cylinder.

Annie glanced at Julia with a slight smile and added, "It's good Esther has befriended Mary Ann. She's an only child who needs company. And I'd rather do Esther's work than have the children underfoot. The girls will keep Nephi out of trouble and protect Susie from wild beasts."

"Of which Nephi is the wildest, though the handsomest," Sister Bryant added with a wry smile.

Annie sighed. "He'll be the death of me."

Julia noticed the dark circles under her daughter-in-law's eyes. "Annie, go and rest."

"I can't. I need to get the children to bed."

"I'll gather them," Sister Bryant quickly offered, "and bring them to you to say good night."

"Thank you." Annie breathed a sigh of relief. "It feels like if I don't lie down, I might fall down."

Julia watched how slowly Annie walked toward the tent. How had she not noticed earlier that her daughter-in-law was exhausted? Together, she and Sister Bryant carried the dishes to the wagon.

"Your wagon is orderly," Sister Bryant said. "My mother always said that a home should be as neat as the cells of a beehive, everything in its place. I'm like her in that respect. I wonder if she ever thinks about me."

"I'm sure she does," Julia commented. She looked at Sister Bryant a bit quizzically. What was inside this young woman? Then she added, "A mother doesn't forget her child, no matter how long they're separated."

"I wish she'd forget her bitterness toward me for joining the Mormons."

"I'm sorry. I'll pray that her heart softens."

Sister Bryant shrugged and straightened her shoulders. She changed the subject. "Sister Annie was sick this morning. I think she's with child."

"Your help is a great blessing to her."

Sister Bryant spoke matter-of-factly. "Sixtus is a little man. Sariah is an angel like her mother. Nephi is an enchanting rapscallion, and Susie is a princess if ever there was one. I am fortunate to be on board with such a crew."

Julia felt a surge of kindness toward Susan Bryant. The young woman was prim and both outspoken and reserved at the same time. When she reached out emotionally, it was for but an instant, with a quick retreat. She must be lonely without a family to share her life with.

Julia suddenly thought of the day when she met Ezekiel thirty-eight years ago. He had been about the same age as Sister Bryant, and even more alone, for he hadn't a testimony of the Savior to bear him up nor the fellowship of the Saints. Julia had become his world, and it had thrilled her. She had never been someone's sun and moon before. She would never forget his hooded sorrow and searing passion. Sister Bryant need not worry about her mother forgetting. As women grew older, memories were like magnets pulling them away from present moments, like flickering lights on the horizon of another time.

* * *

Later that night, Julia lay awake listening to the sound of her children breathing. Her mind would not stop. Was Almera all right? Was her faith firm? Was Sam kind to her?

Julia closed her eyes. She remembered her deceased children, the sounds of their voices and the touch of their hands. Then thoughts of Ezekiel once more rose before her. Was she, through strange sequences of events and characteristics of soul, in part responsible for his unhappiness?

Yet she would not have done anything differently. Through her trials she had come to know God, and this knowledge lit her path and lightened her burdens. It was her very life. Still, these moments came, usually at night when the work of the day had ceased and her children slept, when darkness gathered around her and despite her faith, she felt so very alone.

Would it be possible to visit her kindred while the camp lingered in Dayton? To be with Joel, Rhoda, and Nancy again, to look into their eyes, to feel the warmth of their arms around her, to tell them of the gospel, to see their children—that would be a joy so great that it was scarcely possible to imagine. Yet she had written over a year ago and had not received a response. Did they think she was a fool for joining the Mormons? Would they blame her for the separation with Ezekiel? For her children's deaths? She couldn't imagine such a reception. Not from those whose bonds of affection reached into her earliest memories. Yet it had been so with Susan Bryant and many others. Loved ones had cut cords of kinship, a punishment for following Joseph Smith.

Julia swallowed in the darkness. But not her brother and sister. They would remember. They would not sever the ties that bound their hearts to hers.

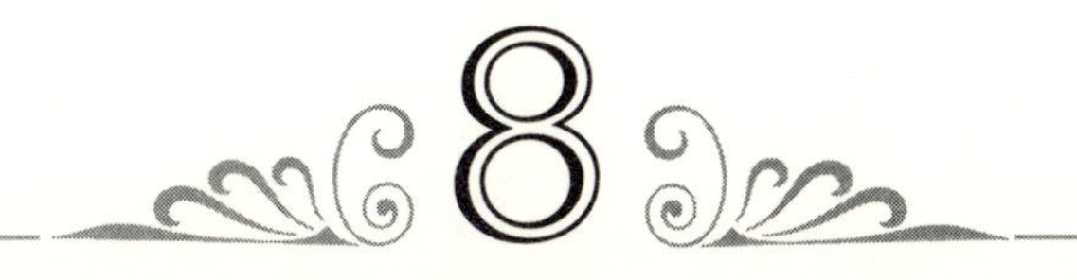

For thy sacred cause, Oh Zion,
Would I give my all below;
Yet the gentile hosts are trying
Thy sweet cause to overthrow.

Joel Hills Johnson

Monday, August 6, 1838

It was nearly noon, and the sun was high in the sky. Julianne glanced over at her husband as they walked hand in hand toward Far West's new, spacious schoolhouse, where a county meeting would be held. Almon looked dashing, dressed immaculately in a dark broadcloth suit and cravat. His cheeks were ruddy from the heat. Today the citizens of the county were meeting to appoint a judge and vote for a postmaster. Earlier Julianne had suggested that Almon wear a cool linen shirt and britches, because it looked to be a hot day. Shaking his head while arranging his cravat, Almon had explained that he planned to hold office one day and needed to look the part now.

Almon and his plans! Julianne smiled thinking of them. Last week Almon had finished building their temporary home, a log cabin on their farmland that flanked the edge of the city. He had built it near the creek within a grove of thick trees. The cellar was as wide as the main floor. All the while, he had talked about the brick mansion he would one day build for her on the middle of their property, with the sun lighting up the windows. He'd eventually turn this cellar into an icehouse and tear down the cabin walls to make a summer kitchen. Their children would play in the yard and run in this grove. Julianne's smile dimmed. If only they had children. If only she was pregnant.

They passed under a stray oak tree. For an instant it blotted out the blazing sun. A messenger boy ran up to Almon. "Here's a letter for you, Brother Babbitt, from Fort Leavenworth. Brother Robinson sent me to give it to you."

After the boy had left, Almon opened the letter. His face broke into a grin.

"Who's it from?" Julianne asked.

"My younger brother, John. He's a rascal if ever there was one. He's close by, working at Fort Leavenworth. Listen to this."

> Al,
>
> General Kearney will hire anyone—free Negroes, Indians, even Mormons. Leave Joe Smith and those blasted Mormons. Here's everything a man could want—drinking, carousing, and women.

Almon eyed his wife. "Perhaps I'll take a holiday and go visit him."

"Over my dead body!"

"On second thought, I'll write John and tell him that my wife is so pretty that it's worth staying in Far West with those blasted Mormons." Taking out a handkerchief, Almon dabbed the perspiration off his brow.

Julianne couldn't help but smile. "Poor boy. You're broiling in that suit," she teased. "Oh, the sacrifices men make in their quest for political power."

Almon grinned and took her hand. "Oh, the sacrifices women make in their quest for beauty. I wasn't the one who slept with my hair tied up in rags last night." Suddenly, he pulled her to him and kissed her.

"You shouldn't do so in public," she chided. "Your reputation is at stake. People will think you a rash young man. Holding hands is bad enough."

Almon cocked an eyebrow. "I *am* a rash young man."

Julianne laughed, glad that he was rash—rash enough to dress so handsomely that it made her pause, rash enough to kiss her in public, rash enough to take her on missions with him, rash enough to pull her from grief to joy.

A few minutes later they reached the schoolhouse. Joseph Smith left the group of men he conversed with and strode up to them. Almon let go of Julianne's hand so that he could shake the Prophet's.

The Prophet greeted them each warmly. "Brother Almon, Sister Julianne, hello!" He too was dressed in a suit, though it was considerably more worn than Almon's.

Joseph continued, addressing Julianne. "Might I have a word with your husband privately before the meeting starts?"

"Of course," Julianne replied.

Almon winked at her. "Save me a seat."

As Julianne walked away, she felt strangely uneasy. Why did the Prophet want to speak with Almon alone? She was certain that he wasn't in the running as postmaster. Was all well? Was Almon going to be called away on a mission? Or was the Prophet reprimanding him for some error? Was that error their missions together?

For the most part, she loved Far West. She loved the fields of green and the wide sky that stretched on and on. She loved the fertile land. She enjoyed being close to Delcena. Yet it felt as if her life were on hold. She remembered the peace she had felt when she had accompanied Almon on missions, when she had been busy and needed. Now a sense of uselessness plagued her. Though she helped Delcena each day, the children cried for their mother, not for her. As Delcena grew large with child, it punctuated her own loss. Julianne longed to do the work of her own life, not someone else's. She wanted children to love and live for. She prayed, telling her Father in Heaven that she was willing to risk the heartbreak she had felt when little David died. She longed to bring His children into the world, to once more hold her own baby close. Then why was she unable to become pregnant? When would her Father in Heaven answer her prayers?

Her thoughts turned to Almon and the Prophet's conversation. What if Almon were called away on a mission without her? What would she do with the hours of each day dragging endlessly on, every dream waiting on God's will? Did she have faith enough to cheerfully accept that? Was there a sliver of hope that she could go along?

Julianne walked into the schoolhouse. It smelled like new, fresh wood. She sat down on a bench near the window and untied her bonnet, placing it on the seat next to her to save a place for Almon. Glancing out the window, she shivered despite the warmth of the day. She watched Almon and the Prophet talk under the shade of a maple tree. Almon wasn't happy. He shook his head briskly at something the Prophet said. Though she couldn't hear him, his hand gestures were quick and pointed. A different prayer entered her heart. She prayed that her husband would accept the Prophet's counsel instead of trying to counsel the Prophet. And now, instead of feeling joy in Almon's rashness, she was worried by it.

Julianne felt a hand on her shoulder. She turned to find Delcena standing there with Lyman. Delcena smiled warmly at her. They exchanged greetings as Delcena and Lyman sat down in the row behind.

Julianne turned around. The room grew full of people. Conversations buzzed. Julianne noticed Lyman glance out the window at Almon and the Prophet. She cleared her throat. "Lyman, do you know what Brother Joseph is talking to Almon about?"

Lyman nodded. There was moisture on the lenses of his spectacles. "I think so. The high council met at the Prophet's house this morning. They discussed the Saints at Three Forks. The brethren believe they settled there against counsel. If the group won't relocate to Adam-ondi-Ahman or Far West, they will no longer be considered one with the Saints."

Julianne took a quick breath. A part of her felt relieved that Almon was not being called on a mission, yet this news would upset him.

A moment later, Almon strode briskly into the schoolhouse. The Prophet walked in behind him but stopped to greet others. Julianne raised a hand in a wave as Almon's eyes roved around the room, searching for her. When he found her, he walked quickly over. After briefly greeting Lyman and Delcena, he squeezed onto the bench next to Julianne. She felt his leg and hip against hers.

"How are you?" she whispered.

"Dandy," he replied shortly, his face flushed.

"Liar," Julianne whispered as she took his hand.

He smiled slightly but without joy. "Woman, you know me too well."

The community leaders gathered in the front of the room, the Prophet among them. The meeting would start soon. Joseph huddled with Sidney Rigdon and George Robinson.

Julianne whispered to Almon. "Lyman told me what's happening in Three Forks. You didn't argue with Joseph, did you?"

Almon shook his head. "Nope, but I told him that those people are faithful and didn't intentionally disregard counsel. And I told him that he and I should go together to Three Forks to talk with them. I want him to see the houses they've built, the stock they've purchased, and the crops they've planted. It's late in the season. If they lose the harvest, how will they eat next winter?"

"Poor Brother Joseph. How difficult being a Prophet must be."

Almon glanced at his wife. "Perhaps even as difficult as being one who follows a Prophet."

The meeting opened. Julianne continued holding her husband's hand. She watched attentively while Judge Elias Higbee was called to the chair and George Robinson was appointed to be his secretary. Sidney Rigdon was recommended as the postmaster of Far West, filling the place of W. W. Phelps, who had resigned.

Following the vote on postmaster, the Prophet stood and spoke. "The time has come, fellow citizens, when it is necessary that we should have a weekly newspaper, to unite the people and to bring us the news of the day. All in favor of establishing this newspaper with President Sidney Rigdon as editor, please show by a raise of hands."

Julianne felt Almon catch his breath. She raised her hand with the rest of the congregation, but Almon hesitated. Instead, he continued to hold Julianne's left hand tightly in his right. Julianne thought about pulling her hand away and elbowing him. Suddenly, Almon abruptly let go and voted with the rest. After the vote, she immediately took his hand once again.

The Prophet continued to speak. He suggested that a petition be circulated to locate the county seat at Far West. There was a rustle of agreement.

Then the Prophet's tone changed as his voice rose decisively. "It is the duty of the brethren to come into the designated cities of Far West and Adam-ondi-Ahman to build and live, and to carry on their farms outside those cities, according to the order of God."

Almon sat stone-faced as the Prophet spoke for a few more minutes on the topic. Joseph closed his remarks and sat down. President Rigdon stood and continued in the same vein, explaining that some brethren had not obeyed the counsel of the Prophet and of the Lord. They had rebelliously established settlements outside the bounds spoken of in the revelations. He warned such individuals of dire consequences. Julianne felt Almon's hand tighten in hers.

After President Rigdon finished, Hyrum arose and with characteristic patience entreated the Saints to build their homes in the cities which the Lord had established and to trust in His Almighty arm for guidance and protection during these perilous times. If they did so, they would receive great blessings.

* * *

On the way to their wagon, Almon set a quick pace as he walked with Julianne, Lyman, and Delcena. A slight breeze broke the sweltering heat. His wife continued to hold his hand as she had during the entire meeting, even through the closing prayer. He knew that she was trying to calm him down. After they both died, she would reach down from heaven, grab his hand, and pull him up to her. That is if his hand wasn't too sweaty from the fire and brimstone. He exhaled sharply.

She led the conversation down any path other than the one where she knew his thoughts fumed.

"I hope that Mother and the others arrive before the cold weather," Julianne said. "Has anyone heard how work on the turnpike is progressing?"

"The council received a letter yesterday," Lyman explained. "They've had a slow start. The men don't have enough tools, and there's sickness in the camp. Fortunately, no one in our family was listed among the sick. They hope to be here by the first of October if all goes according to plan."

"But we all know that things rarely go according to plan," Delcena said.

Almon shook his hand out of Julianne's and turned to Lyman. He was tired of tiptoeing around difficult subjects, of saying everything except that which was in his mind. "That was quite a meeting, wasn't it? My friends in Three Forks haven't an inkling of what's about to hit them."

"Three Forks isn't the only outlying area. There's Haun's Mill and Millport," Lyman added.

"We all know they were talking specifically about Three Forks," Almon countered. "What do you think about Sidney Rigdon's appointments? First he's made postmaster, then editor of the paper."

"I support him," Lyman answered. "He's a talented man and a member of the First Presidency."

"Joseph should have named Don Carlos as editor. Why is he living in Daviess County anyway?"

"Sidney is older and more experienced. Besides, Carlos is needed in the mission field."

Almon shook his head briskly. "It's not right. That's too much power for one man. Sidney's setting policy. Think of the Salt Sermon and Independence Day speech. The power is going to his head. He also convinced the Prophet that Anson and the Canadian Saints willfully disobeyed counsel. That wasn't so."

"It seems like it to him," Lyman countered. "Think of the July revelations. President Rigdon is looking at the facts and trying to support the Prophet."

"He is wrongly interpreting facts and calling his presumptions truth. It seems to me that Joseph isn't running the show anymore, that he's leaving it to Sidney Rigdon and others."

"Joseph is at every meeting. He's counseling the people. Hyrum is right beside him," Lyman countered, his jaw tightening as he strode even more briskly than Almon. Julianne and Delcena dropped behind the men and walked together in silence.

Almon continued. "But Joseph doesn't seem to be making the decisions. Not like he did in Zion's Camp, where he taught us to pursue peace, where he reined in Lyman Wight and those ready to fight."

"Perhaps now is the time to fight," Lyman remarked, his eyes straight forward, "whether we like it or not."

Almon shook his head. "I was ready then. Remember how mad I was before Seth had cholera, when I felt like Joseph was sending us home defeated?"

Lyman looked at Almon. He nodded, and his eyes softened.

Almon gritted his teeth. "But now I'm like Joseph. I just want peace. But the Prophet is giving the militants too much power. The things Sidney says stick in my craw. If I had the money, I'd set up my own paper. It wouldn't hurt to have another voice in Far West."

Lyman stopped abruptly. "I know how you feel. But Joseph is God's prophet. All we can do is trust in his judgment."

"I suppose so," Almon said shortly. His heart beat hard beneath the broadcloth suit. The women caught up. He felt Julianne's smaller hand reach for his and hang on tightly. She wasn't about to let go.

A short time later Almon and Julianne were alone in their wagon, driving home. The wind picked up. By the time they reached their cabin, it blew furiously. While Almon let the horse loose in a field, Julianne hurried toward the cabin, her skirt and hair billowing around her. Almon sprinted after her. When she was at the door, Almon caught up. He took her in his arms as the wind shrieked around them.

"I'll never be as good as you," he whispered into her ear. "Don't ever let me go."

She held his face between her hands and kissed him. He picked her up and carried her inside.

* * *

Tuesday, August 7, 1838

The next morning, the sun blazed in the east and the wind had died down. Lyman rode hard to the Babbitts' farm and found Almon and Julianne cutting and raking hay. Almon's scythe stilled as Lyman pulled his horse to an abrupt halt. Julianne gripped the rake's haft. Fifty yards away, the Babbitts' two horses looked up then continued grazing.

Lyman spoke quickly. "Yesterday afternoon, fighting broke out in Gallatin. The Mormons went to vote, but the Missourians wouldn't allow it, saying they had no more right to vote than a black man. A fight ensued, and two or three of our brethren were murdered."

"Who?" Almon asked.

"We don't know. Word was brought by a non-Mormon. We only know that the men were left lying on the ground and not interred. The old citizens of Daviess County have sworn revenge on our people. Sampson Avard led a group of armed men to ride to find the bodies of the dead. Many brethren are gathering, and George Robinson commands them. Joseph, Sidney, and Hyrum are going with them."

"Then the war has started." Almon's voice was grim. "I'm going. I have to know the extent of the danger. Then I'll ride to Three Forks and warn the people there."

Lyman shook his head. "I came to ask you to stay here and watch over our wives and children. I'm determined to go and stay near Joseph."

Almon's shoulders straightened. "Then we both go. Julianne will take care of your family."

The men turned at the sound of Julianne's rake thudding to the ground. Her brown eyes brimmed with tears as she stalked toward them. "You talk like I'm not here! Have I no say in this?"

Almon turned to her. His voice was firm and his green eyes resolute. "Would you have me stay when our brethren have been murdered? When those in Three Forks are in grave danger?"

"No," she cried out, "I only ask to ride with you. If I must, I'll don a man's coat and britches. I know how to shoot a gun. Betsy Parrish rode with Zion's Camp."

Almon pulled her to him, wrapping his arms tightly around her. His whisper bore into her ear. "Betsy Parrish died with Zion's Camp. Yet if it were possible, I would selfishly take you—keep you by my side to the ends of the earth. But I do not govern this world, nor did I create this war. Stay and get the hay in, tend to our crops. May heaven protect you, my darling."

"I love you," Julianne choked.

"And I you." Almon kissed her gently then let go of her and went to get his horse.

Lyman looked at his sister-in-law and said, "Delcena is frightened. She needs you. The children need you."

Julianne swallowed and nodded. Yet she didn't think that Delcena really needed her. Delcena had the friendship of Emma Smith and other women. It seemed that those with children the same ages were woven together in a cloth of mutual support. She was like a hole in that cloth.

After the men rode away, Julianne didn't go immediately to Delcena. Instead, she lingered in the field. She picked up the scythe and swung it. With tears running down her cheeks, she watched the results of her efforts—live, green stalks falling to the earth.

* * *

Cumulous clouds and a stiff breeze provided the horsemen with alternate sunlight and shade as they rode through Daviess County toward Adam-ondi-Ahman. The group swelled to near fifty as brethren from different parts of the county joined them. Almon and Lyman rode on the east edge of the group where they could scan the countryside.

When they were halfway between Far West and Di-Ahman, the Prophet reined his horse alongside Almon and Lyman. His blond hair blew in the breeze as he pivoted in the saddle and said, "Look around you. This fertile hamlet lies between Marrowbone Creek to the south and Dog Creek to the north. It is to be the City of Seth, named after Adam's faithful son. When I contemplate the name of this place, I think of Seth Johnson, of the peace he sought and found. In this dark hour, I yearn for peace, that the faithful Saints will come here and prosper. Brother Almon, I pray that this journey will end without bloodshed, that we will soon ride to Three Forks together. Perhaps our Canadian brethren will come to settle here or in the valley of Adam-ondi-Ahman."

Almon nodded. "Perhaps. But is it any safer in Daviess County than in Three Forks? Our brethren there died trying to exercise their rights."

Joseph's eyes filled with emotion. "And I don't know their names, nor was I by their side. There is only one thing we can do. We obey God and trust His parental care whether in life or death. He is our Father."

Almon's eyes softened. "God willing, we'll go to Three Forks together."

The Prophet nodded, then his eyes met Lyman's. Joseph smiled despite the lines of worry on his brow. "My friend, it's good to have you near."

A surge of love for the Prophet spread through Lyman. "I will always remain as close as your call."

"May God bless you. May He bless us all," Joseph said. Then he spurred his horse and went back to the front of the group.

Lyman looked around at the peaceful hamlet, the grasses blowing in the breeze, the thick foliage along the creek's banks, and the wild flowers. Seth was an appropriate name for this beautiful place. He looked ahead. Soon they would enter the valley of Adam-ondi-Ahman, armed men on sacred soil. He knew that many of the brethren, like Joseph, prayed for peace, but there were others who were ready for war.

When they passed the trail that branched off toward Gallatin, Lyman and Almon glimpsed a teenage boy hiding behind thick brush. Almon called out a friendly hello, but the boy ran away as if the devil were chasing him. Several men suggested they chase the youth down to stop him from informing the mobs of their position. But the leaders chose not to delay their journey. Let the mobs be wary and know that the people of Di-Ahman would be defended tonight.

An hour later, the air cooled as the horsemen forded the Grand River and entered the valley of Adam-ondi-Ahman. Despite the dire nature of their journey, Lyman felt wonder as he looked ahead toward Tower Hill. What did Adam, who was Michael, the archangel, think of this? Wouldn't God protect this place? Yet God had not stopped Cain from killing Abel. Lyman's thoughts were interrupted when a young man ran out of a cabin and jogged toward him. William Huntington Jr., Benjamin's friend, grinned up at the horsemen.

"Brother Almon, Elder Sherman, hello! It's good to see the two of you."

Lyman and Almon halted their horses as the rest of the company continued up the hill toward Lyman Wight's cabin.

Almon reached down and shook William's hand. "What exactly happened at the election in Gallatin? We heard that some of the brethren were killed, but we don't know who."

"No one was killed, though Riley Stewart and Perry Durphy were busted up pretty good. They'll be all right, though."

"You're certain no one was killed?" Almon's brow furrowed.

William nodded. "Absolutely."

Near the top of the hill, the Prophet, Hyrum, George Robinson, and Sampson Avard had dismounted and were entering Brother Wight's cabin.

Taking in a deep breath of air, Lyman stretched his shoulders in the saddle. The evening air smelled clean. "Joseph will be relieved when he hears the good news."

"Who gave him the false report?" William asked.

Lyman shrugged. "All we know is that the messenger was not a member of the Church."

Almon raised his eyebrows. "Think about it. If a man wanted to stir things up, to get the Mormons to bear arms, which would incite the mobs, that report would be a good way to do it. William, exactly what happened in Gallatin?"

"About twelve of our brethren went to the polls. When they got there, Colonel Peniston, on the Whig ticket, stood up on a barrel and started preaching to the voters against the Mormons—calling us horse thieves and liars, dupes who pretend to heal the sick and cast out devils. He said if the Mormons were allowed to vote, the people would soon lose their suffrage. Sam Brown decided to vote anyway. A drunk Missourian tried to hit Sam, said that Mormons shouldn't be allowed to vote any more than Negroes. All

Sam had to defend himself with was an umbrella. Perry Durphy grabbed hold of the drunk's arms. Then it broke loose. A dozen mobbers attacked Perry, hitting him with fists and clubs and yelling 'Kill him, kill him.' Others joined the fight.

"Think about it," William continued, his eyes flashing with the excitement of the tale. "Twelve of our brethren against a hundred or more Missourians. But we had big John Butler from Kentucky on our side. With the strength of a lion, he knocked down a score of mobbers with an oak club. It's a miracle none of them died. While the other mobbers ran off to get their guns, the brethren scooted out of town. Some of our men hid their families in a thicket of hazel bush and stood guard around them through the rainy night. Now most of them are here in Di-Ahman without any of their property. With you men here, if the mobbers try to drive us out, they'll have a hard time of it."

Lyman felt suddenly weary. The relief he had felt when he learned that no one had died slipped away while the gravity of the situation pressed upon him. Tonight they would sleep with their guns beside them.

* * *

Wednesday, August 8, 1838

The rooster's crow awoke Lyman. For a moment he stared upward at clouds tinged with pink. He was farsighted, and the dawn sky appeared clear and crisp. He turned his head and saw Almon's sleeping form beside him, cradling his rifle in his arms. William Huntington lay next to Almon, having preferred to sleep outside with the men rather than in the cabin with his family. The two men and their weapons blurred together in Lyman's vision, mist-like.

Lyman reached for his spectacles and put them on. He sat up as the world veered into focus. Men were awakening, draining their canteens, chewing on whatever they had to eat—hard tack, pork jerky, or biscuits. Lyman licked his lips. He was thirsty. Last night they had been informed that many of the surrounding wells and springs had dried up. Lyman stretched. The first thing he planned to do was make a trek to the creek for water.

Suddenly six men stepped out of the cabin. Lyman Wight, George Robinson, and Sidney Rigdon stood in sunlight on the front of the porch. Joseph, Hyrum, and Sampson Avard remained in the shadows behind them.

Brother Wight addressed the men. "Brethren, after conferencing most of the night, we're now headed to Adam Black's cabin; near there are the coldest, best springs in Adam-ondi-Ahman. You are welcome to accompany us to obtain water for yourselves and your horses."

"Are we going just for water?" a man called out.

Wight continued. "We go for water and for an assurance of peace. Several of us will pay a call on Mr. Black while the rest of you refresh yourselves."

Now awake, Almon propped himself up on an elbow. "Who's Adam Black?" he asked under his breath.

William Huntington whispered back, "An old resident of Di-Ahman, justice of the peace and Mormon hater. A month ago he knocked on each of our doors and told us to leave or face dire consequences."

Almon whistled lowly. "Looks like we're going to knock on his door now and give him a taste of his own medicine."

Twenty minutes later, on Adam Black's property, they watered their horses. After filling their canteens, Almon and Lyman moved away from the watering hole to make room for other men. As they drank deeply of the cold, crisp water, they watched the Prophet sitting on a rock near the spring, stroking his black horse, Charley, who grazed next to him. The Prophet's blue eyes were focused on Adam Black's cabin.

A number of armed brethren waited on the porch. Inside, Sampson Avard, Lyman Wight, and George Robinson parleyed with Adam Black.

Almon sighed. "Do you find it strange that Joseph isn't in the cabin with them?"

"No. It's best if our enemies don't know which man is the Prophet," Lyman said.

"He's standing back again and allowing the militants to run things," Almon said. Then he added, "Still, maybe it's best that Joseph isn't an eyewitness. If this goes to court, it will go better for him."

A moment later, Sampson Avard walked out and motioned for Joseph to come into the cabin. Joseph handed his horse's reins to his brother and followed Avard.

Five minutes later, Lyman Wight confidently strode out of the cabin with a piece of paper in his hand. Joseph followed him. Sidney Rigdon walked up, and the men spoke together for a moment, then Wight handed the paper to Rigdon.

Rigdon's oratory voice rose loud in the air. "On interrogation, Adam Black has confessed that he has violated his oath as a magistrate and has entered into the following agreement: I, Adam Black, a Justice of the Peace of Daviess County, do hereby Certify to the people, called Mormon, that I am bound to support the Constitution of this State, and of the United States, and I am not attached to any mob, nor will not attach myself to any such people, and so long as they will not molest me, I will not molest them. This the 8th day of August, 1838. Signed, Adam Black, Justice of the Peace."

Then Sidney Rigdon waved the paper in their air, reminding Lyman of both a gentleman waving a flag and an Indian waving the scalp of his enemy.

9

"The Lord bless you!" that sacred sound
Falls sweetly on the human heart,
When friends, by strongest ties long bound,
Are doomed, by fate, awhile to part.

'Tis hard the feelings to control,
And press the hand that has been true,
When soul responsive beats to soul,
In breathing out, "The Lord bless you!"

Joel Hills Johnson

Cincinnati, Ohio—August 1838

Julia, Joel, and Benjamin walked up the steps to the carved, honey-colored door of the white, two-story boardinghouse situated along the riverfront. Smoke rose from the chimney, gray billows meeting blue sky and wind-sped clouds. Tall trees shaded the porch, and the breeze off the Ohio River cooled the air. It seemed almost unreal to Julia—a comfortable, storybook place in the late afternoon of a hot summer day.

"This is it," Joel commented. "Aunt Nancy's place."

"It's nice," Benjamin observed.

Anticipation filled Julia as she raised her hand and lifted the brass knocker. She had not seen her sister in thirty years. It didn't help that she felt scarcely presentable after being on the road five weeks. Still, Julia's knock was sure and her shoulders erect. This was Nancy, her darling younger sister!

The door opened, and her sister stood before her. She was forty pounds heavier, with her graying hair pulled back in a tight bun. It accentuated her face, the fine, sharp features, the fire and life in the eyes. She wore a starched white apron over a navy blue dress. Julia would have recognized her anywhere.

"We're full to the brim," Nancy said with a frank smile. "I can direct you . . ." Then Nancy stopped midsentence, the corners of her mouth turned down, her eyes wide with disbelief.

"It's Julia, Nancy. Dear Nancy."

"Julia! You look so like Mother. I thought for an instant . . ." Nancy began to cry as she wrapped her arms around her sister. Julia felt Nancy's heart beating wildly. She was the same passionate Nancy, not a candle on a candlestick, but a bonfire.

Nancy released Julia, and now, despite her tears, her smile was wide and bright, like a rainbow slicing through the downpour.

"Oh, Julia! I can hardly believe you've come!" Her eyes lighted on her eldest nephew. "Joel Hills Johnson! I'd know you anywhere. Eight years isn't such a long time!"

"No, Aunt Nancy," Joel said with a warm smile. "It isn't long at all."

Nancy hugged Joel tightly then turned to Benjamin. "You're not Seth nor David . . . they've visited me before. You favor the Johnsons more than the Ellises. You could be Joseph or Benjamin, perhaps George."

Benjamin grinned and held out his hand. "I'm Ben. Mother has told us stories of you and Uncle Joel ever since we were small."

"Oh, I hope I'm not always the wickedly spoiled little sister!" Nancy exclaimed as she took Benjamin's hand then pulled him to her for an embrace. "Welcome, Ben. You three must be hungry and tired." Then she turned to Julia. "Supper is nearly ready. We'll eat in my quarters. I hope you're not too tired. We have so much to talk about. Thirty years to make up for."

As she followed Nancy into the building, Julia looked around. The boardinghouse teemed with life. The spacious dining hall contained five long tables lined with benches. Around thirty men sat in small groups, some chewing tobacco, most drinking beer. She passed three men speaking German. An Irishman told a joke as the group surrounding him burst into laughter. Catering to the men's needs were three black women dressed like Nancy in navy dresses and white aprons. A huge black man stood in the corner. His skin glistened with sweat.

Nancy called out to him with a dismissive toss of her head. "Elias, take care of these people's horses." He nodded to Nancy and turned to go. He was the most powerful-looking human being that Julia had ever seen.

Nancy moved around the group, confidently speaking to the patrons as she passed them. "Mr. Braniff, is work on the barracks almost complete?

How long will you and your men be staying? I'll have my man bring you a barrel of whisky tonight.

"Good evening, Mr. Huber. What's that? Your wife and children will arrive this week from the old country. How many rooms will you need?"

When they had crossed the hall, they went through a door into an adjoining apartment. It comprised two small rooms, the door between them ajar. The first room contained a round oak table with four chairs. There was a large cupboard against the wall. The other room was furnished with a bed and a small corner table holding a water pitcher, glass, and basin. It was bare and clean. Nancy's quarters.

"Julia, would you like to lie down and rest before supper? I'll bring you a drink of cider."

Julia declined. "I couldn't rest right now, regardless of how tired I am. I'm like a girl—giddy from the excitement of seeing you. Look at you, Nancy! You run this business by yourself."

"It was hard the year after George died, but now things are thriving."

Then Nancy turned to Julia's sons. "Joel and Benjamin, what would you like? Beer, whisky, or ale?"

"Cider suits me," Joel said.

"And me," Benjamin added.

Nancy suddenly laughed. "That's right. You're Mormons now. Three ciders it is."

Julia looked carefully at her sister. "Then you got the letter I wrote about joining the Mormons? I never knew."

"Yes," Nancy said quickly. "Now I'm off before you wither of thirst."

Julia smiled. "I'm more thirsty to talk with you than anything else on earth."

Nancy's voice cracked as she said, "You are so like Mother! I tried to write you back, Julia. Six years ago. But the carrier returned it unopened. He told me all the Mormons had left New York. I feared that your religion had stolen you from Joel and me. That we would never hear from you again."

Nancy began to weep. At that moment, Julia did not see her as a fifty-year-old woman but only as her baby sister. "Dearest, my prayers and thoughts are ever with you and Joel!"

Julia took Nancy into her arms. They had shared the tender years of growing up. They both had endured great loss and had lived lives full of toil. They were the daughters of Esther Ellis and Joseph Hills, and they stood erect as they cried in each other's arms.

* * *

Two hours later, Nancy listened as Julia and her sons shared the story of their conversion to Mormonism. Nancy's thoughts jumped back and forth, from their lives to her own. It was a fascinating story, a young boy praying to know of truth and being rewarded with a vision from God. A record on plates of gold. Other sheep of a different fold. Nancy, too, labored with the Lord's sheep. Did she dare tell Julia of her efforts?

Now her thoughts slipped back to their childhood. She had always known that God was Julia's friend—like a neighbor living just down the road. Their brother, Joel, had been the scholar and she, Nancy, the pretty, pampered younger sister. Did children naturally categorize others and themselves? Now Julia was here—Julia, who had filled her with jealousy one moment and adoration the next—Julia, whom she had fought with and laughed with—Julia, whom she had ached to be as good as—Julia, who was now so much like their mother.

Nancy watched Julia as she spoke. Her hair was gray, and wrinkles lined her face. Her hands were folded quietly in her lap, and her eyes were just as Nancy remembered: deep brown, oval, and expressive. Earlier Julia had told her about her children's deaths. How had she endured the loss of four? When Nancy's husband, George, had died ten years ago, Nancy had barely survived. Yet Julia had faced such grief four times in the last five years. Which caused more grief? The loss of spouse or child? Could grief be compared, weighted in a balance? No. It could only be endured.

Julia's voice called Nancy back into the moment. "I know that God, our Heavenly Father, lives and loves us. I know that he has restored the ancient gospel of Jesus Christ. I am acquainted with a living prophet of God. This knowledge has brought me joy and comfort, has borne me, as if on eagle's wings, out of the darkness of despair. Dear Nancy, please consider these things."

Nancy listened with tears in her eyes as Joel and Benjamin also bore their witnesses. Then Nancy knew. She knew that she could tell them the truth. She would explain to Julia why she couldn't read the Book of Mormon, why she dare not ask God if Mormonism was true. For if she left her home to join the Mormon faith, too many people who depended on her might lose their way. *Other sheep have I who are not of this fold.*

There was a knock at the door. Nancy stood to open it. The manservant walked in with his hat in his hands. His eyes darted toward the Johnsons. "I've taken care of the horses, ma'am."

"Thank you, Elias. This is my sister, Mrs. Julia Johnson, and her sons, Joel and Benjamin. They are Mormons traveling to Missouri after being driven out of Kirtland, Ohio."

Then Nancy turned to Julia. "And this is my right hand, Mr. Elias Woodberry."

The black man spoke as he bowed his head in respect. "Ma'am. Sirs. It is a pleasure meeting you."

"And you, Mr. Woodberry," Julia and her sons replied.

Elias continued. "I heard a Mormon doctor preach a few years back. When folks was dyin' of cholera. I recall him tellin' of a prophet by the name of Smith."

Joel said, "Our prophet's name is Joseph Smith. He speaks the word of God. Do you remember if the doctor's name was Frederick Williams?"

"I don't recall."

Benjamin scratched the back of his head. "Did he have a team of black horses?"

Elias looked at Benjamin. "Yes, sir. I recall those horses. They were mighty fine animals."

Benjamin nodded. "I made those horse collars."

"Now isn't that something!" Elias returned. "Those were the nicest horse collars I've ever seen."

Nancy smiled and changed the subject. "Elias, are any shipments coming tonight or tomorrow?"

"Not tonight, Missus Taft. But your sons will be sending us a shipment from across the river tomorrow. We'll be getting three large hams and two small ones."

"Is this the shipment you've been hoping for?"

Elias shook his head. "No, ma'am."

"With God's help, that shipment will come soon. For now, could I trouble you to help my nephews purchase some pork? They've been asked to bring back a wagonload of meat for five hundred Mormons waiting in Dayton. They are an oppressed people."

Elias nodded. "It's no trouble."

Joel entered the conversation. "Aunt Nancy, I see no reason to trouble Mr. Woodberry. We're going across the river tomorrow. We could purchase our hams in Newport where you get yours."

Nancy looked briefly at Joel. Was this the time to tell them? Elias's dark eyes met hers. He did not speak or move a muscle, yet a tense silence radiated from him, filling the room.

Benjamin broke the silence. "Do herds of hogs walk the streets of Newport like they do here in Cincinnati?"

"No, they do not," Nancy answered. "Cincinnati is the best place in the country to buy your hams. That's why it's called Porkopolis."

Joel asked, "Then why do you get your meat from across the river?"

Nancy met his gaze. "That's a very good question, but the explanation takes some time. For now, let's get you the best deal we can." She turned to Elias. "Take my nephews. After their business is finished, have them spend the night in our cellar, since all of the beds in the house are full. Tell them the truth. My sister will spend the night here with me."

"Can they be trusted, ma'am?" Elias asked, his dark eyes unreadable.

"Yes," Nancy said with a smile. "I'm absolutely sure."

* * *

Joel glanced over at Elias Woodberry sitting next to him as they rode past Sycamore Street then down a road of dingy buildings where pork was packed and shipped. The black man stared straight ahead, uncommunicative, his jaw jutting forward. Hogs squealed and waddled out of the wagon's path.

"Stop here," Elias stated, pointing to a gray building, a shade less dirty than the rest. The air was rank with the smell of slaughter. Joel halted the team, and the two stepped down from the wagon.

"Don't take the first price he gives you," Elias advised.

"I won't make that mistake," Joel said with a nod.

Benjamin, who had been riding in the wagon bed, climbed down and walked over. "Will you be coming in with us, Mr. Woodberry? To help us get the best deal?"

The black man shook his head. "I'll wait by the door where's I can keep an eye on you gentlemen and the horses. Don't let no one hear you call me *Mister* Woodberry."

"Why? You're a free black man," Joel said.

Elias turned toward Joel. His voice lowered to a whisper. "Treat me like your slave in public. I should have been ridin' in the back of your wagon, not the front. Folks was starin'."

"But you had to give my brother directions," Benjamin interjected. "Besides, you shouldn't worry on our account. We've been stared at all the way from Kirtland."

Elias clamped his mouth shut, ending the conversation.

Joel eyed Elias. He had read about the tensions in Cincinnati. Escaped slaves and free Negroes roamed the streets looking for work. White immigrants rioted, angry about jobs being taken from them by blacks. Southern slave owners crossed the river searching for escaped slaves and furious at the abolitionists who protected them. Where did Elias Woodberry and Aunt Nancy fit into this puzzle? And why did a free man insist on being treated like a slave? He turned to his brother. "From here on out we listen to Elias and do what he says. No questions asked."

Benjamin nodded.

Joel put other thoughts aside and concentrated on the task at hand. The leaders of the camp had given him money with which to buy quality pork for the best possible price. It was a sacred trust. This was the precious, hard-earned cash of his brethren who continued laboring on the Dayton Turnpike. He motioned for Benjamin to come into the packing center with him.

The brothers walked in side by side, tall, lanky, and determined. Scores of hams hung from the rafters. Flies buzzed around them. A thin German man with a thick accent introduced himself as the owner of the establishment.

"I need thirty of your best smoked hams," Joel stated.

The vendor nodded. "Pick them out, sir."

Joel walked around slowly, pointing to thirty of the largest cuts. The vendor notched them with his knife. Then he gave Joel a price.

"That's more money than I have," Joel said. He counteroffered.

The vendor shook his head adamantly. "Not enough. These are big hams. Take twenty-five."

"I'll look elsewhere. I have five hundred people to feed." Joel turned to walk away. Benjamin followed. They gained the door, the vendor's eyes following them. Elias stepped out of the shadows.

The German called out, "Is that Mrs. Taft's man?"

Joel turned around. "Yes. Mrs. Taft is my aunt."

"She's a good lady. Because of her, I give you all thirty hams. I let her nephew rob me any day."

"Thank you," Joel said with a quick smile. He walked back toward the vendor knowing that he had done well for the camp. He paid for the hams while Benjamin and Elias loaded them into the wagon.

As Joel drove the team back to the boardinghouse, Benjamin sat next to him, quiet and observant. Elias rode in the back with the meat. Joel flicked his wrist to keep the horses moving. Rolling his shoulders, he stretched his aching muscles. He had looked forward to sleeping on a feather bed tonight but instead would be on the floor of a cramped cellar. But that was a missionary's fare. He thought of Annie and the children. They were safe, and Susan Bryant was there to help. What of his sisters and brothers-in-law in Missouri? There were rumors of trouble. Would it be a safe haven, the Zion they dreamed of?

Joel took a deep breath. Right now he was in Cincinnati. He was not only here to buy provisions but also to share the gospel with his kin. Tonight his mother would talk more with Aunt Nancy. And tomorrow they would be at his Uncle Joel's place—and most likely on a comfortable bed. But would any of their relatives accept the gospel? All they could do was bear testimony. Then they would head back to Dayton. One thing was certain: his mission to buy provisions had been successful.

Looking south toward the shoreline of the Ohio River, Joel could see the setting sun light the bordering trees a green-golden—aspen, maple, birch, pine, and hickory. The water picked up the crimson colors of the sky.

* * *

It was nearly dark by the time Joel, Benjamin, and Elias arrived back at the boardinghouse. After storing the hams and stabling the horses, Elias lit three lanterns and handed one to each of them. They walked down a path behind the house bordered by thick shrubs until they came to a trapdoor hidden by brush. Joel descended the steep, narrow staircase with Elias leading and Benjamin behind, the humid coolness like still, damp breath against his skin. In the lantern light he saw their surroundings: the cellar was filled to the brim with food with scarcely a place on the floor large enough to sit on, much less lie down upon. *What was Aunt Nancy thinking?*

Benjamin sucked in a breath. "I'll sleep under the wagon, not here."

Elias glanced at the men's confused expressions. "Gentlemen, things are not as they seem."

Elias moved aside a heavy cupboard. Behind it was a door. The men entered the hidden room, the lantern light illuminating one corner then another—a feather bed, basin, pitcher of water, chamber pot, and quilts and provisions piled in a corner, and a lone china doll sitting on a small chair, its skin lily white, its expression frozen.

"Welcome to Sweet Nancy's palace," Elias said, his voice full and deep. "The finest station on the Underground Railroad."

"Then Aunt Nancy is an abolitionist," Benjamin uttered, astounded. "And that's why you wanted us to treat you like a slave. So no one will suspect. Are you a runaway?"

Elias shook his head. "My old master gave me my freedom when he died five years back. But my wife and child are in Kentucky, the property of a different man."

Joel thought of Annie and his little ones. He knew what it was like to be of a hated sect, to be unfairly treated. But he could not imagine what it was like to be a slave. "I'm sorry," he said.

Elias's jaw jutted out. "Them shipments coming across the river . . . they ain't hams, they's people. Missus Taft is a great Christian lady. Your cousins are great Christian men. They's workin' with the Kentucky abolitionists to get my family out. That's the shipment I's hopin' for. Missus Taft bought that doll for my little girl. Misses Taft trusts your mama and you gentleman, so I s'pose you folks is great Christian men and women. Even if you is Mormons."

* * *

Julia lay awake in the dark room, listening to the soft sound of Nancy breathing. The path of their earlier conversation trailed back and forth through her mind, like travelers crisscrossing roads, each on a journey to somewhere unforeseen.

She wouldn't see her brother Joel. Nancy had explained how he left on a merchant ship months ago and hadn't yet returned. This was deeply disappointing, yet Julia looked forward to visiting with Joel's wife, Rhoda, and their children. They were not abolitionists like Nancy and her sons.

Abolitionists. The word stung in Julia's mind. The fact repeated itself. Nancy and her sons were abolitionists. It was a derogatory term. Abolitionists were known for their extreme views, their eagerness to break the law to further their beliefs. They wanted slavery to end immediately regardless of the cost. Earlier, Nancy had tried to explain how it came about.

"That stereotype is based on rumors," Nancy had said. "Much like the public views of Mormons. Most abolitionists abhor violence."

Nancy had spoken of her Presbyterian minister, Lyman Beecher. He believed that slavery was morally wrong but did not advocate extreme methods of fighting it. Rather, he hoped that if it did not spread, it would die a natural death. He had taught Nancy's two sons, Daniel and Thomas, in his seminary where he trained young ministers to win the West for Protestantism. In 1834, students in the seminary debated the slavery issue for eighteen consecutive nights. Many of them, including the Taft boys, became abolitionists, even though Reverend Beecher opposed their radical position. Dan and Tad had left the seminary and moved to Kentucky. Now they brought runaways to Nancy's door in the dead of night.

Julia had been concerned for her sister and her nephews. "Your boys are breaking the law. Kentucky is a slave state. Though I, too, detest the very thought of human bondage, they are stealing what is considered other people's property. I fear for them."

And Nancy had answered, "Oh, Julia. You know even better than I that God's laws are higher than man's laws. These people are God's lambs. I will take a stranger in and clothe the naked and visit those in bonds. This is God's work; I know it just as you know that Mormonism is true. Your path as a Saint is one that you must walk, and I must walk mine as well."

Julia bit her lip. Nancy wouldn't read the Book of Mormon; she wouldn't come to Zion. They might never see each other again in this life. Would they be separated for eternity? Julia knew that the priesthood was restored, that baptism by those in authority was necessary for eternal life, that the way to heaven was straight and narrow. Yet Nancy did what she felt was right with courage, fortitude, and great compassion. Was Nancy lost? Julia could not believe that a loving God would separate Nancy from salvation. Was it possible that her sister was on a different straight and narrow way? Would these paths all converge at heaven's gate one bright eternal morning? How was that possible?

Suddenly Julia heard the click of Nancy's tongue. It triggered a memory, like a flicker of light. It was a signal she and Nancy had used when they were girls to tell the other that they were still awake and wanted to talk. As an adolescent, Julia had often ignored Nancy's click when she was tired of her younger sister's chatter. Julia did not do so tonight. She clicked back.

Nancy spoke softly. "You've hardly mentioned Ezekiel. How is he? Why didn't he come with you to Cincinnati?"

Julia swallowed, her eyes wide open in the darkness. "We've separated. I didn't know how to tell you. After Seth's death we couldn't go on hurting each other."

Nancy's words were direct, but her voice was kind. "How were you hurting each other?"

"He bitterly opposed Mormonism—at least my commitment to it. And his intemperance changed him. When he drinks, he is not the Ezekiel you remember."

"Oh, Julia, how you have suffered!"

"He suffers too, Nancy. He is still a kind father. He has stayed in Kirtland near Almera and her husband."

Nancy let out a deep breath and spoke as much to herself as to Julia. "I remember how much you loved him. And he worshipped you. Is it possible that all this is forgotten?"

Tears filled Julia's eyes. "He hasn't forgotten. Nor have I."

* * *

The following afternoon, the sun was high and bright in Newport, Kentucky, as Benjamin walked with his cousin Benjamin Franklin Hills, called Frank, along the Ohio River, past Mansion Hill back toward his Uncle Joel's comfortable frame house. Earlier, Aunt Rhoda had sent Benjamin down the road to tell Frank to hurry over because his Aunt Julia and her sons had come to visit.

Frank, a large man with red hair and an open smile, had been delighted when Benjamin had introduced himself and had welcomed Benjamin with open arms and immediate familiarity. He had happily introduced Benjamin to Elizabeth, his wife. Their twenty-month-old son, Johnny, was napping. It was then decided that Frank and Benjamin would go back to Mother's immediately. Liz and the baby would come later.

As they walked, Frank chatted amicably. "I've always wanted to meet you. Did you know that our mothers had a friendly argument before either of us was conceived? They both wanted to name a boy after the great patriot. But two cousins named Ben wouldn't do. They solved the dilemma by drawing straws. Whoever drew the shortest had to call her boy Franklin, and whoever drew the longest was privileged to call him Benjamin. Your mother drew the longest. Since I was born first, my mother could have cheated. If she had, you would now be conversing with Ben Hills and I with Frank Johnson."

Benjamin grinned. "Are you certain that your mother didn't draw the longest straw? That Frank wasn't the preferred name?"

Frank laughed. "Not entirely! We shall have the opportunity to ask them this afternoon."

Benjamin took a deep breath of fresh air, feeling a sense of well-being in Frank's company, as if the entire world were as friendly and open as his cousin. Was it possible that Frank and his wife would accept the gospel? How exciting it would be to teach them.

As they continued to walk, Frank pointed to an ornate Greek-style home overlooking the river. It was the fanciest house Benjamin had ever seen. Only the Kirtland Temple compared in grandeur.

Frank explained, "That place belongs to a man named Taylor. They say that he's the wealthiest man in the state of Kentucky."

Benjamin watched the black men and women working in the fields and gardens surrounding the house. This was the first time he had been in a slave state.

"It takes a lot of people to run a place like that," Frank commented.

They passed under the shadow of a sugar maple.

"A lot of slaves?" Benjamin asked.

Other trees now lined the road. They continued walking in dappled sunlight.

Instead of answering the question, Frank changed the subject. "I met your brother-in-law, Almon Babbitt, some years back. He is a fine, talkative fellow. Did he get his license to practice law?"

"He'll have it soon. He's been studying with a lawyer in Kirtland for the past four years. When things settle down he wants to come back to Cincinnati to take the tests. He plans to get a license to practice law in five different states."

"Good for him! I could tell that he was the kind of fellow bound to accomplish whatsoever he set out to do. I think his only failure was that he couldn't make me a Mormon. But no man will. Though Almon tried hard enough."

Benjamin's heart sank as he realized that preaching to his cousin would do little good. If Almon couldn't turn his heart, then Benjamin hadn't a chance.

As if sensing his disappointment, Frank put his hand on Benjamin's shoulder. "And what do you plan on doing, Ben?"

Benjamin was quiet for a moment. How could he explain that he had been given a blessing stating that he would fulfill Seth's earthly mission? That was his purpose, to teach the gospel and follow his Prophet and mentor. But that wasn't the answer jovial Frank Hills was looking for. But it was the truth.

Benjamin said, "Almon encourages me to go into law with him. But I like working with my hands. I've apprenticed with a saddler. I'd like to open my own shop someday. But right now I want to get to Missouri as quick as I can. Joseph Smith is a prophet of God and a noble and great man. I want to be near him and find out where I can be most serviceable to the Lord. I've covenanted to preach the restored gospel of Jesus Christ, to fulfill whatever mission God would send me on."

Frank stopped for a moment and looked directly at Benjamin. "That's noble. But from what I've read in the papers, Missouri is a dangerous place for Mormons right now. They claim you are abolitionists. Have you heard about what happened to Elijah Lovejoy?"

Benjamin shook his head. "I don't know who he is."

"He *was* a Presbyterian minister. Lived in St. Louis, Missouri, and was the editor of the *St. Louis Observer.* He was run out of town when he spoke out against a judge who wouldn't charge the men responsible for a mob lynching of a free black man. Reverend Lovejoy moved to Illinois, and angry men followed him there. He set up another printing press. They burned his press three times; then, last November, they shot him, murdered him. That's when Tad and Dan made a covenant: 'Here, before God, in the presence of these witnesses, from this time, we consecrate our lives to the destruction of slavery!'"

Benjamin was quiet for a moment. Abolitionism was a cause as precious to others as his religion was to him. When he spoke, his voice was also a whisper. "Are you an abolitionist too?"

Frank shook his head. "No. I have a wife and baby who depend on me. I will never jeopardize their well-being."

"That's as noble a cause," Benjamin said.

Frank's countenance darkened. "Is it, Ben? I try to convince myself, but would I do anything differently if I were single and free? I don't like to rock the boat. I value peace and quiet. I live in Kentucky. I'm a Yankee, but I'm friends with slave owners. The Hills blood is full of conviction and courage. It runs deep in Aunt Nancy, Tad, and Dan, and I imagine in your family too. Ideals and purpose are more important than friendship and safety. Caroline, my sister, is the same way. She and her new husband were ready to join the cause after Lovejoy died. But I'm a Partridge like my mother. I don't want the fight, and Mother won't allow abolitionism to be spoken of in her home."

Benjamin thought about how Frank reminded him of his brother Joe. Neither wanted a fight—both wanted to be friends with everyone. Joe had wanted to mend breaks during the Kirtland apostasy when Benjamin had been filled with anger toward those who turned against the Prophet. But Joe was like Aunt Nancy's boys too. He had compassion for the oppressed, especially for the Indian nation. If he lived here, would the injustice of slavery raise his ire?

Benjamin gazed across the river at the free state of Ohio. "Sometimes people don't want a battle," he said, "but they land in the middle of one anyway. And then they have to choose."

Frank Hills looked carefully at his cousin. "You're right. When I was a boy, I was told stories of your mother's kindness and spirituality. You must be like her. Although we don't share the same religion, I'm proud that we share the same given name and the same blood. "

* * *

Julia sat between Nancy and Joel as they ate dinner together at Rhoda's table. Julia studied her niece and nephews sitting across from her. Her brother Joel's children delighted her: Frank favored his mother and laughed like his father; Caroline was an attractive woman with sensitive features and a deep, hearty voice. Then there were Nancy's boys, Daniel and Thomas, called Dan and Tad. As dashing as their father, they charmed her with their wit and passion. They said nothing about abolitionism but asked Joel and Benjamin a hundred questions about Mormonism. Julia wondered what life would have been like if she and Ezekiel had moved to Cincinnati, rather than Pomfret. These cousins would be friends with her children, not strangers. But would she have found the restored gospel of Christ?

As the room darkened, Dan stood up. "Mother, it's time to go. Tad and I will bring the carriage around." He kissed Julia's cheek and shook Joel's and Benjamin's hands. Then he addressed Rhoda. "Aunt, thank you for supper."

Rhoda's color heightened. "You're welcome, Dan. But must you go? What could be more important than staying here when your aunt Julia has come from so far away?"

"Only one thing," Dan responded.

Rhoda pursed her lips, and the room was silent except for Dan's footsteps and the door opening and closing. Tad bid his good-byes and followed.

Nancy stood up. "Rhoda, good night and thank you for dinner."

"Good night," Rhoda responded.

"I'll walk you out," Julia said after Nancy embraced Joel and Benjamin.

Once outside, the moon and stars hung like lamps in the sky. Julia's jaw quivered. Would this be the last time she embraced her sister?

Julia could not stop her tears. "Oh, Nancy, how can I tell you good-bye?"

"Then don't say good-bye," Nancy exclaimed as she hugged Julia. "Only say till we meet again."

"God be with you," Julia whispered. "Until we meet again."

Nancy stepped back as Tad took her hand and helped her climb into the carriage. Julia watched as the carriage moved down the road, its form blacker than the night. She walked back into the house.

Rhoda met her at the door. "They are abolitionists," she cried. "They put themselves in danger."

"I know," Julia admitted as she hooked her elbow with Rhoda's. They walked to the parlor together and sat down.

"I've tried to stop them," Rhoda said. Her skin had weathered with age, but her smattering of freckles still stood out in the candlelight. She sounded very discouraged.

Julia put her arm around her sister-in-law. "Dearest, you can't stop them. Not any more than Ezekiel could stop me and the children from joining the true Church."

Rhoda sighed and closed her eyes. "Joel and I are the only ones who have not changed. If I could, I would have stopped you from becoming a Mormon."

"And I would have made you realize that Joseph Smith is a prophet of God."

Rhoda looked at Julia, smiling slightly and shrugging her shoulders. "Then we are at an impasse."

Julia smiled back. "Except that you are the same, Rhoda, my dearest friend."

"And you, my sweet, stubborn Julia. I'm so glad you came. Must you really leave tomorrow?"

Julia nodded. "I must. Will you give my brother my love?"

"I will. And he'll be very sorry that he missed you. He once said that no one could stop you from being the woman God meant you to be."

10

What's best for me my Father knows
And will my footsteps guide,
And keep me safe from all my foes
And for my needs provide,
His will be done, my spirit cries,
For He is holy, just and wise.

Joel Hills Johnson

Saturday, August 11, 1838

The night shadows on the starlit prairie surrounded Almon as a three-quarter moon rose above the horizon. It had been an uneventful ride from Far West to Three Forks. His companions, Joseph Smith, Hyrum Smith, and Sidney Rigdon rode quietly alongside him. Almon wondered what each was thinking. Along the way, Almon had done most of the talking, describing the personalities and talents of individual Canadian Saints and reiterating their faithfulness.

"This way to John Snider's property," Almon commented as he turned his horse east alongside a dark branch of the Grand River.

"Wouldn't it be better to stay with Brother Call?" Hyrum asked. "He's the leader. If Anson heeds our counsel, things will go more smoothly tomorrow."

"I agree with Elder Babbitt," Sidney remarked. "Sometimes it's better to first gain the ear of one of the more prominent followers—a man like John Snider."

"They're both good men," Almon said, feeling defensive. "I'd wager that we won't have a problem getting either to follow counsel. But we'd get more rest if we stayed with the Sniders. Their children are older and quieter than the Calls'." He glanced toward Joseph. "Tell me which way to take you."

At that instant, the Prophet appeared to be deep in thought. His profile looked kingly in the shadows—the prominent nose and high forehead. Then Joseph's head pivoted toward Almon. "Now I remember John Snider. He once visited us in Kirtland and was a faithful missionary in England. Lead the way to his house."

Fifteen minutes later, John welcomed the men into the cabin. Almon introduced them. Bread, cheese, and strawberries were set out on the table.

"It almost seems as if you were expecting us," Joseph said warmly as he shook John's hand. "Your family's lamp is trimmed."

Almon gazed around the cabin. It was a fraction of the brick house John had built in Canada. He recognized the woven rugs and maple table. Harriet, John's shy, blue-eyed teenage daughter, brought in an oil lamp to brighten the candlelit room. After seating the men around the table, John's wife, Mary, served them bowls of corn chowder.

Following a blessing on the food, Joseph momentarily refrained from eating and explained why they had come. His long-lashed blue eyes were both compassionate and authoritative. He quoted the revelations designating Far West and Adam-ondi-Ahman as gathering places then vividly described the confrontation in Gallatin and the Missourians' threats to outlying areas.

"I come on an errand from the Lord," Joseph said as he looked from John to his wife, Mary. Almon sat silently. Did Joseph realize what he was asking of the women and children? The Prophet continued, looking again at John. "Tomorrow we will counsel everyone to move to Adam-ondi-Ahman or to Far West. Personally, I think that the valley of Adam-ondi-Ahman would be a better place for you. There is land there for a city that shall be called Seth, after Adam's righteous son. I hope that it will become a refuge and inheritance for many."

John looked at Mary, and she nodded. Then he turned back to the Prophet, his large hands resting on his thighs, absolutely still. "We'll make arrangements to move as soon as we can."

"You will be blessed for your obedience," Sidney Rigdon promised. Then he began a discourse on the principle of sacrifice.

Almon yawned. Lately he had felt extraordinarily weary and distracted whenever Sidney preached, regardless of how spirited the oration. Almon glanced around the room, his gaze landing on the loft where the children slept. He realized that he had not yet greeted Eddie and Johnny. Were they already asleep?

Suddenly twelve-year-old Eddie's head popped into view. He was flat on his stomach, like a young cougar ready to pounce. Brown hair totally awry, Eddie's hazel eyes shone brightly when they met Almon's, the candlelight dancing in them. Eddie quickly lifted a box of checkers and pointed silently at Almon and at himself. Almon winked and gave a slight nod.

Then Joseph Smith burst into laughter, interrupting Sidney's sermon. He put his hand on Sidney's arm and pointed toward the loft. "Forgive me, but our young friend has been communicating with Elder Babbitt. When I spied him, I couldn't contain myself."

"Edgar," John said sternly. Eddie slipped back into the shadows.

The Prophet called out to the boy. "Edgar, I see you have challenged Elder Babbitt to a game of checkers. I should very much like to play the winner."

"I'll be right down," Eddie piped up. On his way toward the steps, he elbowed his slumbering brother. "Wake up, Johnny. The Prophet's here."

Their father's brow furrowed. "Brother Joseph, my children have been taught to respect their elders. Edgar ought not to have interrupted our conversation."

Joseph stood up and put his hand on John's shoulder. "Tomorrow is the Sabbath, and we will converse and counsel throughout the day. We will keep it holy as the Lord commands. But this is Saturday night, and a game lightens a man's burdens."

Eddie hurried down the ladder with the game tucked under his left arm. In the loft above, Johnny rubbed his eyes.

Brother Joseph stepped forward and shook Eddie's hand. The boy beamed. After the handshake, Eddie turned to Almon. "Brother Babbitt, I already beat Johnny and Harriet. Give it your best shot. But beware!"

"Oh, Edgar, Edgar, prepare for your doom," Almon said with a laugh so sinister that he could only imagine the intensity of Sidney's frown. Fortunately he wouldn't be brought before the council on a charge of light-mindedness since the Prophet laughed as well.

* * *

The following morning was warm and bright. The day promised to be hot and humid. Almon lagged a few paces behind the group as they walked toward Anson Call's home, where the Sabbath meeting would be held. The air smelled of damp, cut grass. Hay dried in the sun, ready to be raked and piled into stacks. Almon gazed at the stock grazing in the open fields, the acres of corn nearly ready to harvest, and the rich timberland. A feeling of guilt and responsibility cut through him. He had encouraged these people to settle here, and he had failed them. Would all of this—the money spent, the labor, and the crops—be lost? Would the others be as humble as John and heed Joseph's counsel? If they did not, they would be in grave danger. If they did, their children might starve.

But Almon knew these people. He would bet money that they would follow their Prophet. They had followed Almon, and he was half the man Joseph was. Almon gritted his teeth. Had Joseph felt this same way when the Kirtland bank failed? The unspoken guilt pinning you against an invisible wall, making it difficult to breathe? Would they have the sense to hate him for what he, their beloved missionary, had done? Would their families survive the coming winter?

"Elder Babbitt."

Almon turned toward the soft, deep timbre of young Harriet's voice. She was painfully shy, and he could not recall her directly addressing him before. "Yes, Miss Harriet."

The teenage girl continued as if she had the questions rehearsed. "How is Sister Babbitt? Is she in good health?"

Almon nodded and smiled. "She is very well and sends you her love and best wishes."

Harriet glanced down. Then she spoke once more, turning slightly red. "And her family. Are they all well? Do you expect them soon?"

"The last time we received a letter, they were in good health. We look forward to their arrival in late September with the rest of the Kirtland Saints."

"Harriet looks forward to it too!" Eddie teased. "She thinks Sister Julianne's brothers are handsome."

Harriet's face shaded crimson as she looked down at her feet.

"Shame on you," Mary chided Edgar. "If we are lucky, Joseph Johnson will consent to be your schoolmaster, and I will advise him to keep his switch handy if you fail to keep your tongue still."

"I second that advice," Almon said. "And one thing I am certain of—that my brothers-in-law think Miss Harriet very pretty. They are not blind."

A moment later they came to the Calls' stable, situated about fifty yards from the spacious frame house that Anson had recently completed. John signaled for the group to stop. He pointed to five horses. "Those animals don't belong to the Saints. Two of them are property of old settlers named Culp and O'Neil. The pair sold Anson this land. What are they doing at a Mormon meeting?"

Eleven-year-old Johnny cut in. "Brother Call's been sellin' store goods to the Missourians. Billy told me that he don't make them pay till Christmas if they promise to come to Sunday meetings."

Almon couldn't help smiling. Such a ploy sounded like Anson. "That's a missionary for you."

The Prophet's eyes were serious as he turned to Sidney and Hyrum. "Brethren, let us slip in the back and remain quiet during the meeting only partaking of the Lord's supper with the Saints. If we're asked to speak, then we ought only to bear testimony of the first principles of the gospel. Say nothing about the uprising in Gallatin or the gathering places. Afterward we'll meet privately with the brethren."

But it was impossible for Joseph to slip in unnoticed. Anson's eyes widened when he saw him, but at a signal from Joseph, Anson kept preaching and did not introduce the guests. Yet every eye was on Joseph as they sat down.

Almon felt a surge of envy. Joseph's height, his athletic build, his blond hair and expressive eyes, his energy and warmth were like a beacon of light attracting others. Almon, too, would be greeted warmly, but he didn't have Joseph's stature. Yet who did? Even Joseph's brothers Don Carlos and Hyrum hadn't the will and energy that propelled Joseph forward, always forward, that made men struggle to keep up. Was that one of the reasons that the Lord had chosen Joseph?

While they partook of the sacrament, Almon looked around the room, trying to read the old settlers' reactions. John Culp's jaw was tightly set, and George O'Neil's eyes narrowed at the Prophet, his head cocked to the side as he scratched his chin. Was he hatching some sort of plot? Afterward, the two stood up together and made their way out, talking in low voices. Almon tried to situate himself near the door so that he could catch snatches of their conversation, but then he felt an arm around his shoulder.

"It's good to see you, my friend!" Anson Call vigorously shook his hand. "The women are putting together a good meal. Joseph said he is here on an errand from the Lord. I suppose you know what it is."

Hyrum interrupted their conversation, his voice a low whisper. "The brethren are meeting in the east cornfield in ten minutes."

"We'll be there," Almon said quickly, ignoring Anson's questioning look. The stalks would hide and shield them. They would be able to speak privately and hear anyone approaching.

"What's all this about?" Anson asked a few minutes later as he and Almon entered the cornfield, stepping sideways between the tall, green stalks.

"There was a battle in Gallatin."

"We heard about that."

"The Saints in outlying areas like this are being called into Far West and Adam-ondi-Ahman."

"When? For how long?"

Almon shrugged. "I don't know. Joseph will explain. I was watching Culp and O'Neil during the meeting. I didn't like the look in their eyes."

"The fact that we bought this land from them for six hundred dollars and that now it's worth more than two thousand sticks in their craw."

"Have they threatened you?"

Anson shook his head. "No. But they don't have much of the six hundred left. I've given them credit at the store. They ought to appreciate that."

"They don't," Almon said flatly. "Watch your back."

They heard whispered voices. Green ears of corn shuddered in the breeze. Almon and Anson turned, following a path of broken stalks. A moment later they joined a group of twelve brethren. The Prophet stood in the middle. Trampled stalks were under their boots, the sun straight above them, the Prophet's light hair bright gold against the green.

The men quieted as Joseph said, "Anson, how much land do you have?"

"The farm, seven hundred acres of timber, and a mill site. My brother Cyril is on a trip to buy equipment to build the mill."

Joseph questioned the other brethren. They, too, told him the amount of property they owned and their plans for development.

"You've worked hard," the Prophet said. "And this is good country. Perhaps someday it will be a stake of Zion. But not right now. I've come on an errand from the Lord to warn you of approaching trouble. Brethren, there will be difficulties, and you must come into Adam-ondi-Ahman or Far West for safety."

The Prophet continued speaking. Almon felt some comfort knowing that Joseph had listened to him. The Prophet did not accuse the brethren of failure to follow counsel but was appreciative of their hard work and sound judgment. At the same time, Almon wished that he could see into the minds of his friends. Would they be willing to leave? Did they question the necessity of heeding the Prophet's counsel? The Prophet had been wrong about the Kirtland Safety Society. Did they wonder if he was wrong now? Almon felt eyes upon him, unheard voices reaching out.

"Brother Almon, what do you think we should do?" Brother Lathrop asked after the Prophet stopped speaking.

Almon squared his shoulders. This was not debate school; this was real life—life and death. He wouldn't have the blood of one man, woman, or child on his shoulders. But the alternative was daunting: winter would come, the specter of starvation looming near. Yet Joseph Smith was a Prophet.

Almon's voice rose, the oratory timbre, the compelling authority rivaling Sidney Rigdon's. "You are my friends. I know the loss you will endure. But Joseph is God's Prophet. I implore you to follow him. It is necessary for the safety of your families, for your children to gain an inheritance in Zion, for your own spiritual and temporal victory. I've seen the land on which the City of Seth shall be built. If you are never able to return here, I imagine you there, safe and prosperous in the palm of God's hand."

Anson cleared his throat. When he spoke, his words rang clear. "I don't know about you brethren, but I agree with Elder Babbitt. I'll follow the Prophet's counsel."

A moment of silence followed. Then Phineas Young voiced his agreement. "I too."

Harvey Call, Joel Terrell, Theodore Turley, Joseph Holbrook, George Gee, and Asahel Lathrop nodded. Anson called for a vote. Every man raised his right hand. It was unanimous. Joseph's eyes were moist as he went around the group shaking each man's hand.

Then Anson raised a question. "Must we sell our farms immediately?"

Joseph answered. "If I were you, I would not sell yet. Not as long as there is a chance you will be able to return."

"Can we wait to harvest our crops?"

"There is time for you to get away with your families and your possessions. As for your crops, I don't know. All I know is the Lord has commanded me to make these things known to you and to tell you to leave. I do not know if you need to leave within a week or if you would be safe here until spring. Act on your own judgment. I have done my errand and must leave immediately after dinner. May God bless you all."

* * *

Far West

Lyman tried to console two-year-old Seth, who was crying for no apparent reason, while Delcena and Julianne prepared supper. He watched Baby Daniel whine and pull at Delcena's skirt as she tried to take the chicken out of the pot. Julianne put down the rolls and bent down to pick Daniel up, but he only wailed louder.

The noise from the loft added to the commotion. Alvira, Mary, Albey, and the Prophet's son, Joseph III, played charades, acting out the animals from Noah's ark. The game would have been Sabbath appropriate were it not for the neighing, barking, and growling.

Lyman stood and walked to the base of the steps. "Charades is a silent game. You aren't allowed to make any sounds." The noise in the loft suddenly ceased.

"Me can play!" Seth shouted.

Alvira called down, "Seth, I already told you. This game isn't for babies."

Seth cried brokenheartedly. Now Lyman knew the reason for his tears.

"Seth can be on my team," Mary called down.

Lyman carried Seth up the narrow stairs mounted along the back wall. Mary took his hand.

"Blessed are the peacemakers: for they shall be called the children of God," Lyman said, giving Mary a kiss on the forehead. "Hold his hand so he doesn't fall."

Alvira humphed and tossed her head. Lyman eyed her sternly. She ignored her father and announced, "Joseph, your last turn doesn't count because you made noise. You have to go again."

Lyman watched for a moment. Seth was now content in Mary's arms, sucking his thumb. Young Joseph put his hands together, swinging his arms like an elephant's trunk. He was a handsome boy, tall for his age, his coloring and features favoring Emma. Lyman thought about how his children and the Prophet's children had played together a great deal throughout the summer. They were so close in age and configuration. Julia, the Smiths' oldest, was between Alvira and Mary. Albey and Joseph were born exactly one week apart, and Seth and Frederick had been born on the same day.

There was a knock at the front door. Lyman stepped down from the loft. "I'll answer it," he said as he scooped up Daniel. Tears balanced in the baby's brown eyes.

"I hope this doesn't take long," Delcena said. "The children are hungry."

Lyman opened the door to Lorenzo Young, Brigham's younger brother. Switching Daniel to his left shoulder, he shook Lorenzo's hand.

Lorenzo did not smile but spoke directly. "I appreciated your sermon this morning."

"Thank you," Lyman responded, wondering at the purpose of the visit.

Lorenzo continued. "Dr. Avard is holding a meeting this afternoon in the schoolhouse. It starts in thirty minutes. I've come to ask you to attend."

Daniel squirmed and whined. Lyman patted the baby's back, feeling wary. Lorenzo seemed to be an honest man, yet Avard knew that Lyman had avoided taking the Danite oaths. Was Lorenzo a pawn in Avard's hand, sent out to invite Lyman to a meeting where he would be threatened or forced to comply? With the Prophet out of town, was Avard even more aggressive? Had Lyman been targeted?

Holding his restless son gently and firmly, Lyman weighed his words. "I've been to one of Dr. Avard's meetings. I have some differences of opinions and doubt he would welcome me back."

"That's why I want you to come. I've been to a few meetings but haven't taken any of the oaths." Lorenzo's voice became hard. "I won't swear to protect a man regardless of whether he does right or wrong, nor will I covenant to kill a man who breaks his oath. I plan to speak out tonight. I'll need some friends in the room. Can I count on you?"

Lyman nodded. "I'll be there."

Lorenzo declined an invitation to stay for a quick supper and left immediately. Lyman went back into the kitchen. Delcena was putting the chicken and dumplings on the table. Her forehead was wet from the heat. She was seven months pregnant, and Lyman sensed her fatigue. Daniel squealed when he saw his mother and pushed away from Lyman. He began screaming.

"He's hungry," Delcena said, taking him. The baby clutched at her blouse. Julianne brought in bowls of beans and melon.

"Start without me," Delcena said to Lyman and Julianne. "I'll nurse Daniel in the bedroom and come back after he falls asleep."

Julianne nodded and called the other children down for dinner while Delcena walked into the bedroom with Daniel and shut the door behind her.

While Lyman waited for the children to be seated, he noticed that his sister-in-law was not smiling. She had been unusually grim and quiet that afternoon. Perhaps she was worried about Almon. Lyman blessed the food. The meal progressed relatively quietly, the children too busy eating to talk.

Julianne held Seth on her lap. He had dumplings smeared on his face. She suddenly looked up at Lyman. "Who was at the door?"

"Lorenzo Young. He asked me to attend a meeting tonight. I need to go in a few minutes. Thank you for helping us today. Delcena is going to wish that Almon traveled more often."

Julianne smiled slightly, but her eyes were sad. "I can't do much. Your baby boys want their mommy, not me."

Lyman wondered if Julianne were thinking about her little boy, David, who had died. Had he lived, he would now be older than both Seth and Daniel.

Julianne went on. "I'm surprised that Seth is content at the moment. How will you and Delcie manage another?"

Lyman shrugged. "The same as we managed Albey, Alvira, and Mary."

Julianne nodded. "I suppose so. Has there been word from Almon and the Prophet?"

"Not that I know. They should be back tomorrow night." Lyman looked at his pocket watch. He stood up. "The meeting starts soon. I'll tell Delcena farewell. Thank you again."

As he opened the door into the bedroom, Lyman saw Delcena in the rocking chair with Daniel in her lap. But something was different. Lyman realized that the chair was still, both mother and son asleep. Lyman gently picked Daniel up and laid him in the middle of the bed. Then he kissed Delcena's cheek. She started, and the chair creaked.

"Go to bed," Lyman said.

"Too much to do," she returned groggily.

"Your sister's here. Rest while you can," Lyman said. "It's an order."

Delcena smiled and submitted as Lyman put his arm around her waist and led her to the bed. It was too hot to tuck the covers around her. Lyman bent over her and smoothed her hair back. She took his hand and placed it on her abdomen. He felt a gentle roll, the baby moving beneath his palm.

Delcena's eyes were soft. "She's still most of the time—doesn't kick like Seth and Daniel."

"She?"

"Your little girl. Do you like the name Susan Julia?"

"Yes. Have you thought of a boy's?"

Delcena shook her head. "No, I'm almost certain we won't need one. I've dreamed of her, of a quiet, sweet little girl."

Lyman smiled. "We could use quiet and sweet."

As Lyman left the room, he was glad that he hadn't told Delcena the nature of the meeting he was about to attend. It heartened him to know that she was dreaming sweet dreams of a beautiful child. For the moment at least, one of them was in Zion.

* * *

Julianne sent the older children outside to play while she washed Seth's face and hands.

"Where Mommy?" he asked.

"Sleeping with Danny," Julianne said.

"Me sleep too." Seth put his thumb in his mouth and sucked as he walked toward the bedroom door.

Julianne intercepted him. "Stay out here with Aunt Juli."

"No. Mommy," he insisted.

Julianne sighed. Arguing with a two-year-old was fruitless. She also knew that Seth needed a nap. "All right," she said. "I'll help you."

Julianne quietly opened the door to the bedroom. She picked Seth up and set him on the bed by Delcena. Seth snuggled in by his mother and, half asleep, Delcena instinctively put her arm around him. On her other side, Baby Danny lay nestled against her.

Julianne turned and went out the door. A deep ache filled her, a longing to be where Delcena was, sleeping with her babies in her arms. Tears crept down her cheeks as she scrubbed the silverware with ashes. She thought of how many times this summer she had sat silently at quilting bees while Delcena, Emma and other women talked about pregnancy and compared the growth and development of their children.

Julianne closed her eyes and thought of her own little David, of his sweetness and the feel and smell of him. What would he be doing now if he lived? *How long, Heavenly Father?* she prayed. *How long?*

* * *

Sampson Avard spoke to the guard at the door. "Should we let this man in or not?"

The guard looked at Lyman then back at Avard. "Sir, this is Lyman Sherman. One of the Prophet's staunchest defenders in Kirtland."

Avard smiled and put his arm around the guard's shoulders. "Yes, I know. Joseph loves this man. And I've seen their children play together in the streets. But we must know for certain. Some of those closest to Joseph have turned against him in the past." Avard's eyes suddenly darted to Lyman as he pointed straight at his chest. "Lyman Sherman, tonight you shall have the chance to prove, once and for all, whether or not you are friend to the Prophet Joseph Smith."

"Every breath I take stands as witness to that fact," Lyman retorted, his shoulders square and eyes like hot coals burning behind the lenses of his spectacles. He swung open the door and walked past Avard.

Lyman sat down on the end of the bench. He wanted to be where he could get out fast if he had to. He saw Lorenzo Young sitting front and center. One thing he had to admit about the Young brothers—there was no lack of courage.

The meeting began with Avard passionately speaking about the wrongs committed against the Church. The Prophet had suffered vexatious lawsuits and would do so no longer. The Mormons in Jackson County had been violently expelled. No Missourians had been taken before a court and punished for their crimes. The Saints had sought legal redress to no avail. They had lost enough in life and property. They would no longer be buffeted and driven. The Prophet had spoken. The Danites were his army.

They had secret signs to protect and defend themselves. There were penalties. Their lives were the ransom. It had to be so. There was no other way to guarantee the faithfulness of imperfect men who could be swayed by the winds of doubt and fear. They were to never discuss these things outside their meetings, and they must promise this with an oath of everlasting secrecy.

But Joseph never comes to these meetings. The thought reverberated in Lyman's mind. *Those who swear to these oaths can never ask him whether Avard is honest or not.*

"There are some men here who have not made the required covenants," Avard boomed. He pointed to Lorenzo Young. "Brother Young, you are one of those men, are you not?"

Lorenzo stood up. "I am."

"Am I correct in assuming that you have come here tonight to join your heart and soul with this society?"

"Yes. I ask the privilege of speaking to this society that I might tell them my reasons."

Avard was thoughtful for a moment then nodded. "Granted."

Lorenzo took a step forward then turned and addressed the men. "I have come tonight to unite my heart and soul with the brethren here, especially those who belong to this society. I have witnessed secret signs, secret combinations like those told of in the Book of Mormon. We have no evidence that Joseph sanctions—"

"Be seated!" Avard roared.

"Not until I have finished expressing my views!" Lorenzo returned.

"Then I shall put the law of this organization into effect here and now," Avard hissed. "Your life is in peril."

Lorenzo Young's image seemed to grow larger before Lyman's eyes, and his mind went back to the day when he saw and heard Brigham stand against the Kirtland dissenters.

"I have as many friends in this house as you do!" Lorenzo roared, leaping around and standing face-to-face with Avard. "If you make a motion to carry out your threat, you will not live to get out of this house, for I will kill you first."

The color drained from Avard's face. Men jumped to their feet and approached the stand. Lyman was among them.

"I've made no motion," Avard stated. "We haven't come here tonight to fight each other. Too much is at stake."

"Calling Lorenzo a traitor is the same as calling Brigham one. A man shouldn't be killed for a differing opinion!" a voice said above the rest.

"But if we are not one, we are not God's," someone else shouted.

All heads suddenly turned as the guard opened the door and banged it closed. For a moment there was silence. "Dr. Avard," the guard called out, "Brother Robinson has just brought us news. We've received an affidavit. A sheriff from Daviess County is on his way to Far West to arrest Joseph. Brother Robinson asks that you adjourn the meeting and requests that you come speak with him immediately. Joseph must be warned."

Avard was once more in control of the crowd. "Our Prophet will no longer be the victim of vexatious lawsuits! Are you prepared to give your life for the Prophet of God?" Avard thundered.

"Yes!" The men answered as one voice.

"Then this meeting is adjourned for the night. Be ready to answer the call when it comes."

Avard left the schoolhouse before the rest of the men. Lyman and Lorenzo joined the throng headed for the door.

"I'm going directly to Brigham to tell him all that has transpired," Lorenzo said under his breath.

"I'll come with you," Lyman offered.

Ten minutes later the two men found Brigham Young at home. They went outside, behind his house, to talk. After Lorenzo and Lyman relayed all that had happened, Brigham said matter-of-factly, "I have long suspected that some secret wickedness was being carried out by Dr. Avard. For now, you two can go home to your families. I'll go over to Brother Robinson's and offer to ride out with those who warn Joseph."

"I'll go with you," Lyman offered.

Brigham shook his head. "It's best if we don't make Avard defensive. That could divide the brethren. I'll speak to Joseph privately and suggest that Dr. Avard serve the Saints as a surgeon rather than as a general."

* * *

Almon rode backward, turned clear around in his saddle as he pointed the small telescope northeast into the dark woodland where their enemies lurked. Thankfully, his horse obediently followed Joseph's mount. Sidney and Hyrum rode on either side of the Prophet.

The night was still and warm. Twenty minutes ago, as they rode on the edge of the prairie west of the woodland bordering the Grand River, they had realized they were being followed by men a half mile back, shadowed by the trees.

Shielded from view by Hyrum, Almon had turned around in his saddle. They had sung hymns. Their enemies did not realize that the prey knew of their predators. With the scope, Almon followed their movements, watching the changes in the black shadows among the trees.

The men stopped singing. "Looks like they've decided not to give it up," Joseph said quietly, facing forward, his horse marching on. "Can you tell how many there are?"

"Maybe ten. Or twelve," Almon responded. "I'm guessing that they know we plan to go east and stay the night in Di-Ahman. They figure they'll overtake us when we cross the Grand River."

"Then we gallop south, toward Marrowbone," Hyrum said.

"Yes," Joseph agreed.

"Can we outrun so many?" Sidney asked, his voice shaking slightly. Sidney was no longer a young man.

Almon spoke confidently, though his heart pounded in his chest. "We've an ace in the hole. A head start."

"And God as our captain," Joseph added. "Courage, brethren."

Almon tucked the scope into the saddlebag. Then he swung his right leg around to the side and his left leg up and over the saddle's cantle. After poking his toes back in the stirrups, he nodded toward his companions. He was ready.

An instant later, the men pivoted their mounts and with a shout galloped out onto the moonlit prairie, racing southward, creating wind in their faces and swirling grass at their mounts' heels. Behind them, horses crashed out of the brush after them.

"Toward Marrowbone!" Joseph shouted. "Toward safety and friends. God is with us!"

The miles passed in a blur. The men rode up and down hills. Almon did not look back, did not think about the horror which awaited him if his horse stumbled. He was in fate's or God's hands, the victim or victor of the moment. *Mormon boys stick together. Mormon boys stick together.* The four horses thundered on. Could horses see demons? Was that why they spooked so easily and ran so frantically? Could they see angels too? Were David and Seth nearby urging his horse faster and faster? And what angels would surround the Prophet's horse? What was it the scriptures said? "They who are with us are more than they who are against us."

Time passed. The night stilled. The horses stopped, their blood vessels bulging, their flanks foamed with lather. Sweating, the men breathed heavily. They had won the race. Their enemies were gone.

"We've outrun them! Thanks be to God!" Joseph shouted.

"Brother Sidney," Almon said, "do you think our race constitutes breaking the Sabbath? Must we all go before the high council?"

"My boy, we have only pulled the ox out of the mire."

Almon whooped, and the others joined him. It had taken twelve miles for the rabbits to outrun the foxes. Now they were safe, and they rejoiced in the starry night as they walked their horses to Brother Littlefield's farm. The men and their mounts drank deeply from the well, and the horses grazed freely while the men lay down in the barn and slept until daybreak.

* * *

Rain fell softly the next morning when the men awoke. They knocked on the door of Waldo Littlefield's house, where they were warmly received and fed a hearty breakfast. The rain dispersed, and they continued their journey toward Far West. The horses stretched their necks long and low, sleepy on the cool summer morning.

The group rode by the site where the City of Seth was to be built. Clouds billowed in the sky; the air was fresh and misty. Almon wondered how he could feel so peaceful this morning, knowing what he did of mobs and hatred. Would those who chased them last night turn their rage on his friends in Three Forks? How illusory the blessed land of Zion was! Yet it was a lovely morning, and he was on his way home to Julianne. He would grasp the moment and hang on to it for as long as he could.

Ninety minutes passed pleasantly. Then eight miles outside Far West, four men approached them on horseback. Almon recognized Edward Partridge, George Robinson, Brigham Young, and Sampson Avard.

"How did you come so far so quickly?" Brigham asked. "We thought we'd be in Marrowbone before we found you."

"We were pursued on our way to Di-Ahman," Joseph explained. "And rode in all haste to Marrowbone last night."

Sampson Avard cut in. "Brother Joseph, the pursuit has just begun. We've come to warn you. A writ has been issued by Judge King for your arrest and Lyman Wight's. William Penniston has filed an affidavit."

"What laws have we broken?" Joseph asked.

"None." Bishop Partridge took a copy of the affidavit out of his shirt pocket and read a portion of it aloud. "But here are the accusations: 'Armed men, to the number of one hundred and twenty, have committed violence against Adam Black, by surrounding his house, and taking him in a violent manner, and subjecting him to great indignities by forcing him, under threats of immediate death, to sign a paper, the writing of a very disgraceful character; and that they have, as a collected and armed body, threatened to put to instant death this affiant on sight; and that he verily believes they will accomplish that act without they are prevented. And that the body of men now assembled do intend to commit great violence to many of the old settlers and citizens of Daviess County, and that Joseph Smith Jr. and Lyman Wight are the leaders of this body of armed men, and the names of others thus combined are not certainly known to the affiant.'"

"That isn't what happened," Hyrum countered. "No one threatened to kill Black. He has perjured himself."

Robinson continued. "The truth doesn't matter to them. The sheriff from Daviess County is on his way. If you go home, you'll be arrested within the next day or two. A trial in Daviess County will be a mob victory."

"Disappear for a while," Avard suggested. "We have men who will help you, who will not allow their Prophet to be put in prison."

"Being in hiding, being separated from my family and my people, would be a prison as well," Joseph said. "The Constitution of the United States was set up to protect innocent men such as me." He turned and looked at Almon. "But it has not. You are a student of the law. What are your thoughts? What would you do if you were me?"

Almon swallowed. He thought of Julianne and knew exactly what he would do. "I would go home. President Rigdon's Independence Day sermon caused the old settlers to believe that you will not submit to the laws of the land. Prove them wrong. Trust in the law."

"Do you want God's Prophet behind bars? He has said that he will no longer be plagued by vexatious lawsuits!" Avard snapped. "Are you a traitor like Cowdery and Whitmer?"

Almon's fists tightened on the reins. Avard had convinced Joseph to go to Daviess County and confront Adam Black. Avard could have threatened Black before Joseph was invited into the cabin. Joseph was in this fix because he had listened to Avard. Almon bit his tongue, knowing that arguing with Avard wouldn't help the situation. His horse, seeming to feel Almon's tension, pawed nervously.

Almon focused on Joseph. "I would tell the sheriff that you always intend to submit to our nation's laws but that you wish to be tried in your own county, because the citizens of Daviess County are highly prejudiced against you. I would explain that the laws of our nation give you this privilege."

Joseph was quiet for a moment before saying, "Brethren, I should like to employ Generals Atchison and his partner, Alexander Doniphan, as legal counsel as soon as possible." Joseph took a deep breath. "But will the laws of this land protect me?"

"No!" Avard hissed. "And you know it, President Smith. Look at what happened in Jackson County! I have men ready to answer the call. Men who are under oath to obey! To give their lives for you! What has Babbitt been doing while others have covenanted to fight for our rights?"

"Studying the law," Almon returned.

Joseph turned to his brother. "Hyrum, what do you think I should do?"

Hyrum's eyes were troubled. "I don't know. I just don't know."

"Sidney?"

"You are the Prophet, Joseph. Not me."

"Brother Robinson?"

"I stand behind you, whatever you choose. Yet I favor Brother Avard's advice. The people need you free, not behind bars."

"Bishop Partridge?"

"I don't want to see you in prison. You are innocent."

"Brother Brigham?"

"I think that we must avoid war if it is possible. Your leaving could be the spark that lights the tinderbox. If you are tried in Caldwell County, no court will find you guilty."

Almon remembered the debate school incident, when Young had testified against him. Today Brigham agreed with him. It was a welcome change.

The Prophet asked the brethren to pray with him. Afterward, he spoke decisively. "We'll go back to Far West together. I believe that is the best course for now." Without another word, the Prophet spurred his horse forward.

Almon heard Avard curse under his breath, but Avard followed the others as the men followed their Prophet.

11

When I'm feeble, faint and weary
When my heart is filled with grief,
With my prospects dull and dreary,
Then I seek to find relief.

From my cares and toils returning
To my lone and oft retreat;
With my heart and soul desiring
My dear Savior there to meet.

Joel Hills Johnson

Near Springfield, Illinois—September 13, 1838

It was nine o'clock at night. A lone candle burned in the tent as Benjamin soaked a rag in murky water and went to wash Jeremiah Willey's body, to cool the fever that had been raging for nearly two weeks. As he bent down by the low bed, he saw that Brother Willey's face and arms glistened in the candlelight. Brother Willey was sweating profusely. Benjamin's heart jumped—the fever had broken. Was it the quinine that had helped Brother Willey or the prayers of his two little girls who had already lost their mother to typhoid malarial fever? Mary, his sister, had been tending the girls and had told Benjamin of their prayers: "Heavenly Father, make Papa better. Please and thank you." Benjamin sat down on a patch of straw next to the bed.

Brother Willey opened his eyes. His vision cleared as he focused on Benjamin. "Brother Ben."

"Yes." Benjamin smiled slightly as he brought Brother Willey a cupful of water. Supporting his neck, Benjamin helped him take a drink.

Afterward, Brother Willey's words were distinct and slow, like someone who had just awakened from a long sleep and had to concentrate to find his bearings. "You've taken care of me. Thank you."

Benjamin nodded, feeling a bit embarrassed.

"I remember something about Bathsheba. About her dying."

Ben nodded once more. "I'm sorry."

"And my little girls?"

"They're fine. My sister's been looking after them."

Brother Willey put his hand over his eyes. Benjamin did not know if he was praying or weeping. When he spoke, his voice was thick with emotion. "Tomorrow I'll tell them that Papa will take them on to Zion—like their mama would have wanted."

The men remained quiet for a few minutes. Benjamin thought of how he had returned from Cincinnati over two weeks ago to find sickness running rampant in the camp. A few days later, when the work on the turnpike was complete, the camp leaders had decided to move on. With summer nearly over, they didn't have the luxury of waiting until the sick recovered. Just a few days into the journey, Bathsheba Willey had died. It had appeared that Brother Willey would follow, leaving their two little girls orphans. Nothing could be done to relieve his suffering during the day as they traveled over rocky terrain, but Benjamin had been by his bedside every night, determined that if Brother Willey died, it would be with a friend close by doing all possible to ease his passing. But Jeremiah Willey lived.

Benjamin sighed and listened to Brother Willey's even breathing. His patient had fallen into a feverless sleep. After blowing out the candle, Benjamin stretched out on the tent floor, his long legs spanning the width, the crook of his arm his pillow. His thoughts drifted into oblivion as he, too, slept.

Three hours later, Benjamin started at the rustle of someone entering the tent. A moment later he sat up, and his brother Joe stood near him, holding a candle. The candlelight accentuated the hollow lines of Joe's cheeks and the dark circles beneath his eyes.

"Ben, I need to talk to you."

"All right. Brother Willey's fever broke. How's Brother Hale?"

Joe shook his head. "He's dying. I can't do any more for him. Sister Hale's sick too. Do you have any quinine? The camp is out."

Benjamin shook his head. He had given Brother Willey the remainder earlier in the evening. He swallowed, not knowing what to say. No wonder Joe looked haggard. He too had been caring for the sick at night and walking next to the oxen during the day.

"We'll be in Springfield, Illinois, tomorrow," Joe commented.

"Maybe we can get some quinine there."

Joe breathed out, his slender chest deflating as his shoulders sagged. "Sometimes it helps, and sometimes it doesn't. There's been news from Missouri. The Prophet was arrested but released on the lack of evidence. Mobs are threatening DeWitt and Adam-ondi-Ahman."

Benjamin spoke fervently. "I wish I was there with Brother Joseph and the Saints. I'd fight if I had to!"

Joe reached down and placed his free hand on Benjamin's shoulder. "That's what I've come to talk to you about. We're . . . we're not going to Missouri for a while. Joel's been asked by the managers to lease a house for the sick in Springfield and stay here to care for them. Mother and I are staying with him."

Benjamin gaped at Joe. "But we've suffered so long! We can't stop now."

"I don't want to take Mother into a war. Joel has already settled our accounts."

Benjamin's hands clenched into fists. "Why didn't anyone speak to me about it?"

"We scarcely see you. You're behind or ahead of the company, sleeping by the wayside during the day and caring for Brother Willey at night."

"I couldn't leave him alone to die. And now he's getting better. He said tonight that he's going to Zion. Shouldn't we have the same fortitude?"

Joe looked away from Benjamin as he said, "You don't have to stay here with us. Mother anticipated your feelings and told me to tell you so."

A yearning filled Benjamin, achingly intense as he struggled with conflicting emotions. He turned to Joe. "I want to go to the front, to see and hear the Prophet again. But how can I leave Mother and the children?"

Joe swallowed. "I'll take care of them. And George and Will are nearly men. We'll be fine."

"You're sure?" Benjamin asked, the ache hardening into grim determination. He was a man now and would follow his own path—the path trod by God's Prophet.

Joe nodded. "Mother believes that we ought not to hold you back. Besides, Delcena and Julianne are there. You won't starve. Mary will cry, though."

Benjamin thought of Mary. He had grown up between Joe and her, closest to them in age. But while he and Joe had been friends, he and Mary had often been at odds. Yet during the past two weeks, not a night had gone by when Mary didn't bring him supper while he tended Brother Willey. Just yesterday she had suddenly burst into tears and hugged him, asking when he became so kind and so brave, as he used to be so self-centered and exasperating.

Benjamin looked up at Joe. "I'm going to tell her that she can't have a beau until we are together again and I approve of him."

Joe raised an eyebrow. "Warn me first. I don't want to be anywhere near when you get that tongue lashing."

Benjamin chuckled, causing Brother Willey to rustle in his sleep. He stood up and whispered, "Let's talk outside."

The brothers ducked through the entrance. Straightening, they stood together, both tall and slender in the shadowy night. The sky was black and clear, the stars shining brilliantly around them.

Joe no longer smiled but stood as still as stone looking at the stars. Benjamin studied his brother for a moment. What was Joe thinking? Did he understand?

"If you could, would you go to the front with me?" Benjamin asked.

Joe took a deep breath and shook his head. "I don't think so. If Mother were determined to go, then I would and I'd do my best to care for her and the others. But to tell you the truth, I'm relieved. You know me, Ben. I avoid a fight when I can."

"I don't want a fight either," Benjamin said. "But God has strengthened me. And given me the desire and ability to complete this journey. I have to follow that."

"I know." Joe reached down and picked up a pair of boots near the cabin door. Benjamin hadn't noticed them in the darkness. "These are Brother Hale's. They're nearly new. He gave them to us. And his two-year-old colt. He knows he's going to die—he said he won't be needing them for the journey he's making. Take them, Ben. Your boots are almost worn out, and you need a horse."

"Thank you," Benjamin said.

Joe was quiet for a moment. When he spoke again, his voice shook. "I'll miss you and pray for the glad day when we're together again."

Benjamin swallowed back his own tears. "Had God given me a choice of any man to be my brother and friend, I would have chosen you out of all the hosts in heaven."

In tears, Joe embraced Benjamin. "We make a good team. The best. You follow the Prophet like Seth would have. And I'll take care of Mother like Seth always did. May God protect us both until we meet again."

* * *

"Are you sure you won't stay with us?" Annie asked early the following morning as she and Susan Bryant stood together next to the wagons. In a few minutes the Johnsons would separate from the company of Saints to spend the winter in Springfield caring for the sick and raising up a branch of the Church. When Annie's morning sickness had ended, so had her dependence on Susan, yet Annie would miss having this competent friend near.

"When I joined the Church, I resolved to turn my footsteps toward Zion. I will not waver from that decision," Susan answered, her voice stoic, the new sun at her back and her eyes turned toward the west.

Annie took a deep breath. Perhaps Susan thought she would find a man to marry in Missouri. Yet Annie knew better than to speak to Susan of that possibility. Her friend was both reserved and strong-willed. They were like two women cut from separate cloth, so different in looks and nature. But they worked together harmoniously, as if the color of their souls complemented each other. Annie knew without doubt that Susan cared deeply for her family.

Susan turned to her. "When the children awaken, tell them I bid them a fond farewell. Tell them I shall have presents for them when I see them again, if their parents have good reports of their behavior. I will think of your family often and await your arrival. If you need my help in the interim, send me word and I will try to come."

"Thank you, dearest," Annie exclaimed and impusively embraced Susan. "How I shall miss you!" Though Susan returned the embrace stiffly, Annie could tell from Susan's eyes that her heart was full.

* * *

Kirtland, Ohio

Almera helped Rebecca Winters rake the hay into stacks. It was a fine day with the sun high in the sky and a light breeze rustling the trees that would soon change color. So brilliant was the Indian summer that it seemed impossible that fall and winter storms were just around the corner. Yet Almera knew that the season couldn't be trusted. It was illusory—a lovely bridge leading away from summer and warmth.

Her rake stilled as she looked fifty yards away to where Sam and Hiram Winters were forking hay into the wagon. That morning, she and Sam had been invited to help in the Winters' field in exchange for a generous portion of the hay. Almera knew that Rebecca and Hiram were trying to help by befriending Sam. To her surprise, it was working. Sam had accepted the offer and had been friendly today. Was his goodwill to her Mormon friends as illusory as the Indian summer?

For a moment, she watched Sam work—his hair flaxen in the sunlight and his arms strong. She took a deep breath, remembering the time she had fallen in love with him—before he had grown to hate Mormonism, before he had separated her from her family and faith. The wagon was piled high now, and Sam turned and looked at her. She smiled at him, as brave and hopeful a smile as she could muster. If she reached deeply enough into her heart, could she find a way to forgive him?

Sam began filling the Winters' wagon. Almera went back to raking. One thing was certain. Things were better than before—ever since the day when her father had insisted that she help Rebecca Winters with her sewing. It had eased her loneliness in a way that was difficult to describe—like loosening a corset so tightly fastened that it cut off your breath. Sam must have noticed, even cared, for he allowed her to continue the visits. In return, she tried to be a better wife, to be affectionate, to do her duty.

And in the meantime, Rebecca became dear to her. She discovered that Rebecca was much more than the faithful quiet woman whom she had seen on Sabbaths—Rebecca with her narrow cheekbones and square jaw; Rebecca with her eager blue eyes, Rebecca who would snap at her children one moment and cover them with kisses the next. As weeks passed, Rebecca's natural wit and warm smile steadied the winds of emotion that rocked Almera. And slowly, slowly, under the long-suffering tutelage of Rebecca's nature, the icy chill in Almera's heart began to thaw. She raked up the last bit of hay.

Rebecca walked up to Almera and grinned. "We're finished! Each summer, I wonder if we'll ever be done with the hay. Then it's over, and the walnuts are ready. Come over next week. The men will shake the trees, and we'll gather them. You and Sam can have a bucketful."

"All right," Almera said. "And I'll bring you over a bushel of sweet apples."

"Bring them over this week, and we'll make pies."

"I'd like that." Almera smiled back.

Rebecca took an envelope out of her dress pocket and put it into Almera's pocket. "A letter from Julianne," Rebecca whispered. "For you only."

Almera nodded and hugged Rebecca. Her friend understood. There could be things in the letter that would upset Sam. She didn't want to risk that. She turned around to see Sam fiddling with the horse's collar.

"Ready to go?" she called out brightly. Sam looked up and nodded. Rebecca hooked arms with Almera and they walked together toward the wagon. After helping Almera into the seat, Sam amicably bid the Winters farewell and thanked them for their generosity. But when they invited him to come over next week to gather walnuts, Sam quickly declined.

On the way home, Sam started a song:

> Will you wear white, Oh my dear, Oh my dear? Will you wear white, Missus Prescott?
> You won't wear white, for the color is too bright, you won't wear white, Missus Prescott.
> Will you wear green, Oh my dear, Oh my dear? Will you wear green, Missus Prescott?
> You won't wear green, or you'll look like a bean, you won't wear green, Missus Prescott.

Almera smiled. She had never heard that verse before. Sam took hold of her hand and continued.

> Will you wear blue, Oh my dear, Oh my dear? Will you wear blue, Missus Prescott?
> You won't wear blue, for you are not true. You won't wear blue, Missus Prescott.

Sam abruptly stopped singing. His hand tightened around hers. Almera looked down at the hands in her lap—hers pale and white, unable to move when enclosed by Sam's broad, tanned fingers. Their hands stood out starkly against the royal purple of her dress.

* * *

Sam awakened at two in the morning. Rolling over, he reached for Almera, but she was not there. For an instant, panic and rage rushed through him, hot and blinding. Had she left him? He was about to leap from the bed when he noticed something else—the bedroom door was ever so slightly ajar, betraying candlelight in the adjoining room. Silent as a hunter, he slipped out of bed and peered through the crack. Almera sat at the table, her white nightdress glowing in the candlelight, her whole attention focused on the words on a piece of paper. His hands knotted into fists. He had seen Rebecca Winters slip an envelope into her pocket. This was it. How could someone so beautiful and innocent be so deceptive?

He watched her for a moment, his temper smoldering. Earlier he had stayed by her side, acting kind and affectionate, giving her every opportunity to tell him about the envelope. Yet she had hung her dress up quietly without a word, ignoring the weight of the envelope in the pocket.

Then she had donned her nightdress and allowed him to hold her tight, had even relaxed in his arms as he stroked her hair. "Sam, I want things to be as they used to be," she had whispered. He had felt that passion that bound his soul to her and to no other woman. And he had hoped that the envelope contained an innocent recipe, that he had misinterpreted the whispers of the women and their quick embrace: like two men shaking hands after making a secret compact, a covenant that could not be broken.

Almera finished reading the letter and lifted her head. The line of her profile outlined her long lashes and the sweet curve between her nose and lips. Sam opened the door. Her head pivoted toward him, her features betraying her surprise. The fingers of her right hand tightened on the paper.

"Sam? I thought you were asleep."

He stepped quickly toward her. "I'm wide awake."

"I'm sorry that I disturbed you."

"Give me the letter." He reached out his hand.

"It's from my sister." She did not offer it to him but instead folded her arms as if she were freezing, moving the letter tight against her side.

"I saw Rebecca Winters give it to you secretly." Sam's voice rose. "I hoped that you were finished with this falsehood! Give me the letter!"

"I'm not false," Almera said, her jaw quivering, her eyes defiant and pleading at the same time. "But it's addressed to me alone."

"Give it to me."

"It's mine, Sam."

Cat-quick Sam grabbed her left arm and wrenched it away from her body, causing her to gasp in pain. He stripped the letter from her right hand. The flame of the candle wavered then continued burning, illuminating the rage etched in his features. He pushed her away, hard against the chair. "Don't make me beat you like a man breaking his horse!"

"If you lay a hand on me, my father will kill you," Almera threatened.

"He might try! But I wouldn't be the dead one!"

She shrank back; her rage turning to tears. "Don't act this way, Sam. Please. I'm your wife."

He towered over her. "Then act like my wife! The woman bound to obey and love me."

"How can I love you when you frighten me so?"

He took a step back. Then he read the letter aloud, his eyes shadowed with hurt and anger. Almera buried her face in her hands.

Dearest Almera,

I've given this letter to one of the missionaries who has been sent east to raise money to buy land in Daviess County. I've asked him to place it in your hands alone. By buying land from the old settlers, we hope that the conflict here might come to a peaceful resolution. Yet I fear that it won't be so. It would take but an ounce of wind to blow these coals into flame. Already, some brethren were attacked in Gallatin for trying to vote. The Saints in outlying areas are being told to move into the cities for safety. Almon, when traveling with the leading brethren, was chased by a mob on horseback. Brother Joseph was arrested and then released on a lack of evidence against him.

Enough of sad news from Zion. How is your health? How is Papa? Almon and I are well and also Delcena and her family. We thank God for that blessing. We have heard little from Mother and only know that the camp stopped for a time to do work on a turnpike in Dayton, Ohio. We suppose that they have left now, but we do not know how far they have come nor when they will join us. Oh, Mera, it seems that our family, once so close in proximity, is spread now to the four winds.

Delcena is expecting and will deliver in October or November. These days she spends a great deal of time with Emma Smith. Their children are the same ages and as close as cousins. I'm lonely, missing you, Mother, Nancy, and Susan with a longing that I cannot escape. Do you think me childish when your own isolation is so much worse than mine? I know that I have the blessing of a faithful husband, of a sister near, and the Saints surrounding me. I am haunted by the memory of your face, stained with tears, on the day Almon and I left you in the barn. I feel as if we have left you in prison. I pray that Sam repents of his evil toward you. All people, male and female, have the right to worship as they please. Almon and I will come to visit as soon as time and circumstance permit. We will always welcome you into our home.

I hope that my letter has brought you some comfort and cheer. My heart is entwined with yours, my beloved sister. May God bless us all until we meet again.

Julianne Babbitt

Sam slammed the letter down on the table. "My evil toward you! You are the courtesan!" he shouted, the force of his breath blowing out the candle. In the darkness, his voice filled the room. "Married to your religion and sisters, not your husband. But if you dare leave me, if you dare walk out that door, it will be the final threshold you ever cross. Go back to bed. Now!"

Almera stood and stumbled into the bedroom, weeping. Sam followed her and slammed the door behind them. She curled up on the edge of the bed, her body shaking uncontrollably. Sam lay down, staring at the black ceiling, his fists knotted. He would break her if she forced him, but it wouldn't bring him any joy.

At dawn he heard Almera rise and cook breakfast. After they ate in silence, Almera stood up and left the table. Sam followed her. He placed his hands on her shoulders and turned her around to face him. Her cheeks were tearstained, and there were dark circles under her eyes.

"We will forget about last night," he said. "Things will go on between us as before, except for one difference. I'll send word to the Mormons that you are no longer allowed to speak with them. Obviously, Mrs. Winters is a bad influence. Do not defy me, Almera. Next time I will not be so merciful."

Almera did not look at him nor speak. He pulled her close and hissed in her ear, "Do you understand me?"

Her teeth chattered though it was not cold. "I understand."

He let go of her. "Then I'm off. Have a pleasant day."

* * *

Ezekiel heard the front door open and shut as he lay in bed, his head aching after a night at the tavern. It was probably Almera. She usually brought him lunch at the shop, but he hadn't gone in today. He sat up, trying to ignore the stabbing pain through his temple. Yesterday, Thomas Burdick had brought him a letter from his daughter, Julianne. The news from Missouri troubled him. If he figured right, his wife and younger children ought to arrive there in the next couple of weeks, right when things blew apart. He stood stiffly—bitter at the fact that he was growing old, that the best part of his life was over, that his family was gone.

"Almera, that you?" he called out.

"Yes, Papa," she returned. "Are—are you all right?"

He heard genuine worry in her voice. He walked out into the kitchen where she was setting a plate on the table. Her eyes were red from crying.

"Darlin', what is it?" he asked.

"You weren't in the shop. I-I thought something might have happened to you."

He put his arm around her. "Of course not. I'm a tough old coot. Come sit down on the sofa by me for a few minutes. You look like you might be getting sick."

They walked together to the couch. After they sat down, she rested her head on his shoulder, her loose, dark hair falling soft against his aging skin.

"Did you get some of Hiram Winter's hay?" he asked.

"Yes," Almera responded.

"What's it like?"

"Good and clean. Do you need any?"

"No. My barn is full. I got a letter from Julianne."

Almera swallowed. "Me too." She began to cry.

So that was the trouble. She was worried about the situation in Missouri. If she were a man, he would offer her a drink, something to soothe the helplessness. "Your sisters will be all right," Ezekiel said gently. "Their husbands will take care of them." He didn't have the heart to mention her mother, his wife, Julia.

He felt her shudder beneath his arm as her tears continued to fall. "Does it ever quit hurting, Papa?"

Ezekiel closed his eyes as he rested his head on Almera's. He wouldn't lie to her. "No, angel. It never does."

* * *

Springfield, Illinois—early October

It was a simple house: one large room, a small window, a narrow loft, plank flooring, two hearths, and a sound roof. In the yard there was a cellar and icehouse. It was crowded with nine people but would do for the fall and winter. It was as good as any place to live and die in. Outside, the dawn sun squeezed above the horizon, a dash of fire in a dim world.

Julia sat in a chair looking down at the woman in the bed, Mary Cook Hale. Sister Hale's husband, Samuel, had died a week ago, just a few days following their arrival in Springfield. His wife would soon follow him. Julia knew the signs of death. She had heard its rattle last night, had known without doubt that the time was near. She prayed silently for Sister Hale, for her spirit that would soon be free. The children were asleep now. The angels taking Sister Hale home would be uninterrupted. But what of Sister Hale's child, ten-year-old Mary Ann? A few days ago Julia had promised Sister Hale that she would care for Mary Ann. Should Julia awaken Mary Ann to tell her mother good-bye? Or would Mary Ann's tears hold Sister Hale back? Should she wait until after Sister Hale passed away, when the feverish fire in the body had cooled? Julia swallowed. It would be a narrow slot of time when Mary Ann could embrace her mother's precious form without being scorched or chilled. If it were Julia lying there, what would she want? She prayed to know what to do.

Sister Hale opened her eyes. "Mary Ann?" she whispered.

"Do you want me to get her?" Julia asked. A meeting of eyes. A hard gasp for air. A slight nod. Sister Hale was waiting to tell Mary Ann farewell.

Julia went in the other room and took the girl in her arms. She was slim and slight, with blue eyes and wispy brown hair. She was an only child. In the blink of an eye, she would be an orphan. Was she strong enough for this?

Julia gently moved the child's bangs out of her eyes. "Darling, your mama is going to heaven. She wants to tell you good-bye."

Mary Ann opened her eyes. Julia wrapped her arms around her and repeated what she had just said. The child's jaw quivered then tears and a broken sob. Mary Ann's head lay against Julia's chest, against the steady beating of her heart.

"Sweetheart, darling." With a finger, Julia moved Mary Ann's damp bangs behind her ear. "Jesus will give you strength. Mama wants to see you. I'll be right there with you."

Mary Ann swallowed hard and allowed Julia to help her stand. She held Julia's hand tightly. Julia spoke softly. "Don't be afraid. Angels are near, Papa is near to take Mama home to our Heavenly Father."

Tears streamed down Mary Ann's cheeks. Was this too much for a little one? Julia held her on her lap as the two sat down in the chair by Sister Hale's bed. Sister Hale smiled and tried to lift her hand. Mary Ann let go of Julia's hand and grasped her mother's. "Don't go, Mama. Please."

"I love you," Sister Hale whispered. "Sister Johnson loves you too."

Mary Ann clung to her mother while Julia stroked the child's hair. They did not move for ten long minutes until Sister Hale took her final breath and her heart stopped beating. Then Mary Ann let go of her mother and looked up into Julia's brown eyes. "What if you die too?" she gasped.

For an instant Julia did not know what to say. Then she heard her daughter Mary's voice behind her. "Don't worry, Mary Ann."

Julia turned to look at Mary standing near the door, eighteen years old, her blond hair tumbling over her shoulders, her brown eyes brimming with tears. Running over to them, she wrapped her arms around Mary Ann. "If Mama dies, I will take care of you," she promised. "And Joe. And Ben. And Julianne and Delcena in Far West. We have a big family, and you are part of it now. There will always, always be someone to take care of you."

* * *

The next day it was early evening when Joe pulled his coat and boots on. His stomach growled. All he had eaten for dinner was a cold biscuit with watery gravy. He needed to get out of the house, to walk and clear his mind, to go to the general store. And he needed answers—answers to questions that he hated to ask. *Mr. Speed, do you have any more quinine in stock? Do you know of any other employment? Could you give me credit for flour and cornmeal? Will you forgive me for begging so that my family does not starve?*

The sky was thick with clouds. Joe left his coat unbuttoned so that he could feel the bite of the chill wind. His dark hair blew back from his high forehead. They had buried Sister Hale that morning on the edge of the prairie in a pine box, next to her husband. He remembered little Mary Ann Hale, standing with one hand in his mother's and the other holding Esther's, her chest convulsing and her cheeks wet, though hardly a sound escaped her lips. Children should not lose their parents while so young.

Lashed by the harsh whip of sorrow and survival, Joe walked quickly, hoping the wind would dry his tears. He was more emotional than a man ought to be. To be on the right hand of Jesus when He came again, to bear others' burdens when poverty and desperation surrounded you like night—that was the test of manhood, the separation of the sheep from the goats. And this week he had been found wanting. Five days ago, his mother had come to him, saying that Sister Hale had asked her to care for Mary Ann if she died. Joe had balked. *Wasn't there a place for the girl in another family?* He feared another weight on his shoulders, another mouth to feed.

"Joe, she needs us, and I've given my word to God and to her mother," Julia had replied.

He had relented. Of course they would take care of Mary Ann. A realization gripped him with steel bands. Desperate poverty could change a man's nature. He, who used to make another man's suffering his own cause, would have looked at an orphan child and turned his back. He had once called himself Amicus, friend to all; and he had once promised God that he would live his life easing others' burdens, helping them to find joy. What had happened?

Was it the dangers lurking behind the door, demons knocking and demanding entrance? He feared the fever that took the Hales' lives, he felt it in those he touched and doctored, in the air he breathed. He feared it slipping into his family, that his best efforts would once again prove futile. His mother had looked tired at suppertime; the dark circles under her eyes, the deep, exhausted breaths. He remembered the same look in Seth, in David, in Susan, in Nancy. When he asked how she fared, she admitted that her head ached. Joe was afraid. But that was not the only danger near. Starvation threatened to swallow them all.

Joe approached the center of town. The streets were paved with split logs, lying one next to the other, flat sides up. Joe's boots clicked on the wooden plank sidewalk. By the time he reached the general store, the mud had dropped off his boots.

Joe hesitated at the door. He liked the owner, a young merchant named Joshua Speed. He was a cheerful, clear-eyed man with dark, chin-length hair. When they first arrived, he had told Joe where to look for work. During the past three weeks Joe had chopped firewood, sawed stove-wood, made ax handles and washboards. But the jobs didn't pay enough. Joe hated the reason he had come, the need to ask Mr. Speed to sell him goods on credit.

Joe opened the door and walked in. This late in the day, the store was nearly empty. Mr. Speed and a group of four other young men were gathered in the corner, sitting around a blazing fire, talking animatedly. Firewood was piled high to the left of the hearth, plenty to last far into the night.

Joe shuffled his feet and waited awkwardly. He did not want to intrude. One of the men was extremely tall, with the longest legs Joe had ever seen. His cheeks were sunken, his features lank, but his dark eyes glistened as he listened intently to the short, stout man sitting across from him, shaking his cane, shouting that the federal government ought to keep its filthy hands out of state business.

"I would say that depended on what the business was," the tall man rejoined. "If someone threatened to cut off my leg, I should think that was my business. So it is with the United States, with this great experiment in democracy. If the whole falls, so shall the parts."

"Abraham," another man interrupted jovially. He also addressed the tall gentleman. "I heard a rumor that you are suspected of being a Deist. You need to pick out a church and start going now. That is, if you still aspire to be elected to Congress one day."

Speed laughed. "Abraham doesn't like ministers' methods any more than he likes being called Abe." Then Mr. Speed stood up, mimicking a preacher as he raised his hands high above his head and thundered, "All who want to go to heaven, not hell, will stand!"

Laughing, the men around the fire joined the fracas and stood, all except the tall one.

The short fellow raised his eyebrows. "May I inquire where you plan to go?"

The tall man stretched out his legs and smiled benignly. "If it's all the same to you, I believe I shall go to Congress."

The short fellow reddened while the rest of the men roared with laughter. Offering to get them all a drink, Mr. Speed turned. When he saw Joe standing alone, he stopped midsentence. The room quieted.

"Good evening," Mr. Speed said as he immediately stepped over to Joe and shook his hand. "Gentlemen, this is Mr. Johnson, who has newly arrived here in Springfield. Mr. Johnson, before you is a group of Democrats and Whigs. Most are lawyers and some like Mr. Lincoln and Mr. Douglas are members of the legislature. They like nothing better than to come to my store and argue politics on every night save the Sabbath. Don't you think that they would do better spending their time courting?"

"Absolutely," Joe said with a forced smile. He thought about how his family spent their time: watching loved ones die, fleeing hatred, scraping for a meal, nursing the sick, and praying. These men's lives were luxurious, sitting around a warm fire with full bellies, arguing politics and discussing courtship. Such a life would be heaven.

The tall man looked at Joe. "One problem, my boy. I have come to the conclusion that I will never again think of marriage. For this reason: I could never be satisfied with someone who would be blockhead enough to have me."

Laughter again filled the room. Speed shook his head. "Enough of all of you. Mr. Johnson and I have business to discuss."

Speed placed his hand on Joe's shoulder and together they walked to the counter. The merchant spoke cheerfully, like Joe was one of his closest friends. "I was hoping you would come by. Mrs. Lamb came in yesterday. She is looking for a Yankee schoolmaster to teach a congregation of sixty pupils in the winter school. I told her of the genteel Mr. Johnson, a Yankee, who has just arrived in Springfield. She is very anxious for you to begin. If you are up to it."

Emotion sliced through Joe. He felt to shout, sing, and weep all at once. God had answered his prayers. They would not starve. He heartily shook Mr. Speed's hand and thanked him. "I'm up to it!" he exclaimed. "Thank you."

"Think nothing of it." Speed grinned. "Now what can I do for you?"

Flushing, Joe said, "My family needs quinine and cornmeal. But I am out of money. I was going to beg you to extend me credit."

Speed laughed. "Which I shall gladly do considering my sure knowledge of your employment!"

12

Oh my Father, keep and bless me,
Ne'r let troubles on me come, . . .
Do thou guide and safe protect me,
While my foes with wrath shall foam,
And through every step direct me
Till I meet my friends at home.

Joel Hills Johnson

Missouri—October 2, 1838

Benjamin had been reassigned to the first division of the Kirtland Camp. He rode near the front of the wagon train on the lanky, chestnut colt that hardly looked big enough to carry him. His sole possessions included two silver dollars in his pocket, warm clothes stuffed into saddlebags, his new boots tied to a saddle ring, and Old Betsy, his father's silver-trimmed shotgun, which was slung over his shoulder. He looked around at the dips and swells in this fertile, grass-covered land. The dome of blue sky stretched wide and endless. This was a place where one could breathe deeply. This was the land of Zion. At least it would be if it weren't for the depth of shadow on the horizon, the rumors of war.

Six days ago the camp had nearly disbanded. Uncertain of the extent of the danger, they had been hesitant to move on in such a large company. They had debated about what to do. Was there safety in numbers? Or was the camp a huge, crawling caterpillar, vulnerable to anyone who wanted to violently squash the Mormon gathering? Then a Missourian named Samuel Bend had encountered them, had told them of affairs in Far West and

Adam-ondi-Ahman. *A mob was gathering in Daviess County. The governor had called for volunteers.* Following this news, the camp's leaders had decided unanimously to go forward with all haste. The decision proved wise, for now, less than a week later, the journey was nearly over. They were within five miles of Far West.

Benjamin's heart pounded when he saw the riders canter up the rise of the hill. The Prophet led, riding a sleek black horse. Flanking his right was Sidney Rigdon, and on his left Hyrum Smith and Brigham Young. Gladness filled Benjamin. He stretched up in the saddle and waved his arm in a high arc. "Brother Joseph's coming to meet us!"

The Prophet waved back and spurred his horse into a gallop. Benjamin knew that it didn't matter how crowded the streets of Far West were nor how close to their heels the howling mob. Nothing could dim the joy of this reunion, not with the fact that God was with Brother Joseph.

The wagons halted, and Benjamin slid off the colt. He watched as Joseph and his companions dismounted. They greeted the leading brethren with handshakes and embraces.

Then the Prophet's eyes rested on Benjamin. Joseph left the brethren and hurried toward him, wrapping him in an embrace. "Bennie, I've missed you. How is the rest of your family?"

"They were well when I left them. They've stayed in Springfield for the winter, to take care of those too sick to travel."

"Did Joel stay too?"

"Yes."

"But you journeyed on alone?"

"I-I wanted to be near you. To help. In Far West or wherever you need me."

Joseph's smile, the appreciation in his eyes, warmed Benjamin. "It's good you came. Right now I need you in Adam-ondi-Ahman. The Saints there must be strengthened, for mobs from other counties are gathering and threatening them. I feel that you have an inheritance in Di-Ahman. Your friend, William Huntington, is already there."

Benjamin swallowed and nodded. "I'll head there tomorrow."

Joseph rested his hand on Benjamin's shoulder. "As soon as I can, I'll come and visit you. God bless you, Bennie."

"God bless you, Brother Joseph."

Joseph nodded, and Benjamin watched as he moved on and greeted other people. What was it about Joseph that made Benjamin willing to do anything he asked—even give his life? Then a realization struck Benjamin like a beam of bright sunlight. The Prophet's influence lay in the fact that the converse was true as well. Joseph Smith was willing to give his life for Benjamin and for the Saints whom he loved.

Together they journeyed on. Anticipation welled in Benjamin as they approached Far West. Tonight he would be with Delcena and Lyman, Almon and Julianne. And tomorrow he would see William and Zina again. Right now, the Prophet was near. Truly this was Zion. Yet how could he feel so glad when war was so close at hand?

* * *

Friday, October 5, 1838

It was nearly eight in the evening when Delcena finished tucking her three youngest children in bed. She slowly walked back into the kitchen. In her final month of pregnancy, she felt awkward and exhausted as she bent down and placed a log on the fire. Yet it had been a pleasant day. The Smiths had come over that morning, and Emma, sensitive to her condition, had helped Delcena make cider and apple butter. The Prophet had invited Lyman and Albey to ride with him and young Joseph to the south part of the county where he was looking for a location for a town. Emma had left a few hours ago. Lyman and Albey ought to be home soon.

Delcena slowly lowered herself into the rocker. Just yesterday they had closed up the house for the winter. She picked up her knitting. She had purchased a skein of bright blue yarn and was making a scarf and gloves for Albey's sixth birthday. Her fingers moved with the rhythm of the clicking needles as her mind reviewed the past week.

She thought of how Benjamin had arrived on Tuesday evening and left Wednesday morning. He had looked so handsome and healthy, tall and bronzed by the sun. She and Julianne had filled his knapsack with biscuits and salt pork. As he rode away, tears had filled Delcena's eyes, and Julianne had wept. He was on his way to Adam-ondi-Ahman in Daviess County, where the old citizens wanted the Mormons out, where mobs were gathering. If only they could have kept him safe, tucked away in Far West, Caldwell County, among the five thousand Saints here. It was safe for one reason alone. Nearly two years ago, Alexander Doniphan, a representative from Clay County to the Missouri legislature had prepared a bill that created Caldwell County a designated place for the Mormons to settle. Emma and Joseph had been so grateful that they named their baby, Alexander, after Doniphan. But Benjamin couldn't stay. Like Lyman had said, her little brother was a man now, and the Prophet trusted him with a man's responsibility. Surely if the Prophet sent Benjamin to Di-Ahman, God would protect him there.

Delcena turned her mind to other things, to the day with Emma and their growing friendship. Their daughters were the same ages and their sons as well. Yet she didn't think that this new baby would follow suit and be a boy like Emma's infant, Alexander. She and Emma had talked about this, had imagined their little boy and girl growing up side by side. Wouldn't it be something if they fell in love in twenty years? Then Emma had smiled wistfully and said that children had a way of disregarding their mothers' imaginings. After all, Delcena's baby might turn out to be a boy. Then Emma's eyes had become very serious. *And look at what I did to my mother. I eloped with Joseph.*

Delcena's musings were interrupted by the door opening. Lyman walked in carrying Albey on his back. Delcena quickly tucked the yarn in the basket before Albey saw it. He would be six on October thirtieth, about the time the baby would be born. Delcena smiled at Albey as he struggled to keep his eyes open. She would have plenty of time to knit in a few moments, after he was asleep.

"Are you hungry?" she asked Lyman.

Lyman shook his head. "No. We stopped by the Smiths' and ate."

"Albey, come give Mama a kiss good night. Then Papa will carry you to bed."

"I'm not tired," Albey argued as he yawned.

"Tired or not, it's bedtime," Lyman said. He piggybacked Albey over to Delcena. "Kiss Mama quick, or there won't be time for a song."

Albey wrapped his arms around his mother's neck. Delcena held him close and kissed him. Lyman swung his son back up into his arms.

Albey looked up at his father. "You gonna fight tomorrow with Brother Joseph when he whups the Dewitt mob like George Washington whupped the Tories?"

"What is he talking about?" Delcena asked quickly. Her eyes met Lyman's. He looked away. Delcena's heart skipped a beat. What had happened that afternoon? Dewitt was in Carroll County. Had the Saints there been attacked? It was obvious that Lyman didn't want to discuss it right now.

"I don't know about tomorrow, but I know what I'm going to do right now," Lyman said, overly cheerful as he carried Albey toward the loft. "I'm takin' you to bed."

Delcena's hands were frozen on her lap; her knitting remained at her feet. She listened to Lyman's voice singing as he laid Albey down.

When the world in darkness lay,
Lo, Joseph sought the better way,
And he heard the Savior say,
"Go and prune my vineyard, Son!"

And an angel surely, then,
For a blessing unto men,
Brought the priesthood back again,
In its ancient purity.

Even Joseph he inspires;
Yea, his heart he truly fires,
With the light that he desires
For the work of righteousness.

And the Book of Mormon, true,
With its cov'nant ever new,
For the Gentile and the Jew,
He translated sacredly.

Precious are his years to come,
While the righteous gather home,
For the great Millennium,
Where he'll rest in blessedness.

Lyman's voice ceased. Delcena heard him climb down from the loft, his footsteps walking toward her. He sat down in the chair opposite Delcena and looked at her. "Albey's asleep."

"What happened in Dewitt?"

Lyman spoke slowly, his voice very clear, almost like he was explaining something to a child. "John Murdock met us on the road on his way back to Far West. You remember that he moved to Dewitt a month ago?"

Delcena nodded.

Lyman continued. "The Saints in Dewitt are under siege. They're surrounded by a mob who have destroyed property, burned homes, and killed cattle. George Hinkle has sworn to defend them to death, but our people are outnumbered four to one. Tomorrow Joseph will ride to Dewitt with a number of men. He hopes to allay the feelings of the citizens and save the lives of the brethren."

Delcena's jaw quivered. "And you're going with him."

"Yes," Lyman answered.

Delcena shut her eyes and pictured Emma, her dark hair, her almond-shaped eyes, her beauty, and her strength. Emma shared her husband with ten thousand members of the Church. Joseph's life was constantly in danger. Yet every single Latter-day Saint was part of Joseph's family. He gave his allegiance, his life's blood to them all. Delcena swallowed. Emma was her friend and her example. If Emma could do it, so could she.

Lyman's eyes searched hers, wholly pleading for her faith and support. How many times had they had a similar conversation? But tonight Delcena's response was different. "I understand. Of course you will go with Brother Joseph. But what about general conference tomorrow? Will it still convene?"

Lyman's eyes widened. It took him a few seconds to absorb her reaction and answer her question. "Yes. Joseph is meeting with Brigham right now. Brigham and President Marsh will preside. They'll call for volunteers to go on missions as previously planned. The gospel will be preached to the world regardless of the battles raging in Zion."

"But, Lyman, you won't be able to volunteer to go on a mission as you had hoped."

Lyman focused on her, his smile sweet and sad. "No, I'm staying here in Missouri with you."

Lyman arose and walked over to Delcena. He stood behind her and rubbed her shoulders. Then she stood, and he held her in his arms, their unborn child pressed between them. After their embrace, Lyman went to pack his saddlebags with gunpowder, shells, and hard tack. Delcena picked up her knitting and finished Albey's blue scarf.

* * *

Adam-ondi-Ahman—early October 1838

"Hello, Ben. Come look at the map. There aren't very many lots left." Father Huntington's voice was matter-of-fact and friendly as Benjamin stood in front of him and took off his hat. The city had been surveyed, and each man was allowed to choose a lot. Because Benjamin was young and unmarried, he was among the last to pick.

Father Huntington pointed to a place near the center of the map. "This lot is on the promontory, overlooking the Grand River Valley. The Prophet calls it Tower Hill. The trouble is the soil is rocky."

Brother Huntington's finger trailed to the outer edge. "There are a few lots left down here. The land is lower and the soil is good."

Benjamin stood silently for a few minutes, searching the map. The quality of the soil was important, but he didn't want to be on the periphery of the city. Finally, he pointed to the lot on the promontory. "I'll take this one," he said a bit loudly, his voice more confident than he felt.

"It's yours," Father Huntington said as he wrote down Benjamin's name. Then he stood and shook Benjamin's right hand.

After the handshake, Benjamin fumbled with the hat in his left hand. He put the hat on. But there was one other thing he wanted to ask Brother Huntington. "Is Zina home or William?" Benjamin's face flushed, as he knew full well that William wasn't around. Why on earth couldn't he be direct and simply ask to court Zina?

Father Huntington eyed Benjamin as if he were the surveyor and Benjamin the piece of property under scrutiny. After a very long few seconds, he said, "William is gone with the militia, searching for food. Zina is out behind the house picking apples. On your way out, please send the next man in."

Benjamin nodded. "Thank you, sir. I look forward to seeing my lot."

Father Huntington smiled. "There's nothing to thank me for. Joseph was the man who decided to divide the land and give it to the brethren. This is a blessed place. If only we can hold on to it. When are you on guard duty?"

"From midnight 'til eight in the morning."

"Now some of the property you're guarding will be your own."

"Yes, sir." A shiver ran down Benjamin's spine. He had his own piece of land.

A few moments later, he walked behind the Huntington cabin to a small orchard. Zina stretched up to pick an apple. She turned and smiled as he approached. Her coloring was a great deal like Nancy's, but she had a face all her own, with wide, deep-set eyes that made you feel like she cared about you the second they turned your direction.

"Could I help you?" Benjamin asked.

Zina nodded. "I'd like that. We need to pick the rest off the tree before they freeze."

"It's cold for this time of year," Benjamin commented. "Could snow this week." He couldn't think of anything else to say as they emptied the tree of apples.

Zina filled in the gaps of silence, describing the various families living in Di-Ahman, both the Mormons and the old settlers. "Adam Black is the worst," she said with a shiver. "And his wife won't even look at us. Stay away from his cabin, Ben."

Benjamin nodded, then his words ran together. "I've chosen a city lot. It's the highest point on Tower Hill. I haven't been there yet. I was wondering if you'd walk over with me to take a look."

"Of course," Zina said quickly, the color of her cheeks deepening. "I know the place. My little brother Oliver and I go there sometimes to sit and look out over the valley."

They set off together, Benjamin quiet as they walked, Zina humming. Benjamin thought of how she used to sing in the Kirtland Temple choir. He would watch her up there, near Julianne, one of the youngest members, opening her mouth wide, singing with all her heart.

"I remember the temple choir," he said.

"It was wonderful," Zina responded. "Once a corner of the temple was filled with music too sweet for this earth. I think that angels were singing with us. I wonder if I'll hear them again when the Far West Temple is built."

"I hope so," Benjamin said.

Zina turned to him. "But we don't have to wait until then to sing. Do you know the song about Adam-ondi-Ahman?"

Benjamin shook his head.

"Then I'll sing it to you."

Zina's cheerful voice warmed the cold air.

This earth was once a garden place,
With all her glories common;
And men did live a holy race,
And worship Jesus face to face,
In Adam-ondi-Ahman.

We read that Enoch walked with God,
Above the pow'r of Mammon:
While Zion spread herself abroad,
And Saints and angels sung aloud
In Adam-ondi-Ahman.

Zina stopped singing as they hiked up an incline. Then they turned south and walked a short distance down Main Street. Zina's hand reached out from under her cloak as she pointed to their left. "There's your land, Ben, right up there."

Benjamin turned toward where Zina pointed. A knoll rose up about fifty feet from where they stood. Zina continued. "See how it's rounded, like the cope of heaven. There's an old Nephitish altar built in the center of the brush."

Together they climbed the hill. Benjamin studied the mound of rocks, more than three feet high and twice as wide. Some of the rocks were red from a long-ago fire. They were not cut rocks but naturally formed, with dirt filling in the spaces. Bushes flanked the east and west sides of the mound. Trees were scattered around, yellow leaves blowing in the stiff wind.

Zina stepped behind the altar near the edge of the hill. She pointed as she said, "Look how you can see the whole valley."

Benjamin stood beside her but was unable to enjoy the beauty of the view because of the rocks beneath his boots. They spilled in and around the trees, thick, jagged, and hard. What would it take to remove them, to plant or build on this land? He squatted down and pushed rocks aside, only to find more rocks underneath. He dug with his hands, going down six inches then eight—there were rocks upon layers of rock.

"What have I done?" he said dismally as he looked up at Zina, his dark eyes troubled and his voice thick with disappointment. "I should have chosen a different lot."

Zina shook her head. "You're wrong. I love this place. It's the best spot in all of Di-Ahman."

Benjamin swallowed and stood. "But what am I going to do with a lot that's full of rocks?"

"Build a house on it. Love it for what it is."

Benjamin didn't respond. Zina was a woman, and he didn't expect her to understand. She'd always been taken care of. But a man had to provide for his family. He needed an orchard and a garden.

"We'd best head back," Benjamin said.

They didn't talk much as they descended the hill and walked back to the Huntington property. The afternoon deepened into dusk. Zina pulled her cloak tightly around her shoulders.

After thanking Zina for accompanying him, Benjamin trudged back to Lyman Wight's barn where he would sleep. It was growing dark, and Benjamin did not have a lantern or a candle. He quickly ate the remainder of the biscuits that his sisters had packed for him then climbed into the loft. He prayed as darkness enshrouded him. Then he lay down in the hay, bending his arm to form a pillow beneath his head. Exhausted, he shook with cold. His thoughts splintered in different directions. George A. Smith would awaken him at midnight for guard duty. This was supposed to be a garden place, but he had a lot full of rock. He was freezing and hungry. He heard his mother's voice in his dreams. *Benjamin, darling, you're shaking. Why didn't you bring a quilt? Let someone know your needs.* And his answer. *I can't ask. I'm supposed to be a man, and there aren't enough blankets in Di-Ahman to keep the children warm.*

"Ben Johnson?"

The woman's voice startled Benjamin into wakefulness. For an instant he thought it was his mother. The main level of the barn was full of light.

"Benjamin Johnson, are you here?" It was not his mother's voice but Sister Smith's, George A.'s mother.

"Yes." He sat up in the loft, stiff and aching. He forced his fingers and toes to bend. Looking down, he saw her in the center of a flood of lantern light. He blinked. Could it be midnight already? He focused on her. "Is George waiting?"

"No. He's on duty still. It's only nine. He told me that you don't have a blanket."

Only then did Benjamin notice the thick quilt hanging over Sister Smith's arm. She reached up and handed it to him. "It's the warmest we have."

"Thank you," Benjamin said. "I'll never forget your kindness."

Sister Smith chuckled. "We'll see about that. By the time you're old, you forget a good deal."

* * *

Missouri, between Dewitt and Far West—October 11, 1838

Wind pushed Lyman forward. It was Jackson County all over again. A storm raged as more than four hundred people, destitute and ill, walked away from their homes. Lyman walked with them, helping where he could. He had lent his horse to a young family whose oxen had been slaughtered and eaten by the mob. Now the family had no milk to give their children, no animals, save Lyman's, to pull their wagon.

It had been a terrible five days. Lyman, the Prophet, and their companions had been forced to travel narrow, deeply rutted paths because mobs swarmed the main roads. When they finally reached Dewitt, the situation was dire. Many were ill from exposure and starvation. Joseph pursued peace, finding a few compassionate old settlers willing to send messages to the civil authorities. In response, General Atchison immediately sent General Parks to the area with a militia ordered to defend the Mormons. But Park's troops had mutinied and joined the mob. If the Mormons attempted to leave the area to get help, they were shot at. If they stayed, they starved. In desperation, Joseph sent affidavits to the governor.

A day ago they had received Governor Boggs's response. "The quarrel is between the Mormons and the mob. They might fight it out."

On paper, without real money in their hands, the Dewitt Saints sold their lands to the same men they had purchased them from. Their homes had been burned, their livestock slaughtered. Their crops ruined. It stormed the day they left.

Lyman trudged on, exhausted. Last night he had listened to children cry out in fear and hunger. In his dreams they had been his own children. Strange thoughts entered his mind. Recently, Joseph had stripped Sampson Avard of his position. The Prophet was now in command. But the Dewitt Saints didn't have the strength to fight. Lyman thought bitterly of Avard's tactics. He despised the man. But now he wondered if Avard had a point. They wouldn't be suffering like this if they had swept away the people of Missouri like the Israelite armies swept away sinful Canaan. But weren't the Missourians also God's children? Weren't the modern Saints required to live a higher law? But when people lied and authorities upheld them, there was no justice on earth.

The gray, rainy day grew darker. It was early evening, and the wagon train slowed. Lyman watched in horror as Sister Jensen fell dead in her tracks with her husband beside her. She landed on her side, still holding the tightly wrapped newborn infant in her arms. Lyman ran to them and watched helplessly as Brother Jensen crouched over his wife and whispered words which were lost in the cold and swirling wind. Brother Jensen pried the newborn infant from his wife's body. Lyman put his arm on the young man's shoulder.

Brother Jensen turned to Lyman as if he felt a need to explain. "She just gave birth. She was still weak." Then he began to weep. The infant wailed in hunger. A woman with tears on her cheeks walked over and offered to feed the baby. Brother Jensen handed her the tiny bundle. Lyman held the weeping man in his arms.

A short time later, Lyman wrapped Sister Jensen's body in a wet blanket. They had no coffin. When the Prophet found them, he too wept. Lyman helped Brother Jensen bury his wife in a grove of trees as darkness fell and icy rain turned to snow. That night Lyman slept fitfully, dreaming that the body he had buried was Delcena's and the screaming infant his newborn daughter.

* * *

Far West, Missouri—Sunday morning, October 15, 1838

Lyman sat on the bench and listened to the Prophet speak to the priesthood brethren. His face was grim and his eyes bloodshot. He had come home from Dewitt a few days ago to find his family and the Babbitts ill with a stomach disorder. He had been up last night with Mary and Daniel. Delcena was sick as well, and he worried about her condition. Chicken broth was all that she could hold down. Women who lost their strength died in childbirth. The image of Sister Jensen loomed in his mind, still troubling his dreams.

He remembered Delcena's first delivery, the twins she brought into the world. He had been young then with enough faith to cast out his fear. The past five years had changed him. Faith still burned like fire within him, but he realized that death was only a breath away. The choice of each moment was paramount—and the love and life contained therein.

The Prophet's voice rose, bringing his thoughts back to the present. "Greater love hath no man than this, that he lay down his life for his brethren. The Dewitt mob is moving toward Adam-ondi-Ahman. I call upon all who are able to meet me here tomorrow morning at dawn. We will form a militia and ride to Daviess County to defend our people."

Ten minutes later the meeting ended. Heber Kimball said the closing prayer. Lyman stood and walked down the aisle out of the schoolhouse. As he descended the stairs, his thoughts turned once more to his wife. He hated leaving her. How could he explain the need? *Many of the men are sick, but I'm able-bodied. I have to go. Almon and Julianne will be well soon and will help you. Benjamin is in danger.* Lyman drew a deep breath. Benjamin was in danger. Delcena would not argue. But how could he leave her? Wasn't she in danger as well?

"Lyman."

He turned at the sound of the Prophet's voice. Joseph's face was red from the cold, his blond hair ruffling in the wind. Despite hardship and sorrow, the Prophet was strong and hardy, blessed by the Lord.

"Yes, Joseph."

"I want you to stay in Far West. Emma told me that Delcena and your children are ill. Besides, if the mob doubles back, men will be needed here."

Lyman shook his head. "We both know that they'll finish with Di-Ahman first. How can I stay when my brethren are in peril?"

"Your family needs you."

"You have a family too."

There was a look of pain in Joseph's eyes. "I know. I love Emma and the children. But I'm the Prophet. I wasn't with the Saints when they were driven from Jackson County. I will be with them now."

Lyman felt torn—torn between his duty to Joseph and Benjamin and the duty to his family. "Benjamin is in Di-Ahman. Delcena will want me to go."

"Tell her that I'll look after Bennie. Stay here and watch over your family and mine."

* * *

October 15, 1838. Monday evening.

The militia had come from Far West and camped in and around the barn where Benjamin had been sleeping for the past ten days. Old settlers fearful of the Mormons had left their farms. Goods had been foraged from empty houses and barns. There was food for the men to eat. Benjamin finished his meal of pork and bread. The cold weather continued, and the sky loomed dark with clouds. An hour ago he had searched among the militia, hoping to find Almon or Lyman. To the best of anyone's knowledge, neither had answered the Prophet's call. Benjamin felt alone in the crowd, disappointment wringing his full stomach.

Then Benjamin saw William Huntington edge his way through a group of men. He hadn't seen much of his friend since he had been in Di-Ahman. William was usually gone, responding to his father's orders.

"Ben," William said with a grin, "I've been looking for you. The Prophet's asking for you. You're to meet him at Brother Sloan's boardinghouse. He must have a mission to send you on because he said to pack all your things and bring them with you." William laughed. "I told him it wouldn't take you long to pack. You don't have much."

"You're right about that," Benjamin said, brightening. A moment later William left for guard duty. Benjamin took his extra boots out of the knapsack and stuffed his quilt in. He saddled the colt and tied the boots on. Fifteen minutes later, Benjamin arrived at Sloan's boardinghouse. The Prophet was outside saddling his horse.

"Brother Bennie." The Prophet embraced him then nodded toward Benjamin's mount. "Leave the saddle on. Take your things inside and put them in my room. Then we're off to visit that piece of land Brother Huntington tells me you've inherited. There are some things I want to show you and some of the other brethren."

"All right," Benjamin said, his heart beating quickly in anticipation. After gathering his things, he ducked inside the door of the boardinghouse. Brother Sloan frowned when Benjamin asked where the Prophet's room was. "Brother Joseph asked me to leave my things there for now," Benjamin explained. Brother Sloan followed after Benjamin and watched him closely.

Benjamin was relieved to get back outside with Brother Joseph. As they rode to find the other brethren, Joseph explained that Almon was too ill to travel and that Lyman had remained in Far West at Joseph's request.

"I understand," Benjamin said. He thought about how Lyman obeyed the Prophet without hesitation. Benjamin would do so as well. But what would he be asked to do? The Prophet had asked him to bring his things to Brother Sloan's. That must mean that he had a special assignment and would leave from there.

They neared the public square where Heber Kimball and Brigham Young were waiting. Benjamin decided to ask the Prophet before the other brethren joined them. "When we get back, where are you going to send me?" Benjamin asked.

A smile played on the corners of Joseph's mouth. "Nowhere. I want you to stay at the Sloans', where you will have a bed. Where you won't freeze to death."

"You mean inside the house?" Benjamin asked, incredulous.

Joseph smiled. "Yes, Bennie."

Benjamin remembered Brother Sloan's less-than-friendly glance. "But I don't have any money."

"That is the reason that I have invited you to stay in my room with me. If that's all right with you."

Tears pricked Benjamin's eyes. "Yes! But, but other boys are cold too."

"If I could, I would invite every one of them," Joseph said. "But Brother Sloan wouldn't have it. Yet I can help one young man."

"But Brother Joseph, why am I that one?"

Joseph's blue eyes were thoughtful and sad. "I watched how you suffered when Seth died. I, too, lost an elder brother. I made a promise that day that I would watch over you." Then he smiled. "And Emma would have my neck if I left Delcena's younger brother out in the cold. And I love you, Bennie, as I love Don Carlos, my own younger brother."

Benjamin could not speak for the feelings welling up inside him—the memory of Seth, the love for a Prophet of God. A moment later, they approached Brigham Young, Heber Kimball, and a few other men, including John Butler, who had fought valiantly at Gallatin.

"Brethren, come along with us," Joseph exclaimed. "And I will show you something."

Once they reached the top of Tower Hill, the Prophet and Benjamin dismounted, and Joseph led the men to the place where the rocks had been piled high in a mound. Joseph said, "It is true that this was a Nephitish altar, but this place is sacred for another reason as well. It was here, among these rocks, that Adam built a different altar and offered sacrifice. An angel of the Lord appeared unto Adam saying, 'Why dost thou offer sacrifices unto the Lord?' And Adam said to him, 'I know not, save the Lord commanded me.' Then the angel replied, 'This thing is a similitude of the sacrifice of the Only Begotten of the Father, which is full of grace and truth.'"

Joseph continued, his face and hair bright against the dim day. "And it is here where Adam later stood and blessed his children. It is here where they called him Michael. And it is here where he will sit again as Ancient of Days."

Benjamin wiped the tears from his eyes. Zina was right. This was the best spot. Never again would he be envious of anyone's choice for a city lot in Adam-ondi-Ahman.

On the way back, it began to snow. John Butler was on foot. He was a large, powerful man. Instead of shoes, he had green cowhide wrapped around his feet like moccasins.

"John, are your feet frozen yet?" a man asked of Butler.

"They will be soon enough," John Butler said. His voice was deep and rolling, with a thick Southern accent. "We never saw snow like this in Kentucky."

Benjamin remembered that his extra boots were still tied to his saddle. In his rush to leave, he had forgotten to take them into the Sloans' home. He thought of Brother Joseph, of how he would help every man in the camp if he could. But he had chosen to help Benjamin. He thought of how John Butler had fought off the mob in Gallatin, had saved other men's lives.

"Brother Butler," Benjamin said as he pulled his horse to a halt. "I'd be obliged if you'd take these boots off my hands."

John Butler turned and walked over to Benjamin. He examined the boots. "Why, son, I believe they'd fit."

"I hope so, sir," Benjamin said.

"Brethren," John Butler roared. Joseph was riding ahead with Brigham Young and Heber Kimball. "This boy has given me his extra pair of boots! Do y'all think I ought to take them?"

"That I do, John," Joseph called back. "Since Ben has another pair on his feet. And tomorrow I suppose I will follow Bennie's example and set you astride my black horse, Charley."

* * *

That night, for the first time in two weeks, Benjamin slept soundly, other men having relieved him of guard duty. He keenly appreciated the luxury of a soft bed and warm fire. Added to this was the joy of Brother Joseph's presence. Benjamin's rest was deep and dreamless. He awoke early to the Prophet's cheerful warmth. After a simple breakfast, in the company of several other men, they rode to the militia's camp. Five inches of snow had fallen during the night.

When they arrived, guilt crept into Benjamin. The men were freezing, the camp forlorn. Most had bedded down under trees, without tents. Benjamin watched as men crawled out of snow-covered beds, standing up, bone-chilled, as they shook snow out of their blankets and quilts. Lyman Wight stood among them, barking orders.

Benjamin swallowed and dismounted. He walked over to join the men. How could men fight the Missourians if they became sick from such conditions?

The Prophet leaped from his horse. He called out to Brother Wight. "General, let us cheer up these chilly boys! Men, form two lines. General Wight at the head of one and me at the head of the other. We'll have a sham battle, our weapons, snowballs."

Young men whooped and laughed as they fell into line. On the call of "Charge!" snowballs flew. Benjamin dodged as his opponent, a man smaller than himself, threw a snowball at him. He pelted back, the small wiry man dodging and laughing. Out of the corner of his eye, he saw Joseph tackle Sidney Rigdon just as Sidney tried to put snow in Joseph's coat. A snowball glanced the side of Benjamin's head. He fired back then bent down to make another. His opponent attacked, leaping into the air and filling Benjamin's shirt with snow. Old Father Bent, near the campfire, hooted in amusement as the young men rolled over in the snow, until each was thoroughly wet and ready to surrender.

Benjamin scrambled up and looked around. His opponent shook his hand. All around them, men were in good humor and full of mirth. The monotony had broken. The Prophet stood now, watching the fracas with his arm around Sidney Rigdon's shoulder.

"Brother Joseph, look at your pants," a young man called out.

The Prophet looked down to find that his pants were badly torn. He grinned. "While warming up you chilly boys, I've become rather chilly myself." He laughed. Benjamin threw his head back and laughed with the other men. For a brief moment, they forgot the mob gathering and the storm brewing.

13

A whispered word the heart may cheer
And in despair give hope
A look of love may banish fear
And lift the sinking up.

Joel Hills Johnson

October 17, 1838

The morning's snowball fight was a momentary reprieve, like a brief smile before countless tears. As the day lengthened, destitute families flocked into town. The mob, stationed in Millport, burned and pillaged homes throughout the countryside.

Benjamin watched, feeling helpless, gripping Betsy, Ezekiel's silver-trimmed shotgun. He had promised to use her honorably, in defense. But how did a man defend so many: small children with frozen feet wrapped in rags, pregnant women carrying toddlers in their arms, men with angry, defeated eyes, their cattle slaughtered, their crops and belongings destroyed. They found shelter in snowbanks, under trees, and beneath bushes.

Last night's comfortable rest at Sloan's was a distant memory. Benjamin would not be going back. He was a member of the militia. If need be, he would use Betsy to protect the innocent.

"Private Johnson," Captain Seymour Brunson said as he strode up to Benjamin.

Benjamin faced him. "Yes, sir."

"Tonight I want you on guard duty outside Brother Wight's cabin."

"Yes, sir."

"Arthur Millican, our drummer boy, will assist you."

"Yes, sir,"

Brunson turned and began striding toward Lyman Wight's cabin. Benjamin's eyes followed him. A group of men stood outside the door. The Prophet was among them. A man whom Benjamin did not recognize caught his eye. He wore a long bayonet and was dressed in officer's garb, a member of the Missouri militia.

"Captain, who is that?" Benjamin called out to Brunson.

Brunson turned around briskly. "General Hiram Parks. I served under him in the Missouri militia. He was supposed to bring an army here to protect us. Most of them mutinied in Dewitt. The rest when they arrived in Daviess County."

Brunson turned and walked on. Benjamin watched the leaders enter the cabin and close the door behind them. He turned and trudged toward the barn where he had been sleeping, where supplies for the militia were now kept. The sun was low in the sky. He asked the commissary for supper.

The man handed him a slice of bread and a piece of cheese. "This is all any man gets tonight," he said. "We're hemmed in on all sides."

Benjamin thanked him and turned to go. He ate the food, but his stomach still growled. A voice behind him called his name.

"Ben Johnson!"

Benjamin turned as Anson Call walked briskly toward him. Accompanying Anson was Phineas Young, one of Brigham's brothers. Phineas's britches were torn, and it looked as if he hadn't shaved for a week. The men shook Benjamin's hand.

"When did you get in?" Benjamin asked.

"This morning," Anson said. "But it's just me and Phineas. Our families are trapped in Three Forks. We're going back for them as soon as the sun sets. Neil Gilliam and his mobbers are on Grindstone Creek. They don't want us in Adam-ondi-Ahman or Far West. Said they won't harm us if we stay, but will shoot us on sight if we try to leave."

Phineas shook his head and spoke, his voice rueful. "I decided to leave anyway. That's why I'm looking so dandy today. When the mob got wind of it, they came after me. I've been hiding in a cornfield the past four days with Anson bringing me food and water. Yesterday we decided that we'd better risk coming in to Di-Ahman and getting information."

Anson continued. "We crept past the mob last night. We heard that Brigadier General Parks came to protect the Saints. But word is that his militia has joined the mob."

"It's true," Benjamin said bitterly. "Right now Parks is meeting with the Prophet in Brother Wight's cabin. His men deserted him."

Anson gazed at the western sky. The sun was setting, crimson and cold. Anson said, "God willing, we'll be back in a day or two with our families. If we take our wagons out on the northern prairie, we might be able to make it."

"Anson, let's go," Phineas said. "By the time we get through the valley, it'll be dark."

Benjamin watched the two men walk away, their shoulders broad and dark against the setting sun. He walked toward Lyman Wight's cabin.

* * *

It was past eleven, and Benjamin was glad to have company. Arthur Millican, a clean-shaven young man with bushy black eyebrows and dark, wiry hair, took off his gloves and warmed his hands near the fire. The two young men were acquainted. They had known each other in Kirtland and, for a short time, had served together as apprentices in the saddle shop.

"Do you think the enemy will attack tonight?" Arthur asked.

Benjamin shrugged. "We have picket guards down the valley about two miles in every direction. They'll warn us if the mob is coming. We're here to guard General Parks and Brother Joseph."

Arthur stretched his gloves back on. Benjamin noticed that there were holes in the fingertips. Suddenly, he heard a sound to the east, like something dragging through the snow.

"Did you hear that?" Benjamin whispered. Arthur nodded.

They peered eastward, but the night was dark with clouds obscuring the moon and stars. The sound came again, louder now. "I heard that the mob has a cannon," Arthur whispered.

Benjamin raised his rifle. "Who goes there?" he shouted as he fired a shot into the air.

A child screamed. Then Benjamin saw her, a woman staggering out of the darkness. She collapsed to her knees and doubled over. A baby was clutched in her arms. A toddler screamed beside her. Benjamin ran to her. She was a slender thing, shaking uncontrollably, her hair matted, her breathing fast and shallow. Her sopping skirt was turning to ice. The Prophet and others from the cabin sprinted toward them. Benjamin touched her shoulder, and she looked at him. Despite her ragged appearance and the ghostly play of the firelight on her hollow, pain-filled face, he recognized her. She was the beautiful lady that David had hoped to court.

"It's Agnes!" Benjamin cried out. "Don Carlos's Agnes."

* * *

An hour later, Benjamin stood at the door as Agnes told her story. She sat on a stool near the fire, Sister Wight's dress hanging on her, loose and baggy. Though she was wrapped in a quilt, her slender hands continued to shake. Hyrum held her two-year-old daughter in his arms. Sister Wight rocked the baby. Benjamin saw the look of fury in the Prophet's eyes as he listened. Don Carlos was on a mission. Agnes had been alone when the mobbers struck.

"They took hold of me and threw me out into the snow." Her soft voice was the only sound in the cabin. "I ran into the woods while they took the things they wanted from the house. They burned it to the ground. I crossed the river." She squeezed her eyes closed, and tears ran down her cheeks. "It was deep. I almost dropped one of the babies in the water."

"God protected you," Hyrum said gently. "You're safe now."

Agnes began to sob, rocking back and forth on the stool, a plaintive, broken sound. Joseph went to her and knelt by her, taking her shaking hands into his. "Sister Agnes, I will stand between you and harm's way just as Don Carlos would if he were here. If it must be with the sword, then so be it."

Lyman Wight turned to General Parks and said, "What am I to do when you say it imprudent to call upon the militia under my command? And this because of the popular opinion of a mob?"

Brigadier General Parks stared at Agnes's sobbing form. Then he stood. "General Wight, I therefore command you forthwith to raise your companies immediately, and take such course as you may deem best in order to disperse the mob from this county."

Benjamin slipped outside. The snow reflected the moonlight as he walked back to the fire. He explained to Arthur that tomorrow they would fight back. For now, they were allowed to take turns sleeping. Arthur volunteered for the first watch. Benjamin wrapped himself up in the quilt and lay down near the fire. His front side felt burning hot while his backside froze. He lay awake, alternately burning and freezing as he rolled from side to side, thinking of the look in Agnes's eyes when he found her, that look of tension and fear, like an animal that had been beaten.

* * *

October 18, 1838

Pink light rose over the horizon. The fire dwindled to embers. Benjamin glanced at Arthur curled up in a blanket, snoring. He stood and stomped his feet, envious of Arthur's ability to rest in such conditions. Benjamin had endured a sleepless night. As he walked back up to camp, he saw a group of about twenty mounted men. His friend William Huntington was among them. Benjamin jogged up to him. "Where are you going?"

"Come with us and see. Get your colt and catch up," William called out as the company headed north.

Benjamin hurriedly swallowed down a corn cake with a swig of water. The colt, whom he called Jerry, stood still while Benjamin saddled and bridled him. But when Benjamin went to put his foot in the stirrup, Jerry sidestepped, avoiding him. Benjamin staggered and fell, dropping his gun and canteen. Scrambling up, Benjamin bit his tongue. He felt like cursing at the colt and smacking him, but his father's words echoed in his mind. *When you lose your temper with a horse, it generally takes more time to put things right, not less.*

Benjamin let out a deep breath. He stroked the colt, feeling his ribs then running a hand down the long forelegs. The thought struck him that this horse was too young for the heavy work of carrying a man and his supplies, like a boy forced to do a man's labor. Benjamin stroked his nose and said quietly, "I'll be as easy as I can on you. It's just me, my gun, and my canteen. Nothing more."

Another man walked over and stood on the horse's right side while Benjamin mounted on the left. The colt quivered and threw his head in the air but allowed Benjamin to climb on. When Benjamin kicked him forward, he sprang into a gangly gallop, as if he thought running was the fastest way to get this over with. Benjamin leaned forward and directed him north.

Within five minutes, Benjamin caught up to the group of twenty men. William rode near the front. Benjamin fell into rank at the rear behind a youth named Alex as they headed down a trail through the brush along the Grand River.

"Who's in command, and where are we going?" Benjamin asked.

Alex turned around in his saddle. "Seymour Brunson divided the militia into squads who are supposed to root out the mob's ammunition and help the people stuck in Three Forks. Our squad's captain is Cornelius Lott. We'll keep heading north about seven more miles to a place on the Grand River owned by a man named Taylor. If they're storing arms, we'll burn the people out and take what we need. If there's nothing there, we'll leave them in peace."

Benjamin nodded. He thought about the refugees in Adam-ondi-Ahman, about Agnes and all she had suffered. He remembered Joseph's words: "If it must be with the sword, then so be it." This was war, and he had a duty to perform.

By late morning they arrived near the Taylors' property. It was across the river, the house not far from the bank. Benjamin squinted and saw two men dart from the house to a nearby cornfield.

"It's shallow enough to cross!" Captain Lott shouted. "Now!" Icy water flew in arcs as the men galloped their horses into the river. Benjamin's heart beat fast in his chest.

"Men in the fore, surround the house!" Lott ordered when they were on the other side. "Men in the rear, get them!"

Benjamin swung off his horse. He sprinted into the cornfield, knocking over stalks as he raced after one of the men. Suddenly the man doubled back and broke out of the field, heading for the house. As he rounded past a large oak stub, Benjamin darted to one side of the oak, while Alex ran to the other. Alex grabbed hold of one arm while Benjamin grabbed the other.

The man's look of raw terror struck Benjamin. Horrified, the man sank to the ground, losing the contents of his stomach as he begged for his life. He wore linen pantaloons and a wedding ring.

Benjamin loosened his hold and helped the man into a standing position. "Don't be afraid. We haven't come to harm you. We heard that weapons were stored here to be used against our people."

"No, none are here."

Alex said, "If none are here, we'll leave you in peace. If not, we'll burn the house and take the weapons."

"But we won't injure you or your family," Benjamin reiterated.

Two other militia members walked over with a man whom they had captured. Their scarves were pulled up over their mouths, and their guns were pointed squarely at him.

"Search the house and barns," Captain Lott ordered. His wide-brimmed hat shadowed his features. A moment later, two women came out of the house escorted by three members of the militia. One woman was very young and pregnant. Like Delcena, she was near her confinement. She shook like a leaf and was crying. The other woman's jaw was tightly clenched. Three young children clung to her. The oldest child, a little boy about six, broke away from her and ran up to Benjamin, sobbing. "Don't kill my papa!"

Benjamin put his hand on the child's shoulder. "No one will hurt your father. I promise."

The boy spun and raced back to the woman. "He promised, Mama! He promised!" The woman's eyes met Benjamin's, and he saw the fear and pleading in them. Ten minutes passed, quiet except for the rustling of the wind and the crying of the children. Brother Sloan, who owned the boardinghouse, walked up to Captain Lott. "No weapons in the house or barns save this musket and knife."

"Please," the woman with children begged. "We're innocent of your charges. Leave us in peace."

Captain Lott turned away from them. "Search the cornfields," he called out. "Hunt down each shock."

A few minutes later, Benjamin heard William Huntington's whoop. He ran out of a cornfield, shouting, "We found it! A whole cache of guns and ammunition."

Lott turned to the prisoners. "The women may go into the house and get what they can carry out. The others will stay here under guard. Four of you men, take one of the prisoners to saddle their horses."

The mother motioned for her three children to go and stand by their father, the man whom Benjamin had captured. The other prisoner went to the barn under a heavy guard. The women linked arms and walked quickly toward the house, looking straight ahead, the eyes of a dozen men following them.

Ten minutes later, the women came out dragging boxes of food and clothing. There were tears in their eyes. Captain Lott gave his squad permission to enter the house and pack the remaining goods on their own horses. He reminded them that there were hundreds of refugees in Di-Ahman whose homes had been burned and whose belongings had been stolen. This was not plunder. This was survival. Benjamin turned his mind to the children in Adam-ondi-Ahman who shivered beneath snowy bushes, to the helpless terror in Agnes's eyes. He knew the horror of the crimes that had been committed against his people. Then why couldn't he quit thinking about the Taylor women and children who suffered right now in front of him?

When the four horses were brought out, Benjamin helped the prisoners fasten their packs to the saddles. One of the horses was a well-built mare dressed in a fine sidesaddle. She was the intended mount for the pregnant young woman.

Brother Sloan strode over. "I know someone who needs this horse and saddle," he said, taking hold of the reins and leading the mare away.

Tears streamed down the young woman's face, and she bit her lip so hard that it bled. Fury rose within Benjamin. He followed Sloan and tapped him on the shoulder. "Give me the horse."

He looked squarely at Benjamin. "Why?"

"Have mercy. She is near her confinement."

Brother Sloan glared at Benjamin. "Have mercy? Have you forgotten our people's suffering? Have you forgotten Sister Agnes?"

"No!" Benjamin hissed. "But I won't be like those villains! Give her the horse."

"How dare you call me a villain! Whose side are you on?'

"You shame us all!"

"Move aside, boy."

"Give her the horse, or I will move you aside!"

"This is mutiny. Joseph will hear of it!"

"Indeed he will!" Benjamin pushed Sloan away and jerked the horse's reins from his hands.

Brother Sloan staggered back. He turned to Captain Lott and the surrounding men. "Stop him! These people have no rights after what they have done. They would have shot us in the back."

No one spoke for an instant as Benjamin walked the horse toward the prisoners. His face was bright red, and his hands shook with rage.

William turned to the captain. "I think we ought to let Ben be."

Captain Lott looked away from both Benjamin and Brother Sloan and ordered the men to burn the house.

Benjamin took the horse to the young woman. "I'm sorry, but it's our duty," he whispered. "Let me help you up."

She put a shaky arm on his shoulder and stepped into his cupped hands. Benjamin lifted her into the saddle. Then he handed her the reins. The Taylor men were ordered to mount. Benjamin gently handed the children up to them.

"Mister," the little boy said to Benjamin as he sat on the back of the horse with his arms wrapped around his father's waist. "There's a pumpkin with honey in it by the barn. You can have it if you want."

"Hush, Samuel," the father ordered.

It was almost noon, and clouds swelled thick in the sky. Benjamin swallowed, touched by the child's words. It would soon rain or snow. The Taylors had a long way to go before they would find friends or shelter. He gave the mother of the children a leg up. Her dress tore as she went astride the horse.

Benjamin saw a comrade holding a large roll of pillaged homemade cloth—cloth these women had labored to make. Benjamin walked up and took the roll from him. The man nodded and did not argue. Benjamin tied it to the back of the woman's saddle.

As the militia poured kerosene in and around the house, the Taylors rode away. Benjamin's stomach wrung with hunger, and for the first time that day, he realized how tired he was. While flames rose and twisted, Benjamin found the half pumpkin. A beehive was inside. He pulled out some beautiful white comb honey and ate a little as he walked toward his horse.

After the barn was set on fire, Captain Lott ordered the men to mount their horses. Benjamin set the honeycomb on the oak stump near where he had captured Mr. Taylor. This time the colt held absolutely still while Benjamin mounted. His stomach growled. He wished he had time to eat more of the honey.

* * *

On the way home, the company divided in order to scout in different directions. There were ten men in Benjamin's group. The clouds thickened and darkened. Prairie grass rose high around them, rustling in the wind.

Suddenly, a band of stray horses leaped out in front of them. The animals must have been grazing when they heard the company. Their heads lifted high, ears forward, and muscles quivering. The horses galloped away through the tall grasses, forging their own trail. Benjamin's colt whinnied. Other horses called after them. The men halted and calmed their mounts.

"Those are fine-looking animals," William said. He turned to Benjamin. "You've been complaining about your horse. Take your bridle and go get one. I'll halter lead your colt back to Di-Ahman."

Benjamin raised his eyebrows. "I need a horse for heavier service, but who owns those horses?"

William shrugged. "Maybe our own people. They could have run off when their homes were burned."

Benjamin nodded as he dismounted. This was a stroke of luck. Alex and a young man named James with an English accent immediately offered to go with him. Their horses were near twenty years old and wouldn't last much longer. They, too, dismounted and found men to lead their old mounts back home.

Benjamin took off his colt's bridle but left the halter on. He tied a rope to it and handed it to William. Then he gave William his gun. It was heavy and would slow him down.

On foot, the three young men ran down the torn prairie trail blazed by the stray horses. Benjamin led, Alex followed with his musket, and James tripped along behind, his step light and quick.

Hours passed. Benjamin and his companions neared the horses on many occasions, but the animals sensed them first and galloped away before they could be caught. It began to rain: a cold, gray drizzle which would turn to snow over night.

They stopped under an oak tree. "We'd better give it up and head back," Benjamin suggested. He was hungry and exhausted from last night's guard duty coupled with the rigors of the day. The others agreed. They didn't want to be lost at night with mobs roaming the prairie.

As they trudged back the way they had come, Benjamin felt too tired and discouraged to talk. He was the assumed leader of the group, yet he found it difficult to put one foot in front of the other.

"Those horses are like the *ignis fatui,*" James suddenly said.

"The what?" Alex asked.

"The lights on the marshland in Europe. They're always ahead but can never be overtaken. A Russian told me that they are the spirits of babies who died before birth. You can follow them all night but never reach them. Many have lost their way trying."

"I hope we don't lose our way," Alex commented.

"When I was baptized, my father said that it was as stupid as following the *ignis fatui,*" James remarked.

"My father felt the same way," Benjamin said, his mind roving back to Ezekiel. He remembered his father's anger when he had been baptized without permission. And he remembered his father's embrace when he left, the moment when Ezekiel placed the gun in Benjamin's hands. His father would have been proud of him today, of the way he'd helped the young woman. Would he see his father again?

A short time later, they came to a place where the prairie had been trampled in multiple directions. It was growing dark. There was no sunset, just grayness melding into black night without moon or stars to guide them.

"I think this is the way," Benjamin said as they struck a trail. "But I don't know for sure."

His comrades followed in his footsteps through the dark. They walked for hours. Finally Benjamin stopped. "We might be going in the wrong direction. I wish we had a light."

"Alex could light a torch with his musket," James suggested.

Fumbling in the dark, the men bound a bundle of grass together. Alex clicked the trigger of the flintlock musket while Benjamin held the dried grasses to the sparks. The torch ignited, casting light around them. Benjamin's heart sank as he looked around. They were close to a large body of timber. They had not come that way this morning.

"I know this place," Alex whispered. "We're near Grindstone."

Benjamin froze. Had he heard something? Was it his imagination? He immediately doused the light.

"What are you doing?" James hissed.

"I was told that a mob is gathering at Grindstone," Benjamin whispered. "I thought I heard something."

Then they heard and felt it together, the pulse of horses close by, steady and rhythmic. The three young men crouched low and crawled off the trail into the prairie grass. A few rods away, they heard men's voices, some swearing revenge on the Mormons, others calling for caution as they spoke about taking over Mormon lands. Then the voices and the hoofbeats grew distant, fading into silence.

Benjamin stood up. "Let's follow the trail that leads to the timbers. The trees will hide us. I can't go much farther."

Light-headed, Benjamin pushed forward. It must be near midnight. The drizzly mist was icy cold, but it was all that kept him awake. They followed a creek bottom and came to a clearing. Benjamin saw the dark outline of a number of houses. There was no smoke, no light, no sign of animals roaming the yard or of any life at all. The men moved forward slowly and cautiously, crouching low, with Benjamin in the lead. They stopped, tense and silent.

"I'm going to go see if anyone is there," Benjamin whispered. "If they are, I'll ask for food and a place to sleep. I can't go any farther. If I don't come back, either come to my rescue or go report."

"Hurry back," James whispered. Alex was silent. He did not offer Benjamin use of his musket.

Benjamin walked up to the first house and knocked loudly. No one answered. He made his way to the second house and knocked. Still no answer. He walked to the third building. It was a barn full of hay. He made his way back to the first house.

"All's clear," Benjamin called to his companions. His voice sounded like an intrusion. "No one is here."

Alex and James ran to him like dark shadows in the mist.

"The door's barred," Benjamin explained. "Let's check the windows."

Together, they walked around the house, finding the windows barred as well. "We're going to have to force our way in. Alex, hand me your gun." Using the barrel of the musket as both a hammer and a lever, Benjamin butted and pried the window open.

"I guess I'll go in," Benjamin said, thinking that both Alex and James seemed either too cold or too frightened to speak. He put his head through the window and climbed over the windowsill. He felt the floor beneath his feet. It was even darker in the house. He took another step forward and fell headlong into a cellar.

"Ben, are you alive?" James whispered hoarsely after the crashing sound ceased.

Benjamin moaned. "Scarcely. The puncheons must have been pulled up." He crawled to the stairs and stood up. He was bruised but not broken. He could see the outline of the front door, the exterior less dark than the inside. "Come round to the front of the house," he called out to his companions.

Ten minutes later, they were able to start a fire with Alex's gun. They looked around the cabin. "They must have left just a little while ago," James commented. "Everything's here except for the beds, food, and clothing."

"Why do you think they left?" Alex asked.

James's answer was quick and to the point, but the truth of it hit Benjamin like a fist in his stomach. "They probably heard that we torched the Taylors' place."

The old settlers were leaving the countryside because they were afraid of the Mormons. Everyone was afraid. Benjamin saw some deerskins in the corner. With what strength he had left, he pulled them near the fire and lay down. "I can't watch tonight. We might be discovered before morning." Then wet, hungry, tired, and feeling more dead than alive, he tried to say a prayer but fell asleep before the words formed in his mind.

* * *

"Who is there?"

Ben heard the voice in his dreams. Was it Seth calling? Or Joe? Why couldn't they find him?

"Who is there?"

"Me!" Benjamin called out.

"What's your name?"

"Benjamin F. Johnson."

"Shut up," Alex hissed as he rolled over and elbowed Benjamin in the side. Benjamin started and sat up. James's eyes opened, wide and frightened. Alex reached for his gun. The three listened as Benjamin's name was shouted from one man to another. They were surrounded. James closed his eyes, and Benjamin knew he was praying. Benjamin's heart reached out to his Father in Heaven. This was how the Taylors had felt.

"I know him," a deep voice called out above the rest. "This boy's one of ours."

A moment later, the front door opened. The morning light framed John Butler, his large build, dark hair, and light blue eyes the most welcome sight Benjamin had ever beheld.

"Brother Ben," he sang out, "how in the world did y'all end up here?"

Benjamin told Brother Butler about the Taylors' place and how they had been lost after setting out after the horses.

"I should have liked one of those horses myself," Brother Butler commented. "I've borrowed Joseph's horse, Charley, for this commission and shall have to return him when I get back to Di-Ahman."

"How far are we from Di-Ahman?" Benjamin asked.

"About nine miles. You boys nearly made it to the right road. Come on outside, and I'll show y'all."

Benjamin and his companions followed Brother Butler. The Prophet's black horse, Charley, pawed the ground. Benjamin stroked him while Brother Butler spoke to his men. "Go on back to Di-Ahman. I'll stay here with these boys. I owe young Benjamin a debt. He gave me these fine boots."

Ten minutes later, riding Charley, Brother Butler led the three young men about a mile and a half to the edge of the prairie and the smoldering ruins of a house. There were chickens running around and a pile of onions near the well. Brother Butler smiled. "I thought we'd find food here, but we need to hurry."

Benjamin went over to the onions. He was so hungry. His eyes were drawn to the ruined house. Had Captain Brunson found weapons in this place and burned it yesterday? What family had lived here? What was Brother Butler's special commission? He watched as John Butler wrung the chicken's neck and instinctively knew that it wasn't his place to ask these questions. Not here and now. When the war was over, he would talk about it to the Prophet or to Lyman or Almon. Right now people were starving. He was starving. Benjamin peeled the onions with his fingers. Alex already had a fire burning, and James had found a stray pot.

"Cook the food fast, boys," Brother Butler said as he brought over the limp chicken. "Our enemies' camp is nearby."

A short time later, James took the chicken and onions off the fire only half done. "We have to eat to live," he said dryly, "but we had better eat quick if we want to live."

While they ate, Brother Butler walked around the property. He brought back the shell of a gourd filled with salt. "There's a bell cow and a herd of cattle out on the prairie," he announced. "Benjamin, get Charley and follow me. Let's see if we can bring some beef home with us."

Brother Butler jogged toward the bell cow, yelling, "Sook bos! Sook bos!" Benjamin followed, leading the horse. The cow stared at Brother Butler then grunted and started for the salt. He allowed her a lick then took the salt away and mounted Charley. The cow followed Brother Butler. Then forty head of cattle followed her. Benjamin and his companions fell in behind.

When they neared Adam-ondi-Ahman, a cannon fired as if it was saluting them. Brother Butler turned around in his saddle and bellowed, "That, my boys, was the mob's cannon which we discovered and took possession of last night! Our arrival is a godsend indeed! We bring forty head of good beef cattle to a famishing people. Ours is a struggle like Captain Moroni's, for our lives and our families, in defense of freedom and our God-given rights."

As they climbed the hill into the city, Saints gathered round them. Women cried for joy when they saw the cattle. Benjamin felt like a hero. The people would have enough to eat tonight.

An hour later, bone-tired, Benjamin headed for the Huntingtons' cabin to retrieve his horse and gun. On the way he saw a campfire burning near the base of a giant oak. Benjamin looked up. Wrapped in blankets held up by the network of thick branches, he saw a family sleeping. The father sat up and swung down from the tree, leaving his wife and children fast asleep.

Anson Call landed near Benjamin. There were dark circles under his eyes.

"I'm glad you made it," Benjamin said as he shook Anson's hand.

"Me too. We have plenty to thank the Lord for tonight. Our safety." He glanced up at his slumbering family and smiled slightly. "And our accommodations—rather comfortable, considering the circumstances. The trouble is that we had to leave almost everything. There were three families and only one wagon. It's the worst night I've ever had. We inched along, scared that if we moved too fast, the Missourians would hear us. You know John Snider?"

Benjamin nodded. "I've met him." Images rushed into his mind of that day long ago in Ohio when he and Joe had ridden to Anson's land to say good-bye to Almon and Julianne. They'd had breakfast with the Sniders. Joe had noticed their daughter's pretty blue eyes. Joe had told their little boys riddles and jokes. Sister Snider had said she hoped Joe would teach their children someday. A longing for his brother filled Benjamin. Would he ever see Joe again? Would they ever have another bright summer day together?

Anson continued. "John started with us, even pulled his wagon out of the yard. Then he turned back and said he couldn't risk it with his wife and children."

"Do you think he'll make it?" The thought of the Snider family slaughtered sickened Benjamin.

Anson nodded. "I think so. I heard that the mob changed their position when our men went out on the offensive. He'll probably be here by tomorrow morning."

14

When foes combine and Thou art friend
. . . victory is won
Their works of darkness quickly end
Like night before the sun.

Thy praise shall ever be my theme
Thy cause my heart inspires
To glorify thy holy name
Fulfills my chief desire.

Joel Hills Johnson

Far West, Missouri—Sunday, October 21, 1838

The curtains were drawn when Julianne opened her eyes. She wished she could slip back into her dream. Pale sunlight edged around the window. Turning over, she reached for Almon but found him gone. She took a deep, shaky breath. Today was Sunday, and it ought to be a day of peace. Even the mobs would remain quiet on the Sabbath. But Delcena's baby might come. Julianne had spent yesterday helping her sister cook and wash, putting everything in order for the child's arrival. All day she had kept her chin up and had acted cheerful so that Delcena had no idea of her ache inside.

Julianne pulled the quilt close around and closed her eyes, longing for escape. Last night she had dreamed that she was the one holding a new baby in her arms—first it was little David, the baby's eyes so bright; then, in the strange way dreams have of expanding and contracting, she knew it was a girl, her baby daughter. But the dream was gone now, joy evaporated like mist, sent by one's own hopes and fears. Julianne swallowed. If only Almon were next to her, holding her close, causing her to momentarily forget the anger of mobs and the pain of empty arms.

But life went on. It was day now, the Sabbath, with a meeting to go to. Julianne stood and dressed. She brushed her hair and pulled it back into a tight bun. She wrapped her navy cloak around her shoulders. She put her shoes on, stoked the fire, and started the corn mush boiling. When she opened the front door, the day was crisp and clear. She walked outside and found Almon squatting in the yard, sawing rough planks into pieces and nailing them together.

"It's the Sabbath, Almon. Why are you working?" she asked.

He looked up at her, his green eyes as bright as the baby's in her dream. "I'm making a false floor to fit over the opening to the cellar."

She hugged her cloak tightly around her. "But it's the Sabbath."

"When else am I supposed to do it? We're under martial law. Every other day I'm assigned to patrol a road or spy on the enemy's movement. We have to protect our food if the mobs come. We can put this in place, and with the bed and trundle over it, they might not look. If I have enough time, I could nail the floor down."

"But I thought things were getting better. What about the rider who brought word that the mob has been dispersed, that the Prophet and our militia will be home tomorrow?"

"Colonel Hinkle believes our actions at Di-Ahman will inflame the situation. He thinks Joseph made a mistake."

Julianne stood silently, feeling bleak and frightened. Two nights ago, Orson Hyde left Far West, leaving a letter behind explaining his disillusionment. Would this be Kirtland all over again, faithful leaders turning their backs on the Prophet and the Saints? Almon looked down and continued working.

Julianne marched in place to warm her feet. "I keep thinking about Benja. I want him here with us where it's safe."

Almon's hand stilled. He did not look at Julianne but at the new sun in the eastern sky. "Far West isn't safe anymore. I worry about living on the outskirts of town. It's time for you to move in with Delcena and Lyman."

Julianne shook her head. "No. I'll help Delcie during the days, but I'm staying out here with you."

Almon stood up, facing her. "Then if the mob comes, I might have to put you in the cellar and nail the floor down."

Julianne gaped at her husband. "You would bury me alive?"

Almon's eyes were determined. "Don't you understand? I can't be here all the time to protect you."

Julianne stared at the ground, feeling angry and frightened.

Almon studied her and smiled slightly. "You won't obey me any more than your mother obeyed your father. I might have to hog-tie you."

"Almon, this isn't a joke," Julianne snapped. She trembled, ice-cold inside and out.

Almon hugged her, but she was stiff in his arms. He didn't let go. "No, this isn't a joke. I have nightmares of what they might do to you. Angry men hungry for Mormon blood. I have to know you are safe."

Julianne swallowed as her arms encircled her husband. He pulled her closer. "A little longer," she begged. "Let me stay with you a little longer."

Almon stroked her hair. "Perhaps another day or two."

Julianne remembered the pot on the fire. "I have to go or breakfast will burn. Will you be coming to the meeting with me?"

"Not today," Almon said. He kissed her before he let her go.

* * *

Delcena lay on her bed in a cold sweat as the pain passed. Lyman explained that Emma had taken the children after the meeting and that Julianne was here. His lips felt cool and dry as they touched her forehead. "I'll be back when it's over, when the baby has come."

As she looked into his eyes, a moment from years past flitted across her memory. It was the night before Delcena's wedding, when her mother had given birth to her fifteenth child. Delcena had stepped outside on the porch where her father waited, snow swirling around them. "Are you ready for this, princess?" he had asked with fear in his voice as they listened to her mother scream. *Are you ready for this? Birth, death, pain, joy, marriage, children, life? Was anyone ever ready?*

Lyman turned and left. Delcena couldn't think about it—about the mobs beyond their borders, about the terrible whisper in the back of her mind telling her that she didn't have the strength to push this baby out of the womb into the light of day. And if she succeeded, what kind of a world was she bringing this child into? Pain tore through her, a crushing wave then an ebbing tide. *Heavenly Father, help me.*

Julianne walked in with a basin of warm water. She took a damp cloth and wiped Delcena's forehead. Another pain bore down, deeper and unrelenting. "I can't. I can't," Delcena whimpered.

"You can. Bear down!" Julianne commanded.

Hot pain crushed her. Delcena screamed.

"Push!" Julianne cried out. It was so hard, so hard. Julianne stroked her limbs. Delcena heard her sister's voice over the ringing in her ears. "Bear down! Bear down! For the sake of this child, push! Now! Now!" Somewhere in the depth of her being, Delcena found the strength to obey. It felt like time stood still as her baby girl entered the world—a child born on the Sabbath, the day of peace and rest.

The infant screamed. Exhausted and trembling, Delcena watched as Julianne walked over to the basin and washed the baby. Julianne's hands moved so capably, cradling the tiny pink form. Then Delcena saw that her sister wept, warm tears joining the newborn in the water. Julianne lifted the naked infant and wrapped her in a blanket. With tears on her cheeks, she brought her over to Delcena.

"I couldn't have done it without you," Delcena said.

Julianne shook her head. "Yes, you could have."

While Julianne cleaned up, Delcena held her new daughter, realizing that with the Lord's help, she had more strength than she imagined. She examined every part of her. "Susan Julia Sherman," she whispered.

Julianne brought her a drink of water. Delcena took a sip then looked up at her sister. "Do you think Annie will mind another little Susan in the family?"

"No."

Delcena saw that Julianne's face was blotchy from crying. It wasn't like Julianne to weep like this. "Dearest, what is it?" Delcena reached her free hand up toward her sister.

Julianne's jaw trembled. Instead of taking Delcena's hand, she took a handkerchief out of her pocket and wiped her eyes. Julianne tried to smile bravely through her tears. "I-I can't explain. H-her eyes are like Lyman's. I'll go get him." Julianne turned and left the room.

* * *

Lyman hurried to his wife. A new baby when they were on the brink of war . . . would God protect this tiny being, this burden and joy? Would God protect them all? He sat down on the bed next to Delcena.

Delcena handed the baby to him. "She's a girl like I said."

Lyman smiled as he examined the slumbering bundle in his arms, the tiny hands, and the dark shock of hair. "Time will tell if she is as quiet and sweet as you have imagined." The infant stretched and opened her eyes.

"Her eyes are exactly like yours," Delcena said softly.

"I hope not," Lyman said. "Or Susan Julia will have to wear spectacles all her life."

Delcena smiled and sighed. Lyman looked at his wife. She must be tired, yet she looked so alive and at peace. Love filled Lyman, so bright and tangible that it defied war and fear. He held his baby close and sang a hymn to welcome her into the world:

Gently raise the sacred strain,
For the Sabbath's come again,
That man may rest,
And return his thanks to God,
For his blessings to the blest.

Julianne slipped out of the cabin, closing the door softly behind her.

* * *

Wednesday, October 24, 1838

It was eleven at night when Almon and Julianne finished hauling their food and goods into the cellar. The empty cradle was the final item Almon carried down. Tomorrow Julianne would go and stay with Delcena. Almon, at the militia's beck and call, would sleep wherever he could. Almon climbed back out of the cellar. Together they lifted the false floor into place and pushed the bed over it. Almon nailed it down. Then they pushed the trundle underneath, the trundle they had bought when David was a baby, which they had been certain they would need one day.

Julianne poured herself a glass of water while Almon checked his pistols. They were loaded and ready. He looked over at his wife. In the candlelight, her shadow rose against the wall, dark and fragile. Her hair was once again pulled back in a tight bun. It had been weeks since she had curled it. Tonight, she was too exhausted to hold her shoulders erect.

She put the glass down and turned to him. "Can we sleep here tonight?"

Almon nodded. "Yes. It's too late to go into town."

Almon went to the hearth and ran his hand along his musket. When he went on patrol, he took his pistols and his sword, leaving the gun for Julianne. The fire burned down to embers. Earlier in the day, it had looked as if the world were burning, the prairie sky dark with smoke. They had ridden into town to find out what was happening. Word had come that the mob to the south was burning grass and outlying buildings in order to scare the people into leaving their homes so that they could rob and plunder. Almon had decided that it was time to move Julianne into town. They would not wait for the mob. While Almon had organized their valuables in the cellar, Julianne had finished making their cabbage into kraut.

Almon turned and watched Julianne walk over to the bed and kneel down. He knelt down beside her and put his arms around her, listening to her pray, her voice brave and sweet as she begged the Lord to protect them all. They climbed into bed together.

Almon awakened to pounding on the door.

"Julianne," he whispered. "Get down on the other side of the bed." She scrambled to the floor.

He picked up both of his pistols and walked toward the door. "Who's there?" Almon demanded.

"Brother Thompson."

Almon breathed a sigh of relief. He tucked a pistol under his arm and opened the door. Robert Thompson stood before him. A cold blast of air entered the cabin. Julianne arose and lit a fire.

Brother Thompson said, "There's a mob on Log Creek, destroying homes. We think it's Bogart and about seventy-five men. They've taken prisoners: young Nathan Pinkham, William Seely, and Addison Green. They threatened Father Pinkham. He reported that they shot his cow and said they will shoot our boys at dawn. Judge Higbee has issued an order to raise a force to disperse the mob and rescue the brethren."

"I'll get my horse," Almon said. He thought about his cowardice as a boy, about the time when David had wielded his scythe and saved Almon from a beating. Those days were long past. Mormon boys stood together.

When he came back with the horse, Julianne waited at the door. She handed him his overcoat. He buried his pistols in his pockets before stretching into it. The horse snorted. Julianne's teeth chattered from the cold as she belted his sword on him. He felt her hands against his sides and was surprised that they were steady. He stood very still. She walked to the hearth and lifted his musket. She handed it to Almon. "Tonight you need it more than me."

"The enemy is camped a couple miles south of the county line," Brother Thompson explained. "Near Crooked River."

He bid Julianne good-bye. "Try to sleep for a few hours. They won't disturb you tonight. At dawn ride into Far West. I'll meet you there tomorrow afternoon."

"My darling boy." Julianne's hand flew to her mouth. She made a strange sound, a muffled gasp or sob. "Don't get shot. Please."

"My coat is dark, my love. It blends in with the night."

* * *

It seemed more of a dream than reality as Almon rode with his brethren through the darkness. Prairie fires rose in the distance, sending spark-filled columns of smoke into the cold, black sky. Midnight enshrouded them. Swords clanked in their scabbards, and the ground rumbled with the beat of horses' hooves as they cantered across the dry, cracked plain.

When they were within a mile of the enemies' camp, Captain David Patten commanded them to dismount and leave their horses tied to a fence. They divided into three groups. They would take different routes in order to surround the enemy.

"The enemy is camped near the river bank," Captain Patten instructed. "Trust in the Lord for victory." David Patten's white blanket coat stood out against the darkness of the night. "Angels will fight with us this day." But it wasn't day yet, and when the eastern sun rose, it would be at their backs. Was it possible the enemy was unaware of them, or were they marching into their hands?

Almon marched behind Lorenzo Young, one foot after the other, like the tick of a clock. Time never turned back. In front of Lorenzo was a sturdy young man named Patrick O'Bannion. Young Arthur Millican, the militia's drummer boy, followed behind Almon. He carried a gun, not a drum, tonight. Gideon Carter, whom Almon had known when a youth in Amherst, was also close by. Thankfully, Lyman was not with them. He had been detailed to lead a small company north of Far West to guard the road. If Almon did not live through the night, Lyman would protect Julianne. They marched onward, nearing the enemy's picket guard.

"Who approaches?" a voice called out. "Friend or foe?"

"Friend," the captain called back.

"Drop your arms and continue on."

The men clutched their guns more tightly and continued marching. A percussion cap burst from someone's gun, but no shot was fired. Then the crack of the picket guards' rifles split open the morning. Young Patrick O'Bannion fell. Lorenzo Young and John Green broke rank and carried him to the side of the road. Almon continued marching. When the enemy camp was in sight, they formed a line.

"Charge!" Captain Patten shouted. "For our wives and our children! God and Liberty!"

"God and Liberty!" the men shouted. They ran down the hill and clashed with the enemy. Almon snapped his gun twice at a Missourian in a white blanket coat. Had his wife made it for him, just as Ann Patten had made David's? Almon missed. The man dodged out of range while Almon primed his gun.

"Run, you devil, or die!" A large Missourian sprang from the bank of the river with a heavy sword in his hand. He raced toward Almon. Dropping his musket, Almon swept his sword out of the hilt. With quick reflexes, he parried the Missourian's blows. Yet the Missourian was a much larger man and forced Almon back until he could go no farther and stood on a perpendicular riverbank with water gushing ten feet below. The Missourian raised his sword high for one final blow. But before the sword came down, someone hit the Missourian hard in the back. Almon ducked and sidestepped. Men were running amidst the crack of gunfire. The big Missourian leaped down the bank into the water.

A man lay doubled over near Almon. In the darkness Almon could not tell if he was a friend or foe. Gunfire ceased as Almon bent down and spoke to the man. "Which side are you on?"

"God and Liberty," the man whispered before succumbing to silence.

Almon recognized the voice. It was a boy, not a man. He squatted down. "Arthur? Is it you?"

Almon looked into Arthur Millican's face—the thick eyebrows, the smooth chiseled features, the mouth twisted in pain. He was the drummer boy, someone's darling boy.

"My legs," Arthur moaned.

Almon examined the wounds. Arthur had been shot in both thighs. Almon shed his coat and tore his shirt, wrapping the wounds tight to slow the bleeding.

A man ran through the chaos, shouting, "The enemy has fled. Captain Patten is badly wounded! A wagon is being readied for the fallen."

Almon lifted Arthur in his arms as gently as he held his baby son on the day that he had died. He carried him toward the dim outline of a wagon. He saw Lorenzo Young climbing into the wagon with a load of blankets. Two brethren handed Captain Patten up to him. The pink of dawn crept into the sky. Almon waited near the wagon with Arthur in his arms. Captain Patten's white blanket coat was stained with blood. Another wounded man was handed up. Then another. William Seely, one of the Mormon boys whom the Missourians had taken prisoner was among the wounded.

"The devils put him in the line of fire," a man said, answering Almon's questioning look.

Arthur moaned. "I'm afraid to die," he gasped.

Almon spoke with authority. "You're not dying. I stopped the bleeding, and your heartbeat's strong."

"Brother Babbitt, don't leave me."

"I won't."

Almon was motioned over. He carried Arthur close to the wagon and handed him to Lorenzo Young. Arthur gasped and moaned, his face pale in the morning light.

"Grit your teeth, Arthur, and don't be afraid. I'll stay near the wagon. Remember, God and Liberty."

Arthur nodded, and the words were on his lips, though no sound came out of his mouth. *God and Liberty.*

With the rest of the men, Almon walked behind the wagon that bore their wounded and dying. The prisoners had been rescued, but the price of victory was high. Too high. They stopped briefly where their horses were tethered. Before mounting, Almon looked into the wagon. Arthur's eyes were shut, but he breathed steadily. Almon looked around. Patrick O'Bannion was unconscious. James Hendricks had been shot in the neck. Captain Patten was wounded in the abdomen, his torso covered with blood. His eyes were open, but he looked pale as death. Joseph Holbrook had multiple wounds. As they continued to move slowly toward Far West, full daylight spread through the sky. Almon saw Arthur's blood on his hands and shirt and was amazed that he had been able to lift and carry the young man so easily.

* * *

Lyman, with a company of horsemen, accompanied the Prophet, who was in a carriage with Hyrum. There was little talk as they traveled. Shortly after dawn they had received grim word. A battle had been fought. Apostle David Patten and Patrick O'Bannion had mortal wounds. There were other casualties.

They intercepted the company near Log Creek. Joseph and Hyrum left the carriage and climbed into the wagon bearing the wounded. They laid their hands on the head of each man and blessed him. Almon rode up, and Lyman could see the blood on his clothing.

"Are you wounded?" Lyman asked.

Almon shook his head. "No. I carried the drummer boy, Arthur Millican."

"Is there any hope for Elder Patten?"

Almon shook his head again. "No. Nor Patrick O'Bannion."

The Prophet came out of the wagon. "We need to get Brother Patten and two others to a house and bed quickly."

Lyman spoke. "My cousin, Stephen Winchester, lives in the Mirable settlement, two miles from here. He has a comfortable house."

The Prophet nodded. "Good. Some of the wounded are stable enough to continue to Far West in my carriage. But Hyrum and I will accompany the others."

"I'll go with the carriage," Almon offered.

The Prophet turned to him. Grief lined Joseph's features. "Take each man home, except for Arthur Millican. He hasn't a family. Take him to my house. Emma will tend to his wounds."

Four men were helped into the carriage. Together Almon and Lyman lifted Arthur in and propped his legs up as best they could. Almon and another brother climbed into the driver's seat and continued toward Far West. Lyman followed Joseph and Hyrum's group to the Winchesters' home. Once there, the severely wounded were immediately carried inside. Lyman stood near the doorway as women dressed the men's wounds. Ann Patten and Drusilla Hendricks wept by their husbands' sides. Another woman sat beside Patrick O'Bannion as he lay dying.

Sampson Avard, who was also a surgeon, tended to the wounded and dying. Lyman thought of how he had been relieved when Joseph had released Avard from his military duties. Now he watched as Avard worked tirelessly to aid the wounded men and relieve their suffering. Lyman took a deep breath. *How varied are the facets of a man's soul!*

"Ann, don't weep," David Patten whispered weakly to his wife. "I have kept the faith, and my work is done."

The room quieted as Ann ceased crying. She looked into the eyes of her pale husband. "David, do you have anything against anyone?"

A weak smile crossed Patten's lips. "No."

Heber C. Kimball spoke to his fellow Apostle. "Remember me when you go home."

"I will."

"Oh, David," Joseph exclaimed. "You have laid down your life for your friends. How great shall be your reward in the kingdom of God."

Ann stroked David's hair. He looked up at her one last time. "Dear Ann, whatever else you do, do not deny the faith!"

Then he turned to the men surrounding him, the men who bore the priesthood of God. "Your faith is keeping me here. Yet I would go to Christ for it is far better there."

The room grew silent. Tears fell from Lyman's eyes as he prayed for the release of this strong and faithful Apostle of God. David Patten prayed, "Father, I ask Thee in the name of Jesus Christ that Thou wouldst release my spirit and receive it unto Thyself."

A few minutes later David Patten's spirit left his body without a struggle. Ann Patten wept as she held him in her arms. Lyman closed his eyes as a vision opened within his mind. He no longer saw Delcena in the form of the dying Sister Jensen with her newborn in her arms, but he saw her in the form of Sister Patten, weeping beside his own still form. His spirit recoiled. Would he, too, lose his life? This was the second time he had experienced such a premonition. Yet if he had to die, wasn't it best to do so in the service of those he loved? In the service of God? He looked at David's Patten's body. The Apostle was at peace.

* * *

Night had fallen. Almon watched as Sampson Avard took out the tools he would need to remove the bullets from Arthur Millican's thighs. In the adjoining room, Emma bundled up her children. They were far too young for such a sight. Seventeen-year-old Lucy, the youngest sister of the Prophet, sat by Arthur's side. She had spent the afternoon rubbing liniment on his legs in order to keep the blood circulating. Almon had kept his promise and had not left.

Emma opened the door and stepped into the room. She spoke to Almon. "I'll stop at Delcena's and tell Julianne you're here."

"Thank you," Almon said.

Emma glanced over at Arthur as if she were hesitant to leave him.

"I'll wait here until you get back," Almon assured.

Emma nodded. "Lucy, come on," she said.

"I'm not leaving," Lucy responded. "Tell Mother and Father. I'll stay here and wait outside the room until the surgery is over. That's what Mother did when Joseph was little."

Emma took a deep breath and looked carefully at Lucy. "All right," she finally consented. Then she left the house with her children.

A few minutes later, Dr. Avard addressed Lucy. "Miss, it's time for you to leave the room."

Lucy touched Arthur's hand. "My prayers are with you!" she said as she stood up.

Arthur's eyes were fastened on Lucy. She turned and hurried from the room, her hand at her mouth.

Avard spoke to Almon in a low voice. "Tie his legs. Give him something to bite down on and hold his arms. This boy isn't as strong as Captain Patten or O'Bannion. He'll faint before I get the first bullet out. But he'll live to tell the story. They're dead by now."

Fury rose in Almon. He couldn't get David Patten's white blanket coat out of his mind nor O'Bannion's Irish drawl. Why did Patten have to be so fearless? Almon wanted to punch Avard even though this wasn't his fault. "Let's get to it," he muttered.

Arthur did not move while Almon tied his legs down with pieces of cloth. There was innocence in the way he watched Almon, as if Almon were his elder brother or his father, as if all would be well as long as Almon were there. Yet before this day, they had not been close. Almon gave him a whiskey-drenched rag to bite down on. "Scream all you want," Almon advised. "It makes it hurt less. I'll hold you tight, and soon enough the doctor will have the bullets out."

Arthur didn't pass out until Avard started work on his second leg. Almon was sweating profusely when Arthur stilled. Avard finished quickly. He looked at Almon. "The bone is undamaged, and the wounds are clean. He'll be fine."

Avard dressed the wounds and left abruptly. Lucy Smith came back into the room. When she saw the blood, she burst into tears.

"The surgery went well," Almon comforted. "He's sleeping peacefully. With your help, he'll be dancing soon." Lucy controlled her weeping enough to help Almon clean up the blood from the floor.

They had scarcely finished when there was a knock at the door. Almon opened it to find Julianne standing in the frame. Her eyes met his, but she hurried past him and went to Arthur's bedside. She checked the dressings on the wounds and put a hand gently on his forehead. He opened his eyes. "Miss Lucy?"

"No, it's Sister Babbitt." Julianne smiled down at him.

"Is it over?"

"Yes, and you're doing very well."

"How are the others?"

"We'll know more in the morning. Rest now."

Lucy walked over and gave Arthur a sip of water. Julianne went into the kitchen, Almon following her. She turned to him and looked like a different woman from the confident nurse she had been a moment ago. She put her hands to her face and whimpered. "Brother Patten and Patrick O'Bannion have died."

Almon nodded grimly.

"And Brother Carter." Julianne's jaw trembled.

Almon stared at her. "But Gideon wasn't among the wounded."

Tears streamed down Julianne's face. "Someone went back to the battleground. They found his body. He had been shot in the face."

Almon's heart pounded. He had known Gideon ever since he was a child. He felt inexpressibly weary. He reached for Julianne.

She shook her head. "I can't." She squeezed her eyes shut. "I have to help. If you touch me right now, I'll break apart."

Julianne turned and placed a log on the fire. Almon sat down. Brother Carter from old Amherst. Gideon had been left behind.

15

Takes his leave with broken heart
Weeping at the parting kiss.
Turns to go, and finds at last
Something that has slipped his mind
Turns again, his eyes to cast
On his darling left behind.

Joel Hills Johnson

Far West, Missouri—Tuesday, October 30, 1838

Delcena gazed out the window. Gray mist shrouded the sky at early candlelight. The drumbeat echoed throughout the city. Delcena shuddered. It had started half an hour ago, the call for the men to come to the public square. Lyman and Almon had immediately donned their coats and arms. Julianne and Albey had followed—Julianne to bring back news; Albey because he was restless and needed to get out of the house.

The door burst open with a blast of cold air. "Mama!" Albey shouted. "They're marching toward us. We got to get to the square!"

Delcena pulled Albey to her. He shook with excitement, his new scarf wrapped snugly around his neck. It was his sixth birthday. A sob escaped her. *Dear Heavenly Father, help us!*

"Everybody has guns and pistols, Mama. And swords. I want a sword."

"Get your brothers' blankets, Albey," Delcena said. Then she picked up her newborn and put her in a sling around her shoulder.

Julianne entered, her cheeks reddened from the wind. "There's an army a mile away. We have to leave quickly and get to the public square. The men are forming a line. If they attack, we're safer there."

"But General Atchison has always tried to protect us."

Julianne's jaw quavered. "Atchison has been relieved of command. Lucas is in charge until General Clark arrives."

"How many?"

"A thousand. Maybe two."

Delcena spun around to her girls who had stopped in the middle of their checkers game. "Alvira, get Seth." Delcena's heart pounded. *A thousand, maybe two.* "Mary, get some quilts. We're going to the square."

"I won't, Mama!" Alvira said loudly.

"Don't argue. Please!"

"I want to stay home."

Delcena put her hands on her nine-year-old's shoulders. "Don't you understand? We have to do what the Prophet and Papa say!"

Alvira burst into tears. Seven-year-old Mary ran and picked up two-year-old Seth. He was a large child, and his legs dangled as she carried him. He began coughing and crying. Mary put him down and hid her face in her small hands. "Bo Peep!" she said as she peeked out of her hands. Seth laughed.

"Mary, stop playing! Get the quilts!" Delcena said sharply. Mary's face crumbled, but she complied.

Delcena lifted Daniel, who had fallen asleep near the fire. He had a runny nose and was teething. Yesterday he had taken his first step, and they had all cheered. He woke up and tried to push away the baby in the sling. Delcena repositioned him on her hip.

What if Lyman is killed tonight? What if the mob crushes the brethren and ransacks the city? What will they do to us? Delcena's body shook. She felt like she would throw up.

Julianne piled blankets into the children's arms and put two loaves of bread in a sack that she tied at her waist. She picked up Seth, who sat on the floor wailing. The women and children huddled together and went outside. Twenty minutes later they arrived at the public square to find it filled with terrified women and children. They found a narrow spot on the cold ground and sat down, wrapping the blankets around them. The wail of infants drowned out the beat of the drum.

* * *

Lyman's gun was drilled at the approaching enemy. Almon stood next to him, his hands steady and his green eyes fierce. Lyman knew that they were outnumbered four to one. He also knew that if the enemy attacked, each

Mormon would have the strength of five men. God was with them as their wives and children waited behind them on the public square.

"Steady," Hinkle cautioned. "Don't fire the first shot. This might turn out to be a warning, not an attack."

The enemy advanced to within a rifle's shot then halted. They stared at each other, the mob-militia and the Mormon brethren. Lyman's eyes became dry as the sky grew darker. Finally, the mob was ordered to retire to the timber and camp for the night.

* * *

As Delcena nursed the baby, there was chaos in the loft.

"I'm not going to bed," Albey yelled. "It's my birthday! I want to help Papa and Uncle Almon."

"Are they gonna shoot us tonight?" Mary whimpered.

"No!" Alvira said tersely. "Papa said they went to bed in their tents. Don't you remember anything?"

Delcena didn't speak. She kept rocking and nursing her newborn. Julianne paced the floor with Daniel in her arms. Delcena looked over and saw that Daniel was drifting to sleep. Julianne laid him down by Seth, who was curled up near the fire.

The men walked in, their gaits quick and faces grim. Lyman looked at Delcena. "We've hitched up the horses. We're taking Almon's wagon and using it as part of the barricade."

He turned to Almon. "I'll get the barrel in the corner. You bring the house logs."

"How will we keep the children warm if you take the logs?" Delcena asked.

"We'll only take an armful. Where are your embroidery hoops?"

"In the bottom drawer. Why?"

"We're making spears, using the hoops for handles. We'll be at the blacksmith shop tonight unless they need us for guard duty."

"Papa, bring me back a spear!" Albey called out from the loft.

"That's stupid, Albey!" Alvira retorted. "Be quiet!"

"You're stupid!"

"Albey hit me!" Alvira yelled. Mary started sobbing.

"The three of you quit this instant or I'll . . ." Then Lyman abruptly stopped speaking. Delcena looked at him. He stood frozen, staring at the loft. He lifted the lantern and walked over. He stepped up on the ladder.

"Who you gonna spank first?" Albey asked as the light illuminated the children's faces. Mary sobbed brokenly.

"You shouldn't spank Mary," Albey added. "She didn't do nothin'."

"*Anything.* She didn't do *anything,*" Lyman responded with a catch in his voice as he reached out and stroked Mary's fair hair. He continued speaking to his son. "I know it's your birthday, but the spears are for the men."

"I want to go with you."

"You stay here and take care of Mama. When this is over, we'll have a birthday party."

"With Joseph and his Papa?"

Lyman swallowed. "If they can come."

"When will you be home?" Mary gulped.

"In the morning."

"Why are you crying, Papa?" Mary whispered.

"Because you are so beautiful."

Alvira choked, her voice small and confused. "Don't go," she begged. Then she began sobbing even more brokenly than Mary. "Stay here! Please, Papa."

Lyman wrapped his arms around her. "I can't. I have a duty to perform. And now you must be big enough to have faith in God and to help Mama. That's the way to move mountains. When I'm not here, the Lord Jesus will protect you. Promise me you'll remember that."

Alvira wailed. "I can't!"

Lyman kissed Alvira's forehead. "You can, Allie. You will."

Lyman turned around and left the loft. He picked up the barrel and motioned for Delcena to follow him outside where Almon and Julianne waited.

Lyman, Almon, and Julianne loaded the barrel and logs into the wagon. Delcena shook as she held the baby. Lyman wrapped his arms around her. Almon took his pistols out of his pockets and handed them to Julianne.

She took a step backward. "No. I-I can't use these."

"Take them anyway. We'll be back at dawn."

* * *

Far West—October 31, 1838

Lyman's fists clenched in rage as he stood at guard duty in the darkness and pouring rain. He had watched as Joseph, Sidney Rigdon, Lyman Wight, Parley P. Pratt, and George Robinson were led up Eminence Hill by Colonel Hinkle. Joseph had briefly embraced Lyman, explaining that they were going to negotiate. "Pray that this can be settled without bloodshed," the Prophet had said. Then Hinkle had betrayed them. Lyman had heard Hinkle's words to General Samuel Lucas: "These are the prisoners I agreed to deliver up." Then Joseph and the brethren had been swallowed by the screaming, taunting mob.

Now, an hour later, Lyman could still hear the cries of the mob in the distance. They were human hyenas circling their prey, laughing, taunting, and cursing. His prophet, his friend, was a lamb in their hands. Lyman, who would give his life for Joseph, could do nothing. Lyman had to remain on guard duty while Joseph lay in the mud and rain at Goose Creek Camp. But how could any guard protect a body of people after their heart was taken from them?

A man approached Lyman. "Brother Sherman."

Lyman spun at Colonel Hinkle's voice. Rage, raw and consuming, caused the blood to pound in his brain.

Hinkle spoke again. "I'd like a word with you."

"I'd break your neck as soon as speak to you," Lyman hissed.

Hinkle gritted his teeth. "Tonight I will forgive insubordination."

"Are you forgiving treason as well?"

"Blast you, Sherman, they have an extermination order signed by Governor Boggs. We're to leave the state or be killed. Reinforcements are arriving tomorrow morning. There will be seven thousand of them. They would utterly obliterate us."

"Some of us would rather die than become Judas Iscariot."

"Would you rather have your wife and children die as well? Did you hear what happened at Haun's Mill yesterday? They slaughtered our people: men, women, and children."

Lyman shook, the rage inside him turning into something ice-cold and tremulous. He had not heard. Hinkle went on. "They said it wasn't the militia but a vigilante group. If we agreed to their terms, they promised to protect us while we leave the state of Missouri. Before I left to parley with them this morning, Joseph said to beg like a dog for peace."

"He did not know they would take him prisoner!"

"I couldn't risk telling him. Lucas has promised to release the prisoners if Joseph does not agree to the terms. If that is the case, he will come back, and we'll fight."

"They'll shoot him before they return him to us."

"He's a private citizen, not subject to court-martial."

"What are their terms?"

"That we give up the Mormon leaders to be tried and punished. That we sign away our property to pay for damage done by Mormons. That we give up all arms and leave the state."

"And you agreed to that?"

"No. I only gave them our leading men. The rest is up to Joseph."

Lyman stood silently, his jaw tight. Maybe Hinkle was trying to save the people, but the searing pain in Lyman's heart had not diminished; he could not forgive George Hinkle for leading Joseph into a trap.

Hinkle spoke once more. "They want all of the men in the Battle of Crooked Creek to be tried for murder."

"Did you give them a list?" Lyman asked bitterly.

"No!" Hinkle burst out. "That's why I'm talking to you! We must hide the wounded and get the able-bodied out of Far West tonight. The mob is so ecstatic about Joseph's capture that there is a chance of escape."

* * *

"I'm taking Arthur Millican out of the city, to our land. I'll be back as soon as I can," Almon said as he and Julianne stood behind a curtain in the corner of Lyman's house, the mattress that they slept on at their feet. Outside, rain fell in torrents. A few moments ago, Lyman had come with dire news: the Prophet and leaders had been taken captive, and those who fought at Crooked River were in danger. They needed to get the wounded into hiding and the others out of town. Following the warning, Lyman had left immediately to return to duty.

"I-I don't want you to come back here," Julinanne said. "Stay in hiding with Arthur."

Almon shook his head. "That won't work. I have to put the false floor and furniture into place so Arthur has a chance."

Julianne's voice was very soft. "I could do that."

"It's far too dangerous."

Julianne's voice was louder now. "Then flee after Arthur is secure. You can't come back here."

Their conversation was interrupted by a knock on the front door. Almon turned, parted the curtain, and walked toward it. Julianne followed. The only light in the room was the glow of the diminishing fire. They walked past the bed where Delcena slept with Baby Susan. Almon went to the door and looked out.

Brigham Young stood before him, the night black behind him. Brigham's directive was clear and decisive. "Meet Lorenzo and the other men at my house in sixty minutes. Phineas is a master woodsman and will pilot the group."

"I can't make it in time. I'm taking Arthur Millican to my property to hide him in the cellar."

"Then go quickly. I'll tell the men to wait until you come." Brigham was gone before Almon could protest or discuss.

Almon turned to Julianne and pulled her to him. His voice caught in his throat. "In the name of heaven, how can I leave you?"

"For my sake," Julianne begged, clinging to him. Almon took a deep breath. He had to let her go, to move his feet, to get Arthur. But when would he hold her again? This moment would not last any more than Missouri was their Zion.

Julianne spoke as if reading his thoughts. "We'll be together again. God will not forsake us."

But what of Gideon Carter's family? For one of the few times in his life, Almon could not find words to express his emotions.

Julianne trembled, begging him, "Please, please go. The Lord will protect us."

There was an edge of bitterness in his voice. "You still have faith after all of this?"

"Mobs and persecution don't change the truth."

"But what if they kill Joseph? What will happen to your faith then?"

Julianne's voice did not quaver. "Another will be raised up to lead the Church. Nothing will stop this work. Oh, Almon, don't you believe that?"

Bitter tears stung Almon's eyes. "I'm trying to."

Julianne wrapped her arms tighter around him. "Please go, Almon. You need to leave tonight. I know it."

Almon took a deep breath. Julianne was so much better than he was. He could preach the gospel, but her faith and goodness were bound to Jesus' teachings. How could he leave her here alone?

She spoke again. "If you never do anything else for me, do this tonight."

Almon swallowed. He would obey her. "I'll go."

Julianne closed her eyes, taking deep breaths of relief.

Almon stroked her hair. "My brother John wrote that he is working in Fort Leavenworth. I'll get word to him of my whereabouts. If you have to leave before I get back, try to let John know. He can be a rascal, but he will help us. Keep the pistols close by. Lyman will protect you."

"May God go with you." Julianne kissed him.

Almon's heart thudded in his chest. He stepped away from his wife, feeling as if he were fighting against gravity. He put on his coat, and Julianne handed him his rifle. He placed his hand on her cheek, feeling the damp tears sliding silently from her eyes.

"Until we meet again, my darling," he said as he stepped out the door.

Almon ran through the pouring rain. When he arrived at the Smiths', Emma answered the door, her face haggard from grief and sleeplessness. Once in a blessing, Joseph had called Almon a son of consolation. Were there any words that could console Emma this night?

"I've come for Arthur," Almon said gently. "I'm taking him to my land. I have a cellar with a false floor hiding it."

Emma's arms were folded, and she shivered with cold. "Hyrum told me. Afterward are you leaving with the others?"

Almon nodded. "Is Hyrum coming?"

Emma shook her head. "He would rather stay with Mary or be taken prisoner with Joseph." Emma gasped as she stifled a sob.

"God will protect him," Almon said quickly. "Lucas is not the only general. Doniphan is here too."

Emma swallowed and hugged her arms more tightly against her body. Then they both turned at the sound of Arthur limping toward them, a cane in one hand and a grimace of pain and determination on his face. "I can walk now, Brother Babbitt."

"Good," Almon said, crouching down. "Climb on my back."

* * *

Almon moved through the darkness with the weight of a man on his back, first walking then crawling as he carried Arthur past the enemy camp. Joseph lay somewhere there, surrounded by guards, shivering on the ground in the miserable rain. They traversed fields without moon or starlight to guide them. When they arrived at the house, Almon found it in one piece, not burned or ransacked.

After helping Arthur in, Almon lit a candle. Even the furniture was untouched. Almon went downstairs and made a bed for Arthur in the cellar. Then he carried Arthur down. The young man was cold and wet, his wounds bleeding from the trauma of the journey. Almon found the quilt Julianne had made for their son and handed it to Arthur. Almon pointed out the food, the lantern, and the jug of water—everything that he had put in place for a night such as this.

"I won't nail the floor down, but I'll put the rug and bed over it. You can get out if you need to. Good luck, my friend," Almon said as he shook Arthur's hand.

"Thank you, Brother Babbitt."

"May God be with you."

Then Almon closed up the cellar and ran through the wet darkness toward Brigham Young's home. He felt strangely light without a man on his back, yet his legs and back were sore. Almon knew that from that day forward, he would have greater compassion for his horse.

* * *

Thursday, November 1, 1838

At dawn, after three short hours of sleep, Lyman joined the men of Far West at the barricade line. This time Almon was not at his side. They stood behind wagons, barrels, and logs, pointing their muskets at the enemy—the mob-militia marching toward them.

"Don't shoot until you see the whites of their eyes," the captain ordered. "Then do the best you can."

The enemy stopped within rifle shot. The two armies stared at each other, ready to destroy. The Prophet was their prisoner, and this was the final showdown. Lyman's heart thudded in his chest. *I've never killed a man. This is not the way I had hoped to die. What of the converted Lamanites who dropped their swords at the feet of their enemies? The people of Haun's Mill did not have the chance to fight back. I stand between a ruthless mob and my wife and children. I will give my life as David Patten. For Joseph. For my family. For God. There are angels standing with us this day.*

"Lower your weapons!" a messenger said as he ran down the line. "Joseph says to surrender. He would rather go to prison for twenty years or die himself than have the people exterminated."

The blood drained from Lyman's face. The men were silent as death. Slowly, mechanically, Lyman lowered his gun.

The mob formed a hollow square. At the sound of muffled drums, the Mormon men were marched into the square. Each man with a spear thrust it into the ground, breaking off the point and dropping the handle.

When they were all in the square, the general barked out a command. "Throw your weapons down. Sit on the ground, facing inward."

Lyman sat for two hours with his brethren, staring at their firearms littered on the dirt before them, wondering if they would be shot in the back. Missourians swore and boasted about hunting Mormons down like wild animals, about ravaging their women. Others told their comrades to shut up—wasn't it enough that the Mormons were prisoners? Lyman prayed, remembering the revelation Joseph had received years ago, the olive leaf which told of how Moses beheld the God of Heaven weeping, like rain upon the mountains, because men, the sons of God, destroyed one another.

Around noon, the Mormon men were told to stand. They were marched away from their firearms, back into Far West, where they were herded into the public square and placed under a heavy guard. The Mormon men watched in horrified silence as Lucas ordered the exultant mob to search the city for weapons. Over a thousand armed men streamed down their streets, where their wives and children prayed in their log homes, terrified and unprotected. Lyman moaned. *God in heaven, send angels to protect them. Dear God, send angels.*

* * *

Delcena was in the rocking chair, having just finished nursing her infant daughter, when the door was kicked open. Julianne ran to stand next to her. Alriva and Mary grabbed the little boys and crowded behind them, just as they had planned. *Heavenly Father, help us!* Delcena cried inwardly. *Dear God, where is Albey?*

The first Missourian tipped his hat. His face was blackened with soot. "Howdy, ladies. We've come to collect your weapons."

Delcena's mind spun. *One pistol was in a pocket beneath Julianne's skirt. Where was the other? Where was Albey?*

"Cat got your tongues?" The Missourian eyed Delcena, his eyes narrowing as he focused on the infant in her arms. "Your husband one of those men out in the square?"

"Yes," Delcena whispered.

The man laughed, cleared his throat, and spit on the carpet. "Bet you're hopin' he don't get shot today." His gaze shifted to Julianne. "What about you, miss? You got a husband out there?"

"No." Julianne looked at the cabin floor.

"You married?"

Julianne hesitated then said, "No, sir."

"Just think of that. I ain't married either. How 'bout you come with me and we get married today." He reached out to touch Julianne's cheek.

The other man stepped forward. "Pete, search the cupboards for weapons."

"Hang on, Henry. General Lucas won't mind a bit if we have some fun. Look how she stands so straight when she's scared to death. You search the cupboard for weapons while I take her behind that curtain."

The second man shook his head. "No."

Suddenly Albey stepped out from behind the curtain. The pistol in his hand was pointed straight at the Missourian. "Get out of my house!"

"Son, put the pistol down," Delcena begged.

The six-year-old looked at his mother. "I won't."

The Missourian grabbed the pistol out of the boy's hands and smacked it across his face. Albey crumpled, and Delcena screamed. The man raised the pistol once more. As he swung back to hit Albey again, Julianne lunged forward. The pistol hit the small of her back, knocking her off balance. She fell and crawled to Albey.

"Enough!" the other man shouted.

The Missourian turned around and gaped at his companion. "You a Mormon lover?"

"General Doniphan will court-martial men who abuse women and children. These people have a wagon outside. We'll load it with provisions and whatever else we want. But leave them be."

The Missourians ravaged the house. Then they went outside and shot the cow to haul away as meat for the troops. When they had finished, the first Missourian doffed his hat at Delcena as tears streamed down her cheeks. He grinned savagely at Julianne as she cradled Albey's bloodied head in her lap. "No hard feelings, ladies."

* * *

Late that night, Lyman was released to his family with the order to come back into the square at the sound of the drum the following morning. When he opened the door, ashes glowed in the hearth. He could not stop shaking from the cold. In the darkness, he stumbled over to the fireplace and put a log on. It caught flame and he saw Delcena lying in their bed with the three babies. Alvira and Mary slept fitfully on the floor by her feet. Julianne rested on a mattress with Albey. A torn curtain covered them like a thin blanket.

"Lyman?" Delcena opened her eyes, her voice fragile in the darkness.

"Yes." He was so tired that he could scarcely stand.

She crawled out of bed. She went to him with shoulders bent, shaking like an old woman. He held her for a moment. "I have to eat," he whispered.

"There's beans and corn in the pot. I'll get you a bowlful."

While he ate, she told him what the Missourians had done and how they had stolen their provisions except for one barrel of beans and one of corn.

Lyman closed his eyes for a moment. "God has protected you. He has answered my prayers."

Delcena moved the baby boys onto the floor so that Lyman could lie down. But first, Lyman walked over to Albey and examined his wound. Albey winced at the touch and jerked, flinging his arms like he was fighting.

"Papa's here," Lyman whispered, "to bless his brave boy." He put the bandage back on and laid his hands on Albey's head, beseeching the Lord to shield and guide his son.

Julianne awoke and sat up, cringing in pain. "Any word about Almon's group or Arthur?"

Lyman shook his head. "No, thankfully. I'll give you a blessing like Almon would if he were here." Lyman laid his hands on her head and blessed her to heal quickly.

Delcena walked over and kneaded Lyman's shoulders. "What of the Prophet and the others?"

"They arrested Hyrum and Amasa Lyman this morning." Lyman shut his eyes. "There's talk that they'll be either shot or moved to Jackson County. No one knows what will happen."

* * *

Before dawn the next morning, a messenger stopped by with news. Last night at midnight, General Lucas held a court-martial and sentenced Joseph and the other prisoners to be shot by General Doniphan's troops at nine o'clock in the morning. But Doniphan's response had stopped Lucas short:

"It is cold-blooded murder. I will not obey your order. My brigade shall march for Liberty tomorrow morning, at eight o'clock; and if you execute these men, I will hold you responsible before an earthly tribunal, so help me God."

"It was the fear of Doniphan that kept the Missourians from doing worse to us as well," Julianne said, her voice breaking. Delcena reached out and held her hand.

After the messenger left, Lyman knelt with his family. He thanked the Lord for Alexander Doniphan, who had integrity enough to be an instrument in God's hand to save the life of the Prophet and to care about a suffering people. When they arose, it was still dark outside. Lyman swallowed down a few more spoonfuls of boiled beans and corn. Then he turned to Delcena. "I'm going to check on Emma before the drums start."

Delcena stood up and handed the baby to Julianne. "I'm going with you."

"I'm going too," Albey called out. He sounded no worse for wear, despite his injury. "I want to play with Joseph."

Delcena spun toward Albey, her voice fiercer than Lyman had ever heard before. "Stay with Aunt Julianne! Don't you dare take one step out of this house."

* * *

The drum started beating when Delcena and Lyman were scarcely out of the door. "Hurry!" Lyman said as he put his arm around her and they ran toward the Prophet's house.

The door was ajar. Lyman pulled Delcena back when they saw the guards inside. But not before she saw the form of Joseph. Emma and the children clung to him weeping. Delcena put her arm in her mouth to stifle her own sobs.

"Father, Father," little Joseph cried out. "Why can't you stay with us? Father, what are the men going to do with you?"

Delcena heard the clank of a sword drawn from the scabbard and the harsh voice of a guard. "Curse you! Get away, you little rascal, or I will run you through."

Delcena's knees buckled. Only Lyman's arms held her up. A moment later, Joseph was taken from the house, surrounded by the guards. He carried a small bundle of clothes.

"God bless you!" Joseph cried with tears running down his face as he took a last look at his family.

The drumbeat continued.

"They're taking him away," Delcena sobbed, clinging to Lyman. There were tears in his eyes. The drums reverberated as soldiers began to sweep through the streets.

"I have to go," Lyman said, "or they will shoot me."

Delcena let go of her husband. She wiped her eyes on her sleeve.

"Go to Emma," Lyman instructed. "Tell her that as soon as I can, I will follow Joseph. If heaven allows, I will foil any plot laid against him." Then Lyman was gone, walking quickly toward the public square.

Delcena ran into the Smith cabin. Emma fell into her arms.

"My husband," Emma wept. "What will they do to him?!" The children cried uncontrollably.

Delcena cradled Emma tightly, and the two women rocked back and forth in grief.

16

My foes have lies against me forged,
And have in wrath combined
To take my life and have me charged
With sins I ne'er designed

From such ungodly, cruel foes
My safety, Lord, provide.
Since childhood I have always chose
Thee for my God and guide.

Joel Hills Johnson

November 3, 1838

Almon awoke, shaking with cold, in a foot of snow. His stomach growled as snow flurried around him. The twenty men with him were no better off. They had all fled without horses or food, with only their guns and the clothes on their backs.

Some were grateful that they now had meager provisions. Two mornings ago, they had stopped in a clump of hazel brush near Adam-ondi-Ahman. Two men had been sent into town to warn the Saints. The men had returned to camp with a fifty-pound bag of cornmeal. Yet it was far too little to feed twenty men on a 350-mile journey.

Almon stood up and moved his chilled limbs. He watched Lorenzo Young, standing beside the fire, cooking cornbread in a large tin pan. They would each receive a four-inch square piece this morning and another in the evening. Who would perish first from cold or starvation?

"This snow is a blessing," Phineas Young commented as the men gathered around to receive their bite to eat. "The soldiers General Clark sent after us won't be able to follow our tracks."

Almon swallowed the hard, bland food, nearly coughing it up. He drank a bit of water. If he was going to leave, now was the time. If he were captured, the mob wouldn't be able to follow his tracks to the rest of the men. He spoke loud enough for all to hear. "I'm heading out on my own. I'd rather risk falling into the hands of our enemies than freeze or starve. I'll aim for the settlements below Clark's army, pretending I'm a gentleman from the East looking for a place to settle my family in the spring."

"You really think you can waltz into a Missourian's house without a horse or supplies? They'll peg you. You'll be court-martialed and shot."

Almon let out a sharp breath. "Not if I'm lucky. I'll think up a good story. Tell them my horse was stolen."

The men were silent for a moment, digesting Almon's words. He continued. "I plan to cross the Missouri River then double around. I might head toward Fort Leavenworth. I have a brother there. He wrote that they'll hire anyone: free Negroes, Indians, even Mormons. Maybe I'll work for a while. When things settle down, I'll go back to Far West and get my wife."

"You want company?" a man asked.

Almon shook his head. "No. I'd rather go it alone. Attract less attention. But others could head off toward the eastern settlements—either alone or in pairs. Use a false name and make sure that you keep your story straight."

Almon picked up his gun. As he started off through the snow, he thought of how Phineas hadn't offered to send any cornmeal with him. He didn't blame him.

Lorenzo called out, "When you make up your story, don't say it was the Mormons that stole your horse. And, may God protect you."

Almon laughed and turned around, waving his arm through the blur of snow. "Farewell, brethren. We will meet again."

* * *

Tuesday, November 6, 1838

Clouds crowded in the sky and a chill wind blew. At the sound of the drumbeat, Lyman lined up with the other men of Far West in the public square. Missourians drilled their guns at them, reminding them that they were prisoners, not citizens, reminding them that their goods could be plundered, their women raped, and their children abused at the militia's pleasure.

Yesterday, when they had been lined up in this same manner, the names of fifty men had been read. Those men had been arrested with no idea of what crimes they had committed. Would Lyman's name be read today?

Major General Clark cleared his throat. His voice rose as he spoke, his eyes glancing occasionally at the papers in his hands.

"Gentleman, you whose names were not attached to that list of names read yesterday will now have the privilege of going to your fields and providing corn, wood, and so forth for your families. Those who have been taken will go from this to prison, be tried, and receive the due demerit of their crimes. But you are now at liberty, as soon as the troops are removed that now guard the place, which I shall cause to be done immediately."

Liberty. The word staggered Lyman. Where was liberty when you had been robbed and abused, when your friends were shot and your prophet taken prisoner, when you were forced to leave your land or be murdered if you refused? Yet now he would have a bit of freedom. He could move his family to Almon's land, tucked away in the trees and less visible to marauders. They would have food there, and they could care for Arthur Millican until he regained his strength.

General Clark continued to speak, and as he did so, Lyman wondered how many of the lies the general actually believed. "The orders of the governor to me were that you should be exterminated and not allowed to remain in the state, and had your leaders not been given up, and the treaty complied with before this, you and your families would have been destroyed and your houses in ashes.

"There is a discretionary power vested in my hands which I shall exercise in your favor for a season; for this lenity you are indebted to my clemency. I do not say that you shall go now, you may stay here for the winter. But you must not think of putting in crops, for the moment you do this the old citizens will be upon you. If I am called here again, in case of a noncompliance of a treaty made, do not think that I shall act any more as I have done—you need not expect any mercy, but extermination, for I am determined the governor's order shall be executed. As for your leaders, do not once think—do not imagine for a moment—do not let it enter your mind that they will be delivered, or that you will see their faces again, for their fate is fixed—their die is cast—their doom is sealed.

"I am sorry, gentlemen, to see so great a number of apparently intelligent men found in the situation that you are; and oh! That I could invoke that Great Spirit, the unknown God, to rest upon you, and make you sufficiently intelligent to break that chain of superstition, and liberate you from those fetters of fanaticism with which you are bound—that you no longer worship a man."

Lyman took a deep breath. He did not worship a man. Joseph was a mortal man, a beloved friend. Lyman's fists clenched. He would obey Clark on one account; he would not *imagine* that he would see his leaders again. Instead, he would *go* to them. He would see Joseph and help him, even if it cost his life. For it was through this Prophet that God was made known to Lyman, not as some great spirit or unknown being, but as two distinct personages: a Father who succored His children in their needs, and a Savior who gave His life in the past and spoke to a prophet in the present. Lyman did not fear to leave his family in the hands of such a God.

* * *

Adam-ondi-Ahman—November 7, 1838

It was nearly two in the morning as Benjamin stood guard two miles from the city, down in the Di-Ahman valley. An icy wind blew flurries of snow. The thick, shoulder-high prairie burned on the opposite side of the road. The fire reached the sky, illuminating the dark clouds above. He gripped Old Betsy, his father's gun. The inlayed silver on the rifle reflected the crimson flames.

It was difficult doing his duty in the smoke and freezing wind. He felt more lonesome and afraid than ever before in his life. He did not know what Clark's and Lucas's militias had done to the Saints in Far West—to his sisters and their families. He trembled when he thought of Brother Joseph, who had been taken captive. Was he alive?

Suddenly, Benjamin jolted to attention. He heard the crunch of horse hooves on the hard prairie and the rhythmic hum of wagon wheels. He left the open road and moved toward the woodland.

"Who goes there?" he shouted a few moments later as the wagon and horsemen approached.

"A family of refugees from Far West."

Benjamin ran out from behind the brush, relieved that they were his people. He greeted them with a handshake. The men were exhausted. The women and children slept in the wagon. Benjamin accompanied the family to Di-Ahman. On the way, they told him about the many arrests and the plundering and atrocities.

"Do you know anything about the families of Lyman Sherman and Almon Babbitt?" Benjamin asked.

"I've seen Elder Sherman in the street but haven't seen Brother Babbitt. I don't know what's happened to him. Are they family?"

Benjamin nodded. "Their wives are my sisters."

"I'm sorry, son. People are in hiding. Some have been shot. You can't walk the streets much. The old citizens know we're not armed."

"Are you sure they've taken Joseph and the brethren to Jackson County?"

"Yes, but there's rumors that they'll move them to Richmond. Brother Joseph left word for the people in Di-Ahman. He doesn't want you to fight. When the army comes, you're to surrender and leave the state."

* * *

Adam-ondi-Ahman—November 8, 1838

They came the next morning: General Robert Wilson and nearly seven hundred men. They forced John D. Lee, a prisoner, to lead them to Di-Ahman. Brother Lee had a written letter from the Prophet: "Do not oppose them. Accept whatever terms they propose. Surrender and leave the state."

With every Mormon man in the settlement, Benjamin was marshaled into rank and marched with all arms into Wilson's camp, where the soldiers had formed an open square. Once inside the square, the Mormon men, on command, laid their arms inversely upon the ground. Benjamin stared at Old Betsy. Ever since he was a child, she had been part of his life, part of his father. She was a straight shooter, the finest gun in the pile.

The men were then marched from the square where old citizens from Daviess County jeered and spit on them as they walked by. Suddenly Benjamin was pulled out of rank. A colonel stood in front of him. With the colonel was a man whom Benjamin immediately recognized. His name was Taylor.

"This is one of the men who burned my father's place," the man said.

"Is that so?" The colonel's eyes drilled into Benjamin.

"Yes, sir," Benjamin answered.

The colonel drew his sword and pointed in the direction of Wilson's camp. "Step quick," he commanded with the tip of his sword touching between Benjamin's shoulder blades. They marched to the general's marquee.

Benjamin was left outside with four armed men pointing their rifles at him. They called him a "cursed Mormon and a stinkin' Yankee." Benjamin stood silently, over six feet tall, clean-shaven and slim-framed, more genteel than robust. Mr. Taylor had followed him over. He glanced at Benjamin with pity rather than loathing, then he ducked into the general's marquee.

* * *

The following morning, Benjamin sat on a stool in Adam Black's cabin with two men pacing around him as they continued the interrogation. One was tall and loose-limbed and wore a dark, broadcloth suit. Earlier he had introduced himself as the state's attorney from St. Louis. He had accompanied General Wilson to this godforsaken place. The other man was short and broad—Doctor Carr of Gallatin. At the crack of dawn, they had questioned him separately. Now together, they asked him the same questions, twisting the structure of their sentences, trying to trip him up, to determine whether or not he was lying.

Benjamin answered the best he could. All last night he had prayed while the guards mocked him as he sat on the snowy ground without blanket or overcoat. Now he knew that God had heard his prayers. His thoughts were clear in spite of his terror. He remembered every answer he gave. Inwardly he continued to pray, beseeching the Lord to help him speak as truthfully as he could without implicating any of the brethren.

"The man who led you to the Taylors'? Give me his name. Now. If you want to live," Dr. Carr pressed him.

"I have just come to this place," Benjamin said, swallowing, "and know only a few people. I heard others call the man Captain Cornelius."

The doctor glanced at the attorney, who motioned with his head that they should leave the room and speak privately. Benjamin closed his eyes. Had he done wrong? Would they be able to determine that Captain Cornelius was Cornelius Lott? Benjamin's eyes stung. Brother Lott was over fifty, hardy and good humored. Benjamin didn't want to betray him, to hurt him.

The attorney and Dr. Carr came back. Rather than pacing, Dr. Carr sat down in the chair opposite Benjamin and looked at him searchingly.

The attorney placed his hand on Benjamin's shoulder. "Young man, we have questioned you over and over again, and you have in no way contradicted your statements. Mr. Taylor has also told us how kindly you treated them as prisoners, how you assisted the women and even quarreled with your own companions for their sake. We believe that you tell the truth, that you have been raised an honorable man.

"We also know that your situation is terrible. There is little hope for escape from conviction. You're the only prisoner here, and this army expects a bloody revenge. You are the only one to answer for the burnings and raids upon the old settlers. We may not be able to save you, but we will try."

That night a snowstorm struck Di-Ahman. Shaking uncontrollably, Benjamin wondered if he would live until dawn. His drew up his knees and rested his head between them, his arms wrapped around himself. Eventually Benjamin dozed. The guard changed. He was rudely awakened.

"You ready to die, boy!?" The handle of a corn cutter pressed hard into Benjamin's side.

The other guards laughed. "Rogers, how you goin' to use that cutter?"

"Please," Benjamin begged. The crimson flame of the guard fire danced in the snowy wind.

"He says *please*!" a guard cursed. "Did the Taylors' say *please* when you burned them out!"

Rogers swung the corn cutter in front of Benjamin's eyes. "I used this last at Shoal Creek on an old man by the name of McBride. I shot him with his own gun then cut off his fingers, his hands, then his arms. I split his head open. My friends here fired into the smithy shop, killed more Mormon stink that you can count on your fingers and toes."

Rogers squatted near Benjamin's face and thrust the cutter at him. Benjamin jerked away. Rogers spit as he leered, his yellow teeth grinning, his breath hot and vile. Benjamin turned his head, and his hands flew up, trying to erase the spittle, trying to shield his eyes from unimaginable evil. Another man grabbed Benjamin's arms and pinned them back. He yanked Benjamin to his knees.

There was laughter and cursing, Rogers in front of him hissing like a demon. "See the blood on this cutter! I ain't never going to wash it. I'm just goin' to add more Mormon blood to it. Yours!"

The man shoved him. Benjamin fell, retching with the smell of blood and spittle in his nostrils. He curled into a fetal position, an unimaginable hell spinning around him, as men bragged about murdering his friends, shooting a woman, finding a boy behind the blacksmith's bellows and blowing off the top of his head. The cutter whizzed over Benjamin's body again and again as Rogers laughed and described how he would dismember him.

Immersed in hell, Benjamin waited to feel the searing pain, to die in snow drenched with his own blood, to join Seth in heaven where he would be free from an evil so black that he could not bear it. Hours passed as the ordeal continued.

Then suddenly it stopped. Other men walked up. The guard changed. Benjamin gulped down cold air. The wind blew and snow swirled, but nature was not strong enough to clear the air of the vile evil that had twisted in the firelight around him. His body heaved time and time again.

When morning came, snow continued to fall. The new guard stared at Benjamin, curled up and shaking. "Mormon," the guard commanded, "see that hazel brush over there. Cut some and make a bed for yourself. No man ought to lie in this snow."

Benjamin complied, though his vision blurred. He could not get the taste of blood out of his mouth. Finally, he curled up in his hazel brush. He closed his eyes but could not sleep for the horrible images that rose before him, writhing and shrieking in his brain.

Hours later he shrank back at the touch of a hand. Shaking, he realized that it was not a demon but the old slave who cooked for the militia. The black man held out a bag containing fragments of beef and cornbread. He placed it in the snow near Benjamin. "I'll bring you more soon as I can," he whispered before slipping away.

* * *

Far West, Missouri

Lyman sat in the Youngs' small log house with two of the Twelve, Brigham Young and Heber C. Kimball. Heber began the conversation. "We just received word that they're moving Joseph and the prisoners from Independence to Richmond. The fifty brethren who Clark placed under arrest are there as well. We are asking for volunteers to go. Yet there is great risk."

"I planned to go anyway," Lyman interrupted. Two days ago he had moved his family to Almon's house. They were relatively safe and had food.

"Good," Brigham said. "Leave at nightfall. And be careful. Mobs scour the roads. They won't let Mormons come and go. We figure they don't want us to get to a courthouse. In a week, time runs out on our preemptive land rights in Daviess County."

Heber shook his head and breathed out sharply. "Don't they realize Joseph told us to leave the state—that our property means little to us compared to the life of our Prophet and friends?"

The men talked for a few more minutes. Worry and responsibility lay heavy on their shoulders. They had to find a way to help Joseph. They had five thousand people to organize and remove from the state. Then Brigham and Heber placed their hands on Lyman's head and blessed him with protection on his mission, promising that he would see his family again.

With a heavy heart, Lyman left his friends. When he stepped outside, the cold wind sliced through him. He turned his coat collar up and began the long walk home. He had only taken a few steps when a horseman emerged out of the blur of snow. The stranger carried a gun.

"You Lyman Sherman?"

Lyman looked up at him. He was a young man with unkempt hair and beard; his lips were crusty and his face wind-burned. He had been waiting for Lyman. "Why?" Lyman gritted his teeth. "Who wants to know?"

"Me. John Babbitt."

"I'm Sherman." Lyman stared at the stranger. Was this man Almon's kin, or was this some cruel ruse?

The stranger glanced around furtively to make sure no one was listening. "I got a message for my brother's wife. You know where I can find her?"

Lyman nodded. "Give me the message. I'll make sure she gets it."

John Babbitt shook his head. "I'll take it myself. I figure she'll give me sumthin' to eat. There ain't enough in this town to keep a dog alive."

Lyman recognized the shrewd brightness of the man's eyes. They were like Almon's. "Mrs. Babbitt is my wife's sister and under my care. You can have supper with us. But tell me one thing first. Does Almon live?"

The stranger nodded brusquely. "Of course he's alive."

* * *

Julianne heard the two quick knocks then a pause and three more. She stopped stirring the soup. It must be Lyman. This was the signal to get Arthur out of sight. Julianne helped Arthur to the stairs. His steps became stronger each day. Julianne prayed that Arthur would be safe as he disappeared in the cellar. She put the false floor into place and the rug over it. She left the bed alone, since moving it would make too much noise.

Lyman knocked again.

"Just a moment," Delcena called out.

Baby Susan whimpered as Delcena stopped nursing. Her other children gathered round. "Who is it, Mama?" Alvira asked.

"It's Papa," Delcena said. "He probably brought someone home to eat supper with us." They stayed by her. Even Albey dared not run to the door. Julianne hurried to Delcena and placed a hand on her shoulder. "I'll unlatch it," she whispered.

Julianne opened the door. The children watched as their father walked in with the rough-looking stranger. Julianne's heart leaped in her chest. There was something about this young man . . .

Lyman spoke to her. "This is John Babbitt. He's come with news of Almon."

"Where is he?" Julianne said, shaking like a leaf in the wind.

John took his hat off. "Either in Booneville or Richmond. Some fellows brought this letter to me in Leavenworth." John reached into his pocket and handed Julianne a wadded square of paper. Her hands trembled as she smoothed it open and began reading.

> Johnny, you know that I've journeyed alone to Missouri from the east. I've run into some difficulty. A group of ruffians waylaid me and took my horse and supplies. I'm recovering in Booneville with a Christian family by the name of Drake. Soon, I will go to Richmond as planned. The Drakes warn me that travel is dangerous right now due to the Mormon war. They are certain that it was Mormons who accosted me. Could you get word to my wife that I am alive and well? No mail can reach her from here, but perhaps from Fort Leavenworth. I will be staying at the Richmond tavern.
>
> Your brother,
>
> Manny

"Who's Manny?" Albey piped up.

John eyed Albey and grinned. "It's what I called your uncle when I was your size. He'd tell me not to call him Manny since his name had an O in it. Said to call him Money instead; said he'd have a hoard of it when he grew up."

John looked at Julianne. "Ma'am, I hate to interrupt your cryin', but I'm starved. Could we discuss my brother's difficulties over supper?"

Julianne nodded and wiped away her tears. "Of course." She turned and quickly set the table. Delcena brought out the cornbread and bean soup. The children's fear turned to curiosity as John magically pulled a penny out of each of their ears.

John ate without waiting for a blessing on the food. Lyman's children stared at their father, waiting for him to reprimand the guest. Instead, Lyman picked up his spoon and started eating. Albey grinned and took a large bite of corn bread. Lyman watched John Babbitt carefully. The more the man interacted with his family, the more he reminded him of Almon. But was he trustworthy?

Lyman cleared his throat. "Almon was a member of Far West's militia. Just before the city fell, he left with a group of men who thought they might be arrested, court-martialed, and shot. From the sound of the letter, Almon has set out on his own."

John nodded. "I heard about the problems here. When I got the letter, those first words, 'You know,' tipped me off. He used to say that when he wanted me to lie to get him out of trouble. *You know, Johnny, that I never set foot out of this house. Tell Mama.* I covered for him every single time. He paid me back by teaching me how to read." John looked at Julianne and chuckled. "He's a scoundrel, ma'am. I guess you know that by now."

Julianne smiled back. "Precocious and high-spirited. But not a scoundrel."

"Well, there's one thing he didn't lie about. You are as pretty as he bragged. I'm heading toward Richmond tomorrow. If he's not there, I'll go on to Booneville and find him."

Julianne's eyes shone with tears. "Mr. Babbitt, you are an answer to my prayers."

John's ruddy complexion deepened with embarrassment. "I don't know about that, ma'am." He turned to Lyman. "Mr. Sherman, I s'pose I'll stay here tonight."

Lyman glanced at Delcena. She was blowing on a spoonful of soup then feeding it to Daniel. He had not had a moment alone with her—had not told her that he would be leaving tonight. "Mr. Babbitt, you'll have to ask the ladies. I won't be here. I'm also heading toward Richmond in about at hour. It will be safer for me to travel at night. Our Prophet, Joseph Smith, is one of the prisoners who has been taken there. I will do all I can in his behalf."

Delcena looked up. She met Lyman's eyes but didn't speak.

John shook his head. "You won't get far. When I came through, the men on the road said they were shooting any Mormons who came or went."

"I'll stay off the main roads. Travel under cover of darkness."

"Do you have a gun?"

Lyman shook his head. "No. They took our arms. We have a pistol. But I'm leaving it with the women."

"What about a horse?"

"They took our stock. Even killed our cow."

"Then I'll tell you what. Let me get a few hours of shut-eye, and we'll travel together."

Delcena swallowed as her voice cracked with emotion. "Thank you, Mr. Babbitt. You are an answer to my prayers as well."

John laughed out loud. "Manny always said that there's miracles aplenty in Mormonism. John Babbitt answering two women's prayers beats them all!"

* * *

Springfield, Illinois

George lay still with the fever raging in his brain. He knew his mother was near. He could feel her hand moving back his long bangs, placing a cool rag on his brow. He could think a little clearer with the rag in place. He opened his eyes. Julia came into focus. Her black hair, streaked with gray, fell down around her face. Her brown eyes were misty. When she saw that he was focusing on her, she smiled. It seemed to George to be the loveliest smile in the world, a smile that said, "I love you. You mean the whole world to me." He wondered if he would ever be able to find a girl who smiled like that. If he did, he wouldn't ever let her go.

"Son, you're getting better. Now take some nourishment." She helped him sit up and gave him warm soup and a cool drink of water. Afterward, George lay back down and fell into a dreamless sleep.

* * *

The next day, Joe walked home from the schoolhouse with his siblings Amos, Esther, and William. Mary Ann Hale accompanied them as a part of their family. Joe shivered in the thin sunlight. During the day, he had been so consumed with teaching that his fears were kept at bay. Now they flooded his mind. That morning before he left, George's fever had subsided, but Julia had been stricken. Mary had stayed home to take care of her. Joe could not remember another time in his life when his mother had not arisen from bed.

When they neared the house, Will and Amos immediately went to the barn to feed and milk. Mary met Joe and the girls at the door. Her eyes were red, her blond hair hanging limp down her back. She wore an apron and held a stirring spoon.

"How is Mother?" Joe asked.

"She's worse. She can't hold any food down. Oh, Joe, what will we do?"

Mary Ann and Esther stood wide-eyed and frightened, holding each other's hands.

"Nurse her back to health," Joe said. Then he turned to the younger girls. "Worrying won't do a bit of good. Go on and set the table."

Mary spoke again, her voice low and shaky. "That's not all. The neighbor brought over a newspaper. Things are bad in Missouri. It says that the Mormons burned a whole county and killed hundreds of men at someplace called Crooked River. It says that the Mormons are going to attack Richmond and that they're sending the whole state after them." Mary began to cry.

"Those things happened two weeks ago. What happened to Juli, Delcie, and the kids? Lyman and Almon? Ben could already be dead!" A sob shook Mary.

"He's not dead," Joe stated as he put his arm around her shoulders.

"We don't know that!" Mary cried.

"I know," Joe said stoically. "I would know if Ben was dead. Somehow, someway, I would know. We have to be strong right now. Go on and get supper on the table while I check on Mother."

When Joe entered Julia's room, she lay on her side with her knees drawn up to relieve the cramping. Her cheeks were red from the fever. She moaned in her sleep. George sat beside the bed, his bangs hanging over his eyes as he held her hand. He looked thin and exhausted.

"George, you shouldn't be in here. You should be resting."

George looked up at Joe, his eyes large in his gaunt face. "She wore herself out nursing me."

"She nursed other people too."

"And they died."

"She's not going to die," Joe said. "Get back to bed. That's what she would want."

After George left, Joe spent most of the night with his mother, trying not to think about Benjamin, about his sisters in Missouri. He only focused on her, on how to relieve her suffering and keep her alive. Over and over again he saturated a cloth with thin broth and squeezed the liquid into her mouth. He also cooled her body with damp rags.

Mary relieved him a few hours before dawn. After a bit of sleep, Joe arose and woke his younger siblings. They ate a cold breakfast, and Joe told them to get ready for school. Joe dressed carefully and combed back his hair. One thing was certain. He couldn't lose his teaching position. It was their only sustenance.

Before leaving, Joe went into his mother's room. Mary was asleep in the bedside chair, her head cocked at a strange angle. Joe placed a hand on Mary's shoulder, and she startled awake.

"Give her a bit of laudanum this morning, then broth every hour," he instructed her. "Make sure the broth is thin and has been boiled for at least ten minutes. Then cool it until it's warm, not hot."

"All right."

"Don't forget. Nothing to eat except broth. Keep a cool rag on her forehead. Give her a tinge of laudanum."

"You already said that, Joe. I'm not stupid."

"I didn't say you were."

Joe bent down and kissed his mother's cheek. He heard her whisper a name. But it wasn't his name, it was Benjamin's.

* * *

Exhausted, Joe could scarcely keep his thoughts straight in the early afternoon. Suddenly, the schoolhouse door flew open, and a slim, young woman wearing a stylish black dress walked into the room. Holding her hand was a little boy about three years old.

"Mr. Johnson," she said confidently, although there were dark circles under her eyes. "My name is Mrs. Ann Forquer. You have probably heard of my late husband, George Forquer, who was formerly secretary of state for Illinois."

"I'm sorry, ma'am. I'm from Ohio and only recently moved here." Joe continued to look at her, feeling stupid. She was very pretty and didn't look much older than his sister Mary.

She waved her hand. "No matter. Since Mr. Forquer's recent death, I have found it necessary to occupy my mind by helping those in need. Mr. Speed and my sister, Mrs. Lamb, have told me that you are a young Yankee schoolmaster and a fine teacher who manages sixty scholars. I would like to buy books for your school. Do you mind if I observe with my son George?"

"Not at all," Joe said with a slight bow, wishing that he could simply ask this lady to come back another day. Instead, Joe continued teaching an arithmetic lesson to the older scholars while William tutored the smaller children. Amos raised his hand often, brightly answering the questions. It touched Joe's heart—the way his little brother was trying to help him impress this heiress.

When her son grew restless, Mrs. Forquer stood and shook Joe's hand. "You are nurturing some rising scholars. I'll purchase readers for you."

"Thank you," Joe said with another bow. As soon as she was gone, Joe breathed a sigh of relief.

In the late afternoon, still battling fatigue, he dismissed the students, stretched into his overcoat, and walked home. When he arrived, he found Julia no better but not any worse. After supper Joe felt too tired to stand on his feet.

"Go to bed," Will said. "Mary and I will tend to Mother."

Out of necessity, Joe complied. That night he dreamed that he was galloping a horse through a large field. His mother stood in the middle with her arms wide open.

"Benjamin!" she cried out.

"No, Mother, it's me, Joe."

"Of course it's you, Joe," she smiled. "Look, Benjamin is behind you."

Joe turned, and Benjamin rode up behind him, grinning.

"Why Joe!" he shouted. "You came to Zion."

Then a shot sounded, and Benjamin fell from his horse. Joe ran to him. "Don't worry, Ben, you'll be all right."

"I know it, Joe. I know you'll pray for me."

Joe awakened, sweating profusely. He knelt down and begged his Heavenly Father to protect his brother and to heal his mother.

* * *

Mentor, Ohio

In the morning, Almera stoked the fire and set the water to boil while Sam slept. Lately, he had been spending his evenings at the tavern and coming home after midnight. He would crawl into bed beside her, smelling of liquor, and instantly fall asleep. She preferred the evenings of solitude to her husband's company. They had little to talk about, and the hurt she had endured at his hands had hardened within her. She would rather be alone to read, sew, or just hold the cat by the fire. And sometimes, when she was very lucky, Rebecca Winters would ride by and see that Sam's horse was gone. On these occasions, her friend knocked at the door. Rebecca's visits made Almera's life bearable.

Almera checked the boiling water in the pot, and with a ladle she placed the eggs in one by one, very gently. Sam sauntered into the kitchen and stretched. His forearms were bare and muscular. Even in the winter he wore his shirtsleeves rolled up. He walked up to Almera. She allowed a quick kiss then turned her head away, smelling last night's whiskey on his breath.

"There's news," he said. Did she hear a triumphant edge to his voice? "The Mormons are in trouble."

Almera glanced at him. She had not heard from anyone in Missouri since the letter from Julianne. "What do you mean?"

"It's all over the papers. The Mormon army devastated an entire county, attacking a militia that tried to protect the citizens. More than fifty soldiers were killed. The state is sending out thousands of men to squash the rebellion. Joe Smith says his people will fight until the death."

The ladle shook in Almera's hand, rattling the egg. "That couldn't be true."

Sam put his hands over Almera's. The egg stilled. He took the ladle from her and released the egg in the boiling water. "Fortunately you're safe here with me."

Almera swallowed. "Does my father know?"

"He was at the tavern. He heard the talk. He drank a good deal of whisky last night."

"After we eat, I'll take him breakfast."

Sam moved behind her and took her slender shoulders between his powerful hands. It was strange, the way his voice sounded jaunty, callous, and threatening all at the same time. "Suit yourself. But don't stay long. I'll be waiting for you."

* * *

Almera walked into Ezekiel's house without knocking. He sat at the kitchen table with his head resting in his arms. He had been in that position for hours—ever since he had returned home from the tavern. Ezekiel lifted his head. Almera sat down across from him, placing a loaf of bread and six boiled eggs between them.

With bloodshot eyes, he focused on her. Her face was so thin and pale. She began questioning him about their family in Missouri, repeating the same things he had read in the paper last night.

"Is it true, Papa?" she demanded as if he would know. Didn't she realize that he was an old, useless drunkard?

"Just because it's in the paper doesn't mean it's true," he answered. "Remember when the paper reported that Joseph Smith had been killed with Zion's Camp? It was a bold-faced lie. For the life of me, I can't imagine Joseph ordering his men to murder and plunder. If it happened, his back must have been against a wall, or he thinks he had a vision."

Almera blurted out in tears. "He doesn't just *think* he has visions. Papa, I can't stay here. Sam frightens me. There is no love between us. Julianne said she would come back for me. If she does, if she lives through this, I'm leaving. I can't stand being here alone, not knowing if my family is alive or dead. I'd rather be in Far West with those who love me, surrounded by a thousand Missourians."

"How does Sam frighten you? Does he threaten you or strike you?"

"No, Papa. I-I can't explain." Almera's hands shook.

Ezekiel reached out and took her shaking hands in his. He thought of his mother, of how she had lived in a house without love, with a husband who was cruel to her. Yet his mother had told no one. In Almera's case, Sam was the husband, the head of the family. That was his right. Ezekiel did not think he would physically hurt Almera. Yet would she tell him if Sam did? Almera was his daughter, and she suffered. He could see it in her eyes, in the way she had grown thin and nervous. He had not given her life to leave her in sorrow.

He thought of Julia, of how she had refused to leave Kirtland and join him in Chicago, of how she had struck off without him and had headed for

Missouri. He thought of himself, of how he had run away from home at age fourteen. Now Almera sat before him, passionate and determined to leave. She was certainly their daughter. She had the will to leave Sam forever. But Ezekiel did not have the will to lose her, the only part of Julia he had left.

"When that day comes, I'll go with you," he said quietly.

"Thank you, Papa," she said, weeping now as she squeezed his hands. "Thank you."

* * *

Adam-ondi-Ahman, Missouri

What was the attorney trying to *do?* Benjamin stood at trial before Adam Black, the justice of the peace. General Wilson watched the proceedings with Dr. Carr. The attorney spoke of districts, the Caldwell prisoners, and the likelihood of a conviction. Adam Black glanced toward Benjamin with a look of disgust. *Black was an enemy, but was the attorney a friend as he had claimed?*

"You understand," the attorney went on, "that if the prisoner is found guilty and committed to the magistrate, he will be sent to a different district in the opposite direction of Far West and Richmond, one hundred miles away?"

Benjamin's hands broke out in a sweat, and his heart drummed in his chest. More than anything, he feared being taken away. If he had to, he could stand up like a man and die beside the Prophet. But to be subject to other men like Rogers with the corn cutter . . . to suffer all alone . . . His face felt hot as he started to shake, his knees locking.

General Wilson whispered something to Dr. Carr. The doctor stood, tapped Benjamin's shoulder, and pointed to a chair. "Sit down."

The attorney went on, describing more hypothetical situations. Now that he was sitting, Benjamin's mind cleared. He realized that the attorney was trying to keep Black from making a decree—he was trying to keep Benjamin here, in Adam-ondi-Ahman, as General Wilson's prisoner.

Black hit his fist on the table. "Do you purposely befogg and entangle me!?"

"Forgive me," the attorney replied humbly. "I'm only trying to explain the law. This prisoner is a citizen of the state of Missouri. In order to extricate ourselves from eventual lawsuits, we all need to clearly understand this situation. I am not speaking of the prisoner's guilt per se but of the rights of citizens under a judicial system. Surely you understand. Yet if the general tries him in a military court as a private in the state's militia . . ."

Black suddenly stood up and turned to face General Wilson. "Do what you want with him! Court-martial him! Shoot him! Get him out of my sight."

Black left the room. Wilson frowned deeply as his eyes locked on Benjamin. Then he turned to the guards. "You may take the prisoner back now."

* * *

It was snowing outside when Julia awakened to find Joe looking down at her. His face was thin, and there were dark circles under his eyes, but he was smiling, her happy, kindhearted Joe. She felt a surge of love for him so strong that it brought tears to her eyes. Joe's nursing had kept her alive, and his hard work had saved all of them.

"How are you feeling?" Joe asked.

"Better than before," Julia said. "Has there been any word from the family?"

Joe shook his head. "No letters."

She could tell that there was more, that Joe was not telling her something. "What's happened?"

"Just newspaper reports. You don't need to worry right now."

"But I am worried."

Joe took her hand in his but didn't say anything.

"Please, son, it's better to know the truth."

Joe sighed. "There was an article in today's *Sangamo Journal.* The Saints have surrendered."

"Please bring it to me."

Julia closed her eyes while Joe left to get the newspaper. She thought of Delcena, Julianne, and Benjamin, of her grandchildren and Brother Joseph. What had they suffered while she had been too sick to even pray for them? *Father in Heaven, preserve their lives as Thou hast preserved mine. Oh, that I could see them once more!*

Joe returned and read the article aloud. His voice shook slightly at times then continued:

"'The Mormon war has been terminated by a surrender of the Mormon leaders. On that day, about 3,000 men, being part of the army of 5,000, ordered out by General Clark, comprising General Atchison's division, made their appearance before the town of Far West, the county seat of Caldwell County, where the Mormons were entrenched. Six of the Mormon leaders avowed their willingness to surrender, in the expectation that the Mormons would be unharmed. Their names are Joseph Smith, Sidney Rigdon, George Hinkle, Lyman Wight, Parley P. Pratt, and Mr. Knight. The Mormons assembled at Far West comprised 700 men under arms.

"'The reports vary as to what happened after that surrender, in fact, our intelligence does not come down clearly to a period, later than the day of capitulation.

"'However, it is stated that, about the time of the surrender, a company of men—200 in number—fell upon a body of the Mormons on Shoal Creek, about 20 miles from Far West. The Mormons, it is said, were 36 in number, and the story runs that all but four were put to death. Some of the names of the killed, as reported to us, are David Evans from Ohio, Jacob Fox from Pennsylvania, Thomas McBride and his father, Mr. Daly, M. Merrill and his son-in-law, Mr. White, all from Ohio.

"'The facts about Bogart's fight are not as previously reported. Two of his men were killed—one died outright, one died of his wounds. At the same time four Mormons fell—among them the captain of their band—Bogart's company were stationed on the line of Ray County. They had captured four Mormons; and to rescue these, the attack was made upon them by the Mormons.

"'The disposition of the captured Mormons present a case of great difficulty. They are generally poor—at least they have but little money and few means besides their stock and crops to preserve them from starvation. The presence of several thousand troops in their vicinity must have reduced them greatly. The proposition—so it is given out—is to remove them from the state of Missouri. Are these 5,000 men, women, and children—without any means and literally beggars—to be thrust upon the charity of Illinois, Iowa, or Wisconsin?

"'It is said that the leaders are to be put to trail. We hope that a searching operation will be applied to the guilty on all sides. It is only in such a way that the government and people of this state can place themselves in a just and dignified attitude before their sister government and fellow citizens of the Union.'"

Joe's voice stopped. Tears slid down Julia's cheeks. The Prophet was in chains. Were her children and grandchildren all right?

Joe looked at her. "Mother, you shouldn't be burdened with this when you're ill."

She tried to explain. "It's better to know. Then I can pray for them."

Joe went on. "The news was worse last week. It was a terrible time. You were so sick, and we knew that the Missouri governor had issued an order to exterminate the Mormons or drive them from the state. The reports were that Joseph and the people would fight to the death. We knew we might lose you and were afraid that Ben, Juli, and Delcie were dead. Now you are getting well, and there is hope that they live. These are answers to our prayers."

Julia nodded and wiped away her tears. "Joe, would you pray right now?"

As her son prayed aloud, Julia thought about Zion. It was not just a place but the pure in heart. Was it possible that somehow within these terrible events God had not forsaken Zion but was preserving it instead? Was it possible that her family would be together again someday?

17

My God to Thee my soul looks up
Thy grace my thoughts employ
Thou art my glory, life and hope
And found of every joy.

Joel Hills Johnson

Adam-ondi-Ahman, Missouri

Hours passed as the snowy world dimmed and the wind howled. Night would soon fall. Benjamin wondered how many hours he had been sitting on the log shaking as an impenetrable chill knifed through him. The cook edged toward him then shrank away as two new guards strode up, one stout and the other lean. Scarves wrapped their faces, making their features indistinguishable.

Less than ten feet away, the stout Missourian lifted his gun. An inner steel coursed through Benjamin as cold as the ice around him, freezing his blood and nerves. If they killed him now, he had less to fear. He would not freeze to death. Rogers could not return in the darkness with the corn cutter.

The man pulled off his scarf. His face was scarred, and wrinkles lined his mouth. "You give up Mormonism right now, or I'll shoot you."

Benjamin shook his head. "No."

The man aimed and pulled the trigger. An explosion occurred as the gun misfired. Benjamin sucked in his cheeks, realizing that he was still alive. Why was he shaking when he felt calm? Benjamin folded his hands tightly and prayed for it to end quickly, for Seth to come.

The Missourian cursed as he examined the lock and replaced the priming. Muttering, he spoke to his companion. "I've had this gun twenty years, and this never happened." He smirked at Benjamin's form and pulled the trigger again. The wind whistled. The gun remained silent. He tried again. Still nothing.

"Come on, you can kill this cuss!" his companion roared above the sound of the wind.

"I'll put in a fresh load."

Benjamin looked away, out toward the snowy valley, toward the place where Adam walked. They would be here soon. Seth, David, Susan, and Nancy. He felt Seth's eyes upon him and heard David's laugh in the wind. Was it Susan and Nancy's touch that thawed the ice within him? Tears stung his eyes. Then he saw something. The general running toward them, his shouts lost in the wind.

The Missourian cursed at Benjamin and pulled the trigger. The gun exploded in his hands. Through the flames, Benjamin saw the man fall back. He saw the shock and terror in his eyes. The general barked out orders as Missourians ran to the aid of their companion. As they put out the fire and lifted the unconscious man covered with burns and blood, Benjamin heard the general command, "Take him to my tent where the surgeon will attend him. Do not harm this prisoner."

That night, Benjamin could not sleep. He rocked back and forth on his bed of hazel brush as he shook with cold. Why was he still alive? Why? And his siblings were gone once more, memories in a night so dark and cold that it seemed it would never end.

* * *

November 12, 1838

It was late at night as Brigadier General Robert Wilson sat in the shanty that the Mormon's called the bishop's storehouse and composed a letter to Major General Clark. A fire glowed in the hearth, but the room was cold. His pen stilled for a moment, and his brow creased. In his late thirties, he was one of the richest men in the state. He had come here with General Clark to do his duty. Clark had commanded him to investigate the crimes committed against the old settlers and to bring the Mormon perpetrators to justice. If the need arose, he was to help enforce Governor Boggs's extermination order.

Wilson frowned deeply as he thought of the young prisoner. The boy was brave, intelligent, and utterly alone. He had a name: Benjamin Johnson. Yesterday, from a distance, Wilson had watched one of his own men point a musket at Johnson. Wilson had shouted as the gun fired, his voice lost in the wind. The prisoner had not fallen, for the gun had backfired, fatally injuring the soldier. When Wilson arrived at the scene, the Mormon boy sat there, shivering in the cold but solemn and dignified after staring death in the face. Wilson had not spoken to him. Yet he had known at that moment that Benjamin Johnson was everything a man could wish for in a younger brother or a son.

General Wilson continued his letter:

> It appears that the most guilty Mormons have previously escaped, they having ample opportunity, as I am informed that the town had not been under guard before our arrival. The investigation is still progressing, but with but little hope of affecting much, as the Citizens seem to be unable to identify but few.

Wilson paused. Was it right to leave out Johnson's name? General Clark would not care that the boy had shown compassion—had even argued with his own companions for young Mrs. Taylor's sake. On the other hand, the old settlers justly wanted vengeance for the wrongs against them. Would he be able to stop a wholesale massacre? Perhaps this boy's blood would appease the rightful citizens of Daviess County. A lamb at the slaughter. Johnson claimed that he had not been here long and knew few people. He had no names to give his interrogators. It seemed true enough as no mother, father, brother, or sister begged for his life. Would a single Mormon mourn his death?

Wilson's head ached. He was tired of the freezing rain in the afternoon and the unyielding snow at night. He was stuck in this hovel, compelled to order the death of an innocent lad. He closed his eyes, remembering another time when he had felt equally powerless. Despite his worldly success, he had been helpless in stopping the death of the woman he loved or the little brother he cherished. The image of Johnson rose again in his mind. Benjamin.

Robert Wilson lifted the pen and finished the letter to General Clark. He folded the communication, and with wax from the candle, sealed the envelope.

* * *

A few nights later, following six days of storm, the sky began to clear. The following morning Benjamin offered to help a more humane group of guards cut and haul wood for the fire. As they worked, he talked with them, trying to show them that he was a man, not a hated fanatic.

When they had finished, a young guard jovially told Benjamin that he was a "regular Yankee Doodle" and began singing the song. Benjamin joined him. The guard danced, kicking up his heels in the snow.

Yankee doodle keep it up
Yankee doodle dandy,
Mind the music and the step
And with the girls be handy.

After the song, the black cook walked over and gave Benjamin a handful of leftovers. Benjamin sat down and ate hungrily. The oldest of the guards, a man in his early thirties, leaned on his gun and gazed at Benjamin. "I won't find any satisfaction when you're shot. They say you'll be court-martialed soon."

Benjamin raised his head, his eyes meeting his guard's. Benjamin took a shaky breath. "How soon?"

The guard shrugged and glanced toward the general's marquee. "Not long. Look over there. The general's watching us; his mind's on you. Before my duty, he told me that he wants this ended. If you turn over the names of others and help to convict them, he'll let you go free. Otherwise, the old settlers won't rest unless you pay."

Benjamin did not respond.

"Don't you value your life? 'Tis better to be a living coward than a brave dead man."

Benjamin stared at the ground, the scent of hazel and smoke mixing with the chill air, his mind turning in circles. The taste of death that he had already experienced, but escaped, haunted him. What did God want from him now? Should he seek to stay alive? But how could that possibly take the form of turning over the names of other Saints and becoming a traitor?

A thought struck him: *Which would require the greatest bravery? To stand up like a man and be shot or to live like a dog and be despised by those you love?*

Benjamin raised his head and looked into the fire at the twisting flames. A longing for his own life, young and precious, filled him. What would happen if he were a traitor? How would his father feel? Benjamin knew the answer. Ezekiel would be ashamed. His mother, Joe, and his sisters would weep for his dishonor. And what of those who had died and begged him to be faithful—Seth, David, Nancy, and Susan? And the Prophet? Brother Joseph would forgive him but would never fully trust him. It would be a living death.

Benjamin broke out in a cold sweat. He imagined himself standing by some large trees in an open space as weapons of death were raised against him. This time they did not backfire. He saw himself falling—falling into the cold snow, his blood red against the white. The loss of his own life rose as a phantom before him, an incomprehensible sorrow. Yet he could not picture another way; he was not brave enough to ever meet those he loved who were good and pure, knowing himself to be a traitor.

"Ben."

At the sound of his name, Benjamin's head turned. William Huntington walked near the guard fire. He raised his hand up in a barely perceptible wave. The guard looked at Benjamin then at William.

Benjamin's soul ached. Would this be his last chance to see William in this life? "Sir, could I speak with him?"

The guard nodded gruffly. "But not alone."

Benjamin motioned for William to come near. William approached, shuffling his feet, tense and fidgety. Benjamin didn't blame him for being nervous with the guards close by, their muskets loaded and ready.

"Can you sit for a few minutes?" Benjamin asked.

William nodded and sat down next to Benjamin on the hazel brush.

"How are things?" Benjamin asked.

William shrugged and Benjamin saw the bitterness in his eyes. After glancing at the guard, William began in a low voice. "The Calls are still living in the big oak. Last night, two Missourians come to the tree when they were sitting on the branches, eating their supper. One cocked his gun and stuck it in Brother Anson's face. When his wife and children screamed, the Missourian rode off but said he would come back and kill him later. That's how things are. How are they with you?"

"I guess they'll shoot me too," Benjamin said and quietly added, "They already tried." He thought about asking after Zina, but could not do it. The thought made him want to live too much.

William turned to Benjamin. "My family has a pass to remove to Far West. They want all the Saints gone within the next three days."

Benjamin's heart sank, and he swallowed. The familiar terror of isolation pressed upon him.

William spoke again. "The owner of the boardinghouse sent me. He's worried about the state of your soul. He wonders if you want revenge against him because of your business disagreement."

Benjamin stared. William was talking in riddles. Brother Sloan owned the boardinghouse. What business disagreement? Then Benjamin knew. He and Sloan had argued at the Taylors' home. Brother Sloan was afraid that Benjamin would give his captors Sloan's name.

"He need not worry," Benjamin muttered.

William continued. "Other men wonder the same. They can't sleep at night, not knowing."

The blood drained from Benjamin's face. His people thought he would prove a traitor. While he stood alone in the prospect of death or worse and remained faithful, instead of praying for him, they spoke evil against him. Unable to control his emotions, Benjamin's body jerked as a sob tore from him.

The older guard turned and looked menacingly at William. "It's time for you to leave."

Benjamin gulped in air with tears streaming down his face. He no longer cared if the guards listened on not. "Tell the people to have no fears. With God's help, my soul is true. But instead of praying for me, they prophesy evil against me."

"Leave him, now!" The guard pointed his musket at William. With a stricken look in his eyes, William stood and walked away.

The guards stood silently as Benjamin wept. After a couple minutes, the older guard let out a quick breath. "The general is right. Those Mormons ain't your friends. I hope you realize that before it's too late."

* * *

An hour later, the guards who participated in the Haun's Mill massacre were once again on duty. For the past five days, their duty had been during the day, tempering their brutality. As they sauntered over, Benjamin felt too exhausted to even raise his eyes.

Immediately, one of the guards poked his gun in Benjamin's ribs. "Git up! We need more wood for the fire. March!"

Benjamin stood. He walked over to the large maple tree they had cut that morning. He picked up a heavy load of wood and hefted it onto his shoulders. Due to the deep snow, combined with emotional and physical exhaustion, he had difficulty walking. Benjamin trudged slowly toward the fire.

Rogers grinned fiendishly. "This boy needs to hurry."

Another guard picked up the cue. He came up behind Benjamin. "Step faster, or I'll stick this bayonet into you."

No longer caring about his own life, a terrible revulsion swept over Benjamin. Heat and fury pounded in his brain. He spun around and threw down the load of wood. "I will not carry another chip!" Benjamin shouted. "If I had a sword, I would split you from end to end!"

Suddenly, General Wilson stepped out of his marquee and quickly strode over. Benjamin's heart raced.

"General, this prisoner has threatened me!" The guard spit on Benjamin.

The general turned to Benjamin, speaking sternly. "What happened here?"

With his heart still pounding, Benjamin said, "Sir, I was packing wood for the guard fire, and this man threatened to bayonet me if I did not move faster."

The general turned to the guards. "If you do not, from this time forward, treat this man as a prisoner ought to be treated, I shall put you all under guard!"

* * *

That night, Benjamin fell asleep as soon as he lowered himself into the hazel brush. Utterly spent, he did not feel the cold. Instead of dreaming of violence and death, he dreamed of an island of light, of inexplicable peace. Words of a revelation filled his mind. *Look unto me in every thought. Doubt not, fear not.* When he awakened, he thought of the guardian angel the Prophet had spoken of when he blessed him so long ago in Kirtland. Opening his eyes, Benjamin saw William Huntington running toward him. Benjamin scrambled to his feet as the guards gave William leave to approach.

This time William embraced him tightly. "Yesterday I went home," he exclaimed in a low voice. There were tears in his eyes. "And told Zina what you said. She cried and said that you have been horribly neglected. Then she walked through the streets and told everyone who felt like it to come to Father's house and pray for you. The house was full, Ben. People came in groups and prayed for you throughout the night. All of the Saints prayed for you. We prayed that you would be released and live."

"I felt it, Will," Benjamin said. "Tell Zina that I felt your prayers."

At noon, the aide-de-camp came up to the guard fire. He spoke directly to Benjamin. "The general wishes to speak with you privately."

Walking alone into the general's marquee, Benjamin's hands shook slightly. How would this end? Would the general try once more to extract information from him? When he could not, would the general order him to be court-martialed and shot? But Benjamin's friends had prayed for his release. He thought about the feeling of peace last night. Would death be his release, the place full of light?

Once inside the marquee, General Wilson invited Benjamin to sit down at the table across from him. The general drummed his fingers on the surface. Then the fingers stilled. General Wilson looked directly at Benjamin and said, "Mr. Johnson, I believe that you have been well-raised and have good parents. It appears to me that you have been truthful and honest, and your actions at the Taylors' house burning stand very much to your credit. After speaking with the state's attorney, I have wanted to help you for some time. But the citizens of the county and some of my own militia were expecting Mormon blood. I knew it was necessary to wait to avoid mutiny. Now ten days have gone by, and every Mormon is required to leave the county."

The general was quiet for a moment. He stood and walked around Benjamin, deep in thought. Benjamin swallowed, afraid to trust the hope for life that rose like a wave within him.

General Wilson stopped walking and turned to him with an earnest look in his eyes. "Benjamin, I'm a very rich man. I have watched you closely this past ten days. I like your appearance very much. I would like you to come and live with me, as if you were my younger brother or my son. If you will leave the Mormon faith, I will give you a pass and sufficient guards to take you directly to my house. I can help you become one of the finest and wealthiest men in the state of Missouri."

There was a moment of silence save the sound of soldiers jostling outside the marquee. The muscles in Benjamin's jaw tensed as he tried to control the emotions coursing through him. Tears gathered in his eyes and fell silently down his cheeks. Finally Benjamin said, "Thank you, sir. But—but I have parents in the East who I've never been separated from till now. If I am ever free again, I know that I must go to them; for—for they will fear I'm dead. Please do not think me ungrateful. As long as I live, I shall remember your kindness."

General Wilson nodded slowly. "I understand. I'll take full responsibility for your release and will write out a pass. But you must wait until night to leave, for the old citizens will kill you regardless of any paper I sign. An hour before sunset, I'll send a guard to take you to your friends. Leave from there. You may go now."

Benjamin stood and saluted. "God bless you, sir."

The general stood and returned the salute.

* * *

That evening after sunset, William was outside watching the road while Sister Huntington fed Benjamin a full bowl of corn chowder. As Benjamin ate, the night deepened, casting long shadows throughout the cabin.

Brother Huntington sat down next to Benjamin. "There's a house four or five miles distance where you can build a fire and keep from freezing." He gave Benjamin directions then reached into his pocket and handed Benjamin three matches. "I wish I had an overcoat or blanket for you, but the mob took nearly everything."

"I'll be all right. I'm used to it."

Benjamin stood up. It was time to go. Zina walked over. She looked up at Benjamin. The kindness in her eyes reminded him so much of Susan. "Be careful," she said. "I know that Heavenly Father will shield you."

"Thank you for holding that prayer meeting," he said awkwardly, wishing that he could tell her that he hoped to see her again. "I know the Lord softened the general's heart."

"No doubt." Zina nodded.

"I'd better go," Benjamin added. He thanked Brother and Sister Huntington and bid them good-bye.

Once outside, William shook his hand warmly. For a moment they stood together, watching the moon's reflection on the snow as they looked down into the starlit valley of Adam-ondi-Ahman.

"My family's leaving on Monday," William commented.

"Do you think we'll ever come back here?" Benjamin asked.

William shrugged. "I don't know. It was hard for Father to sign over his land. He thought this was Zion—that we would be here forever, that if we had to fight, the Lord would fight for us. But he did what the Prophet asked. He wouldn't have given up his land or his gun for anybody else."

Benjamin thought of this, of how he, too, would give up anything for Joseph. Did they do this because of love for the Prophet or because Joseph spoke for God? Perhaps it was for both reasons.

He thought of his lot, that rocky place overlooking the valley. He remembered complaining to Zina about it, then later accompanying the Prophet there. He remembered the thrill he felt when the Prophet explained that this was the place where Adam had built an altar and blessed his posterity. After that, Benjamin wouldn't have traded his land for any on earth.

Benjamin suddenly realized that he had never signed it over. He had been a prisoner on the day that the men had been forced to relinquish their property. But that didn't matter. It didn't help to own land if you were killed claiming it. The land was gone from him, all except for its history, and that belonged to God.

"Where will you go?" William asked.

"To my sisters in Far West."

"You won't be able to stay. Far West will be the first place they'll look."

"I know," Benjamin said. "Maybe I'll try to get to Springfield, Illinois."

"That's a long way from here."

"I'll figure it out."

The young men shook hands and embraced. A hard north wind blew as Benjamin set off in the darkness.

* * *

The wind shrieked around him. Benjamin was able to find his way by moonlight. It was slow going because of the deep snow. When he found the cabin, he realized that someone had been there before him. Not only had the wood been burned, but the chinking of the house as well. Plodding through the snowy yard, he looked for wood, but found nothing but one damp log. He brought it in and tried in vain to start a fire with his matches. For a moment, he pondered his predicament. Did he have the strength to travel ten more miles to Marrowbone, to the halfway house in the skirt of timber between Di-Ahman and Far West? What other choice was there?

It was well past midnight, and Benjamin was chilled to the bone when he arrived at the halfway house. Even in the moonlight, he saw that fences were gone, dissembled to use as firewood. Smoke rose from the chimney. Benjamin knocked on the door. There was rustling and low voices. A man cracked it open and peered out.

"I'm Ben Johnson," he explained quickly. "I was a prisoner in Di-Ahman. General Wilson let me go. I'm on my way to Far West to find my kindred. I need a place to spend the night."

The man's shoulders sagged. "Son, I would help you if I could. But I can't even fully open the door. People are wall to wall, sitting on the floor and sleeping. Only the most ill are lying down. Look."

Benjamin peered inside. There were people everywhere. How could they sleep like that, propped against each other? His heart sank. He was so cold.

The man said, "There's another house owned by Elisha Groves. It's just a mile away through the timber."

Benjamin listened as he was given directions. He set off but took a wrong turn. After walking for over an hour, he arrived back at the house from which he had started. This time, after his knock, the man squeezed through the door and walked with Benjamin until the path was plain.

It was nearly morning when Benjamin arrived at Brother Groves's home where he was warmly received. However, the house was frigid, for the wind forced its way in where the chinkings between the logs had been broken out. Benjamin tried to sleep, but the floor felt hard and cold beneath him. He lay awake wondering why he could sleep on hazel brush in front of a guard fire but not here in a house.

In the morning, Brother Groves shared his breakfast with Benjamin, but it was only a bit of boiled corn. As Benjamin started off, the air was full of frost, and through the mist the sun looked pale and chill. The wind was terrible and full in his face. He mechanically lifted one foot after the other through the unbroken snow over miles of frozen prairie.

Hours passed. Benjamin walked backward trying to keep his breath. Then he stopped, too benumbed and exhausted to take another step. He stood on a high, bleak prairie, with no signs of life in either direction, not even a tree or shrub. Benjamin doubled over. Did the angel of death stand before him, just beyond the veil of wind? He had heard that people felt warm before they froze to death. How long would it take? Then Benjamin prayed in his heart. He prayed for God to give him hope and strength or to take him home. *Look around,* a voice whispered in his mind. He turned and saw to his left a small, deep swale where grass stood high above the snow.

Why didn't I save just one match? At the thought, he felt in his pocket and found one match that he thought he had already used. He stumbled to the high grass, wiped the snow off his boots, and lit the match. He fired the grass. As the flames spread he inhaled the heated air. The warmth spread through his body, loosening his numbed limbs. Even the wind abated. Benjamin went on. Just before dark, he knocked on the door of Julianne's house.

* * *

Julianne prepared the corn bread as she looked around her cabin at the place she and Almon had lived and dreamed in. Those dreams were scattered, like shattered glass. Yet she and Delcena kept up a front, forcing back their terror for the children's sake, pretending everything would be all right. But her dimming ember of faith was so hard to keep alive.

Julianne glanced over at Delcena, who sat near the fire, roasting potatoes and parching corn with her children. Arthur Millican read the Bible in a chair nearby. It had been ten days since Johnny had come and gone with Lyman. Then, five days ago, the mobber Captain Bogart had come to the house with his men. Julianne blinked back tears. The Missourians had not found Arthur. Instead, they had come looking for Almon, saying he was needed in Joseph Smith's trial. They said that Almon had last been seen in Richmond, but they had reason to believe that he was back in Far West. A couple of the Missourians had camped outside the house for two days. Then they had left without incident. Almon had not come home, and Julianne did not know where he was. Where was her faith? She ought to be grateful that he was not in the Missourians' hands. But yesterday's news had broken her heart.

Emma and young Lucy Smith had come. Lucy had sat near the fire talking with Arthur. The two had looked so young and hopeful side by side, their heads inclined toward one another. Then Emma had told them. Refugees were arriving from Di-Ahman.

"Was Benjamin among them?" Julianne and Delcena had asked at the same time.

"No," Emma had said, sorrow and compassion lining her brow. "He was the only man taken prisoner."

Julianne had run outside, leaving Emma to grieve with Delcena. Staring at the cold moon and stars, she had shivered in her cloak and had wept for her younger brother. The thought of him spending the winter alone in a freezing prison or being court-martialed and shot was unbearable. Then she had felt Emma's and Delcena's arms around her.

Suddenly Julianne's thoughts jerked back to the present. There was a knock at the door. It was not the rhythmic knock that signaled a friend. It was the blunt knock of a stranger. Arthur started for the cellar. Julianne lifted the pistol from the hearth and tucked it into her apron pocket. Delcena told the children to run and hide on the far side of the bed. Quickly Julianne and Delcena laid the piece of wood over the cellar hole, put the rug in place, and pushed the trundle bed over it.

There was another knock.

"Who is it?" Julianne called out as she checked to make sure that the pistol was not visible.

"Ben."

Julianne gasped as she flew to the door and flung it open, shaking uncontrollably. Benjamin tottered. She wrapped her arms around his waist, holding him up. He wasn't wearing an overcoat. He felt so cold. Julianne was afraid she might not be strong enough to keep him from falling.

Then Delcena was with them, her arms around them both as she wept. Together they helped Benjamin to the fire.

"Benja, Benja," Julianne sobbed. "We thought we would never see you again."

* * *

Benjamin lay on a mattress. Delcena and Julianne sat by him, rubbing his hands and feet until they were warm again. He watched the fire, the flames twisting and sputtering. Arthur offered him a cup of warm broth. Benjamin sat up and took the cup, feeling the heat on his hands, the warmth spreading through his body. Alvira and Mary served him a baked potato and corn mixed with honey. He ate, savoring each bite as he turned his head and looked at his sisters through a sheen of tears. How was it that he was alive? That he was safe and free?

His nephew Albey squeezed in beside him and asked a hundred questions. "Uncle Ben, did the rascals try to shoot ya? Did they beat you up? How'd you escape? If they find ya, will they hang ya? We got a pistol! Uncle Almon gave Aunt Juli two, but I was gonna shoot one of the rascals when he took it and hit me. See this?" Albey pointed to the scar on his head.

"Albey, wait until morning," Delcena begged. "Uncle Ben's tired."

Benjamin took a deep breath. "I don't mind." He didn't want the moment to end, this heaven of being loved and cared for. Memories of leering faces, of a corn cutter stained with blood, of a musket backfiring, entered his mind. Two opposite worlds on the same planet. "Some men wanted to shoot me, Albey, but God was with me." Haltingly, Benjamin told bits and pieces of his story. Albey didn't say a word but wrapped his little arms tightly around Benjamin. When Benjamin finished talking, Delcena and Julianne were crying again.

"God was with me," Benjamin repeated, so tired that his words slurred together.

"Of course he was." Delcena wiped her eyes and hugged his shoulders. Julianne squeezed his hand, still crying.

Arthur said, "In a couple of days, you and I can head to Fort Leavenworth. Word is they'll hire Mormons."

Benjamin nodded, weariness bearing down upon him.

"Benja, lie back down," Julianne said gently.

Delcena brought over a quilt. Albey helped her tuck it around. Benjamin felt Julianne's tears as she kissed his hand. His sister's words were soft as down. "Night, dear Ben. Sleep well, Benja."

As Benjamin drifted into sleep, the voices of his loved ones slipped into oblivion. But another voice rose within him. Was it Seth? The whisper of his mother's prayers? The Holy Spirit? The vibrant echo of his own faith? The voice spoke so clearly that the words were etched forever into his soul:

Providence has preserved your life. It is the direct hand of the Lord for His own purpose and glory.

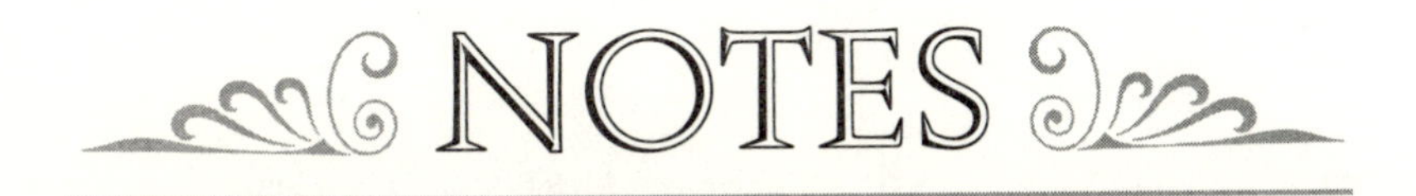

NOTES

A Banner Is Unfurled Series Timeline (Vols. 1–3)

1787
Fourteen-year-old Ezekiel Johnson runs away from home, leaving his mother and abusive stepfather.

1797
Ezekiel Johnson travels to Grafton, Massachusetts, and meets Julia Hills.

1801
January 12
Ezekiel Johnson and Julia Hills marry.

1820
Early Spring
The Prophet Joseph Smith receives the First Vision in a grove of trees in Palmyra, New York, near his home.

1827
January 18
Joseph Smith marries Emma Hale.

September 22
Joseph Smith obtains the gold plates from Moroni at the Hill Cumorah.

1829
January 15
Ezekiel and Julia's youngest son, Amos Partridge, is born.

January 16
Delcena Johnson and Lyman Sherman marry.

May 15
John the Baptist confers the Aaronic Priesthood on Joseph Smith and Oliver Cowdery in Harmony, Pennsylvania.

May
Joseph Smith and Oliver Cowdery receive the Melchizedek priesthood from Peter, James, and John near the Susquehanna River between Harmony, Pennsylvania, and Colesville, New York.

June
Translation of the Book of Mormon is completed. The Three Witnesses and the Eight Witnesses are shown the gold plates.

1830
February
Joel and Annie decide to move to Ohio.

March 26
The first printed copies of the Book of Mormon become available in Palmyra, New York.

August
Delcena and Lyman Sherman have twins, a son and a daughter. (The baby boy dies that first year.) Nancy is thrown from a horse and is told by the physician that she will never walk again.

September
David goes with Joel to Ohio. They settle in Amherst, Loraine County, Ohio. Joel partners with John Clay in building a saw mill.

October
David returns to Pomfret to help move Annie to join Joel. He finds Ezekiel is drinking more, Nancy is not well, and there is increased stress in the Johnson home.

November
Seth and Ezekiel leave to spend the winter in Cincinnati.

December
David returns to Amherst with Annie and Sixtus.

1831

March

Annie attends the "Mormonite" meetings and is the first in the family to be fully converted. In time, Joel joins her at the meetings, critically yet faithfully, comparing the doctrine of the Book of Mormon and the Bible. David meets Don Carlos Smith, reads the Book of Mormon, and also gains a testimony of the truthfulness of this new, controversial religion.

May

Annie is baptized.

June 1

Joel is baptized by Sylvester Smith. David's baptism is performed by Edson Fuller, who is distracted during the ordinance. David feels dissatisfied with the circumstances of his baptism.

July

Almon Babbitt is healed by Jared Carter.

August

A letter from Joel, with a copy of the Book of Mormon, arrives in Pomfret, informing the family of his, Annie, and David's conversion. Seth and Julia write back to Joel and express their concern.

September and October

In Pomfret, Julia and her children study the Book of Mormon while Ezekiel stays in Fredonia to work. Seth struggles inwardly about the truth of the book. Most of the family receives a testimony of the book.

September 20

Joel is ordained an elder.

October 25–26

Joel Hills Johnson meets the Prophet Joseph Smith in Orange, Ohio, at a general conference of the Church. Orange is located fifteen miles south of Kirtland; about sixty-five members of the Church live in that area.

Fall/Winter

Joel and David, with Almon Babbitt, arrive in Pomfret to share their testimonies with the family. Missionaries Joseph Brackenbury and Edmund Durfee stay in the Johnsons' home. Lyman Sherman and Julia decide to get baptized. Shortly after their baptism, Seth's prayers are answered as he receives a witness of the Book of

Mormon. Ezekiel returns from Fredonia and does not allow the younger children, who are not of age, to be baptized.

1832

January

Seth, Nancy, and Julianne are baptized shortly after Lyman's and Julia's conversion.

January 7

Elder Brackenbury dies of "bilious colic." The night after the funeral of Elder Brackenbury, during the middle of the night, the Johnson men check the graveyard and intercept medical students attempting to dig up the body of their beloved missionary.

February 18

Annie gives birth to baby Sariah.

Spring

There is great persecution of Church members in Western New York, some focused specifically on the Johnson family's baptism and the inability of members to heal either Elder Brackenbury or Nancy. Benjamin returns with Joel to Amherst.

Summer

Seth, Ezekiel, Susan, and others travel to Kirtland. Ezekiel seems to be favorably impressed by Joseph Smith. In Amherst, at Joel's home, a "mania" overcomes Seth.

Ezekiel returns with Seth to Pomfret while Benjamin stays in Amherst to help Joel with the coming harvest. In New York, David is rebaptized by Jared Carter.

October 30

Lyman and Delcena's son Albey Lyman Sherman is born. Seth is stronger and chooses to go and bring Benjamin back from Ohio. Ezekiel tells Seth that he is going to sell the farm in Pomfret and move the family to Chicago.

1833

January

The first School of the Prophets is organized in Kirtland. (D&C 88)

February 27

The Word of Wisdom (D&C 89) is revealed in the upper room of the Whitney store where the first School of the Prophets is held. Joel Hills Johnson is in attendance.

March–May 1833

Hurlbut goes on a mission to Erie County.

March 13
Hurlbut visits the Prophet Joseph at his house in Kirtland, Ohio, and discusses the Book of Mormon.

March 18
Hurlbut is ordained an elder. Sidney Rigdon and Frederick G. Williams are called as counselors to Joseph Smith.

May 1
School of the Prophets is closed and is to commence again in the fall.

Late Spring
A letter from Ezekiel with instructions to move to Chicago is lost. Forced to leave the farm in Pomfret and having not heard from Ezekiel, Julia and her children move to Kirtland, Ohio. The family meet the Prophet and move into a home that Joel has purchased for them on the Kirtland flats.

31 May
Orson Hyde files charges against Hurlbut with the Church leadership for immoral conduct which Hyde alleges took place on his mission in Pennsylvania.

June 3
Hurlbut's case is brought before the bishop's council. Although Hurlbut is not present following the testimony of Orson Hyde and Hyrum Smith, D. P. Hurlbut is excommunicated.

June 5, 6
Joseph Smith presides at a conference discussing the building of the temple. The trench for the walls of the temple is dug.

June 21
Joseph Smith calls a special council to hear Hurlbut's case. Hurlbut makes a public confession of his wrongdoings and is rebaptized, reordained, and restored as an LDS missionary and resumes his mission without a companion.

June 23
A general council is convened in Kirtland where several members testify that Hurlbut has boasted of making a false confession and is deceiving Joseph Smith. Hurlbut is excommunicated a second time.

July 20
The persecution in Zion culminates with the burning of the printing press. The Saints living in Jackson County are ordered to leave.

July 23
Cornerstones of the Kirtland Temple are laid. The *Journal History* records that Joel and Don Carlos Smith participated. In *My Life's Review,* Benjamin states that Lyman and Almon were also involved in the laying of the cornerstones.

In Jackson County, Missouri, the Saints "bearing a red flag . . . led by the Spirit of God, and in order to save time, and stop the effusion of blood, entered into a treaty with the mob, to leave the county within a certain time." They agree to leave by the next January.

August
D. P. Hurlbut collects information about the Spaulding manuscript and begins his anti-Mormon lectures.

Fall
The Saints in Kirtland begin work on the temple. Joel is called upon to to make brick for the temple. The initial plans for the temple call for building the temple out of brick.

October 30
David Johnson dies. Don Carlos Smith is present with him at the time of his passing and witnesses a spiritual manifestation.

November 4–6
The Latter-day Saints are violently forced from Jackson County. The Battle of Big Blue in Missouri takes places November 4. During the following days, women and children are forced to flee for their lives.

November 13
"The Night of the Falling Stars," a magnificent meteor shower that lights the sky, occurs. This sign from heaven gives hope to the Johnson family, the homeless Saints camped near the Missouri River Bottoms, and the Prophet Joseph in Kirtland.

November 25
Orson Hyde and John Gould arrive from Missouri and bring news of the expulsion of the members of the Church from Jackson County.

December 12
Nephi Johnson, son of Joel and Annie, is born in Kirtland.

1834
February 24
Joseph Smith receives a revelation commanding a relief force be sent to Missouri.

The force is to consist of at least one hundred and as many as three hundred volunteers. (see D&C 103)

April 9
The decision of a court case between D. P. Hurlbut and Joseph Smith is announced in favor of the Prophet. Hurlbut is fined and ordered to keep the peace for six months.

May 6–7
After requesting and being refused help from the president of United States, Zion's Camp begins its 800-mile march to Missouri. Seth Johnson, Lyman Sherman, and Almon Babbitt are all members of Zion's Camp.

June 26
Zion's Camp is disbanded due to the outbreak of cholera, and members are sent to different areas around Clay County.

July 3
Joseph instructs General Lyman Wight to give an honorable discharge to every man who has proven faithful. The members begin to return to Kirtland.

Summer
Nancy Johnson is healed by Jared Carter.

November 3
Almon Babbitt and Julianne Johnson marry.

Winter
Seth teaches school in Willoughby, Ohio.

1835
February 14
The members of Zion's Camp meet together and the Twelve Apostles are called. Almon Babbitt and Lyman Sherman are in attendance. Seth Johnson is ill.

February 19
Seth Johnson dies.

February 28
Organization of the Quorum of the Seventies takes place. Lyman Sherman is called as one of the seven Presidents of the Seventies. He receives a blessing.

March 1
Seth Johnson's funeral is followed by another meeting of the former members of Zion's Camp. Almon Babbitt receives a blessing and is called as a Seventy.

March 7 or 8

Blessings in the temple are given to those who have worked on the building of the temple. Joel H. Johnson and Benjamin Franklin Johnson both record this experience in their life histories.

April 3

Patriarchal blessings are given to the family in the Shermans' home by Joseph Smith Sr.

Spring

Sometime in 1835, most likely after Seth's death, Ezekiel and Julia Johnson separate, and Ezekiel moves to the bordering town of Mentor. Benjamin Franklin Johnson and Joseph Ellis Johnson are baptized.

May

Almon takes Julianne on his mission to New York.

July 31

David Homer Babbitt, son of Almon and Julianne, is born (possibly on their mission or as soon as they return).

August 19

The council reproves Elder Babbitt and instructs him to obey the Word of Wisdom, follow commandments, and tells him that it isn't advisable for any man to take his wife on his mission.

August 26

Joel H. Johnson leaves on a mission to southern Ohio.

October

Benjamin Johnson and Almon Babbitt leave for a mission to Pomfret, New York. Before leaving, Benjamin receives a blessing from the Prophet Joseph.

December

"The Debating School Incident" is recorded in *History of the Church.* Joseph Smith discontinues the Kirtland debating school, causing an "altercation" between him and his brother William. Lyman Sherman, Almon Babbitt, and probably Benjamin, are present.

December 26

Doctrine and Covenants 108 is an answer to Lyman Sherman's request "for a revelation to make known his duty."

1836

January 21–22

Lyman Sherman, as one of the seven presidents of the Seventy, receives his anointing and blessings and is witness to the great endowment of power which is received prior to the dedication of the Kirtland Temple.

February 22

The sisters sew the veil of the Kirtland Temple.

March 16

Susan Ellen Johnson dies. The Prophet Joseph Smith attends her funeral and records it tenderly in his journal.

March 27

The Kirtland Temple dedication details are in the *History of the Church* (II:410–28). There are many glorious manifestations before and after the dedication.

April 3

Joseph Smith and Oliver Cowdery receive a vision in the Kirtland Temple of the Savior and past prophets. (D&C 110)

May 26

Almon commences preaching in Madison, Ohio, and within three months baptizes a branch of twenty members, including Anson Call's family.

June 30

Seth Sherman, son of Delcena and Lyman Sherman, is born.

July 11

Susan Ellen Johnson, daughter of Annie and Joel H. Johnson, is born.

October 16

Almera Johnson and Samuel Prescott are married by the Prophet Joseph Smith. (See notes in *Glory from on High*, 298.)

October 30

Nancy Maria Johnson, oldest daughter of Julia and Ezekiel Johnson, dies.

November 2

Brethren in Kirtland draw up articles of agreement in preparation for a bank—the Kirtland Safety Society. Sidney Rigdon is elected president and Joseph Smith Jr. as cashier.

November 29
Baby David Homer Babbitt, son of Julianne and Almon Babbitt, dies.

December
Orson Hyde attempts unsuccessfully to obtain a bank charter from the Ohio State legislature.

1837
January 4–8
First Kirtland Safety Society notes issued.

January 8
At the Sunday morning meeting in the temple, Lyman Sherman sings in tongues with 1,500 attendance.

January–February
As soon as the Kirtland Safety Society is opened officially, Grandison Newell and other anti-Mormons target it for failure. He and others bring up bank notes, demand coin, causing panic and a run on the bank. The capital behind the bank is land, not gold, and Kirtland Safety Society script becomes worthless.

February 19
The Prophet returns, having been on a mission in Michigan, and powerfully speaks in the temple answering the rising criticism that is mounting against him within the leadership of the Church.

Spring
There is increasing criticism mounting toward the Prophet Joseph, including leaders and members of the various quorums. All Ohio banks suspend payment as a banking panic which starts in New York moves westward. Although the banking failures are not unique to Kirtland, Joseph Smith receives the blame for the failure, and lawsuits are drawn up against him.

April 6
Seventh anniversary of the Church's Restoration.

Mid June
Mary Fielding, a recent convert from Canada, writes home mid-June that "truly my heart has almost bled" for Joseph. Besides facing dissidents, he is struck down by a nearly fatal illness. In early June, he is incapacitated while his critics revile him in meetings.

August

Riot in the Kirtland Temple. While the Prophet, Sidney Rigdon, and other leaders are out of town, apostates threaten and attempt to forcefully overtake the temple during the Sabbath service. Many members of the Church have lost significant amounts of money in the bank, and there is a "civil" war between members—those claiming that Joseph is a fallen prophet and those loyal to him. The Johnsons remain loyal and support the Prophet.

October 2

Lyman Sherman is called and ordained a high priest.

October 11

Daniel Sherman, son of Lyman and Delcena Sherman, is born.

October 22

Joseph Ellis and Benjamin Johnson are reprimanded by the Kirtland Council for "recreation unlawful to the church"; they are listed as having attended dances in Kirtland. They both answer humbly to the council, resolving the situation.

November

The doors of the Kirtland Safety Society are closed for the last time.

December

Brigham Young leaves for Missouri because of the threats that come as a result of his verbal support of the Prophet Joseph.

1838

January 12

Joseph Smith and Sidney Rigdon flee to Clay County, Missouri, faced with a warrant for their arrest on a charge of illegal banking, just ahead of an armed group out to capture them. A pregnant Emma follows Joseph in a wagon.

January 16

The Church printing office goes up in flames, destroying many copies of the Book of Mormon. Benjamin Franklin Johnson states that his brother-in-law Lyman Sherman is responsible.

NOTES

Chapter 1

Based upon Benjamin Franklin Johnson's account in *My Life's Review* (22), the incident of Lyman Sherman setting fire to the printing office in Kirtland was told in the previous volume of this series. See *A Banner Is Unfurled Volume 3: Glory from on High*, 267–72.

Luke Johnson, one of the original latter-day Apostles (not a blood relative to the Ezekiel Johnson family), leaves the Church in 1837, probably due to the Kirtland bank failure. In 1846, after the Prophet's death, Johnson came to Nauvoo, wanted to rejoin the Saints, was rebaptized, went west with Brigham Young's first company, and settled his family in Tooele County, Utah. Although alienated from the Church, as a constable in Kirtland he used his authority in two separate incidents to protect the Prophet Joseph and his father, Joseph Smith Sr. from arrest, allowing them to escape and safely leave Kirtland (Smith, *History of Joseph Smith by His Mother*, 367–68; *History of Luke Johnson by Himself*). Luke Johnson wrote,

> January 12th, 1838, I learned that Sheriff Kimball was about to arrest Joseph Smith, on a charge of illegal banking, and knowing that it would cost him an expensive lawsuit, and perhaps end in imprisonment, I went to the French farm, where he then resided, and arrested him on an execution for his person, in the absence of property to pay a judgment of $50, which I had in my possession at the time, which prevented Kimball from arresting him. Joseph settled the execution, and thanked me for my interference, and started that evening for Missouri; this was the last time I ever saw the Prophet." (*History of Luke Johnson by Himself*)

These two incidents inspired the fictional story of Benjamin's, Delcena's, and George's interaction with Luke, as constable, warning Don Carlos and his family to leave Kirtland. The timing of the departure of Don Carlos's family is historically based.

The Huntington family's home in Kirtland became a "Mormon underground," providing safety for many of the brethren who needed to leave Kirtland quickly. Oliver B. Huntington writes that Lyman Sherman and others were concealed in his father's home during this time period. "Numbers lay concealed in our house day after day, until their families could be got out of the place, one after another would come and go until we had served a variety with the best we had, and were glad of the privilege of showing favor to the righteous; among which number was Benjamin Wilber, Lyman Sherman, old father Smith, Samuel and Carlos Smith" (*Autobiography of Oliver Boardman Huntington*).

The fictional scene with Almon Babbitt, William Law, and John Snider brings these three men together in a probable way. John Snider was a Canadian Saint well acquainted with Almon (Berrett, *Sacred Places, Missouri,* 364). William Law was taught and converted in 1836 through the efforts of John Taylor and Almon W. Babbitt (Cook, Lyndon W., *William Law, Nauvoo Dissenter,* 48). Almon continued to have a relationship with William Law and John Snider throughout the Nauvoo years.

Anson Call relates the experience of meeting General Wilson on a steamboat and being introduced to Governor Boggs and the Missourians (Barney, *Anson Call and the Rocky Mountain Prophecy,* 52). The conversation in the text is based on the specific conversation that Anson records. Almon Babbitt's presence is fictional, and he was not among those Anson listed as present on the steamboat. He and Anson Call worked closely together in locating and purchasing land and bringing their families with the Canadian Saints to Missouri.

Chapter 2

Joel Johnson, a Seventy, would have most likely been involved in the organization of the Kirtland Poor Camp. "Perhaps the greatest work achieved by the First Council of the Seventy in their organized capacity was the organization of the Kirtland Camp, and leading it from Kirtland, Ohio, to Adam-ondi-Ahman, Missouri, a distance of 860 miles" (Roberts, *First Year Book, The Seventy's Course in Theology,* 13). He and his mother, Julia, are listed as head of households (*HC* 3:92).

The letter referred to in the chapter, written by the Prophet Joseph Smith from Far West on March 29, 1838, is found in *The History of the Church* (3:10–12). The quotes in the text are directly from that letter.

The actual date, time, or circumstances of Delcena and Lyman's departure to Missouri are not recorded, nor are the details of their journey to Missouri known. Being "mired" in the mud and the experience of the prairie fire were found in Luman Shurtliff's autobiography. Luman Shurtliff records that near "Indianapolis, the capital of Indiana, we overtook several families of saints . . ." It is possible that the Shermans were among these families. Regardless, they would have traveled the same route and may have had experiences similar to the Shurtliffs. Luman descriptively writes,

> We . . . crossed the Wabash River and soon came to 24 miles of prairie. These prairies were low and soft, and in many places, covered with water. Sometimes our teams would mire down and also the wagons. We would have to carry out the wives and children on our backs, then wade in, unharness and get out our horses, then hitch a chain to the tongue, put two or three span of horses, and draw the wagon out. The first night on this prairie we camped out of sight of any house, tree, brush or inhabitation that we could see, and we could see as far as the sight of man could reach . . . [We] were wet and cold and we had nothing to make a fire with. We could see at a distance to the west of us a fire burning the grass. We were camped in a spot where the grass had been burned. We fed our horses grain and when nearly ready for bed, the grass fire came so near that we came to it and warmed and practically dried our clothes; we followed up the fire until it passed our wagon, then we laid down and slept nicely and awoke in the morning by the cooing of prairie hens and croaking of frogs, bull snakes and many things that make the noises the like I had never heard before . . . (*Biographical Sketch of Luman Shurtliff*)

The Shermans, established in Far West, greet Benjamin in the fall of 1838, when he arrives with the Kirtland Camp.

CHAPTER 3

The Lord's will regarding the Kirtland Poor Camp, a large group of Saints which would travel together to Missouri, was made known during a quorum meeting in March 1838. The *History of the Church* records,

> The Spirit of the Lord came down in mighty power, and some of the Elders began to prophesy that if the quorum [Seventy] would go up in a body together, and go according to the commandments and revelations of God, pitching their tents by the way, that they should not want for anything on the journey that would be necessary for them to have . . . President James Foster arose . . . He declared that he saw a vision in which was shown unto him a company (he should think about five hundred) starting from Kirtland and going up to Zion . . . The Spirit bore record of the truth of his assertions for it rested down on the assembly in power . . . (*HC* 3:88)

The information about other visions circulating in Kirtland is found in Zerah Pulsipher's life history. The incidents strengthened the faith of those who could not travel on their own, assuring them that the Lord would journey with them to Zion.

Early in 1838, Anson Call planned to go with the Kirtland Camp (his name was on the original roster). However, plans changed, and he stayed in Missouri to purchase land and buy crops. He instructed his family to come with Almon Babbitt's company, which included the Canadian Saints (Barney, *Anson Call,* 44–47). The details of Almon Babbitt's leadership and the exact date that the company left Kirtland are unknown; however, their arrival in Missouri, where they settled, and their involvement in the Missouri War are documented in several sources (*HC* 3:48, 55, 242, 245; and Berrett, *Sacred Places,* 417, 463–67).

CHAPTER 4

There is no historical evidence indicating whether Joseph Smith ever knew who was responsible for the fire at the Kirtland press. On March 29, 1838, the Prophet wrote to the Saints in Kirtland, "We have heard of the destruction of the printing office, which we presume to believe must have been occasioned by the Parrish party, or more properly the aristocrats or anarchists" (*HC* 3:11). Benjamin Franklin Johnson is the sole source indicating that Lyman set the fire (*MLR*, 21–22).

Although the meeting of Lyman and Joseph Smith is fictional, the death of Thomas Marsh's son did occur on May 7, 1838, as recorded in the *History of the*

Church. "James G. Marsh, son of Thomas B. Marsh, age fourteen years, eleven months, and seven days, died this day, in the full triumph of the everlasting Gospel" (*HC* 3:28).

The Independence Day celebration of 1838 as found in the text—which includes a processional of all the Saints, the setting of the liberty pole, the laying of the Far West Temple cornerstones, and Sidney Rigdon's inflammatory speech—is based upon Luman Shurtliff's biographical sketch, Mosiah Hancock's autobiography, and the *History of the Church* (3:41–42). The words of the Prophet's revelation concerning Far West and the temple are taken directly from the Doctrine and Covenants 15:7–8, 10. Luman Shurtliff's account does not list the names of the other men who participated with him in preparing the liberty pole, and the *History of the Church* does not specifically name those in the procession. Lyman and Delcena Sherman have not left any records, and so it is not known to what degree Lyman participated. Thus, to include Lyman in the proceedings is logical because of his calling and his role in similar ceremonies in Kirtland. In the text, Lyman is represented as helping with the southwest cornerstone. This cornerstone is laid by the presidents of the elders, "assisted by twelve men" (*HC* 3:42).

Luman Shurtliff's description provides great insight into the observations and feelings of the body of Saints that day:

> On the 3rd of July [1838], I, with several others of my company, went into the timber of Goose Creek, got the largest tree we could and made a liberty pole, and on the 4th of July, 1838, the brethren and their families assembled in Far West to celebrate the day and to lay the cornerstone of our temple in the city of Far West. Early in the morning we raised the pole, raised the Stars and Stripes and then laid the cornerstone of our temple. We then assembled under the flag of our nation and had an oration delivered by Sidney Rigdon. This orator became quite excited and proclaimed loudly our freedom and liberty in Missouri. Although Sidney was a great orator and one of the leading brethren, his oration brought sorrow and gloom over my mind, and spoiled my further enjoyment of the day. After the services, the multitude dispersed. This was on Saturday. On Sunday a cloud came over Far West, charged with electricity, and lightning fell upon our liberty pole and shivered it to the ground. When the news reached me, I involuntarily proclaimed, "Farewell to our liberty in Missouri." (*Biographical Sketch of the Life of Luman Shurtliff*)

Parts of Sidney Rigdon's speech that day, as recorded in *Comprehensive History of the Church* (1:440–41), were used in the text of the chapter. Mosiah Hancock recollects in his autobiography that his father, Levi, and his uncle Solomon Hancock sang a song that the Prophet Joseph had asked Levi to write for Independence Day. The words of the song used in the text were taken from the eighteen verses that were originally written (*Autobiography of Mosiah Hancock*). Lightning did actually strike and splinter the liberty pole, and the Prophet was heard to say that as he walked "over the splinters" of the liberty pole, the Saints would "eventually triumph over their enemies" (Berrett, *Sacred Places Missouri,* 312).

The "Danites, a paramilitary organization" (*The Joseph Smith Papers,* 1:293) discussed in the text by Lyman Sherman and Luman Shurtliff, were organized around the time of Sidney Rigdon's sermon on June 17, 1838, warning dissenters to leave Far West (293, Baugh, "Call to Arms," 79–80). Luman Shurtliff's understanding of this group is explained in his autobiography:

> About this time I was invited to unite with a society called the Danite society. It was gotten up for our personal defense, also for the protection of our families, property and religion. Signs and passwords were given by which members could know the other wherever they met, night or day. All members must mend difficulties if he had any with a member of the society, before he could be received. (*Biographical Sketch of the Life of Luman Andros Shurtliff*)

Of those who joined the secretive group, Historian William S. Hartley in *My Best for the Kingdom, History and Autobiography of John Lowe Butler, A Mormon Frontiersman,* writes, "Danite use of secret signs and passwords has been disparaged, but, again, such rituals serve pragmatic purposes in wartime [Missouri 1838]" (50).

The gathering of the Kirtland Camp on July 5th, prior to their departure, took place on a piece of land just south of the Kirtland Temple. Details are found in the *History of the Church.* "The night was clear and the encampment and all around was solemn as eternity . . ." (3:98–99). Benjamin, although wanting to go with his family to Missouri, worried that his poor health would be a burden to the camp and decided "it would be better to stay" with Ezekiel and Almera. "While lending all aid possible and assisting in their starting with the company" at the time of departure, Benjamin did go because he was needed to help drive some "refractory stock" (*MLR,* 23–24).

Anson Call met his family twenty-five miles west of the Mississippi River to greet and help them as they arrived in Missouri. They went to Far West for a few weeks and then moved to Three Forks of the Grand River (Barney, *Anson Call,* 54–55). About twenty-two families, a total of 145 people, settled in Three Forks, in Clinton County (county lines changed in 1841 and this area is now in Gentry County) about thirty miles straight northwest of Adam-ondi-Ahman. The settlement was located where the west, middle, and east forks of the Grand River join together. This was beyond the area designated for the Saints to settle. Anson Call, his parents and family, John Snider, John Young Sr., Phineas Young, Hannah Flint (Anson's sister-in-law), and Joseph Holbrook were among these families (Berrett, *Sacred Places,* 463–65). Julianne and Almon stayed in Far West near the main body of the Saints.

Chapter 5

The dates of travel and many details of the Kirtland Camp are found in the *History of the Church* (3:86–145). July 9, 1838, was a hot day, and several children had been sick, "some dangerously so" (101), for a few days. "Brother and Sister Wilbur's little son died, aged six months and twelve days . . . He had been sick two or three days, and some other children in the camp had also been sick, but all recovered excepting Brother Wilbur's son" (104). A little south of the village of Hudson, the Hales' wagon tongue broke. Joel H. Johnson's oxen failed and were left behind." One was sold for slaughter for ten dollars and the other recovered (102, 103). On July 10, resolutions were drawn up for the camp, which included those listed in the chapter "that every company in the camp is entitled to an equal proportion of the milk whether the cows are owned by the individuals of the several tents or not" (103). July 11 brought rain for the first time and "the whole company got thoroughly wet" (104). Benjamin relates that his health improves on the journey of the Kirtland camp: "And such was the increase of my health and hopes that I felt that I could *do* or *endure anything* to prove my gratitude to the Lord for His blessings" (*MLR*, 25).

Chapter 6

It is not known if Lyman Sherman joined the Danite Society. However, it is highly probable that he was invited to their meetings. Sherman is portrayed as deciding not to join Avard's group because there is no evidence linking him to the more militant factions during the Missouri period. Although many prominent brethren joined the Danites, others questioned Avard's motives.

Sampson Avard was a relatively new member of the Church when he entered the Missouri conflict and became a leader in the secret Danite organization. To join the group required oaths and commitments of secrecy. While outwardly defending the Saints, he also engaged in unlawful and vigilante activities for a brief period beginning in June 1838 and ending in November when he testified against the Prophet Joseph Smith. Avard's testimony contradicted the oaths and covenants which he secretly enforced within this group. His testimony was a factor in the Prophet and others being imprisoned for months in Liberty Jail.

Richard Bushman, in *Rough Stone Rolling,* presents historical facts, explanations, and questions concerning the Danites (349–55). Because of the secrecy of the organization and "obscurity of records" (350), there are many questions regarding the exact situation and any involvement of the First Presidency. Avard played upon the members' loyalty to Joseph Smith and required an oath to be completely submissive to the Presidency (351). It is very unclear as to what Joseph knew, for there is no account of him attending a Danite meeting or being aware of the Danite oaths. One consistent theme in his speeches throughout the year was to warn the brethren "not to act unlawfully" (355).

The complexity of the conflict, the interpretation of the laws, and the hostility toward the Saints made it difficult to know what was lawful or not. Because of the many threats against the members of the Church in Missouri, they found it necessary to defend themselves, their property, their families, and their very lives. Bushman explains the situation:

> With the threat of mob attacks rising in the summer of 1838, the Mormons teetered on the boundary between law and war. They feared they would come under attack again . . . The governor told them that neither the courts nor the state militia could give assistance to such a hated people. How should they react to an attack? Could they rely on the courts that had always failed them? Should they allow themselves to be forced out again? . . .
>
> They had lived in the South long enough to know that southern officials ignored the crimes of rioters. Judges and sheriffs closed their eyes to the crimes of the people. As one student of mobs has written, "The more mob violence accelerated in deadliness in the South, the less likely authorities were to interfere, or if they did, they took the side of the mob" . . .
>
> The Saints lived in a world where rioters acted with impunity. Aware of the realities, Joseph decided that the Saints could not back down again. They could not allow themselves to be driven repeatedly from place to place. (Bushman, 354)

CHAPTER 7

Benjamin's experiences while traveling with the Kirtland Camp are based upon his description in *My Life's Review.* Benjamin does not record the exact dates of these incidents, but they are consistent with July 28–29 in the day-by-day account of the Kirtland Camp found in *The History of the Church* (3:116–17). He served in helping the sick and learned "in some degree the use of medicine" (*MLR,* 25), as he cared for Brother and Sister Willey. Another important event during this time was the opportunity he had to share the gospel with the people he met. He describes,

> On one occasion while passing through a town of considerable size in western Ohio, I stopped before a large tavern to answer a question. I was covered with dust, without a coat, and barefoot, and feeling mortified at my appearance wished to hurry on, but other questions were asked and I could not leave them unanswered . . . And when I ceased and looked around there were hundreds before me and all windows were open on both sides of the street, and crowded with listening women; and all appeared to wonder at the dirty, barefooted boy. But no one marveled more than myself. (*MLR,* 25–26)

History of the Church provides detail of the Sabbath day meeting, stating that "numerous spectators" (3:117) were present. Benjamin's account says, "The next day being Sunday, a number of carriage loads of people came from town to our meeting in camp, stayed for a time and enquired for the young man who had preached to them in town the day before, of which no one knew anything. I saw them come and go again but was too bashful to attract their notice or speak to them" (*MLR*, 26).

Rebecca Winters's and Almera's interactions are fictional; however, the Winters and Burdick families were baptized by Lyman Sherman in Jamestown, New York, and most likely knew his family in Kirtland. The Winters and Burdicks stayed in Kirtland, not far from Mentor, where Almera and Ezekiel resided. It is very possible that there was a relationship between the two women.

The Kirtland Camp remained in the Dayton, Ohio, area while the men were employed working on the national turnpike (*HC* 3:118). According to George Washington Johnson, the stay in Dayton, while working on the turnpike, allowed the sick to rest and recover (Johnson, George W., *Autobiography*, 3).

Chapter 8

The meeting on Monday, August 6, 1838, is recorded in *History of the Church* (3:55–56) and details included in this chapter are taken from this account. Although there is no specific record of Almon and Joseph Smith's discussion of Three Forks during the public meeting, Joseph Smith does write of the early morning council. During this meeting there was discussion of "certain Canadian brethren, who had settled on the forks of the Grand River, contrary to counsel" (*HC* 3:55).

That same day, August 6, twelve Mormon men, including the Prophet's brother, Samuel H. Smith, went to vote in Gallatin, Daviess County. Gallatin, 4.5 miles southeast of Adam-ondi-Ahman, the county seat of Daviess County, was settled one year before the Mormons moved into that area. The Whig candidate, William Peniston, concluding that the Mormons would not vote for him, denounced the Mormons and their right to vote. A fight broke out, and false rumors that several Mormons had been killed ignited "fears on both sides [which] intensified an already violent and dangerous situation" (*Joseph Smith Papers Volume 1,* 299). The Gallatin attack on the Mormons, as presented, is documented in several sources (*The Joseph Smith Papers Volume 1,* 298–301; *HC* 3:57–58; Berrett, *Sacred Places,* 480–83; Hartley, 54–57). Joseph Smith stated,

> About one hundred and fifty Missourians warred against from six to twelve of our brethren, who fought like lions . . . Blessed be the memory of those few brethren who contended so strenuously for their constitutional rights and religious freedom, against such an overwhelming force." (*HC* 3:59)

Mormon John L. Butler, feeling his body strengthened during the skirmish, recalls, "Many thoughts ran through my mind . . . I never in my life struck a man in anger . . . I did not want to kill anyone, but merely to stop the affray . . . thinking when hefting my stick that I must temper my licks just so as not to kill" (found in Hartley, 54). Hartley explains how John saw his role in the incident:

> "I never struck a man a second time," John noted. He had felt a surge of almost super human power while defending his brethren. "I felt like I was seven or eight feet high and my arms three or four feet long, for I certainly ran faster than I ever did before and could reach further and hit a man, and they could not reach me to harm me." In retrospect, and with a strange twist of logic, John wondered if perhaps God had used him at Gallatin to save the souls of the Missourians by preventing them from becoming murderers. John said that later, while in Nauvoo, "the thing opened up to my mind that I was operated upon by a spirit to save them by knocking them down to keep them from killing the Saints which would have sealed their damnation." (Hartley, 57)

With the news of the election-day battle in Daviess County and rumors of many deaths, volunteers and recruits from Far West and neighboring areas gathered and rode to Lyman Wight's property in Adam-ondi-Ahman to assess the situation and protect their brethren if necessary. Sampson Avard, a Danite general, led the initial group of men whose immediate purpose was to recover the corpses of the rumored victims for burial (*Joseph Smith Papers Volume 1,* 299 referencing Sampson Avard, Testimony, Richmond, MO, Nov. 1838, "Evidence" & Joseph Smith, Affidavit, Caldwell Co., MO, 5 Sept., 1838). Colonel George Robinson, a Danite colonel and also a colonel in the Caldwell County regiment of the state militia, led the larger group of volunteers. Joseph Smith also said the recruits traveled in small groups, "two, three, and four in companys, as we got ready" (*HC* 3:71). Although we have found no specific information as to their involvement, it is likely that Almon and Lyman were a part of this armed Mormon Militia.

Adam Black, non-Mormon and justice of the peace in Adam-ondi-Ahman, earlier that summer joined the mob effort to drive the Mormons from Daviess County. He was visited by Lyman Wight and Cornelius Lott shortly after the Gallatin election brawl. Wight and Lott, Mormon leaders in Daviess County, desired a commitment from Black that he would be fair, as justice of the peace, to the Mormons living in that community. They were unsuccessful but returned with over one hundred armed Mormon men, those same ones who had come to investigate the situation at Gallatin. The situation continued as

> Sampson Avard, a leading Danite, led a group of two or three men into Black's house, presented him with a written statement promising to uphold the law, and Black reported later, threatened to kill him if he did

> not sign. It appears that only after Black refused to sign the statement was Joseph Smith brought in to break the impasse. A compromise was reached in which Black drew up his own statement. (*The Joseph Smith Papers Volume 1,* 300)

That same day, August 8, Adam Black signed another statement, an affidavit accusing the Latter-day Saints of surrounding his home and threatening to kill him if he didn't sign; he named Joseph Smith and Lyman Wight as the leaders of the hundred-plus armed men. Joseph states in his affidavit, in September, that in the meeting with Black there was no bad language and that he wanted to make sure that there were not "any unfriendly feelings" (*HC* 3:72). In Joseph's affidavit he does not directly accuse Avard of wrongdoing but is clear that Avard was specifically involved in this incident. He was relieved of his military duty sometime within the next few months. Avard, later in November during the Richmond trial, testifies against the Prophet.

Chapter 9

Julia, Joel, and Benjamin did go to Cincinnati while the Kirtland Camp stayed in Dayton, Ohio, for a month. This is based upon Benjamin's statement that he went twice during that time to "visit his kindred and do business for the company" (*MLR,* 24); George Washington Johnson's statement that "his mother and my brother Joel made the trip to Cincinnati, Ohio, to visit my mother's sister and other kindred living there" (*Autobiography of George Washington Johnson*, 3); and a letter written by Julia on March 13, 1839, to her half-sister Diadamia Forbush: "I went to Cincinnati last summer and there found Nancy and Rhoda. Rhoda is in Newport across the river from Cincinnati, they are well" (Cluff & Gibson, *Johnson Gems,* 24). Julia does not mention her brother, Joel Hills, who was married to Rhoda, nor Nancy's husband, George Washington Taft.

In the 1830 census, Cincinnati Ward 2, Hamilton, Ohio, a Nancy Taft is listed as the head of household. In her household are two women between thirty and fifty (Nancy would have been about thirty at the time of the census); ten males between the ages of twenty and thirty; two between forty and fifty; and two younger boys (one under five and the other under ten). Because of the multiple males between the ages of twenty and thirty, it is assumed that her residence was probably a boardinghouse, as presented in this chapter. There is an 1801 marriage record of Nancy Hills (b. 1785) and George Washington Taft (b. 1783). Other documents, including census records, are difficult to find regarding her family. Her sons, Tad and Dan, are fictional because there is no information about Nancy's children except from the 1830 census, which indicate her children were most likely boys. Because there is no older male in the household, and because Julia does not speak of Nancy's husband in the 1839 letter, in the novel it is stated that her husband has died. More information is known about Joel and Rhoda Hills and their family. Rhoda and the names and ages of her children are correct according to later census and family records. Benjamin Johnson and Joseph Ellis Johnson continued contact with Franklin Hills years later as adults (letters in Joseph Ellis Johnson file at the University of Utah).

Nancy's involvement in the abolition movement and as a participant in the Underground Railroad is fictional. However, Cincinnati was a primary stop for runaway slaves as they traveled north during the 1800s. Cincinnati's location on the Ohio River put it at the crossroads between North and South and the journey to freedom. It was a major hub of activity, enabling thousands of slaves to find hope in a new free life. Today, the National Underground Freedom Center is located in Cincinnati.

The nickname "Porkopolis" was coined in about 1835 and given to the city of Cincinnati. In 1818, Elisha Mills opened Ohio's first slaughterhouse there. Salt pork, packed in brine-filled barrels, became a U.S. food staple, and within a decade, the city earned the nickname "Porkopolis." Joel and Benjamin had been sent to Cincinnati for business (see *MLR,* 24), and although records do not indicate what kind of business, it makes sense that they were sent to get supplies of pork which would be of great value to the Kirtland Camp and Saints in Missouri.

Joel Hills Johnson, as a child, did live with his uncle, Joel Hills, in Newport, Kentucky (across the river from Cincinnati, Ohio), from the fall of 1813 until the spring of 1815. In *A Voice from the Mountains: Life and Works of Joel Hills Johnson,* he says, "I cannot relate many incidents of the journey, being small, but recollect passing the Allegany Mountains in the state of Pennsylvania and coming to Pittsburgh, where my uncle then bought a flat boat . . . We then descended the Ohio River to Cincinnati, which was then a small town" (13).

Lyman Beecher, the father of Harriet Beecher Stowe, as represented in the novel, was a Presbyterian minister and did have a school in Cincinnati in 1838. In American history, Elijah Lovejoy was martyred for his opposition to slavery.

CHAPTER 10

Joseph Smith records on August 11, 1838, "This morning I left Far West, with my council and Elder Almon W. Babbitt, to visit the brethren on the Forks of the Grand river, who had come from Canada with Elder Babbitt, and settled at that place contrary to counsel" (*HC* 3:62). In *The Joseph Smith Papers Volume 1,* George Robinson writes that the First Presidency left with Elder Babbitt for Three Forks of the Grand River, "to give council as needed" (302). Anson Call, his family, and friends (twenty-two families) had begun farming a large tract of land. These families consisted of the group of Canadian Saints Almon Babbitt led to Missouri, who arrived in Far West during the middle of July. After staying for about one week in Far West, they had without the consent of the First Presidency gone to settle the land that Anson Call acquired (303). Anson purchased preemption rights for a thousand-acre tract of land from George Washington O'Neil and John Culp. There were seven hundred acres of timber and a site for a mill. Preemption rights allowed one to settle, occupy, and improve the property, guaranteeing first rights to buy that land from the federal government when surveys were completed and the market opened (Barney, *Anson Call,* 53–54). November 12, 1838, was the date that Anson would have had to finalize the purchase of the land by signing the appropriate papers.

After arriving at Three Forks, the Prophet wrote, "I continued with the brethren at Forks of the Grand river, offering such counsel as their situation required" (*HC* 3:62–63). Although there is not a specific list of the brethren who attended the meeting, it would have been men representative of the twenty-two families that had settled there also. In addition to Anson Call and John Snider, some of the men in these families were Harvey Call, Joel Terrell, George Gee, Asahel Lathrop, Joseph Holbrook, Theodore Turley, John Young Sr., and Phineas Young. The names of the Missourians, John Culp and George O'Neil, were used in the text because they were the individuals who had sold Anson Call the land. The details from the meeting were taken from Anson Call's autobiography:

> I received a visit from Joseph, Hyrum and Sidney Rigdon. Joseph stated that he had come to visit on a special errand. It was on the Sabbath; the day of his arrival the brethren were congregated at my house for the purpose of meeting in connection with a number of Missourians.
>
> After meeting was out he [Joseph Smith] told me he wished to see the brethren together, on which he availed himself of the opportunity of slipping off into the cornfield with about 12 of the brethren. He then stated to us we must leave for there were going to be difficulties. We inquired of him from what source. He said it was not for him to say; the message he had received was for us to leave and go to Far West or Adam-ondi-Ahman. We unanimously agreed to do so. We then inquired whether it was necessary for us to go forthwith or whether we could stay and save our crops and see our farms. He said you need not sell your farms and he presumed we should have time to get away, but how much time he knew not. They then immediately left us after dinner. (*Anson Call Autobiography* as found in Berrett & Parkin, *Sacred Places,* 465–66)

Joseph Smith's words in conversation with the Three Forks brethren are taken from a statement written by Anson Call to B. H. Roberts. He writes saying that Joseph was pleased with the land, that Three Forks may one day be a stake of Zion, and counseled them not to sell but to leave because of the difficulties. "The Lord has commanded me to make this known to you and to tell you to leave." When asked about when, Joseph answered, "I don't know but what you can [remain] 'till next spring or I don't know that you can stay one week. Act on your own judgment—I have done my errand" (Call statement to Roberts, 10–12 as found in Barney, *Anson Call,* 56).

The scene of the Danite meeting is based upon Lorenzo Dow Young's account in his autobiography. It is not known whether Lyman was present at this meeting, but his fictional opinion is consistent with the fact that he is not listed in any accounts of being involved in the secrecy of the Danite group led by Avard. Lorenzo Young had met Avard on his mission and felt that he "was a dishonest, hypocritical man." He then went on to describe his interactions with Avard in Missouri:

> The Doctor attracted no further attention from me until my arrival in Far West. In the latter part of the summer, I found he was in Far West among the saints holding secret meetings attended by a few who were especially invited. I was one of the favored few. I found the gathering to be a meeting of a secret organization of which, so far as I could learn by diligent inquiry, he was the originator and over which he presided. At one of these meetings he stated that the title by which the members of the society were known, "Danites," interpreted meant "Destroying Angels" . . . At different times new members were sworn in by taking the oath of secrecy and affiliations. The teachings and proceedings appeared . . . in direct antagonism to the principles taught by the leaders of the Church and the Elders generally. I felt a curious interest in these proceedings and determined to hold my peace and see what would develop. The culmination finally arrived. At one of the meetings Dr. Avard particularly required that all present who had been attending their meetings, should at once join the society by making the required covenants, and I was especially designated. I asked the privilege of speaking, which was granted. I began to state my objections to joining the society, and was proceeding to state my reasons and in them to expose its wickedness when Dr. Avard peremptorily ordered me to be seated. I objected to sitting down until I had fully expressed my views. He threatened to put the law of the organization in force there and then. I stood directly in front of him and was well prepared for the occasion. I told him with all the emphasis of my nature, in voice and manner, that I had as many friends in the house as he had . . . He did not try to put his threat into execution, but the meeting broke up. From the meeting I went direct to Brother Brigham and related the whole history of the affair. He said he had long suspicioned that something wrong was going on but had seen no direct development. He added, "I will go at once to Brother Joseph, who has suspicioned that some secret wickedness was being carried on by Dr. Avard." Dr. Avard was at once cited before the authorities of the Church . . . He turned a bitter enemy of the Saints. (*The Biography of Lorenzo Dow Young*)

Sometime prior to the Crooked River Battle, Avard was relieved of leadership and served only as surgeon to the Mormon Militia. It was not until the Prophet and other leaders of the Church were in prison that they learned the extent of what Avard had promoted in this organization. In the *History of the Church,* the Prophet Joseph writes that on August 13, on their way from Three Forks to Far

West, they were "chased ten or twelve miles, by some evil designing men, but [they] eluded their pursuit" (3:63). After returning to Far West later that week, he turned himself over to the sheriff because of a warrant that was issued resulting from "misrepresentations" at Adam's Black home on August 8. Rumors had spread that the Prophet would not answer to the law. However, he clearly stated, "I intended always to submit to the laws of our country, but I wished to be tried in my own county" (3:63).

Chapter 11

In *My Life's Review,* Benjamin Franklin Johnson provides insight into his care for the sick in the Kirtland Camp:

> On returning from my last visit [to Cincinnati], I found much sickness in camp and some deaths already occurred. The wife of Benj. Willey had died and brother Willey was very sick . . . And as I had now become well and strong physically I adopted the sick as my especial charge . . . For three weeks in this manner did I care for and nurse the sick by night and travel on foot by day, only obtaining sleep by the roadside as I got in advance of the company, or while bating the teams at noon" (25).

"Benj." Willey was actually Jeremiah Willey, as listed on the Kirtland Camp Register (*HC* 3:91) with four people listed in his family. Information about the Willey family is taken from family group sheets and from the 1830 and 1850 census. In 1839, Jeremiah Willey married Anson Call's sister, Samantha.

The Kirtland Camp, having traveled 575 miles, stopped in Springfield, Illinois, on September 14, 1838. Joel H. Johnson, his mother, and several other families stayed because of illness (*HC* 3:139–40). After struggling with the decision to stay with his mother in Springfield, Benjamin said, "I felt like going to the front, where I could again see and hear the Prophet" (*MLR,* 26). He did go on to Missouri while the rest of his family, who traveled with the Kirtland Camp, stayed in Springfield.

Mary Ann Hale's parents died in Springfield, leaving her to be cared for by the Johnson family. She lived with Julia and eventually married Benjamin in November 1844 as his second wife (*MLR,* 26).

The scene when Joe encounters and meets Abraham Lincoln and Stephen Douglas is fictional. However, both men were living in Springfield during this time period. Joshua Speed owned a successful store, where Abraham Lincoln, a young lawyer, boarded. Young lawyers and politicians in Springfield, including Lincoln and Douglas, would meet in Speed's store to visit and debate. It is probable that the Johnsons interacted in some way with one or more of these historical figures, though it is not mentioned in any of the Johnson journals. Joseph Ellis Johnson describes their stay in Springfield:

> Mother and other members of the family were taken sick, and with little means to help us we had a very hard time. I was forced to resort to any light employment I could obtain, and among other things chopped wood, sawed stovewood, made axe handles and washboards, and was finally induced to act as "yankee schoolmaster," which I did through the winter with much satisfaction and success, having 60 scholars, mostly small. (*JEJ: Trail to Sundown,* 64)

George Washington Johnson says that "through the following winter [in Springfield] there was much sickness. My mother and myself were very nearly dying with Typhoid Fever" (*Autobiography of George W. Johnson,* 3). The Johnsons stayed in Springfield for about one year until the summer of 1840 and then moved directly to Illinois to gather with the body of the Mormon Church.

CHAPTER 12

The details of the Kirtland Camp's arrival in Far West are found in *History of the Church* (3:147). On October 2, 1838, five miles from Far West, they were met by the Prophet. In *My Life's Review,* Benjamin says they arrived and were greeted by the Prophet on October 20. This is most likely an error because other records are consistent with the Kirtland Camp Record found in *History of the Church.*

"Joyful salutations" (*HC* 3:147) came when the Prophet and other leaders rode out five miles to meet the camp. Benjamin says, "On approaching Far West we were met by the Prophet, who came out to meet us, and I felt certain joy in seeing him again" (*MLR,* 27). Sidney Rigdon, Hyrum Smith, George Robinson, and Isaac Morley (patriarch of Far West), and several other brethren "received us with open arms, and escorted us into the city" (*HC* 3:147).

Benjamin had planned to stay with his sisters in Far West; however, the Prophet counseled him to "proceed to Diahmon, to assist, with others, in strengthening that place against mobs gathering there from adjoining counties" (*MLR,* 27). The camp continued the next day to Adam-ondi-Ahman. Joseph Smith's history says, "The camp continued . . . I went with them a mile or two . . . accompanied by Elder Rigdon, brother Hyrum, and Brigham Young, with whom I returned to the city, where I spent the remainder of the day" (*HC* 3:147; *The Joseph Smith Papers,* 330).

Benjamin writes substantially about his time in "Diahmon," which is Adam-ondi-Ahman, also referred to as Di-Ahman. The text is consistent with descriptions of his experience in choosing his lot of land, suffering with cold while sleeping in Lyman Wight's barn, and being brought a blanket by George Albert Smith's mother, the Prophet Joseph's aunt. His relationship and affection for Zina, as seen beginning in this chapter, are taken from Benjamin's words: "We formed a mutual attachment . . . grew into feelings of reciprocal love, with hopes, which although not realized in full did not hinder our being ever the warmest and truest of friends" (*MLR,* 47).

Lyman and Delcena's conversation about the problems in DeWitt and the conference of the Church to be held in Far West, presided over by Brigham Young, were taken from *History of the Church* (3:152–54).

Mormon families first moved into DeWitt in July 1838. George M. Hinkle and John Murdock were the priesthood leaders in this Mormon settlement of Carroll County. This area grew rapidly with a number of groups moving into the area. "Conflict seemed inevitable as the rapidly growing Mormon population caused resentment in the minds of the 'old settlers.' The Jackson County experience was about to be repeated" (Berrett, *Sacred Places Missouri,* 508). DeWitt in Carroll County was the most exposed Mormon settlement. When the Mormons there were threatened with expulsion, they asked for help from the government. A petition to Governor Lilburn W. Boggs was sent, and the answer in the Prophet's words "from His Excelleny" given: "The quarrel was between the Mormons and the mob," and that "we might fight it out" (*HC* 3:157). Historian Richard Lloyd Anderson said,

> The real story of the Mormon exile reduces Governor Boggs to a tool of the strong first-settlers' party in upper Missouri. This group deserves identification and a name; it existed in active and dormant forms for at least two years in about ten counties that ringed the Mormon area. Governor Boggs catered to this faction, to the point of allowing them unlimited freedom against Latter-day Saint settlements, and finally adopting their goals and slogans in his extermination orders. (Anderson, "Clarifications of Boggs's 'Order' and Joseph Smith's Constitutionalism," edited by Garr and Johnson, *Regional Studies in Latter-day Saint Church History Missouri,* 27)

When it became apparent that no help would come, they agreed to leave. The Saints, most of whom had only been there less than three months, left on October 11, 1838, in a winter storm. The story of the death of Sister Jensen is found in *History of the Church*: "That evening [October 11] a woman, of the name Jensen, who had some short time before given birth to a child died in consequence of the exposure occasioned by the operations of the mob, and having to move before her strength would properly admit of it. She was buried in the grove [where the Saints had camped for the night], without a coffin" (3:160).

When Joseph heard of the situation of the Saints in Carroll County, he rode with a hundred men under the command of Seymour Brunson and Lyman Wight. Although not historically documented, Lyman Sherman may have ridden with the Prophet in this group to aid the Saints from DeWitt. The old settlers secured a cannon and, after driving the Saints from DeWitt, looked to continue their extermination of the Mormons in Daviess County (*HC* 3:159–60). "General Atchison, Mormons, rank and file in the settlers' party, and bystanders all said that illegal forces freed by the Carroll capitulation would now move against Daviess County Mormons" (Anderson, 41).

Shortly after the Prophet's return to Far West from DeWitt, he was informed by General Doniphan that the old settlers were marching for Adam-ondi-Ahman. On Sunday, October 14, he preached, calling for those who would stand by him and defend their brethren to assemble at the public square the next morning (*HC* 3:162). Benjamin does not report that either of his brothers-in-law came to Adam-ondi-Ahman at this time.

Ben did write of Joseph Smith's arrival, though: "Soon the Prophet came to Diahmon and called for me to come and board at Br. Sloan's, the place at which he stayed" (*MLR,* 28). Benjamin records the attention which the Prophet gave to him during this very critical time. Joseph Smith also took Benjamin to his lot and showed him the loose rocks "as ones of which Adam built an altar and offered sacrifice upon this spot." This was comforting to Benjamin, which is seen in the following statement: "then I was not envious of anyone's choice for a city lot in Adam-ondi-Ahman" (*MLR*, 27). Joseph Smith's ability to love and sense the needs of an individual is poignantly admirable considering the serious crisis he was dealing with at that time.

Several other men accompanied the Prophet and Benjamin to Adam's altar that Sunday, October 21, 1838. These included Hyrum Smith, Brigham Young, Heber C. Kimball, John Taylor, Vinson Knight, Edward Stevenson, Henry Herriman, Chapman Duncan, Henry W. Bigler, William Moore Allred, and possibly Lorin Farr (Berrett, *Sacred Places,* 387). Heber C. Kimball was one of several in the group who wrote of the experience:

> The Prophet Joseph called upon Brother Brigham, myself and others, saying, "Brethren, come, go along with me, and I will show you something." He led us a short distance to a place where were the ruins of the three altars built of stone, one above the other, and one standing a little back of the other, like unto the pulpits in the Kirtland Temple, representing the order of three grades of Priesthood; "There," said Joseph, "is the place where Adam offered up sacrifice after he was cast out of the garden." The altar stood at the highest point of the bluff. I went and examined the place several times while I remained there. (Whitney, *Life of Heber C. Kimball,* 222)

Benjamin and Edward Stevenson, a seventeen-year-old soldier of the Caldwell County Mormon Militia, both slept in Lyman Wight's barn. The barn and surrounding land became the campground of the Mormon militia in Di-Ahman. "Lyman's spring and well [was] nearby, cabins of local Saints close at hand, plenty of trees to supply firewood, the Grand River a quarter of a mile away, and a ravine to protect the militia from cold winds" (*Sacred Places Missouri,* 447). Stevenson wrote that the barn was close to Adam's altar, and knowing this inspired their commitment to defend their families, friends, sacred liberties, religion, and God. He also told the story of a snowball fight the morning of October 17, 1838. The details in the novel about this snowball fight as described in Stevenson's journal are found in *Sacred Places Missouri*. "After drilling the inexperienced militia, Joseph the Prophet on the campgrounds was to be seen cheering up the chilly boys. Thus, the Prophet was cheerful, often wrestling with Sidney Rigdon, and he had his pants torn badly, but had a good laugh over it" (Berrett, 449).

Chapter 13

The conditions of the Saints in Daviess County became desperate during October 1838. The success of evacuating DeWitt continued as the efforts of the anti-Mormon vigilantes identified Daviess County next, beginning with raiding isolated homes of the Latter-day Saints (*The Joseph Smith Papers Volume 1,* 331). State militia commander Alexander Doniphan admitted that he could not protect the Saints and their property rights (*The Joseph Smith Papers Volume 1,* 331*)*. Twenty-five to forty homes or other buildings belonging to the Mormons were torn down or burned in October according to several sources as listed in *Sacred Places* (450–51). Benjamin Franklin Johnson records,

> The people who lived around within miles of town had all fled; and all the Saints who had bought farms through the more northern portion of the country or elsewhere were now flocking into town some of them bringing little more than their lives. It being . . . very cold for the season, a heavy snowstorm came upon many families with nothing but brush as a shelter, for the aged or the sick, or the mother with her babes, and in this terrible condition some children were born. This to me was an appalling condition but a still worse was upon us, for we were being hemmed in all sides by our enemies and were without food. (*MLR*, 28)

This chapter illustrates historically based experiences of the Saints in Adam-ondi-Ahman and Three Forks, including that of the sister-in-law of the Prophet, Agnes Smith, as well as the adventures of Anson Call and Phineas Young. The way was blocked between Adam-ondi-Ahman and Far West by the mobs and there was a watch on the Three Fork Saints to make sure they did not leave (Barney, *Anson Call,* 58–59). Anson wrote,

> We were watched by day and night to see that we did not leave the country. They sought to kill Phineas Young. He hid himself in a bunch of corn stalks. I carried him food and water for four days, and we became uneasy and dissatisfied with our situation. We could not get any intelligence from the Missourians as to what was going on in the county. They told us that if we stayed we should not be harmed, but that if we attempted to go away, it would be death. (*Autobiography of Anson Call*)

Anson and Phineas secretly left to obtain help for the Saints in Three Forks but realized they must return and get their families out, as is told in this chapter.

General Hiram Parks of the Missouri State Militia arrived in Adam-ondi-Ahman on October 17 to keep the peace (Berrett, *Sacred Places,* 404). His arrival intersects with the heart-wrenching story of Agnes Smith, Don Carlos Smith's wife, as told by her brother-in-law Hyrum:

> On the evening that General Parks arrived in Diahman, the wife of my brother, the late Don Carlos Smith, came into Colonel Wight's about 11 o'clock at night, bringing her two children along with her, one about two and a half years old, the other a babe in arms.
>
> She came on foot, a distance of three miles, and waded Grand river. The water was then waist deep, and the snow three inches deep. She stated that a party of the mob—a gang of ruffians—had turned her out of doors and taken her household goods, and had burnt up her house, and she escaped by the skin of her teeth. Her husband at that time was in Tennessee [on a mission], and she was living alone. (*HC* 3:408)

Benjamin did stand guard in Adam-ondi-Ahman, and he was on "picket duty" (*MLR,* 29). However, his interactions with Agnes Smith, Arthur Millican, Seymour Brunson, and Anson Call are imagined, although all of these individuals were in Adam-ondi-Ahman with Benjamin at this time. General Parks's orders to Mormon Colonel Lyman Wight as written in the chapter are consistent with Hyrum Smith's continuing account of that evening:

> The cruel transaction [Agnes Smith's persecution] excited the feelings of the people of Diahman, especially of Colonel Wight and he asked General Parks in my hearing how long we had got to suffer such base treatment. General Parks said he did not know how long.
>
> Colonel Wight then asked him what should be done. General Parks told him "he should take a company of men, well armed, and go and disperse the mob wherever he should find any collected together, and take away their arms." Colonel Wight did so precisely according to the orders of General Parks. (*HC* 3:408)

Lyman Wight and Hyrum Smith vividly describe what happened to Agnes Smith (*HC* 3:442–43; 408). However, it is not known who was at the Wight cabin when Agnes arrived. The conversation between Lyman Wight and General Parks actually took place the following day after Parks witnessed the destruction of Agnes's cabin (*HC* 3:442–43).

The Mormons mounted a preemptive strike in Daviess County beginning in mid-October, targeting the property of vigilantes (*The Joseph Smith Papers Volume 1,* 331). On October 18, the Mormon Militia took action against three small settlements: Millport, Gallatin, and Grindstone. Benjamin Johnson goes into detail about his own involvement and feelings about the raid on the Taylors' farm in Grindstone. His account in *My Life's Review* is very detailed, and these details are specifically woven to create the storyline of Benjamin's adventure this night (*MLR,* 29–33).

Chapter 14

Susan Julia Sherman was born October 21, 1838 (Lyman and Delcena Sherman family records), only ten days before the fall of Far West. The Babbitts and Shermans did not leave accounts describing the events they witnessed during this time. However, the fictional descriptions of their experiences are consistent with journal accounts of other Saints during this time period.

The details of the Battle at Crooked River were taken from several firsthand, individual accounts including those of Parley P. Pratt, Lorenzo Dow Young, Nancy Tracy, Drusilla Hendricks, and Heber C. Kimball. Nancy Tracy described the sounding of the alarm, "when about midnight, we heard the drumbeat on the public square, which was a signal for the brethren to come together . . . to the square (*The Life History of Nancy Naomi Alexander Tracy).* Their order, as decreed by the judge of Caldwell County, Elias Higbee, was to intercept and "re-take the prisoners" (Baugh, 88). About sixty men total answered this call.

Historian Alexander L. Baugh in an article entitled "The Battle Between Mormon and Missouri militia at Crooked River" explains the background information of the "skirmish" which "fueled the civil strife between the Mormons and the Missourians" and was a primary factor in "bringing about the forced expulsion of the Latter-day Saints from the state" (Baugh, 85). In his examination he finds that the DeWitt expulsion of the Mormons and their reciprocal aggression in Daviess County were the preliminary events to the Battle of Crooked River. Samuel Bogart, militia commander of Ray County in patrolling the border between Ray and Caldwell Counties, may have planned to force the Mormons into an aggressive act by taking three young Mormon prisoners and positioning his men defensively at Crooked River. The Mormons quickly responded to what they thought was a mob attack and the "result was armed conflict" (98). Baugh quotes Ephraim Owens, a Latter-day Saint who believed that Bogart's plan was to have the Mormons believe they were a mob, "and thus draw them to an attack, that they might have a lawful pretext to call out the forces of the State to expel the Mormons, as they knew the Mormons would not willingly come in contact with the militia" (86).

Almon's fictional experience in the Crooked River Battle was drawn greatly from Lorenzo Dow Young's following description:

> We kept the road to a ford on Crooked River, twenty miles distant, where we expected to find the mob. As day was breaking we dismounted about a mile from the ford, tied our horses . . . We marched down the road some distance when we heard the crack of a rifle. [Patrick] O'Banion

> [the Mormon militia's guide], who was one step in advance of me, fell. I assisted John P. Green, who was captain of my platoon, to carry him to the side of the road. We asked the Lord to preserve his life, laid him down, put a man to care for him, ran on and took our place again . . . Colonel Patten at this time was in the advance at the head of the company. As we neared the river the firing was somewhat lively, and he turned to the left of the road with a part of the command, while Captain P. P. Pratt and others turned to the right. We were ordered to charge, which we did to the bank of the river, when the enemy broke and fled. I snapped my gun twice at a man in a white blanket coat . . . A tall, powerful Missourian sprang from under the bank of the river and with a heavy sword in hand, rushed toward one of the brethren . . . crying out, "Run you devils or die!" . . . He defended himself well, but his enemy was forcing him back toward a log over which he would doubtless soon have fallen and been slain. I ran to his aid. (Little, *Biography of Lorenzo Dow Young*)

On October 25, 1838, in the Battle of Crooked River, Apostle David W. Patten, Patrick O'Bannion, and Gideon Carter of the Mormon militia were killed. Moses Rowland of Bogart's mob-militia was killed (*HC* 3:169–72). Even though the Mormons lost more men than Bogart, the Latter-day Saints were considered the victors by recovering the three kidnapped Mormon boys and dispersing the mob. "The firing ceased . . . and the wilderness resounded with the watchword, 'God and Liberty.'" They dispersed the enemy "who left their horses, saddles, camp and baggage in the confusion of flight" (*Pratt,* 154) and freed the prisoners. Newspaper articles in Missouri falsely claimed, "between 50–60 men were massacred by the Mormons" (Berrett, *Sacred Places,* 268), and rumors spread that Mormons would burn Richmond. These false reports led to Governor Lilburn W. Boggs issuing the extermination order, the attack and fall of Far West, the arrest of the Prophet Joseph, and expulsion of the Saints from the state of Missouri.

Those injured were taken to the Stephen Winchester home to recuperate for a short time (Baugh, *Heber C. Kimball,* 94). Although Winchester was Lyman's relation, Lyman's suggestion to take the wounded there is imagined. Arthur Millican was shot in both legs just above the knee and taken to the Smith home to be cared for (Newell and Avery, *Mormon Enigma: Emma Hale Smith*, 73). Two years later in Nauvoo, he married Lucy Smith, the Prophet Joseph's youngest sister. Although Almon's involvement in Millican's rescue is fictional, Arthur was with Julianne and Delcena during at least a portion of the time he spent in hiding. (*MLR*, 42–43; Thayne, *Dissertation on Julia Hills Johnson,* 97).

CHAPTER 15

Governor Boggs issued the initial extermination order on October 27, 1838, "in response to this mythical Mormon offensive [rumors of Missouri militia being slaughtered during the Crooked River Battle]" (Anderson, 47–48). All instructions were sent to General John B. Clark that the "Mormons must be treated as enemies" and must be exterminated or driven from the state "if necessary for public peace" (46). With these directives, Clark replaced David R. Atchison as "commanding general of the Mormon expedition." Atchison and Doniphan, both lawyers, had been hired by the Mormons previously and knew Church leaders and were working to legally help them. Atchison was criticized by the settlers for seeking solutions with the Mormons (see 47), even during their more directive, self-defensive measures in Adam-ondi-Ahman. This seems the reason for his release during this critical time in the conflict.

After Generals Atchison, Lucas, and Clark wrote to Governor Boggs that it was critical "to be here," Boggs replied that other duties kept him from coming. Five days later after the first order, Boggs issued another letter to Clark explaining the extermination order. He told Clark to "execute without delay" his earlier orders. In this military command he was given "full power . . . to take whatever steps you deem necessary" (39). This included making an example of the Mormon leaders, specifically Joseph Smith, the First Presidency, and those known to have fought in the Battle of Crooked River. Anderson states that "Boggs reiterated this extermination order after he was in possession of more accurate facts" (48), indicating that he was keenly aware of the false rumors and was answering to the interests of the Missouri majority and not the legal rights of the Latter-day Saints.

These directives moved so quickly that Clark was not in the immediate area when Generals Lucas's and Doniphan's troops marched to Far West on October 31, 1838, to surround this Mormon community. George Hinkle, John Corrill, and others tried to negotiate with General Lucas. He demanded their surrender and took seven prisoners, including Joseph Smith, Sidney Rigdon, and Lyman Wight. Hyrum Smith was arrested the next day. On November 1, Joseph addressed the Saints and counseled them to lay down their weapons. General Lucas then held a court-martial for those seven men. Excerpts from Lyman Wight's journal state,

> Sometime about the hour of eleven o'clock [PM] General Doniphan called on me . . . and said to me, "your case is a d——d hard one; you are all sentenced to be shot tomorrow morning at eight o'clock on the public square in Far West, by fourteen to seven, and for this reason I wash my hands against such coolblooded and heartless murder." And also said he should move his troops, numbering three hundred, before sunrise the next morning, and would not suffer them to witness such hardhearted, cruel, and base murder. He then shook hands with me and bade me farewell. (Anderson, 50)

Doniphan's strong feelings of opposition halted the immediate execution of the Latter-day Saint leaders. Boggs, three weeks later, stated that they were not to be tried by the military but in civil court (Anderson, 57).

The personal details of these events as written in this chapter are taken from records and stories of individual Latter-day Saints living in Far West during the siege. Some of their experiences, reactions, and feelings are given voice by the Lyman and Delcena Sherman family, and by Almon and Julianne Babbitt. Luman Shurtliff goes into great detail in describing making spears out of hoop handles, their subsequent surrender on November 1, and the details of being forced to face inward with their backs to the enemy (*Luman Shurtliff Autobiography*). Joseph Holbrook said, "November 1, 1838, the brethren laid down their arms . . . and all the town of Far West was put under guard. That day the troops, some 5,000, all mounted on horseback, marched through the town in the principle streets, abusing the Saints when they could meet with them" (*Joseph Holbrook Autobiography*). Mosiah Lyman Hancock, although only a child, as an adult writes of terrible acts of trauma and abuse committed on the women and children. He painfully writes of his own abuse, which included being left for dead (*Mosiah Lyman Hancock Autobiography*).

One of the purposes of the Far West siege was to gather the men who had participated in the Crooked River Battle and other conflicts. Hyrum Smith, Brigham Young, and Lorenzo Young met on the public square that night, and Hyrum counseled those involved in the Crooked River Battle to leave because they may be court-martialed and shot (Little, *Biography of Lorenzo Dow Young*). About seventy-five of those men who were involved in the Battle of Crooked River and the Daviess County conflict left Far West during the night. The Missouri militia realized this and searched for the men. It is not historically known that Almon leaves this night as written in the chapter; however, Benjamin notes that he meets Almon and his brother John in Fort Leavenworth. Many Mormon men fled there for protection and to earn money to leave Missouri the following spring (*MLR*, 44).

Delcena's and Julianne's experiences regarding the search of their home is also based upon the memories of women and children. When in Far West, men were herded into the square and placed under guard while the army entered the city. Nancy Tracy recorded,

> We had been smitten and driven about, the women and children suffering and cold and hungry, until it was unbearable, and what was to be done? . . . I had my door open and looked out upon the scene as the army marched into the city. As I lay in my bed sick, I thought the end of them would never come. They stationed one company near my house and there camped. I was alone except for my little children. My husband had to leave, for all those who were in the Crooked River battle were being hunted for by the soldiers. So I was at their mercy. Still they assured me that I would not be molested. However, they searched the premises and put a double guard around my house. So I was a prisoner in my own home with no one to care for me but my little boy. Everyone had all he could do to look out for his own. (*Nancy Naomi Alexander Tracy Autobiography*)

The details of shooting the cow and having stock and provisions stolen to feed the army were recorded by numerous Saints. Sister Young (wife of Lorenzo Young) experienced the following after her husband fled from Far West: "Disappointed in not finding him they shot down the only cow . . . within a few yards of the cabin door. From that time the family had little else than frozen potatoes and corn bread to satisfy the cravings of hunger" (Little, *Biography of Lorenzo Dow Young*).

Although fictionalized, the connection between the Lyman Sherman and Joseph Smith families has some historical basis. Albey Sherman recalled that he spent a great deal of time in the Smiths' home during his childhood as he and Joseph III were the same age. Lyman was a close companion to the Prophet Joseph and was described by Heber C. Kimball as "a good man—a noble man—and Joseph's right hand man" (*MLR,* 191). The scene of Joseph Smith's departure from his family in Far West is well documented. However, the Shermans' witnessing Joseph being taken away and the final scene between Emma and Delcena are fictional.

Chapter 16

The details of the escape of those who fought at Crooked River are found in Lorenzo Young's account. The men stop in a hazel bush, and near Adam-ondi-Ahman are given fifty pounds of "chopped corn" or "unsifted cornmeal." Lorenzo describes the snowstorm that night:

> In the night snow commenced falling and appeared to come down in sheets instead of flakes. In the morning it was about a foot and a half deep. A part of the company at first regretted this but others felt that the hand of the Lord was in it. My brother Phineas at once declared that it was the means of our deliverance. We started on, the wind began to blow, drifting the snow so that our tracks were completely covered soon after they were made. We afterward learned that our pursuers encamped where we had rested, on the opposite side of the prairie from our night encampment. In the morning they pursued but found it impossible to follow our trail. Thus were we saved by a friendly interposition of the elements. (Little, *Biography of Lorenzo Dow Young*)

Although it is not known if Almon was in this group, the details and timing, including Almon's decision to depart on his own, are consistent with Lorenzo Young's account. Young says that some men left their group because they "would rather face the chances of falling into the hands of their enemies than take chances of perishing with cold and starvation" (Little, *Biography of Lorenzo Dow Young*). Young also reported that those men went to settlements either east or south, crossed the Missouri River, and made their way to safety. Although the writers' choice to have Almon write from Booneville, Missouri, is fictional, it is not arbitrary. Boonville is east and south of the involved settlements. It is also across the

Missouri River, just as Young described. Almon had a personal connection to this city, for it was the place where his parents died in 1859 and 1867 (LDS Family Search). Almon's comings and goings are pieced together from a few facts that have been taken into account in writing the continuing storyline. Almon is in Richmond sometime during this period. A letter from Joseph to Emma (November 12, 1838) states that "Br [Almon] Babbit" is waiting for the letters. Interestingly, Richmond is on the road between Far West and Booneville. It is also known that Almon and his brother John did work together in Fort Leavenworth that winter (*MLR,* 44).

On November 6, 1838, General Clark "paraded the brethren at Far West," called out and arrested specific men, and gave a speech. *History of Caldwell and Livingston Counties, Missouri,* written by St. Louis National Historical Company in 1886, as quoted in *History of the Church,* states,

> A few days after his arrival General Clark removed a portion of the restraint he had imposed upon the Mormons, allowing them to go out for wood, provisions, etc. He assembled the multitude on the temple square and delivered to them a written speech, a copy of which is here given. It goes far to prove that General Clark was ordered to "exterminate" the Mormons, not excepting the women and children, and burn their houses and otherwise destroy their property. (*History of Caldwell and Livingston Counties,* 140, as found in *HC* 3:204)

This speech, as written in the novel, is taken directly from *History of the Church* (3:202–4).

General Wilson arrived in Adam-ondi-Ahman on November 8. The Prophet reported that "General Wilson ordered every family to be out of Diahman in ten days, with permission to go to Caldwell, and there tarry until spring, and then leave the state under pain of extermination. The weather is very cold, more so than usual for this season of year" (*HC* 3:207).

In Benjamin Franklin Johnson's *My Life's Review,* he wrote a comprehensive account, relating personal feelings and insightful thoughts about this very tumultuous time (34–42). This chapter mirrors the details of his experience. In the notes, only a small portion is quoted, but all can be read in *My Life's Review.* Benjamin wrote that the gun he gave up in Adam-ondi-Ahman was not his own and was the finest in upper Missouri. The storyline detail that the gun was his father's silver-trimmed shotgun Betsy is imagined but very possible. Oliver Huntington described the gun in detail: "Benjamin laid down probably the most valuable rifle owned by a Mormon at that time. Besides being a true shooting gun it had sixty pieces of gold and silver inlaid upon stock and barrel" (*Deseret News,* 16 October 1897, as found in LeBaron, *Benjamin F. Johnson Friend to the Prophets,* 23).

Benjamin wrote that one of the guards was "the fiend Rogers who killed Father McBride with the corn cutter, by cutting off his fingers, hands, arms, and then splitting his head." Other details of Roger's atrocities are contained in the writings of those Saints, including Joseph Young, who witnessed the massacre at Haun's Mill. Benjamin continued to speak of the evil that surrounded him that night:

> That same corn cutter, still crimson with blood hardly dry was swung over my head once and again, with it boasting of what it had done and what it would yet do, and with oaths and cursings picturing the fate that awaited me. No fancied horror could equal the real horror of the presence and words of those fiends; and I have ever felt that presence and their words, with the corn cutter covered with blood, was the most terrible ordeal through which I have passed . . . it was a something that grew out of being with and subject to those monsters: so much worse than the vulture to the giant pinioned to the rock, that there are no words to express it. (*MLR*, 36)

George Washington Johnson wrote that while in Springfield during the winter "there was much sickness. My mother and myself were very near dying with Typhoid Fever" (*Autobiography of George W. Johnson*, 4). The Johnsons in Springfield did not leave a record describing what they knew about the parallel Missouri events. However, rumors and exaggerations were reported in the local newspapers. Springfield's *Sangamo Journal* (November 10, 1838) reported the exaggerated accounts of the aggression of the Mormons, the threats to burn Richmond. Another article in the *Sangamo Journal*, on November 17, 1838, formed the basis, almost word for word, of the newspaper article read in the text by Joseph to Julia.

With the financial collapse of Kirtland in early 1838, Mormons were flowing into Missouri and looking for affordable land. Daviess County, north of Far West, specifically Adam-ondi-Ahman, became the focus of their new settlement. At this time northern Missouri was largely unsurveyed land. This allowed the Saints "to settle on the land and qualify for preemptive rights that did not require payment until the surveys were completed" (Walter, *Mormon Land Rights in Cladwell and Daviess Counties and the Mormon Conflict in 1838: New Findings and New Understandings*, 5). The timing of when the surveys were completed and the opportunity of the Saints to finalize the payment of their land explains some of the frantic efforts of the Missourians to expel the Saints in November 1838. The dates of the siege of Far West and the Richmond trial, including the restriction of travel and communication of the Saints during this time, made it impossible to complete the payment which came due on November 12, 1838. Through recent study of documents and research, it seems that this was known and most probably planned by the leaders of the anti-Mormons in Missouri. Walker states, "While the causes of the Mormon conflict in 1838 may be multifaceted, the result was not. Some Missourians enjoyed a financial windfall by getting clear title to the Mormon's land in Daviess County. While the primary motive is still unclear, it is an undisputable fact that key Missourians involved in the Mormon expulsion immediately seized a financial reward" (46).

CHAPTER 17

The story of the gun misfiring is not described in *My Life's Review* but is found in *My Heritage* (study book for The Church of Jesus Christ of Latter-day Saints) and in E. Dale LeBaron's book *Benjamin F. Johnson: Friend to the Prophets.* Both accounts are taken from an article in the *Improvement Era* (8:337–40) written by his son-in-law, James H. Martineau:

> While sitting upon a log one day a brute came to him with a rifle in his hand, saying, "You give up Mormonism right now, or I'll shoot you." Receiving a decisive refusal he took deliberate aim not 10 feet distance and pulled the trigger. No explosion occurred, and he cursed fearfully, saying he had used the gun 20 years and it had never before missed fire. He examined the lock, put in fresh priming and again essayed to shoot Johnson but without effect, and a third time with the same result. A bystander told him to fix up his gun a little, and then said he, "You can kill the cuss all right." "Yes," said the would be murderer, "I'll put in a fresh load." He did so and again essayed to kill Johnson. This time the gun bursted [sic] and killed the wretch upon the spot, and a bystander was heard to say "You'd better not try to kill that man." (LeBaron, 25)

Brigadier General Robert Wilson of the Missouri militia assigned to Adam-ondi-Ahman wrote a letter on November 12, 1838, to report his response to the orders given by General Clark. This letter is found in the Missouri State Archives with the Mormon War Papers 1837–1841. He began by stating that after his troops' arrival on November 8th, he "immediately placed a guard around the Town & ordered the Mormons to parade." Wilson's letter blames the Mormon people for the situation in Daviess County but states that his actions to give them a permit, assuring their safety to Caldwell County or out of the state, was the only course to prevent a "total massacre." It is evident from this letter that part of the order was to investigate and arrest those guilty of crimes in that area. He admits the difficulty, saying, "The most guilty had previously escaped," but states that some investigations are proceeding with little hope "of affecting much" because the citizens could not identify individuals involved. Benjamin Johnson's name is not mentioned, and it appears from personal records and accounts that Benjamin's was the only arrest in Adam-ondi-Ahman. Robert Wilson, a wealthy Missourian, later became a lawyer, a politician, a Unionist, and a United States senator for the state of Missouri.

In *My Life's Review* Ben addressed his struggle to remain loyal to the brethren he served with, even when he thought he would be shot. He was a young man with his life ahead of him, but powerfully came to the following conclusion, as written in his own words:

> Which would be the greatest bravery—to stand up like a man and be shot, or like a dog live to be despised by all who loved me. To make my parents who now loved me ashamed to own me, and my brothers and darling sisters, to think how they would weep for my shame, and those who had died and begged me to be faithful. Could I endure such a living death? Every feeling within me responded, "No! I am too great a coward ever to meet those I love, who are good and pure, and feeling myself a traitor." And my whole soul gave the verdict that I would not save my life at such a price. (*MLR,* 38)

The storyline follows very closely to what Benjamin wrote in his personal history. He described how some guards treated him with civility and others with cruelty, threatening to "stick a bayonet" into him if he did not step faster. He defended himself and was protected by a colonel, which has been changed to General Wilson in the text. Ben "sought to keep a cheerful face," drew guards into conversation, and occasionally sang. He sorrowed deeply due to the "injustice" when his friend William Huntington visited. Benjamin recorded that William "conveyed to me that the fears of the people that I would prove a traitor . . . I had stood there alone in the prospect of death . . . and I had been true, and now instead of praying for me and giving me their faith they were prophesying evil . . . and a flood of grief gushed out of my eyes before I could hinder it." He rejoiced in Zina's prayers. Additionally, General Wilson, after offering to take Benjamin into his home and family, was understanding of Benjamin's refusal and wrote a pass for him to travel to Far West. Wilson told Benjamin to leave secretly at night because the "old citizens around Diahman would certainly kill me if they found I was set at liberty" (*MLR,* 39–41). Benjamin's journey through the cold, past Marrowbone to his sisters' home in Far West is consistent with the details which he gives in *My Life's Review* (41–43). The last line of the text is Benjamin's own words: "All the providences attending my imprisonment and liberation are ever remembered as the direct hand of the Lord . . . to his own purpose and glory (*MLR*, 42).

SELECTED BIBLIOGRAPHY

Backman, Milton V., Jr. *The Heaven's Resound: A History of the Latter-day Saints in Ohio, 1830–1838.* Salt Lake City, UT: Deseret Book, 1983.

Barney, Gwen Marler. *Anson Call and the Rocky Mountain Prophecy.* Salt Lake City, UT: Call Publishing, 2002.

Berrett, LaMar C., and Max H. Parkin, eds. *Sacred Places, Missouri: A Comprehensive Guide to Early LDS Historical Sites.* Salt Lake City, UT: Deseret Book, 2004.

Bradley, Martha Sonntag, and Mary Brown Firmage Woodward. *A Story of Mothers and Daughters on the Mormon Frontier.* Salt Lake City, UT: Signature Books, 2000.

Bushman, Richard Lyman. *Joseph Smith: Rough Stone Rolling.* New York: Alfred A Knopf, 2005.

Collier, Fred C., and William S. Harwell, eds. *Kirtland Council Minute Book.* Salt Lake City, UT: Collier's Publishing, 1996.

Garr, Arnold K., and Clark V. Johnson, eds. *Regional Studies in Latter-day Saint Church History Missouri.* Brigham Young University: Department of Church History and Doctrine, 1994.

Hartley, William G. *My Best for the Kingdom: History and Autobiography of John Lowe Butler, a Mormon Frontiersman.* Salt Lake City, UT: Aspen Books. 1993.

Huntington, Oliver B. *History of the Life of Oliver B. Huntington: Also His Travels and Troubles Written by Himself.* L. Tom Perry Special Collections, Harold B. Lee Library, Brigham Young University.

Johnson, Benjamin F. *My Life's Review, Autobiography of Benjamin Franklin Johnson.* Provo, UT: Grandin Book Company, 1997; and Benjamin F. Johnson Family Organization, 1999.

Johnson, George Washington. *Diary of George W. Johnson.* L. Tom Perry Special Collections, Harold B. Lee Library, Brigham Young University.

———. *Jottings by the Way.* St. George, UT: C. E. Johnson, 1882.

Johnson, Joel H. *Diary of Joel Hills Johnson.* L. Tom Perry Special Collections, Harold B. Lee Library, Brigham Young University.

Johnson, Joseph Ellis. *The Papers of Joseph Ellis Johnson,* special collections department of University of Utah Libraries.

Johnson, Rufus D. *J. E. J. Trail to Sundown, Casadaga to Casa Grande, 1817–1882, The Story of a Pioneer: Joseph Ellis Johnson.* Salt Lake City, UT: Joseph Ellis Johnson Family Committee, printed by Deseret News Press, 1961.

Kimball, Heber C. *The Journal of Heber C. Kimball.* Originally published: Salt Lake City: Juvenile Instructor Office, 1882.

LeBaron, E. Dale. *Benjamin Franklin Johnson: Friend to the Prophets.* Provo, UT: Grandin Book Company, 1997.

Little, James A. "Biography of Lorenzo Dow Young." *Utah Historical Quarterly* 14 (1948): 25–132.

Pratt, Parley P. *Autobiography of Parley P. Pratt.* Salt Lake City, UT: Deseret Book, 1973.

Roberts, B. H. *First Year Book in the Seventy's Course in Theology.* Salt Lake City, UT: Deseret Book, 1931.

Shurtliff, Luman A. *Biographical Sketch of the Life of Luman Andros Shurtliff.* L. Tom Perry Special Collections, Harold B. Lee Library, Brigham Young University.

Smith, George Albert. *History of George Albert Smith.* L. Tom Perry Special Collections, Harold B. Lee Library, Brigham Young University.

Smith, Joseph. *History of The Church of Jesus Christ of Latter-day Saints. 7 vols.* Edited by B. H. Roberts, Salt Lake City, UT: Deseret Book, 1980.

Smith, Lucy Mack. *A History of Joseph Smith by His Mother.* Salt Lake City, UT: Bookcraft, 1958.

Tracy, Nancy Naomi Alexander. *Life History of Nancy Naomi Alexander Tracy Written by Herself.* L. Tom Perry Special Collections, Harold B. Lee Library, Brigham Young University.